Small Town

SLOAN WILSON

ARBOR HOUSE
New York

17610

Dedication

To my wife, Betty, who makes all my visions of beautiful, fascinating women seem no more than simple realism.

To my children, Lisa, Rebecca, David and Jessica, who make my portraits of mixed up young people an obvious triumph of fiction over fact, but who give me great banks full of youthful charm to draw upon when I write a book.

To my grandsons, Benjamin, Joseph and Eli, who save me from believing that the future must end with me.

To the memory of my father, Albert F. Wilson, who celebrates somewhere, I am sure, every time I write a book.

To the memory of my mother, Ruth D. Wilson, who traveled all over the world, but who always secretly lived in the small town where she had been brought up.

S.W.

ACKNOWLEDGEMENTS

I would like here to thank Don Fine for being such a good editor.

I want to thank Dr. Jon Moldover, Becky's husband, for giving expert medical advice whenever any of the characters in this book got sick.

S.W.

Author's Note

In the past half century I have lived in five small towns and I have worked as a reporter in many more. These towns were in my native state of Connecticut, in Rhode Island, where I learned the newspaper trade, in Florida, where my parents lived for a long time, and in upstate New York. My memories of all these places helped me to imagine the town of Livingston in this novel. This entire story is, of course, fiction. As my mother used to say, I tend to talk fiction even when I am trying to tell the truth, so there is no danger of this work of the imagination being sullied by anything so mundane as accounts of real people or any one real place.

S.W.

1

As soon as Ben got off the plane in Albany, he saw Ephram waiting for him. The old Indian was wearing dungarees, a blue work shirt and an ancient chauffeur's cap.

"Bens!" Eph said, his craggy, copper-colored face breaking into a smile of great warmth. "Good to see you, boy!"

No one else had ever called Ben "Bens," and it had been some time since anyone had called him "boy." He was forty-five years old and weighed 222 pounds, a big powerful man who was just beginning to worry about gaining too much weight.

"Eph, you haven't changed at all!" Ben replied, and it was almost true. The Ephram who had taught him to fish and hunt thirty-five years ago had not looked much different from this gnarled, curiously ageless man who now insisted on taking the small suitcase from his hand.

"You got more baggage?" Eph asked.

"No. I left in a big hurry."

"No real need. You know how your mother is."

Eph led the way to a high Cadillac, old but well polished. "You want to drive? My eyes ain't what they used to be."

Ben got behind the wheel. "Just what's going on at home?" he asked.

"Nothing much to worry about. Your boy's all right. A little wild, maybe, but who the hell ain't at his age?"

"Where is he staying now?"

"That's what all the fuss is about. He was supposed to stay with your mother till school lets out, but you know how your mother and Liz can keep at a kid. He tried living in your old house. When your mother raised hell about his being alone there, he started to spend most of his time at his girl's house."

"Who's the girl?"

"Ann Kelly, old Dan Kelly's youngest."

"Do you know anything about her?"

"Her old man has raised a lot of hell around here—that's what has your mother scared. The girl herself is a pretty little thing and she's got a nice sister who works at the office in the mill. Of course, you can hear talk about them, but you know how that goes. They talk about everybody here, even the dead."

Feeling a little like the pilot of a ship, Ben steered the old Cadillac onto the Northway and began the hundred-mile drive from the Albany airport to the village of Livingston, a town high in the Adirondacks where he had been born, and had spent more than half of his life.

"How long you going to be with us?" Eph asked.

"Just until I can get things straightened out. I'm going to try to take Ebon back to California with me. I can't just let the boy look after himself."

Eph smiled. "Good luck," he said.

"What does that mean?"

"His mother tried to get him to move to Florida with her. Ebon's got a mind of his own."

After passing Schroon Lake on the Northway, Ben turned onto a state road that twisted through the mountains. Although it was early May, mounds of snow could still be seen where cliffs and pines shielded them from the sunlight. White birches and maples were just coming into full leaf. The wind that came through the open window of the car was chill but

4

fragrant with spring. After descending a steep hill, the road paralleled a rushing river with seething pools and steps of small waterfalls.

"God, I still think this is the most beautiful place on earth," Ben said.

"That's what everybody who don't live here says. If you like it so much, why don't you settle down?"

"If I could find a way to make a living here, I damn well might."

Ephram spat out his window, a gesture of disdain that made Ben feel defensive. "A small town is no place for a photographer," Ben concluded.

"Why don't you take over your daddy's old paper again? Pete has run it clear into the ground."

"A small town is no place for a single man to live."

"You forgot how easy it is to find women here?"

Ben laughed. "I guess that I've been traveling so long that my feet won't quit running, Eph. If I ever get them under control, this is where I'll settle down."

They drove through a thick stand of huge old pine trees. Although the river was invisible, they could hear the roar of a fifty-foot waterfall about a quarter of a mile away. In his youth Ben and Heidi, whom he had married at the age of twenty-one, had often visited it. After walking through the fragrant shadows of the pine forest, they had swum in the pool at the bottom of the falls. Climbing the slippery rocks, they had stood behind a rushing curtain of water, surrounded by a rainbow of spray. After diving into the small, dark, deep pool at the bottom of the falls, they had swum fast through the icy water to a natural terrace of gray granite that had preserved the warmth of the sun even in moonlight. The only trouble was that Heidi had got a terrible case of poison oak there and he never had been able to get her to return.

He was seventeen when he fell in love with Heidi, the same age that Ebon, their son, was now. The realization of that would make it no easier to deal with his son's problems.

5

If Ebon were as blindly infatuated as Ben had been at his age, there wouldn't be much anyone could do.

Ben sighed. It was ridiculous to feel that his personal history always had to repeat itself. Maybe Ebon would just have a sunny little friendship with this Ann Kelly, and let it go at that.

After passing the giant pines, the road twisted up a steep mountain. This was the place where his father liked to test a new car. To help it make the ascent in high gear, Steve Winslow had raced around curves as fast as possible, arriving in triumph at the summit, but with his wife screaming in indignation. To calm her and to enjoy the view, his father often parked at the peak. The state had now widened that area and marked it with an iron sign which read (apparently for the sake of the shortsighted) SCENIC VIEW.

Ben stopped the old Cadillac here. The panorama was so beautiful that it almost gave the impression of being artificial, like a Walt Disney landscape. Between two ranges of snow-capped mountains in the distance, there was a glint of silver to betray the presence of Lost Lake, a series of connected ponds, really, which led deeper into the Adirondacks. Between Ben and Lost Lake the valley stretched level and green with spring. The river, still white with its rush from the mountains behind him, embraced the village in a semicircular curve. From this distance, Livingston looked like a stereotype of a New England town, which it was not. The steeples of the five churches rose above the elms and maples which surrounded them. The brick high school stood like a fortress between its battlefields for football and baseball. A rectangular village green in the center of town was surrounded by Victorian mansions, some of which had been turned into cheap apartment houses, a fact which was not apparent from the mountaintop.

About four miles beyond the village, a paper mill in the distance looked like an ill-assorted jumble of brick blockhouses. From its tall stacks only a wisp of saffron smoke

6

escaped, an improvement over the days when it had spewed out clouds of foul-smelling gases. In a wide circle around the town and the mill there were small houses, many of them surrounded by blossoming fruit trees and gardens. A stranger viewing the town from the mountaintop could never have guessed that many of these dwellings were impoverished shacks, trailers or abandoned farms.

Ben Winslow was as incapable of viewing the town with a critical eye as he would be of taking a clinical look at his aged mother. On her side, he was a Livingston, a descendant of the man who had founded it more than a century ago. For Ben the village was, among other things, a collection of emotion-loaded personal landmarks. The house on the green with the widow's walk was the one where he had been born, and where his mother still lived. In that high school, which his father had politicked to build, he had won top academic honors, admission to Harvard, where he had spent four lonely years, and a girl who had dominated half his life. The church where he had been married, the courthouse where he had been divorced, and the house where his son was probably waiting for him now—all were within a stone's throw of each other. The paper mill that had formed the basis of his mother's fortune still filled the air with a faintly acrid stench, even though the black smoke had disappeared.

As he stared at this view, Ben suddenly found himself moved almost to tears. There was so much that he loved in the town and so much that he hated! He didn't know whether he wanted to live forever here where almost everything was familiar, or to run back to California, where almost nothing was.

"This is a damn good place to take a woman," Eph said, gesturing toward the view. "You ever set here on a moonlight night with the right company?"

"Yes," Ben said, forced a grin, and started driving down the hill to the village.

Although no one could call Livingston beautiful at short

7

range, there was much about it that Ben still loved. The unpainted shacks and trailers were the homes of poverty, but they had an air of snugness and independence. A family could live in them on almost nothing. With a garden, a deer rifle, a fishing pole and the ability to do odd jobs for the summer people out at Lost Lake, a man could get by in one of those shacks without having to ask for relief. Even those on relief could live in relative comfort because they had no rent to pay and could cut their own wood for heat. If one had to be poor, Livingston was about as good a place to do it as anyone could find.

"You going to see your mother or Ebon first?" Ephram asked.

Ben wanted to see his son without delay, but he would probably get involved with him, and his mother would be hurt if he didn't see her right away.

"Mother, I guess."

The main street of Livingston was more like the set of a Western movie than a New England village. Many of the stores had flat roofs with false fronts to make them look higher and fancier. Here, unchanged, was the Empire movie theater, to which Ben had taken his girl on so many Saturday nights. Here was the office of the Livingston *Recorder*, where his father had taught him the beginnings of the newspaper trade and of photography. Marston's Jewelry Store, where he had at the age of twenty bought an engagement ring on credit, Dr. Bill's house with an office in the rear, the Livingston Economy Store, where he had bought his first tuxedo—all these establishments subjected Ben to storms of nostalgia. Livingston was one of the few places in America where the landscape of a middle-aged man's youth stood unchanged.

Oak Street which led to the village green was lined by substantial colonial and Victorian homes owned by lawyers, physicians and the managers of the mill who were able to prosper in the midst of a regional depression. Howie Hewat, the leading politician, had added a new glass wing to his big brick house and a garage big enough for his three cars, two snowmobiles and his boat. Near it was a stone house owned by Ben's brother, Pete. A crew of men and a drag hoe were digging in the backyard.

"What's Pete building?" Ben asked.

"A swimming pool. With the lake so near, it sounds crazy to me, but they say he's going to heat it and swim most of the year. I think he's trying to get his wife to stop nagging him about moving to Florida."

Ben was ashamed to feel a pang of something like envy. After years of roaming the world and after a divorce, he was coming home more nearly broke than he had ever been, while Pete had developed a prosperous law practice. After decades of dull work, Pete no doubt deserved whatever success he had, and Ben wished that the competitive spirit of his family didn't surface to make him resent his brother's good fortune.

"Pete and old Howie are thick as thieves these days," Ephram said. "Damned if the two of them aren't going to end up owning most of the county."

"What are they going to do with it?" Ben asked.

Ephram laughed. "Damned if I can guess. You know, this Adirondack Park Agency thing is trying to make this whole damned valley into a zoo. Maybe old Pete and Howie will be the keepers."

In the center of the village green was a white bandstand and four monuments commemorating wars in which men from this valley had fought. A magnificent bronze Indian stood as a memorial to the French and Indian War, much of which had been fought in this region. A soldier in a three-cornered hat stood at attention to honor the Revolution, and a general on horseback still rode to the battles of the Civil War, for which the foundries of Livingston had produced cannon. After this the town's urge to build memorials had apparently subsided. Only a big block of granite which looked like a giant's tombstone marked the two world wars. Caught

9

up in its depression, the village had done nothing to commemorate the wars in Korea and Vietnam, despite the fact that many good local poor boys had died in them.

The house of Ben's mother stood at the eastern end of the square. Although the lawns and the flowering fruit trees were well kept, Ben was shocked to see that the old Victorian mansion was badly in need of a coat of paint. As far as Ben knew, his mother still possessed a fairly large share of the fortune which had been made when her father sold the paper mill some fifty years ago. For years, his brother, Pete, had been managing her funds. Had he somehow managed to dissipate them?

As he parked the old Cadillac in front of the house, Ben was annoyed by the fact that he was thinking about money while preparing to see his mother for the first time in two years. He hurried across a wide porch, where the planks were almost as weathered as those in abandoned farmhouses. Before he had a chance to knock at the door, it was opened by Elizabeth, a tall, somber housekeeper who had worked for his mother for some forty years. Elizabeth greeted him with as much warmth as she could muster, for Ben had often taken her side when his mother wanted to fire her, as the old lady did every year or so. For decades there had been rumors that Elizabeth was a lesbian, and every time old Virginia fell into a fit of moral indignation, she wanted to dismiss the housekeeper, despite the fact that she couldn't find anyone else who would keep the house as spotless as she demanded, put up with her dictatorial whims, and maintain the customs of servants she remembered from her youth.

"It's good to see you, Ben," Elizabeth said with her thin smile. "We all were so relieved when we learned you were coming home!"

He wondered whether that hinted at crises about which he had not yet heard. The curtains had been drawn, and as always, the dimly lit nineteenth-century rooms seemed an appropriate setting for some sinister drama, even when absolutely nothing was happening there. The house had a peculiar smell which often came back to him in dreams. A variety of medicines, mothballs, cooking odors which could not escape because no one in the house liked open windows, furniture polish—all these were mixed with the sweetness of many vases of flowers, lilacs and apple blossoms.

As Ben climbed the red-carpeted circular staircase, he had the peculiar sensation of regressing to his early childhood. He felt guilty, guilty as hell, though he had no idea of what he had done. He was scared, and at the same time impatient with himself. When a forty-five-year-old man visits his seventy-nine-year-old mother, he should be thinking of how to give comfort, not of his own ridiculous fears.

"Benny? Is that you?"

Her voice had not aged at all. Still strong, still imperious.

"Yes, mother."

"Come in, come in!"

When he opened the door to her bedroom, he got a shock. Virginia Livingston Winslow had suffered a series of small strokes and had aged sadly in the past two years. She had changed from a big, stocky woman to a wisp with a gray wig which did not sit quite straight on her head and a brown silk dress which was so big that it seemed almost empty. Her face felt dry as autumn leaves when he kissed her. Immediately she sat down in a wooden wheelchair.

"So, Benny!" she said, peering at him through silver-rimmed glasses.

"So, mother," he replied with a smile.

"You've put on weight. Don't get fat the way your father did. That's one thing that killed him."

"I'll try."

"Have you seen Ebon yet?"

"I just got in."

"Benny, I can't tell you how worried I am about that boy."

11

"I rather got that impression when you called me."

"And I'm furious at Heidi. What kind of a woman would just run off and leave a seventeen-year-old boy on his own?"

Although Ben had suffered his moments of bitterness about his former wife, he did not like to hear her attacked unfairly. "Mother, I think that Heidi acted in a fairly reasonable way," he said. "She married a man who lives in Florida. Ebon didn't want to move down there with her, at least till the end of his school year, so it was agreed that he could stay with you. What's wrong with that?"

"What's wrong is, he didn't stay with me and no one can do a thing with him! He lives alone in your house some of the time, but most of the time he lives with his girl. Do you approve of that for a boy seventeen?"

"I believe he's staying with the girl's family."

"Some family! You ask Mary about Dan Kelly. She won't even let him into her saloon. The man's notorious."

"Well, I guess lots of good youngsters have bad fathers."

"Ha! There's talk about this Ann Kelly, too, lots of talk! Elizabeth knows about her. You just ask her."

"Mother, there always has been talk about me in this town and about Elizabeth and even about you. If you're alive in this town, you cause talk and as Eph said, even when you're not, sometimes."

"What did they say about me?" she demanded.

What they had said was that Virginia had bought herself a handsome husband, treated him like a chauffeur and had driven him to drink, but this obviously did not bear repeating.

"Rumor had it that you were a real hell-for-leather horse-back rider," he said with a smile.

"I never hurt a horse. Now don't get me off the point, Ben. What are you going to do about Ebon? I can't manage him. He ought to be with his mother, with you, or in boarding school."

"What I'm going to do is to talk with him before making any decisions," Ben said. "I'll see you later, mother."

"Wait a minute! I have a lot more I want to talk to you about! Pete is giving me a terrible time, and I keep hearing the most terrible things about Elizabeth."

"We'll have a long talk soon, mother, but first I want to see Ebon. He's mostly why I'm here, after all."

As he emerged from the dark shadows of that strangely sweet and sour smelling house, Ben could understand why his son had been unable to spend more than a few hours there. He himself, after all, had erupted from it when he was not much older than seventeen.

Ephram was still sitting in the Cadillac. "I'll take you to your place before putting the car up," he said. "I told Bert down at the garage to charge up the battery of your old jeep. It's rusted out pretty bad, but it ought to get you around for a while."

The house where Ben and Heidi had spent many of the twenty-four years of their marriage was on Miller's Road, which paralleled the river. Built of gray stone, it was surrounded by tall lilac trees. The whisper of the rapids which lapped against a high bank at the end of the garden could be heard in every room.

In the driveway of this house Ben saw an ancient pick-up truck on which there were many faded bumper stickers and decals. A sign on the rear said GOD, GUTS AND GUNS WON AMERICA. LET'S KEEP ALL THREE! The front bumper said SUPPORT YOUR LOCAL POLICE! American flags and emblems of the Sheriffs' Association decorated the windows.

"I wonder what patriot belongs to that?" Ben asked wryly.

"That's the Kellys' truck," Eph said. "I guess old Dan put that stuff on. Maybe he's trying to make up for not even being a citizen. He keeps going back and forth from Ireland, and he never did get his papers."

As Ben walked across the lawn to the front door of the house, he noted that the place looked deserted. The grass had not been cut recently, and a trellis of rambling roses on the front porch had blown down. When Heidi had lived there,

13

she always had insisted on keeping everything so neat! She had infuriated him by asking him to interrupt his work for household tasks.

It seemed strange to ring this front doorbell like a stranger, but he did not have a key. After a few moments he heard footsteps. The door opened, and there stood Ebon. How tall he was! In the year since Ben had seen his son, the boy had shot up. A lanky youth who must be well over six feet, Ebon was barefoot in blue jeans and a T-shirt. His curly brown hair, so much like his mother's, was cut just short of his shoulders. His narrow face was almost too sensitive and delicate for the young athlete's body, but there was also strength and great vitality there. Ben's first emotion was pride. This apparently was one aspect of his life which was turning out right, no matter what anyone said.

For a fraction of a second the two men stared at each other, trying to join visions of present and past. Ebon was astonished to see that his father was a little shorter than himself, as though he had shrunk, but Ben was still a man of massive strength, with shoulders wider than the son's might ever be. With his iron-gray hair cut short, Ben looked more like a general than a photographer.

"Well, if it isn't the old Iron Mountain himself!" Ebon exclaimed with a grin, and gave his father a playful right to the shoulder.

"You're leaving yourself wide open, boy," Ben retorted with a laugh and flicked his left at his son's chin, opening his fist at the last moment to deliver not a punch but a caress.

How strange that they should revert to old boxing lessons after all this time! Neither of them had ever really given a damn about boxing.

The two men exchanged a brief, embarrassed hug, like fighters clinching in the middle of a ring.

"By God, you really are taller than I am," Ben said. "How are you ever going to look up to your father now?"

14

"I still wouldn't want to mess with you," Ebon said. "Want a beer?"

They walked to the kitchen. The house looked as though a party had been held recently without a clean-up crew. Empty glasses, beer cans and overflowing ashtrays were everywhere. Ben was annoyed at himself for feeling the beginnings of anger. Sure, Ebon should have kept the place neat, but what seventeen-year-old boy would?

The cold beer tasted good. In an ashtray on the kitchen table Ben saw, half buried in the ashes, some pinched butts of marijuana cigarettes.

"If you're going to smoke grass, I'd get rid of the remains," he said. "The cops around here like nothing better than a chance to make a pot bust. Nothing else can make a boozed-up cop feel so virtuous."

"I'll take care of it," Ebon replied, and all the old tensions of a father-son relationship were suddenly reestablished. There was a moment of silence before Ebon added, "Why did you come home?"

"To see you."

"To take me to California?"

"Not necessarily. To find some solution for you better than living alone."

"I'm not alone. I've got a girl."

He made those two short sentences sound beautiful. A child of divorce Ebon might be, but he had found a solution. Suddenly swept back to the days when Heidi had rescued him from despair shortly after the death of his father, Ben was not inclined to be critical. Those old words still sounded pretty good: "I'm not alone. I've got a girl."

"I'm glad," Ben said.

Having expected objections from his father, Ebon was confused. "She's a wonderful girl," he added uncertainly.

"I'm not a bit surprised."

"Her mother is dead and her father lives in Ireland, but

15

she has a wonderful older sister who takes care of everything and a grandmother. I've been living with them."

"So I've heard."

"It isn't what a lot of people try to make it, dad! They're decent people, the best people I've ever met, all of them! You can't believe how good they've been to me."

"I'm grateful."

"But you're disapproving," Ebon said.

"I just wonder what you plan next."

"They said I can spend the summer there. I'm going to paint their house."

"Good."

"In the fall I'll go to college. What is there to worry about?"

He didn't really know how to answer that question and there was a moment of silence.

"Please don't give me the lecture about how terrible it is to get married young. Muth already did that."

"She ought to know."

"Besides, I doubt if I can even get Annie to marry me ever, dad. You'll have to meet her to understand."

"When can I?"

"We can stop by the farm now. At five I have to pick up her sister at the mill. I have their truck."

Ebon drove the old pickup, handling it with skill and apparent pride. They jounced to the outskirts of the village, where they turned down a dirt road that led toward the river. An ancient orchard of gnarled apple trees bloomed on their right. In a grove of maple trees ahead, Ben saw an old-fashioned farmhouse. Behind it were some sun-silvered unpainted barns and a silo which leaned like the Tower of Pisa. Surrounded by green fields, the place had something of the beauty of an ancient sailing ship, the survivor of many storms.

"This place hasn't been farmed in years," Ebon said. "They're just trying to hold onto the land. They have about

16

three hundred acres on the river." He spoke almost with proprietary pride.

They parked by the front of the house. Chickens and ducks made way for them as they walked across a yard toward a porch which was stacked high with firewood. Opening the door without knocking, Ebon motioned for his father to follow. The dimly lit living room was fragrant in a way that only rooms which are heated by wood stoves can be.

"Grammie," Ebon called. "Annie!"

An old woman in a wheelchair propelled herself briskly from the kitchen.

"Annie's out in the back pasture with that damn horse," she said. "If you give the bell a ring, she'll come back."

Ebon was so eager that he strode toward the back door without introducing Ben.

"I guess you be Eb's father," the old woman said, peering at him intently.

"Yes. My name is Ben."

"Ben Winslow. I knew your father and liked him too. About the Livingston side of your family we won't say much."

Ben laughed. In the backyard he heard an old farm bell ring loudly. Joining his son there, he looked out over the ocean of green grass and gently rolling hills.

"She's exercising her mare out there," Ebon said. "She'll be back before long."

They waited. Although it was not yet four in the afternoon, spring peepers were beginning their chorus. The air was fragrant with apple blossoms. On the bank of the river, willow trees, still more yellow than green, bowed over the water.

"Here she comes!" Ebon said.

The chestnut mare and rider appeared suddenly on the crest of a distant hill. They galloped swiftly toward the farm, disappearing in valleys and bobbing up like a boat. The girl wore a white shirt which gleamed in the afternoon sun. Her long hair, almost the same color as the chestnut mare, streamed out behind. She wore dungarees, no shoes, and rode bareback. That surprised Ben less than the fact that she also rode without a bridle. While still a hundred yards away, the horse slowed to a walk and proceeded to munch grass. With easy agility the girl jumped to the ground and walked toward them. As she came closer, Ben saw, with something like a sinking heart, that this was indeed more than an ordinarily pretty teenager. Shining hair, glowing skin, near-classical features, and a figure really too good to be true—all this with laughing eyes and that smile some Irish girls have patented— poor Ebon! How could he get his thoughts and feelings together when confronted by *this* country girl?

"Dad, this is Annie," Ebon said in tones of vast understatement, a real throwaway line.

"I can't imagine what you see in her," Ben replied with a smile. To his astonishment, the girl looked stricken. "That's a joke, young lady," he quickly added. "I haven't seen such a spectacular horse and rider even in the circus!"

The girl's face abruptly became radiant. Her blue eyes sparkled. "Thank you, Mr. Winslow," she said. "I've wanted to meet you for a long time."

"She's a photography nut, dad," Ebon said. "She collects your collections, and she has a whole gallery of her own stuff."

Annie blushed, a pleasant phenomenon. Suddenly she sat cross-legged in the grass and put a green stalk in her mouth. She said nothing, but her mischievous eyes never left Ben's face.

"May I see this gallery of yours?" Ben asked.

"No! It's nowhere near good enough."

"That's not true," Ebon said. "Some of her shots are terrific."

Annie kicked his knee gently with one bare foot. "I'm just a lousy amateur," she said. "I don't even have any equipment.

18

I take great snapshots with an Instamatic, if you don't mind pictures of people without any heads."

He laughed and she joined him. Her words and blushes were appropriately shy. Her laughing eyes were not. With a girl that pretty, Ben thought, it would be difficult for any man—never mind a seventeen-year-old—to tell what kind of a person she was. Was she intelligent or hopelessly naïve? Was she essentially seeking or giving? At first few men would really care. Girls that pretty were a born entrapment. Whether they wanted to or not, they started a relationship by blinding a man.

"Eb, could you get me a drink of water?" the girl asked.

"Sure," Ebon replied, jumping up.

"And my coat's in the kitchen. It's getting chilly."

"In a second."

He ran toward the house. There was no reason why he should not run such errands, but there had been a note of command in the girl's voice.

"How long are you going to stay in Livingston?" Ann asked.

"I don't really know yet."

"I'm sure that Sis would love to have you stay here at the farm with Ebon and us if you want. We have plenty of room."

"That's very kind. I'm afraid I have to stay with my mother for a while."

Ebon returned with a glass of water and a denim coat. As he solicitously helped the girl to put this on, Ben found himself envying him. Maybe he was just infatuated, and maybe young love would turn out no better for him than it had for his father, but it was a beautiful afternoon in May and only fools could think that the passion of seventeen-year-olds was somehow spurious. Perhaps it would turn out to be transitory, but without doubt Ebon would remember this girl all his life, perhaps with gratitude, perhaps with regret, or the usual mixture of the two. Whatever the future, Ebon was obviously exuberant now as he helped Ann on with her coat. She momentarily arched her upper body while she put her hands through the sleeves. When would a full-figured girl like this be more beautiful than when she was seventeen? Every line of her was full of an innocent sensuality which made even Ben conjure up dreams of long ago and moonlit fantasies which he thought he had forgotten. How must a seventeen-year-old boy, already on fire with youth, stay cool in this kind of aura?

Rather ashamed of his thoughts for suddenly turning almost clinical, Ben found himself wondering whether Ann and his son were already full-fledged lovers. They both looked so fresh-faced and young that the very question seemed wrong, yet the circumstances of both their lives were mixed up enough to disturb ordinary patterns, and, at any rate, the girls and boys of this lush valley commonly did not stay away from each other long, as he well knew. Still, he found himself wishing that they would not get too deeply involved too soon. Probably there would be no way to tell them that the years of innocence were awfully short, why try to live like adults before you had to? ...

Now the two young people started walking toward the horse, automatically joining hands as their fingers touched. Suddenly Ben found himself wondering how long it had been since he had held hands with anyone. With the people he had met in California, almost any embrace but that was easily available.

2

As the girl led the horse toward the barn, Ebon returned to his father.

"Time to go get Rosie," he said cheerfully. "Want to
come?"

"Sure."

"What do you think of my girl?"

"I envy the hell out of you. It's always hard to tell how
things will work out in the long run, but right now I wouldn't
care either."

Ebon laughed. "What's to worry about in the long run?"

"Well, you know, Fitzgerald said that the rich are different
from other people. I don't know about that, but I do know
that great beauties are different from other people."

"Sure, they're better looking."

"It's more than that. They grow used to a lot of attention
and to getting their own way. They affect men differently.
It's a subtle syndrome."

"I'll take my chances," Ebon said with a grin, and got into
the cab of the truck.

As they drove toward the paper mill, the acrid smell grew
worse. At close range the mill itself looked like a city block
set down in the country. Driving through a wire gate, Ebon
stopped in front of a brick building with a sign which said,

"Administrative Offices." Almost immediately a door opened and a slender woman about thirty years old came out. The first thing which Ben noticed about her was her energetic, gracefully hurrying walk. Holding herself erect with her shoulders back, she pumped her arms almost as though she were running. She was wearing a sweater of beige cashmere and a brown tweed skirt. As she came closer, Ben saw that her face resembled Ann's but was pale and tired-looking. Her figure was less buxom than her younger sister's, and curiously because of that, almost more youthful, more like an adolescent's. Her hair was much the same color as her sister's, but curled and cut short in a way which displayed her graceful neck. Unlike her sister, she had brown eyes and high cheekbones. As she approached the truck, her face broke into a smile of great warmth. She had great eyes, all full of flash and humor.

"Hi there!" she said. "You're right on time."

When Ben looked out from the cab, she added, "You're Ebon's father. I heard you lecture at the high school ages ago."

"I bet I was a bore."

She laughed, throwing her chin back, and Ben found himself liking her intensely, just like that, for no real reason he could name. There was something about this brisk, obviously tired but laughing woman—something, well, gallant, warm and wise, which made the charms of her sister's extreme youth seem no more than a prelude.

Rose sat crowded between the two men in the cab of the truck. "I've wanted to meet you for a long time," she said to Ben. "I have all kinds of nefarious schemes in which I would like to involve you."

"Like what?"

"I'll need time to explain. You'll have dinner with us, won't you?"

"I'd like nothing better."

The heartiness with which he gave this reply made her give

22

him another smile. Her teeth were just a little crooked, saving her smile from looking like a toothpaste advertisement. While her figure looked younger than thirty, her tired face looked older, with a delicate etching of lines which took away all blandness. He would like to photograph that face, he decided. Ann's beauty had the effect of masking her character, but Rose's appeared to reveal it.

"It's a nice day, isn't it?" Ebon suddenly asked, with a smile.

"No, it most definitely is *not* a nice day," Rose replied firmly. "Only an ass could think it was. And I don't like your tone of voice, young man! Shape up or ship out!"

Increasing Ben's bewilderment, they both laughed.

"You have to understand that I am the public relations girl for the mill," Rose explained. "After being terribly, terribly sweet to people all day, I'm just aching to tell somebody off. Eb knows that it's better if I do it before I get home."

Ben found himself envying his son's close relationship with Rose, as well as her younger sister. Obviously Ebon had found himself not only a girl, but a whole family. From what he had seen of these people so far, they had a lot more to offer than anyone in the boy's real family. Perhaps the best thing he could do for his son was to go back to California and let him alone. The thought made Ben feel suddenly cold. In Santa Barbara he had many friends and his profession enabled him to meet some of the most beautiful women in California, but maybe because of his own inadequacies, he had been able to form no close ties with anyone. He had no sentimental longing for his former wife, but ever since his divorce, he had felt himself alone even in the merriest company.

When they got back to the farmhouse, Rose said, "Would you like a drink? I hid a bottle of Scotch on dad the last time he was here. Maybe I can find it."

The Scotch was in a cupboard so high that she had to use a stepladder to reach it. He noticed that there was never anything awkward about the way she moved. As she perched on the ladder, he observed that she had a compact, nicely rounded rear and wished that he knew her well enough to compliment her on it.

"Rose, you're a fine looking woman!" he said on impulse.

"Ah, all the boys say that when I give them whiskey," she replied with her smile. The lilt of her Irish accent seemed to come and go unpredictably. Bottle in hand, she stepped gracefully down from the ladder. Taking a dish rag from the sink, she wiped it.

"I'll say one thing for my father," she said. "When he's around, I never have to dust the whiskey bottles."

After she prepared his drink, he sat at a big, round kitchen table. Putting on a yellow apron, Rose began to get dinner. Soon Grammie arrived from another room in her wheelchair and started to set the table. Some of the dishes were on shelves too high for her to reach and her old hands kept dropping the silver. Without apparent irritation, Rose helped her, interrupting the process of making biscuits and peeling vegetables.

"Let me do the potatoes," Ben said. "When I was in the army, I got the potato peeling medal with two oak leaf clusters."

She gave him a big bowl, potatoes, a scraper and a paper bag for the peels. While he worked, he studied the big old country kitchen. Rose was using a cast-iron wood-burning range which heated the room. Beside it was an ancient gas stove, apparently for summer use. The soapstone sink was almost big enough to serve as a bathtub. In a row beside it were modern washing machines for clothes and dishes, as well as a dryer. Net bags of potatoes, carrots and onions hung from shelves. The room was fragrant with spices, apples which filled several wooden bowls, and a roasting chicken Grammie had put in the oven and which Rose now basted. Soon baking biscuits added their aroma.

Ben had never been in a kitchen like this in his life. In his mother's home, servants had done the cooking and he had rarely been allowed in their domain. In his own home Heidi

24

had designed a kitchen which looked like a laboratory and had made such a virtue of hating housework that no one had felt comfortable there. If this old-fashioned kitchen, with its padded maple chairs and the enormous table was not part of his experience, why did he feel so at home in it? Had he read of kitchens like this in forgotten books and longed to come home to one?

Rose too had an air of familiarity about her, though he had never known a woman any way like her. At the age of seventy, his mother had triumphantly announced that she had finally learned how to boil an egg and make coffee on the maid's day off. Heidi had been an excellent cook when she put her mind to it, but usually played the grim part of a martyr when she had to abandon her painting, her piano and her sculpturing to get meals. Rose not only cooked with apparent pleasure but did it after a full day's work in an office. She was playing the roles of both husband and wife while taking care of both the old and the young in her family. She was *responsible*, and though that might seem a dull word to apply to a good-looking woman, it made her almost unique amongst the women he usually met at cocktail parties, on beaches and in his studio. She was also humorous and competent in all sorts of small ways as she prepared food without having to consult books and briskly repaired an eggbeater which had jammed. It was curious to discover that he had reached a point where a woman who was responsible, humorous and competent was a lot more desirable and downright sexier than all the beauties with beehives of blonde hair and plunging necklines.

Although such thoughts were of course premature, Ben found himself wondering what would happen if he tried to get to know this woman better. The very qualities he admired in her would probably make her very self-protective. A fling with a divorced man considerably older than she who could be expected to return to California at any moment would not be her style at all. Probably she had an understanding with some

25

earnest thirty-year-old engineer in the mill who was saving his money for a carefully considered marriage. This woman, almost as much as her younger sister, was for him to admire, but not touch, a thought which made Ben feel more restless and lonely than ever.

He was somewhat encouraged, though, to see that Rose was not entirely indifferent to him. As she moved about the kitchen, she often glanced at him, then looked away with a smile when their eyes met. Under what he suspected was iron discipline, she was perhaps naturally flirtatious. Her face, which was really very pale for a person living in the country, flushed during one moment when her glance met his.

Ebon came in to fill the woodbox.

"Thank you, dear," Rose said. "Call Annie now and we'll eat."

Well, Ebon certainly had been accepted in the family, Ben thought, and realized he felt something like a touch of envy. He was almost alarmed to find that his food tasted unusually good, something which always happened when he started to fall in love. This time there were more prosaic reasons, though. He had forgotten how chicken tasted when it had been fed on corn not chemicals, and when it had never been frozen or trucked for hundreds of miles. He had forgotten what home-baked biscuits were like with fresh, unsalted butter. Wild strawberries canned at home, with real whipped cream, made a shortcake better than any he had ever tasted.

While they drank their coffee, Annie rinsed the dishes and Ebon stacked the dishwasher, something he had never done at home. Annie had none of the verve with which her sister worked in the kitchen. Her mind obviously on higher matters, she seemed almost to be in a trance as she scrubbed pots with a rag instead of a scouring pad that would get them clean.

"Let me do that," Ebon said, sounding slightly annoyed.

In the end, he did most of the work. Ben didn't know whether that meant that Annie was clever or merely abstracted.

26

After coffee, grammie retired to the television set in the living room and the young people began to do their homework on the kitchen table.

"Would you like to take a walk?" Rose asked Ben. "We have some new lambs out back."

"Oh, let me show him the lambs!" Ann said.

"How about your homework, honey?"

"I don't have much. Come on, Eb, let's show him the lambs! I bet you'll want to take pictures of them, Mr. Winslow!"

She ran ahead. Rose and Ben followed her on a dirt path that led to a fenced-in portion of the pasture. The spring twilight was still bright and a chill wind blew from the north, ruffling the grass like gusts on a lake. The throbbing of tree frogs was so intense that it drowned out all other noises, even that of distant traffic. The mill had shut down for the night and the acrid smell no longer cut the sweetness of spring blossoms in the air.

The sheep were huddled together in a corner of their pasture. As Ann approached, she called, "Here Baby, here Cotton, here Daisy!"

As though they knew their names, three lambs detached themselves from the flock and came bounding toward her. Unlocking a wire gate, she went in, knelt and embraced first one lamb, then another. Standing up, she began to jump up and down.

"Come on, lambs! Jump! Jump with me. Jump!"

Obediently the lambs began to bounce up and down in the lush green grass as though they had springs for legs. Ben had *heard* of gamboling lambs, and had occasionally seen a lamb play in this way, but never three together and never on command. The pretty young girl and the lambs made a distinctly joyous sight.

Their exuberance was infectious. Suddenly Ebon was jumping with them. Almost immediately Rose followed with a laugh, gracefully bounding about. Before Ben knew it, he himself was skipping about like an agitated rhinoceros. Ap-

27

parently enjoying the competition, the lambs whisked about, kicking their feet in all directions.

Ben was thinking that even in his youth he had never celebrated spring with *this* sort of elation. Suddenly his right foot slipped into a woodchuck hole, and he fell heavily in the grass, his right ankle throbbing painfully. Everyone, even the lambs, stopped jumping.

"What's the matter?" Ebon asked.

"Are you hurt?" Annie said.

Without saying anything, Rose knelt beside him and began taking his right shoe off. Her fingers were nimble as she pulled off his sock.

"Move the foot as much as you can," she said.

He wiggled it, clenching his toes with pain.

"I think it's just a sprained ankle," she said. "We'll soak it in warm water and Epsom salts. Eb, help me get him up."

With his left arm around his son's waist and his right arm on Rose's shoulders, Ben hopped toward the house. Although Rose was only about five feet three inches tall, she was a good person to lean on, literally. Ebon's tall thin body seemed a little embarrassed by his father's embrace, but Rose's small shoulders were solid, unflinching under his pressure.

When they had helped him to sit by the kitchen table, Rose poured him a whiskey and filled a galvanized iron washtub with hot water. Ebon helped her to carry it to Ben's chair. Rose tested the temperature of the water with her hand before telling him to put his foot in it. The heat felt good, easing the pain a little. With a towel over her shoulder, Rose knelt by the tub.

"Eb, go get some Epsom salts before the drugstore closes," she said.

"Can I go with him?" Ann asked.

"You go to your room and do your homework."

"I apologize for being so much trouble," Ben said.

"Blame it on the woodchuck. Do you mind if I try massaging that ankle underwater?"

28

Her touch was both gentle and firm, seeming to understand every sore spot. She caressed not only the ankle, but the sensitive instep and the toes. The thought occurred to him that a woman who could touch a man's foot like that must have infinite possibilities, but he did his best to banish it.

"Does that hurt?" she asked.

"If it does, I love pain."

She laughed, low, throaty. He liked the way she laughed, and that was another danger sign. First his appetite improved and then everything a woman did seemed marvelous. Those were the first two steps of infatuation. Often the third step was the discovery that everything the woman did seemed terrible. Beware!

"Look, this feels great, but don't let yourself get tired—"

"I'm all right. Just tell me where it feels best."

It was difficult to resist the temptation to make a rather bawdy reply, but he did, pressing his lips sternly together. She glanced up at him and blushed before she began to laugh.

"I didn't say anything," he protested.

"No, but I can tell you have a dirty mind," she said. "I like that. When a girl meets a clean-minded feller, there's no way she can tell what he's thinking."

He laughed. "Rosie, I like you!"

Her eyes widened. "Why?"

"I don't really know why, but you make me feel good. I was forty-five going on sixty-five when I met you. Now I think I'm forty-five going on twenty-three."

"Ah, but you're a beautiful man to say that," she replied, her Irish lilt returning. "Would you like a cup of tea while your foot soaks?"

"That would be fine."

As she poured water from the kettle into two cups, her face was serious. Putting a steaming cup in front of him, she said, "And when are you proposing to go back to California?"

Suddenly it seemed to him that he had made a move of sorts and that this was her sensible refusal.

"I have no real plans," he replied. "I just came to check on Ebon. Do you mind putting him up here all summer?"

She sat beside him and stared into her teacup for a moment before answering. "I don't know," she said with a small shrug.

Having expected bland reassurances, he was surprised. His face showed it.

"Look, I love Eb," Rose hastened to say, "but I'm not sure it's such a smart idea to have him and Annie in the same house all the time."

"Are you worried about them?"

"A little. Young love isn't always all that it's cracked up to be. Annie's a pretty complicated lady right now and there's nothing simple about Eb. Sometimes they make each other happy, sometimes pretty miserable."

"Isn't that par for the course?"

"I'm not sure. I've never played much."

"Do you think the kids should be separated?"

"I'm not even sure whether that would be possible. Eb said he'd hitchhike home if you sent him to Florida or California."

"Does Annie welcome all this attention from him?"

"Sometimes, and sometimes I'm afraid that she resents it. He's much more intense than she is, but I guess that's usual for kids their age."

"Probably, but I can't allow him to impose on you."

"It's not that. He makes himself very useful around the house. To tell the truth, I think I'm more worried about him than about her. She's shy and actually more than a little scared of boys. The high school is pretty rough these days and she's had some bad experiences. Annie doesn't want to grow up, and Ebon can't wait. In a way I wish he could find himself a less complicated girl."

"Well, he'll be going to college in the fall. I hear that colleges are full of uncomplicated girls these days."

"Do you really believe that?" she asked with a smile.

They were interrupted by Ebon, who delivered the Epsom

salts before retreating to his room to do his homework. After emptying the bottle into the tub, Rose again massaged Ben's sore foot.

"I don't want you to think that Eb isn't welcome here," she continued in a low voice. "Whether we kept them apart or together, we would have worries. I guess I just find it a relief to have someone I can worry with for a change."

"You'll never find a more expert worrier. What I think you've been trying to tell me, Rose, is that Eb is infatuated with Annie, but Annie doesn't really respond all that much."

"That's part of it. I was also trying to say that maybe Annie isn't grown up enough to love anyone right now. This is no time to go into it, but she's had a good many problems."

"So has Eb . . ."

"It's still spring and they're still young," Rose added with her smile. "Who are we to feel sorry for them?"

"It's spring for us, too! When you do that to my foot, I feel sorry for everyone in the world who hasn't just sprained an ankle."

She laughed. "Do you want Eb to take you home tonight, or do you want to stay with us? I don't think you should try to travel far."

"My home consists of an empty house full of empty beer cans. Do you mind putting up yet another refugee from the Winslow family?"

"No. Since you gave me a compliment, I guess I can say I like talking with you. I wish to hell that you weren't heading right back to California. This town really needs you."

"In what way?"

"We're both too tired to go into it much now. But, in a nutshell, Howie Hewat is taking over the town."

"Have you talked to my brother, Pete, about it?"

"Pete is Howie Hewat's righthand man. Forgive me, but does the chicken go to the fox for help."

"What do you think I could do about it?"

31

"If you took over the *Recorder* again, you'd have a big voice. And people will always listen to you around here, Ben. You've not been forgotten."

"I'm afraid that I'm not much of a reformer. Anyway, I doubt whether anyone can change this town. Do you ever think of getting out?"

"How do you get out when you've got two dependents and three hundred acres of land you can't sell?"

"That riverfront should bring a good price."

"You've been away a long time. The Park Agency has all but confiscated it. I'll tell you about it later. Right now I'm going to light up the stove in your room."

While she was gone, Ebon came into the kitchen. "Can I take you home, dad?"

"Rose has invited me to spend the night here."

"Here?" Ebon echoed, and he looked annoyed before he caught himself. "Well, I guess with your foot it's a good idea," he added.

Ben realized then that he was in a sense invading his son's territory, forcing him to share this miraculous island of warmth he had discovered all by himself, sort of usurping his place as the man of the house.

"I'll be going home in the morning," he said, but the sentence sounded flat. Ebon was alert enough to suspect that from now on Ben might be at least as important a part of the Kelly family as he was. He turned without speaking and went back upstairs.

When Rose returned, she added hot water to his footbath and sat across the table from him for perhaps an hour while he soaked his ankle.

"Tell me about California," she said.

"That's a big subject."

"I just want to know about your part of it. What do you like so much?"

32

He'd never before seriously tried to describe his life on the West Coast.

"The town of Santa Barbara is supposed to be about as close to Utopia as you can get," he said, "and in some ways it is. Beautiful mountains come down to great beaches. All the flowers seem to be about twice as big as they are anywhere else. It never gets really cold and rarely gets too hot. There are so many handsome men and beautiful women on the beaches that they sometimes seem to me to be a different race. Almost no one seems poor. The poor folk drive Cadillacs instead of foreign cars."

"And how can little old Livingston compete with that?"

"I don't know, but I actually dream about Livingston almost every night when I'm out there. Curiously enough, my dreams keep track of the seasons. In winter I dream about snow and in the fall, I dream about the foliage on the mountains. I've often toyed with the notion of coming home, but I'm rather suspicious of my reasons."

"Why?"

"To be honest, I'm afraid that I miss the sense of importance I feel here. This is the only place in the world where I can cash checks anywhere and where I can at least make myself heard if I get mad. . . ."

He found himself telling Rose a story he'd never told to anyone. He had a daughter, Laura, now fourteen years old, whom he had always adored, but as so often happened, the girl had sided with her mother during the divorce two years before. She hadn't answered his letters and had declined to visit him until her mother, who wanted a few months without children, had insisted. A tense, fragile thirteen-year-old, Laura had seemed not at all impressed by her father's beach cottage. Bored and listless, she seemed relieved when he enrolled her in a nearby private school.

This august institution was far ahead of anywhere she had been, but Laura was a good student and worked hard. This

33

pale, silent little girl from the East made few friends, but she at least seemed to enjoy her classes. So he was shocked when the principal telephoned him one afternoon to say that Laura "had had a little accident" and was in the hospital.

The child's face was bruised and she had a cut above her right ear. Lying in the hospital bed, she had seemed oddly stoic when Ben asked what had happened.

"Some kids threw rocks at me," she said.

"Why?"

"They got mad."

"*Why?*"

She had been riding in a school bus on the way to a museum. When they had stopped at a traffic light, some Chicano kids had thrown rocks at the bus, breaking a window but hurting no one. The bus driver had collared one of the children and a truck driver had caught two more. The police had come and had asked the students on the bus if they had done anything to provoke the incident. Everyone said no, everyone but Laura.

"Some of the kids were yelling *wetback* at them," she had told an officer.

According to her schoolmates, she had ratted. When they came to school the next day, three of the boys had brought rocks in their pockets and during recess, in the playground, they had used them.

"That's terrible," Rose said.

"Bad enough, but the strange thing was the feeling of powerlessness I had when I tried to get those boys punished. The principal wanted to forget the whole thing. The boys apparently came from prominent families and he didn't want trouble. When I went to see him in his office, he said a report was being written and when I asked to see a copy of it, he said it would not be available to the public. The guy couldn't or wouldn't get my name straight. Every time I phoned him, he called me Williams or Warren, or some damn thing. I didn't get anywhere until I took pictures of Laura's face and threatened to call a news conference. Even then, the kids who threw those rocks got nothing but a brief reprimand. That just made them madder, and everywhere Laura went in school, she heard whispered threats. She was furious at me for making a fuss. Needless to say, she was glad to go back East, and hasn't visited me since."

"You think that couldn't happen here?" Rose asked.

"Not to me, or my kids. Here we're the, well . . . the prominent people. Look, I *know* that sounds terrible and ridiculous, but no special credit to me it's also pretty true. . . . Maybe that's why I've stayed away from here so long. Maybe I long to be some kind of small-town aristocrat, but I'm not too proud of myself when I start falling into that role—"

"These days you might find that fairly difficult anyway. . . . Howie Hewat is the current king of the hill."

"I went to school with Howie. I just find it hard to take him seriously."

"If you ever try to do anything around here without his approval, you'll be cured of that."

"I know. There's always been one guy who controls everything around here. It might be fun to try to knock him over, but can you understand, Rose, that I'm tired? And confused about my family and everything else. I never see my daughter. My son has had to be practically adopted by you, and I literally don't know whether I'm coming or going. I guess I'd like to straighten my own life out before I take up any great do-good causes."

"I can understand that," she said. "God knows . . ."

A banjo clock on the wall struck three, but the hands pointed to ten.

"I guess I better be hitting the old hay," Rose said. "Can I help you to your room?"

"I'd like that."

After drying his foot, she helped to pull him up from his chair and offered herself as a crutch as he hopped down the hall. Because he could brace himself against the walls, he

35

didn't really need her, but welcomed the excuse to put his arm around her firm, warm shoulders. They laughed almost like teenagers as he hopped along, holding his injured foot a few inches above the floor.

The room she had prepared for him was only about ten feet square. It was filled almost entirely by a brass double bed and an ancient barrel-shaped Round Oak stove which emanated a dry heat which was welcome in the damp old house. He sat heavily down on the edge of the bed and she helped him to turn and get his feet up.

"Does your ankle hurt now?" she asked.

"Yes! Terribly! It needs to be massaged!"

She laughed. "In the morning if we have time before I go to work. Good *night*."

"Rose, wait a minute! I want to thank you. You've kind of rescued my son. You've fixed my ankle and I can't tell you how you've raised my spirits—"

"I'm glad," she replied with a smile.

"Will you have dinner with me tomorrow night?"

"It would be easier if you ate here. I have to see to my family."

"They ought to be able to take care of themselves for one night. Sit down a minute. Do you have to go right away?"

She perched on the edge of the foot of the bed. "I'd have to get home early," she said. "Grammie needs a good deal of care."

"I'll bring you back anytime you want. . . . You know the idea of my moving back here isn't beyond possibility. Santa Barbara may be a Utopia, but there are two things wrong with it for me: it seems to press me into being mostly just a slick commercial photographer, and I can't seem to find anybody to talk to out there. I have absolutely no doubt that it's my own fault, but in the two years I've been there, I can't seem to break out of . . . myself. It's easy to find people to drink with, eat with, swim with and fish with, even to sleep with, but I can't seem to establish any communication—"

"I have the same trouble here," she replied with a rueful smile.

"If I could get control of the *Recorder*, is there any chance that I could hire you away from the paper mill?"

"Don't talk like that."

"Why?"

"Not till you've thought about it enough to be serious. I've wanted to work on a newspaper all my life. For a PR girl, that's like a chance to go straight."

"It shouldn't be hard to get the paper back. It still legally belongs to my mother, and Pete has never really liked running it."

"You may have trouble."

"How?"

"Pete works for Howie, and through him Howie controls the paper. He likes that. He won't give it to you without a fight."

"I'll see Pete tomorrow about that."

When Rose left him with the light out, Ben struggled out of his clothes and lay watching the flickering yellow light that the open draft of the stove cast on the ceiling. The pine logs snapped and crackled, and a thin fragrant wisp of smoke escaped the lid of the old Round Oak. The delightful warmth made him drowsy. As he drifted off to sleep, he found himself eagerly looking forward to the morning. How long had it been since he had felt that way?

3

Eʙᴏɴ awoke Ben at seven.

"Time to get up, dad! Rosie has to get to work and we have to go to school. It's your turn in the bathroom."

The stove was out and the room was chilly. Throwing a blanket around his shoulders, he started to walk down the hall toward the bathroom. A dull ache reminded him that he had turned his ankle, but he found that he could walk with only a slight limp and there was no real pain. Coming from the other direction in the hall, Rose met him. She was wearing a jade-colored dress of Irish linen which was high-necked enough to be prim and close-fitting enough to counteract that effect entirely. When she saw him in his blanket, she laughed.

"How's the ankle?"

"It needs countless hours of massaging."

"I guess we'll have to run you straight to the hospital. Seriously, how is it?"

"Almost entirely cured, unfortunately. Your treatment worked."

"Good! . . . I'll get you dad's bathrobe. Here's a razor and a new toothbrush. I'll put a shirt and shorts on your bed. They belong to dad too, but I think they'll fit."

Her father's clothes did fit him almost exactly, a fact which Rose exclaimed about, apparently regarding it as an omen,

38

though whether a good or bad one he couldn't tell. When he showed up at the breakfast table, he found her in her apron frying bacon while Annie dreamily stirred a pitcher of frozen orange juice with a wooden spoon. Ebon was briskly supplying each stove in the house with firewood. Grammie was making toast, cursing heartily as she burned her fingers.

"Can somebody take me to the doctor at one o'clock?" grammie asked.

"The kids will be in school, but I guess I can get away from work," Rose said.

"Let me do it," Ben said. "I'll have my jeep."

Ebon let an armful of wood fall into the woodbox with a little more noise than usual.

"Hell, I could do it during my lunch hour," he said.

"No need, son."

"And could you do some grocery shopping while you're at it?" Rose asked Ben. "I'll give you the money and a list."

"Fine," Ben replied. "And I'll pick you up outside your office at five."

"I *always* do that," Ebon said.

"But tonight Ben and I are stepping out together," Rose said. "I'll get you guys some spaghetti and meatballs. Do you want anything else?"

"We'll be all right, Sis," Ann said. "Have a good time."

"Yeah," Ebon said, and Ben wondered whether he was enough smitten with Rose, as well as Ann, to be jealous, or whether he just thought that his whole little harem was being invaded by his father.

As soon as breakfast was over, Ebon and Ann climbed into the back of the pickup truck while Ben and Rose got into the cab. Since the school bus did not stop near the farm, they drove to the high school. As the young couple, both dressed in sneakers, dungarees and white shirts, walked toward the door, Ebon put his arm around Ann's waist. She did not melt toward him, but also did not object. They appeared to be

39

idyllic young lovers, except for their faces, which to Ben seemed rather tense and strained.

Next stop was Ben's house, where Ephram had left his old jeep in the driveway. Ben used it to follow Rose as she drove her truck back to the school, where she left it in a parking lot for Ebon. After she had climbed into the jeep beside him, he headed for the paper mill. It was a bright May morning, but still chilly enough to make him grateful for his overcoat. The tattered top of the open jeep did not offer much shelter from the wind, and the heater did not work.

Rose wore no coat over her thin jade dress.

"Aren't you cold?" he asked.

"I feel too good to be cold. Isn't it a gorgeous morning!"

"It is that, but you've got goose bumps on your arms."

"I like feeling the sunshine and the air." Her lips were parted. "Look at those terrific poplars"—she smiled shyly—"I wish I had waving branches and leaves that could shiver in the wind—"

"What you've got are nice pink arms that are shivering in the wind." Stopping by the side of the road, he took off his overcoat and handed it to her.

"Won't you freeze?" she asked.

"My sports coat is heavier than your dress." He helped her put on the overcoat.

"It does feel great," she said. With a smile that might have been coquettish, she added, "Are you always so beautifully gallant, or is this what I get for rubbing your foot?"

"I play the point system."

"What does that mean?"

"Every time I do something nice for you, I get points. Lending you my coat is probably worth ten points. Giving you flowers might be worth five."

"How many points are you trying to get?"

"A thousand."

"What happens then?"

"I'll get a prize."

40

"Like what?"

"Oh, we'll think of something."

She laughed. "That's terrible."

"Not if you play the game too. I've already been giving you points for all the nice things you've done."

"Like what?"

"Playing den mother for Ebon is worth five hundred points at least. Fixing my ankle is worth three hundred. Giving me two good meals and putting me up for the night is worth another hundred. You only have a hundred to go."

"Then what happens?"

"Like I said, you get a prize."

"I won't ask what it is," she replied with a laugh. "Like you said, we'll think of something."

At the mill he told her he'd see her at five, and kissed her chastely on the lips. "Do I gain points or lose them for that?"

She laughed. "I'll tell you later," and walked briskly toward the door of the mill, her arms moving as though she were running.

He felt younger than when he had been young.... Well, his first job of the day, he decided, was to find some woman who would clean up his house in time for the dinner he wanted to prepare for Rose that night. Remembering that there was a big bulletin board in the country store where cleaning women and sitters advertised their services, he drove there. The first name he saw was Mrs. Martha Lansky, who wrote only CLEANING with her telephone number.

"I don't have no car," a gruff voice answered his call. "Can you come and get me?"

"Sure."

"Can I bring my daughter? She's seventeen and can help real good."

"Fine."

The Lansky home proved to be a tarpaper shack so covered by vines and surrounded by flowering bushes that it looked almost pretty. Martha Lansky turned out to be a stout but

41

strong-looking woman with straight gray hair cut short and ill-fitting false teeth, which she kept adjusting as she talked, the way one might adjust a television set for volume and clarity.

"Say, you're Ben Winslow, ain't you?" she demanded as she approached the jeep.

"Yes. You're..." He peered sharply at her but did not recognize her.

"Martha Lansky now, but my born name was Kolisky. You used to go with my cousin Katie, when you was both kids. I bet you haven't forgotten her."

"I sure haven't!" Ben replied, remembering a fragile blonde girl who had been sixteen years old that summer of his own sixteenth year. She had lived in a shack much like this one near the place where the river ran into Lost Lake, on the edge of the valley. Her father weathered the Depression by catching night crawlers, frogs and crayfish to sell as bait. They had had an old flat-bottom rowboat, and on moonlight nights, Ben had rowed with Katie in the black-water marshes on the edge of the lake. He could still remember the way she had inhaled sharply sometimes between kisses and her miraculous ability to say yes.

("She is not a suitable girl for you at all," his mother had said. "If you persist in seeing this girl, you'll regret it all your life.")

"Of course I remember Katie," Ben said. "What is she doing now?"

"Dead," Martha replied as she climbed into the jeep. "She had seven kids, too many for her. Put on way too much weight, and then she got the sugar. She had clots of some kind and Dr. Bill cut her leg off. She never really got over that."

"I'm *sorry*," Ben said, sounding as shocked as he felt.

"Well, that's life, ain't it? She used to follow you in the papers and in the magazines, Ben. Every time she saw one

42

of your pictures, she'd cut it out. I found a lot of that stuff when I went through her things."

Ben felt deeply touched, and guilty. After a summer of discovering love together, he had gone off to a year of boarding school. The next spring he had become involved with Heidi, a much more fashionable girl, the daughter of friends of his parents. He had, he supposed, been ashamed of Katie, and had never gone near the marsh again.

"Just stop at the trailer on the right side of the road at the foot of the hill," Martha said. "I want to pick up my daughter, Fern. She cleans good and she could use a few bucks."

Ben started the jeep. If she had saved his pictures, Katie could not have hated him too much. She had been a naturally sunny girl, mild and quick to forgive. If he had had the sense to stick with her, their whole lives might have been different.

"Just stop here for a second," Martha said. "Blow the horn. She expects us."

A pretty, round-faced girl about seventeen or eighteen came out. She was about five months pregnant, and was followed by a little boy. "Can I bring Jimmy with me?" she asked. "I can't find no one to take him today."

"Bring him along," Ben said.

Fern climbed into the back of the jeep with the child. "You don't have to worry about Jimmy," she said. "He never makes no trouble."

The boy sat as still as a sandbag beside his mother, and his impassive little face seemed to see nothing, to care about nothing. When the car started, he gave one guttural cry of alarm, and clung to his mother's arm.

"He don't get a chance to ride in cars much," the girl said. "You don't have to worry about him, though. Jimmy can just set in a corner all day without bothering anyone."

The boy's face was curiously thick, Ben saw, and guessed that he was autistic. In the cities they had autistic children too, but the cleaning lady didn't often bring one to work . . .

43

and in the city one wasn't so apt to run into a reminder of a childhood love affair.... Ben wasn't sure whether he liked it or wanted to escape it, but in Livingston, he always had the feeling of being more deeply involved with people than he was anywhere else.

As he drove toward his house, Ben remembered that when he had come home from the Korean war, a newly successful photojournalist, he had thought of putting together a book of photographs to be called *Small Town*. His inspiration had been Agee's book, *Let Us Now Praise Famous Men*. Every aspect of small-town life would be presented, including the hollow-cheeked mothers who were only in their twenties, the men stirring the stinking vats of pulp in the paper mill, as well as the pretty girls diving into the lake or riding horses bareback, the way Annie now did. The project had been in his imagination for years, but no publisher had been interested in a book about Livingston, and he had needed money too much to devote months to such an ambitious project on speculation.

If he returned to Livingston now to run the *Recorder*, he might have time to begin the *Small Town* project again. Certainly it would be better to attempt something ambitious than to finish his career by doing flattering portraits of celebrities and society women, which was the bulk of his work in Santa Barbara. Now that Heidi had remarried, he no longer had to pay alimony, and there was no real need to make so much money.

These thoughts helped to cure the depression into which the news of Katie's grotesque death had put him. After he let the cleaning women and Jimmy into his house, he telephoned his brother, Pete. Until he talked to him, after all, he would not know whether his old job at the *Recorder could* be his again.

"Ben!" Pete said. "I heard you were in town. When can we get together?"

"Are you busy right now?"

"Never too busy to see my brother. Come on over for a cup or glass of whatever you want!"

His words were certainly cheerful enough, and Ben wondered whether he were imagining an undertone of irony or mockery.

As Ben drove toward his brother's house, he reminded himself that Pete had plenty of reason to feel all kinds of emotions about him. Pete, after all, had been the one who stayed home and took care of his mother's affairs, while Ben went off to take every photographic assignment he could get. When he got his Pulitzer prize for his work in Korea, Ben had been given a welcome-home parade in Livingston, and had ridden up the main street in a Cadillac convertible with his mother and wife. Pete had been offered a place in the front seat.

"No, Ben," he had said. "You're the hero. Make the most of it as long as it lasts."

His bitterness could have had many sources. Pete had been born small, while Ben had always been big enough to find athletic competence easy. Pete, like Ben, had been infatuated with Heidi while she was growing up, but Ben had married her. When the marriage had gone sour, Pete had made a big point of telling Ben how faithful and reliable his own wife, Lucy, was.

"Don't compare women," Ben had snapped. "They have different temperaments, different temptations."

Since Lucy was both stolid and exceedingly plain, those words were easily taken as an insult. Pete had flushed and had given his thin grimace of a smile.

As if all this weren't enough cause for bad blood, their mother, Virginia, often used Ben as a court of last resort when she quarreled with her younger son.

"I'll tell Ben," she'd say if Pete was not quick to have, say, the floors in her house waxed. And Virginia kept scrapbooks of Ben's work everywhere and photographs of him and his

45

family. If one toured her house, one could not tell that she ever had a younger son.

I think that if I were Pete, I'd hate me, Ben thought. He has all kinds of grievances, and I don't really have any.

Except suspicions. Ben had always been embarrassed and somehow ashamed even to think about his mother's money, but she had inherited a good deal from her father. For years Ben had somehow suspected that his brother would arrange in some legal way, or apparently legal way, to get most of this. Since Virginia's decline into senility, she would sign anything put before her by one of her sons, and Pete had power of attorney. In such circumstances it would be possible for a clever lawyer to arrange almost anything.

The thought of the investigations which would be necessary to find out whether his suspicions were justified made Ben so uncomfortable that he had simply given up on the whole situation. In good years, at least, he could make as much money as he needed. It would be better to content himself with that than to lie awake nights worrying about an inheritance and his brother's possible dirty tricks.

But where, Ben thought as he parked in front of his brother's house, was the money for this sleek residence and the heated swimming pool coming from? He shrugged his shoulders and walked toward the massive front door, which had a brass knocker in the shape of a lion's head.

A black houseman, the only black man in Livingston County, opened the door. Ben wondered why his brother insisted on hiring a black man in a place where his life must be very lonely and complicated. The people of Livingston had many virtues, but respect for anyone much unlike themselves wasn't one of them.

The entire ground floor of Pete's house was his office, an arrangement which guaranteed tax advantages. It was furnished with beautifully reconditioned antiques. A fire had been laid in a big fieldstone fireplace, but had not been lit.

Pete sat behind an ornate Italian desk by a large bay win-

46

dow. He must have heard the houseman let his brother in, but did not stand up until Ben was ten feet away.

"Well, welcome home, Ben!" he said. "It's been a long time."

Ben found himself studying his brother closely. Pete had gained no weight. His thin body, which had seemed scrawny in youth, had become an asset. His hair had turned white and was starting to recede, giving him a scholarly appearance which was increased by steel-rimmed bifocals. He was wearing an expensive suit of dark blue worsted which looked as though it came from Brooks Brothers, where he was probably the only regular customer from Livingston County. His black English shoes were highly shined, and his tie was a dark Italian silk which matched the blue of the suit. To Ben, he looked curiously like a little boy all dressed up for a funeral. In a town where even bankers often were informal, did Pete get himself up like this every day?

"You're looking good, Pete," Ben said, slapping him on the shoulder. "I wish I could keep the pounds off the way you do."

Silently smiling, Pete sat down and Ben sank into a leather armchair nearby.

"Have you seen Ebon yet?" Pete asked.

"Yes."

"How is he?"

"Fine!"

"Where is he staying these days?"

"Out at Rose Kelly's farm."

"You think that's a good idea?"

"So good I stayed there myself last night. Charming people, the Kellys."

Pete cleared his throat. "Ben, perhaps I know more about these people than you do. The younger sister there has quite a reputation at the high school. The older sister is a real . . . well, firebrand."

"In what way?"

"She's been trying to sue the Adirondack Park Agency, for one thing. She's always carrying on about something."

"I like her. You could use a few more rebels around here."

"If you like her, you'll love her father. Last time he was here, he slugged a state trooper."

"I don't think that has much to do with me."

"Maybe not now. Are you going to leave Ebon out there, send him south with his mother, or take him back to California with you?"

"I don't know yet. To tell the truth, I've been thinking of moving back here myself."

"Wonderful!" The irony was unmistakable.

"What would you think if I wanted to be editor of the *Recorder* again?"

"Well, there would be a lot to think about, Ben."

"I didn't know you had any interest in journalism."

"To be honest, I don't like it, but the paper has been my responsibility for a long while."

"I appreciate that."

"You can't just hop into the editor's chair and out of it whenever you feel like. I'd need reassurances. . . ."

"I appreciate that."

"There also is a question of whether your brand of journalism would be just right for a paper owned by an old lady's trust fund. Somehow I doubt whether this is just the right time and place for a crusader. Howie Hewat is one of the officers of the trust. He may have something to say about that."

"You mean, I now need Howie's approval before I can get dad's old paper back?"

"He has a legal right to voice an opinion. We also have our present editor to think about. I think that Scottie's been doing a pretty good job."

"Leave him as editor and make me publisher."

"I'm the publisher. You know more about journalism, but

I'm a better businessman. Frankly, our income has almost doubled since you left."

"Come on, Pete! The radio station died. You picked up a monopoly on advertising."

"That's part of it. I'm not saying we don't want you, Ben. I'm saying that Howie and I have to think it over."

Finding himself at the mercy of his brother and Howie Hewat bothered Ben more than was reasonable, but his father had trained him for work on the paper. During the years he had edited it, he had won awards for excellence, and his father had often assured him that the publication would some-day be his. No one else in the family or the town knew as much about running a country weekly as he did. That was a fact.

"Pete, I appreciate all the work you've done for the family," Ben said, "but don't try to take over too much. And don't try to impress me with the authority of old Howie Hewat. It won't work."

Pete gave his thin smile. "I'm sorry you don't like Howie. He speaks well of you."

"Ask him if he remembers the time he threw a football helmet full of water from the toilet at me in the gym at the high school."

"You better put that charming question to him yourself. Do you have anything else you want to talk about, Ben?"

"Why don't you have mother's house painted?"

"She won't allow anyone but Tom Trudeau to work on the place. She says she had a contract with him. When any other workman appears, she gets all excited and chases him off."

"Then why not hire Tom Trudeau?"

"He's been dead about ten years. I've tried to explain that to mother many times, but apparently she just can't believe it."

"Can't you get mother out to Cliff House on the lake and have her place painted while she's gone?"

"She never leaves home now. And the doctor says we must try not to get her upset. I hope you remember that if you intend to contest control of the paper."

"Like you, I have a lot of thinking to do."

"Well, come see Lucy now before you go."

Ben followed his brother up a wide stairway to a living room where Lucy was watching television. A stout, plain woman who still wore a pink bathrobe, she had a curiously touching smile, like that of a hurt, fat child.

"Did Pete tell you about our swimming pool?" she asked.

"No."

"It's going to have a glass roof like a greenhouse that can be closed in winter, open in summer. We'll be swimming the year around, just as though we lived in Florida. Isn't that wonderful?"

"It sure is."

Before he left, Pete insisted on showing him his recreation room in the cellar, where he had pinball machines, a billiard table and a ham radio set.

"I can talk to people all over the world," Pete said.

Ben was going to ask what he said, but thought better of it. His brother's life suddenly seemed so drab that he had a temptation to hug him, despite their differences, but after so many years of chill, this was impossible.

It was almost eleven o'clock as Ben left Pete's house. Since he didn't have to take grammie to the doctor until one, he decided to visit the *Recorder* office to see what kind of paper Pete had been publishing, and what kind of editor he was employing. The stairs to the second floor office of the newspaper had changed not at all since his youth. They were hot, airless and steep, but so many memories were associated with them that they seemed almost beautiful. Here on cold winter afternoons when he was a boy he had often waited for his father to finish work. Later, when he was learning to be a reporter and a photographer, he had often sprinted up these stairs, taking them two at a time, to meet a deadline, or just to show a good story to his father. Later still, he had often walked with Heidi up these stairs late at night, when they had known the office would be deserted. There had been all the excitement of the forbidden as they opened the door and, without putting on a light, had settled onto the old horsehair couch in the reception room.

Now the horsehair couch had been replaced by a sofa covered by fake leather. Instead of a receptionist there was a bell button and a sign which said PLEASE PUSH FOR SERVICE. Efficiency had arrived in Livingston.

"What can we do for you?" a girl who looked like a high school student said.

"May I see the editor?"

"Regarding what?"

"Business. My name is Ben Winslow."

"Are you Pete's brother?"

"I guess that's as good an identification as any."

The girl led him across a big room with five oak desks, three of them empty. A ginger-haired man about forty years old sat at the big rolltop which had belonged to Ben's father. His feet were on one corner of it as he leaned back and drank from a bottle of beer.

"This is Ben Winslow, Pete's brother," the girl said.

The man looked Ben up and down as though he were a prospective employee. His feet remained on the desk.

"What do you want, Mr. Winslow?" he asked in a dry, nasal voice.

"I want to see your files of back issues," Ben replied, trying to control his anger. His father's desk, he saw, had rings left by bottles all around the typewriter.

"Why?"

"What's your name?"

"Fitzgerald. They call me Scottie."

"Why?"

"You know, the writer . . ."

51

"Well, I guess you're his final indignity."

"You trying to be funny?"

"Where's the morgue? I want to see what's going on around here. Don't disturb yourself. I'll find the way myself."

The old morgue was a mess, with open filing cabinets disgorging folders. Stacks of cardboard cartons apparently stored correspondence. Through an open door was a big room where the linotype machines had once stood. Here were piles of back issues in hard binders of imitation leather. Ben found the current year and began reading at random. It wasn't necessary to examine many issues before discovering that the paper had been turned into little more than a cheap throwaway full of handouts from the mill, advertisements and boilerplate copy from cheaply syndicated columnists. There was hardly any real local news, nothing from the police blotter, and no political articles except releases from Howie Hewat, whose heavy face smiled from almost every issue. Ben could imagine the comments of his father, who had worked so hard to give the paper a statewide reputation for excellence.

Tossing the bound copy aside, Ben walked out to the big room, where Fitzgerald still lolled with his feet on the rolltop desk, beer bottle in hand.

"Did you find what you want?"

"Not exactly. Do you know that you're editing a throwaway or are you meeting your own personal standards of excellence?"

"Pete told me you'd be a pain in the ass."

"I can be that literally. If you don't get your feet off that desk and get rid of that beer bottle, I'll give you a demonstration."

"Pete said I don't have to pay no attention to you."

"Just ignore me then," Ben said as he reached out his foot and shoved the chair from under the man.

Fitzgerald jumped up just in time to avoid being dumped on the floor. His face was scarlet. "You son of a bitch!"

"Maybe so, but I can't stand seeing a crumbum unskilled

so-called newspaper man with his feet on my father's desk. And we never allow drinking in this office, not where people can see it, anyway."

"Why don't you wait until you get rank before you start throwing it around?"

Picking up the beer bottle which Fitzgerald had left on the desk, Ben slammed it into a tin wastepaper basket with a resounding ring. Then he walked to the door and the stairs. He was halfway down before he began to regret his grand ... grandstand ... display of temper. Big Ben Winslow had marched up the hill and down again, leaving behind a humiliated little man who probably had no idea in the world what it was all about anyway.

Feeling oddly shaken, Ben went across the street to Joe's Bar for lunch. Joe's father had established this saloon long ago in a firehouse which had been used in the days when the engines were drawn by horses. It was the biggest tavern in town and sold the best hamburger, a huge slab of ground steak grilled to order and served on fresh Italian bread. Although it was not yet noon, the bar was already crowded. As Ben sipped a beer and waited for his sandwich, he studied the other patrons, his eye sharpened by his persistent thoughts about the possibility of doing a book of photographs about a small town. This crowd was much more varied and picturesque than any one would be likely to find in a suburb or city, which commonly catered to only one neighborhood or class. Lumbermen who cut logs for the paper mill, and who tended to look a little like big brown bears, stood next to real estate salesmen in brightly colored sports coats, trout fishermen with hats full of dry flies, paper makers in clean coveralls, the local dentist and a gaggle of neatly dressed lawyers. There seemed to Ben to be an unusually large number of pretty young women, some of them in tight white T-shirts. The red jackets of the Livingston Volunteer Fire Department were worn by many of the men. The babble of conversation was so loud that Ben could barely hear the jukebox, on which

53

a girl with a nasal voice was singing, "I'll always keep you in my heart, although you've gawn away."

Joe, a tall, thin man who looked startlingly like his father, who had served Ben in his youth, brought out his sandwich. "I thought it was you, Ben," he said. "How the hell are you?"

"Happy. Happy to be home."

"How long are you going to stay?"

Before Ben had a chance to answer, there was an abrupt hush in the big saloon. Turning, Ben saw that Howie Hewat had just come in. While still a high school student, Howie had been six feet two inches tall, but already had been too overweight to be a good athlete. Now he was even taller and had become a powerful-looking fat man who, Ben guessed, might weigh close to three hundred pounds. He was wearing a spotless fawn-colored gabardine suit and his brown hair was still thick. His big face was somewhat bloated, but he was still an imperious-looking man. Suddenly he grinned and waved his big hand.

"Hi, everybody!" he said, with a wave. "We sure got ourselves a great day, don't we?"

"We sure do, Howie!" Joe said and there were murmurs of assent.

Slowly the babble of voices picked up as Howie made his way to a table in the corner, and sat down with several young lawyers. Almost immediately Joe brought him two hamburgers and a pitcher of beer.

Ben was rather glad that Howie had not seemed to notice him. He wasn't quite sure what kind of relationship he should try to establish with his old schoolmate. One thing was certain: if Howie could produce a hush in Joe's bar simply by entering the place, he certainly had accumulated enormous power in the past few years.

After finishing his lunch, Ben went to a nearby grocery store, where he bought the food on Rose's list and the few good things he needed for the simple dinner he planned to serve in his own house that night. Arriving at the farm at a

54

quarter to one, he found grammie by the front door, all ready to go to the doctor.

"Just lift me into your car," she said. "I don't need the wheelchair. They have one at the doctor's office."

She was so light he felt as though he were carrying a small child.

"You can just leave me at the waiting room," she said. "You don't have to hurry back to get me. I like all them magazines there, and that office is the only place where I meet people who got more troubles than I have!"

There was a pause as he turned onto the county road.

"You going to stay around here long?" she asked suddenly.

"I'm not really sure yet."

"You got money? Your folks always did."

"I'm afraid that it still belongs to my folks."

"Your father was a good man. Drank too much, but what man don't? I'd say you done your share of drinkin' yourself."

"How do you deduce that?"

"I can tell a drinkin' man as far as I can see him. I should. I've known enough."

"I've had my share of troubles with the booze, but I've been all right for a long while."

"Is that why your wife left you? Booze?"

Ben laughed. "I think it was more complicated than that. You don't pull any punches, do you, grammie?"

"I'm too old to beat around. Do you like Rose?"

"Yes."

"Do you have idears about her?"

"What kind of ideas?"

"Now come on. Don't you beat around! Rose is a good-looking woman. I used to have a figure like that, and if I don't know it gives men idears, then nobody does!"

"Well, I have to admit, she gives me idears, but I'm too old to act on every idear I have. I like your Rosie, grammie. I'm not going to hurt her."

"Ha! There's hardly been a man who didn't say that!"

55

"If anybody gets hurt, I think it's likely to be me. I guess that your Rosie is well able to take care of herself."

"Maybe. But you don't know much about her, young feller. She's had a hard life, a really hard life. She's held up the world for a lot of people, and one thing she don't need now is trouble."

Parking near the door of the doctor's office, he carried her in, and a receptionist helped to settle her in a wheelchair.

"Good to see you, grammie," the woman said. "Is Rose coming in today too?"

"She didn't say nothing about it," the old woman snapped.

"Is she getting any more rest these days?"

"You know nobody can make Rose rest!"

"Well, you tell her that Dr. Bill wants to see her. If she won't follow doctor's orders and come in for a checkup, he can't be responsible."

A woman with two children entered, and Ben withdrew. He remembered how pale and tired Rose had looked, and felt the first stirrings of worry. Although he had just met Rose, his misgivings brought back an echo. In his boyhood, Dr. Bill had always been telling him to have his father come in for a checkup or he "couldn't be responsible."

4

THAT night, when he met Rose outside the offices of the paper mill, however, she did not look tired. Smiling, she came toward him with that peculiarly energetic walk. His father, who had loved horses, would have called her "a high-stepping little mare," and though many modern women would regard that as an insult, there was a fondness intended in the phrase which still made Ben like it.

"Hi!" she said. "Do you mind running me home before we go to your place? I want to change my clothes and make sure that everything is all right."

Small bits of mica in the new road from the mill gleamed like diamond dust in the late afternoon sunlight. A young man was mowing the lawn of a farmhouse as they passed, and the smell of new-cut grass was sweet. When a woman, Ben thought, made a man feel so much more alive than usual, he could be sure that there was great joy or trouble ahead, probably both.

"Did you get grammie to the doctor all right?" she asked.

"We had a fine time."

"Did she talk your head off?"

"Not really. She just wanted to know whether I have money, whether I drink, and whether I have 'idears' about you."

"Oh God!"

"For your information, I said that my family has money but I don't. I used to drink too much, but have it fairly well under control. And I definitely do have 'idears' about you, but I am trying hard to keep them under control."

She laughed, that lovely full laugh that in itself seemed larger than her small body.

"She also seemed worried about your health," he said. "I know I have no right to bring that up."

"What did she say?"

"It wasn't grammie so much as the receptionist at the doctor's. Damn it, I wasn't going to bring it up. Obviously, it's none of my business."

"Cora wanted me to come in for a checkup and said the doctor couldn't be responsible, et cetera? Hell, I've had a mild rheumatic heart condition since about the age of six. Dr. Bill has wanted me to pay monthly dues ever since as though I'd joined some kind of a club."

When they got home, they found Annie and Ebon preparing their dinner while grammie shouted instructions from her wheelchair. They were using the wood stove and the kitchen was hot. Ebon was wearing only his bluejeans, and his tanned upper body was more heavily muscled than Ben remembered it. As a photographer—hell, as a father—Ben was impressed by the beauty of his son's lithe young body, but he was chagrined to find that he also was a little envious. Ebon could match the symmetry of his girl; at forty-five, Ben wasn't in the ballgame. The thought of his own middle-aged body filled him with more humility than he wanted.

"Dad, could I talk to you a minute?" Ebon asked, and led the way out the back door.

"What's on your mind?" Ben asked.

"First of all, can I bum some money off you? It's Annie's birthday day after tomorrow and I want to get her something."

"How much do you need?"

58

"Well, you know how good she's been to me, putting me up and all. I'd like to get her a nice camera. How much would one cost?"

"A really good one would run to several hundred dollars and I doubt whether you could find such a thing around here. Wait a minute! I left a bunch of cameras in my old dark room. Let me see what I can dig up for you."

"Thanks," Ebon replied, but he sounded subdued. Realizing that he had robbed him of the fun of buying a gift, Ben added, "Why don't you buy her something else? Go ahead and charge anything you want."

"OK. Dad, have you made any plans yet? About what you're going to do, I mean."

"About going back to California?"

"That and about me."

"I'm sort of investigating the possibility of moving back here for good. How would that strike you?"

"What would you do?"

"Maybe take over the paper again, and do some of my own work. Do you like the idea?"

"Of course!" Ebon replied, but he sounded more thoughtful than exuberant. "When will you know?"

"There are a lot of things to check out. I'll have to go back west to see what I could do with the house and the studio. These aren't exactly decisions to make overnight."

"I guess not. Dad, do you mind if I ask where you're going with Rose tonight?"

"Just to our house for dinner."

"Do you like her?"

"Who wouldn't?"

"She's been awful good to me. . . ."

"Eb, I'm not going to fuss anything up. Is that what you're afraid of?"

"No. It's just . . . I don't know. I'm sorry."

"And your mother has told you some fairly lurid things about my behavior. Right?"

"Well, sort of. I guess that she sort of got it in for photographers in general, or at least a lot of your friends."

"I know. Photographers, poets and artists are all crazy and live surrounded by beautiful nudes. Unfortunately, that's somewhat exaggerated."

"I don't think muth really believes it, but when she gets mad..."

"I get the picture. Eb, I've been worried, too...about you and Annie...look, *all* fathers worry when their kids fall in love. And now you're worried about me and Rosie. Well, since we can't do much about each other's morality, don't you think it might help if we both relaxed?"

Ebon laughed, and they were still feeling the moment of closeness as they returned to the kitchen. Rose, who was now wearing a light tan trench coat, was waiting by the door.

"Are you all set?" she asked.

"All set."

When she got into the jeep, she added, "This is the first night I've had off since I can't remember when. I feel quite giddy."

A new moon was climbing just above the tops of the trees as they turned into his house. Both white and lavender lilacs were blooming everywhere, as well as apple and pear trees. Their perfume was sharpened in a not unpleasant way by the distant scent of a skunk which had been chased by a foolish poodle.

"Would you like to look around the property before we go into the house?" he asked.

"I'd love to."

There was a small greenhouse with several panes broken, a large garden which had not been tilled recently, and on the bank of the river, a terrace of old brick. Just before picking Rose up this evening, he had carried lawn furniture from the garage to the terrace and had stocked a small portable bar. She sat on a wrought-iron bench and sipped white wine from a crystal goblet, while he poured a Scotch into an old-fashioned glass. A chill wind blew from the rushing river and they both were grateful for their coats.

"I feel quite theatrical," she said as he sat down on another white wrought-iron bench. "The river, the lilacs, a man who drinks from a glass, not a bottle. This can't be Livingston. Where are we?"

"I don't know. In all the years I've lived in this house, I somehow have never felt at home here. You know, it doesn't really belong to me anyway."

"Who does it belong to?"

"Mother, or the family trust. She gave the use of a house to Pete, and of one to me, but the gifts are never outright. Her father started that custom. I think that one idea was to keep his relatives in Livingston. If we leave, we get nothing."

"That's strange."

"It's a way to keep control."

"But you left anyway."

"Many times, but I always seem to come back."

"Because of this house partly? You never could find a more beautiful place to live."

"Because of the town. Because I'm always a stranger anywhere else. I think that feeling brings a lot of people home."

"I felt that way in Boston, but sometimes I loved it," she replied.

"You lived in Boston?"

"I had one year at Boston University. Then a lot of things happened and I had to come home."

"Do you feel trapped sometimes?" he asked. "Sometimes I feel a stranger anywhere else and trapped when I come home."

She shrugged. "I really love Annie and grammie and dad. That takes the curse off it."

"Haven't you ever wanted to get married? I know that's an idiotic, insensitive, impertinent question! But one bad thing about any small town is that single people have so little choice...."

"After the questions grammie asked, I guess you have a

61

right to ask anything," she replied with a smile. "Sure, I've always wanted to get married, but I'm pretty picky about it, and most men aren't just dying for a bride with dependents."

"I never even thought of that," he said, thinking that Annie at least would be rather pleasant to have around.

"When I was younger I always had a kind of dread of joining the Twenty-three Club," she continued. "Have you ever heard of that?"

"No."

"Well, most girls get married around here when they're eighteen, whether they're pregnant or not. They live in trailers and have babies while their husbands try to find work or start out at the mill. At the end of about five years of trying to raise kids with practically no money, the husband often takes off and the wife gets disgusted. After five years of marriage and three or four kids, she's twenty-three years old and on the loose. She spends most of her time at Joe's bar, trying to pick up somebody else's husband. That's why they call it the Twenty-three Club."

"I'm glad you didn't join."

"I've been engaged twice, both times to engineers at the mill," she continued. "Each time my father showed up, and that was the end of that. As you may have heard, dad can be a little off-putting. I wasn't too upset because I figured that if a man couldn't handle dad, he'd never be able to handle me for long."

She shivered and pulled her coat tighter around her.

"Would you like to go up to the house?" he asked.

Before taking the cleaning women home earlier that afternoon he had had them fill vases in the house with lilacs and apple blossoms. The stately living room was fragrant.

"It must do something to you to live in such surroundings," she said, admiring the high ceilings, the blue satin curtains, the Persian rugs.

"It makes you crazy. At least something made me crazy when I was living here."

"Maybe it's the fumes from the mill. They've made me climb a few walls."

He helped her take off her trench coat. She was wearing a dress of an off-white silky material, clinging and cut low enough to quicken his pulse in a way which even nudes had not done in a long time. "Now that dress is no fair," he said.

"I made it myself in a mad moment last year, but to tell the truth, this is the first time I've dared to wear it."

"I feel honored, but don't blame me if all my 'idears' about you are beginning to sound like inspirations."

She laughed. He put a collection of Johnny Mathis records on the phonograph. He was beginning to feel unusually tense.

"Do you want another drink before I put dinner on?" he asked.

"I think I'll try a Scotch," she said.

The flowers, the music and the bottle made him suspect that he was arranging a stereotyped seduction scene. He did not understand why he felt so sure that this should not happen so fast with this woman, who apparently was as lonely as he. This, however, was not California, not New York nor Rome.

"You sit here while I start dinner," he said.

"Can't I help?"

"For once you do no work at all. It won't take a minute."

The potatoes had already been baked, and a mixed green salad with endive was ready in the refrigerator. All he had to do was to put the two Delmonico steaks he had bought in the broiler.

"How do you like your steak?" he asked.

"I know I should say rare, but I like it well done."

He laughed. "I bet you don't like your martinis to be too dry."

"The more vermouth, the better."

"And you don't like Mercedes-Benz or Jaguar cars."

"You can't get parts for them around here and no one can fix them."

63

"Would you like to dance?" he asked. "My dancing is old-fashioned. I stopped learning the latest steps when I dislocated my back while trying the Twist."

"Just don't try any dips. I never could handle them."

When he put his arms around her, he paused without moving his feet for a fraction of a second. She felt good. Why she should feel better than any other young woman, he had no idea, but she fitted into him in a way that made him revert to the delightful confusions of his youth. Slowly he began to dance. Her hair had a distinctive fragrance he did not recognize, something very clean and natural, like the lilacs and apple blossoms all around them, but with just a hint of musk. He began to dance cheek to cheek.

"This is silly," he said, stopping suddenly.

"Why?"

"You've got me dying to ask you to the senior prom. Will you accept my fraternity pin?"

"Only if you won't try to go all the way." Mischief in her eyes. "Remember, I'm a nice girl."

He turned the steaks in the broiler and returned to the couch, where he held her hand. That too felt good. She was an excellent hand-holder, showing great understanding of an act of love which the sex manuals never explained. Her hand was neither listless nor agitated. Her fingertips delivered a caress so subtle that he had to concentrate to feel it, but it was there, all right.

"I better take the steaks out," he said.

The main course consisted of nothing but the steaks, the baked potatoes and the salad, with a good burgundy. Still feeling like an actor in a seduction scene, he lit a silver candelabra which held six red candles.

"This is good!" she exclaimed, but she did not seem in the least hungry. He, on the other hand, had to fight a temptation to wolf his food. He kept glancing at her in the candlelight, where she looked demure as a bride. For some reason it was difficult to make conversation. His fork clattered loudly on his plate. A grandfather clock in the corner ticked solemnly.

"Did you see your brother today?" she asked.

"Yes. I think it may be pretty difficult for me to get back the paper."

"I figured that. You can bet that Howie wants to keep the county's only paper in his pocket."

"I can't help being angry. My father sort of trained me to run that paper."

"Have you ever thought of starting a new one?"

"The town could never support two papers, and the *Recorder* is a habit with people."

"Ticonderoga supports two papers. It has for five years or more. Ti is no bigger than we are."

"It would take a lot of money."

"Not necessarily," she said. "With photo-offset, you wouldn't have to buy any presses. I know a place where you could get all the equipment you need for camera-ready copy for only a few hundred dollars."

"You sound as though you've thought a lot about this."

"I told you, every PR person dreams of starting a newspaper. I just don't have enough guts to do it alone."

"It would take more persistence than anything else," he said. "Sometimes a weekly can be a damn boring job."

"I think Howie would relieve the boredom for you. If you ever criticized him, or exposed some of the things he's done...."

"What could he do?"

"If I tell you, you'll think I'm just being melodramatic."

"I've been around here long enough to know that there's nothing unrealistic about melodrama in these here mountains."

"Did you hear about the radio station?"

"I heard its tower fell down in a blizzard and they couldn't afford to put up a new one."

65

"Their news man criticized Howie. A good many people think that the turnbuckles on the guy wires of the tower were tampered with."

"Any proof?"

"Not really. The state police talk about metal fatigue. The damn thing wasn't insured. There may be a story in that, too. The business manager of the station is now working for Howie. I can't prove much, but I can prove that Howie was doing everything possible to scare the station's advertisers away. He just couldn't stand an independent voice around here."

"I never knew him to be so—"

"He's got a lot tougher lately. I think he has a big deal cooking and won't let anybody get in the way of it."

"Do you have any idea what that is?"

"It's complicated, but fundamentally it's the damndest land grab you ever saw and a plan to put something big on it. I think Howie has figured a way to beat the zoning and the Park Agency."

"I always figured he'd find some way to convert political power to money."

"If you don't mind my being even more melodramatic, I'll tell you that Howie has assembled quite a collection of hoodlums for doing little jobs like toppling radio towers. He defends a lot of tough types in court, supposedly as an act of charity. He has quite a few friends who wear funny leather jackets."

"Have there been any other acts of violence?"

"Several, including the usual hunting accidents and car crackups. I don't know whether any of them were engineered, but a lot of people around here think so. One thing is sure: Bert Greer, who was shot in the woods last fall, was the most effective enemy Howie ever had. He was a good DA and he was building up a case. Now do you think I'm paranoiac?"

He took a sip of wine and wiped his lips. "No, but we both may be falling for the small-town disease of believing all the most sinister rumors. People around here have to have a devil to hate, even if they have to invent one."

"If we had a paper that could pin down the truth, maybe the rumors would lose some of their power. We're all still whispering in the dark."

She cut a piece of steak, but did not eat it.

"You give me quite a challenge. I don't know if I'm young enough to be a crusader."

She smiled. To Ben there seemed to be an inference that if he was young enough to aspire to be a lover, he must be young enough to be a fighter. Suddenly he was annoyed at her and annoyed at himself. She asked too much and he was too lazy. After clearing the table, he brought in bowls of mixed fruit and melon balls with sour cream.

"I wish you didn't serve such good food with such little effort," she said. "You're sort of upstaging my act."

"Actually, this is the one, the only, meal I know how to make.... Rose, you'd be wrong to think of a small-town paper as a great crusader. If we dug into the Hewat thing, we probably wouldn't find one fact we could print. Most of the time we'd just be back to covering church suppers and American Legion meetings."

"I'd like that too," she said.

"Would you work with me if I started a paper?"

"I'd love to, but I couldn't afford to take much of a pay cut."

"How much are you getting now?"

"About eight thousand."

"I guess I could manage that for a year at least. After that ..."

"I'd be willing to take a chance," she said.

There was a pause.

"I've got to be responsible," he said. "I can't promise anything now. I'm not even sure what I want to do yet. If I started a newspaper, I'd have to sell my house out in Santa Barbara—that's the only real money I have. I'd have to sell

67

my studio. Damn it, I don't really believe that I'd even be thinking of any of this if you weren't wearing that damn dress! I shouldn't get a business and a woman all mixed up in my head!"

She laughed. "Would it help if I took the dress off?"

"Not likely!"

"I apologize for pressuring you. I confess that I do want you to move back here and I do want to work on a newspaper with you, but that of course shouldn't be a major consideration for you. I guess I'm mostly thinking about myself . . . take a good look at me, Ben. I'm a small-town spinster stuck in a lousy job at a paper mill. Some of the men I meet are perfectly grand looking, but their idea of ambition is to get a new motorcycle or to form a rock group to play at Joe's bar Saturday nights. I want something that lets me at least hope beyond that. . . ."

Without thinking he got up and kissed her, bending awkwardly over her as she sat at the table, not much more than brushing her cheek with his lips. She stood up and came to him and kissed him properly.

"I always knew there was a lot of literal truth in that old 'Stardust' song," he said, feeling himself still at the high school prom.

"How's that?" she asked, her lips back against his.

" 'When our love was new and each kiss an inspiration . . .' "

" 'The nightingales told their fairy tales,' " she quoted on. "Will I make you furious if I say that my mother simply loved that song?"

"Ah! You are a mood murderer!"

"Do you want to sing 'My Wild Irish Rose'? My father just adores that!"

She was, he realized, deftly taking some of the steam out of the atmosphere. But the atmosphere would not stay unsteamed. A sudden silence fell. She glanced at the floor and, unaccountably, blushed. Sitting beside her, he touched her shoulder and she was in his arms again. It was the sort of hearty but simple embrace which could happen to a wandering man hundreds of times in a lifetime without leaving even a memory, or it could be a moment he could never forget, a kiss and embrace like a passionate exchange of marriage vows, without a word being said.

She broke away and took a deep breath. Now her face was anything but pale, and she was breathing more quickly, and her chestnut hair, alive in the candlelight, was in delicious disarray for a woman who was commonly so brisk and controlled, he thought. When he kissed her again, his hand touched her breast and she pressed it firmly there, at the same time caressing it.

"Let's go upstairs," he finally said.

There was a moment of silence before she gently pushed his hand away and with apparent regret said, "No. Not in this house."

"We could drive somewhere."

"I want to wait. Don't be mad at me. I'm no tease, but it will be no good if we feel rushed and crazy."

"I understand."

"I want you to take me somewhere where you've never been with a girl." She smiled before asking, "Is there anyplace like that anywhere in this whole damn county?"

"Is that the kind of reputation I have?" he asked with a laugh.

"According to grammie, I must take every precaution."

"Well, the old lady is usually right. At any rate, I know a good inn in Vermont. They have great food and I've always wanted to spend the night."

A sharp intake of breath. "Let's go!"

"When?"

Her eyes turned mischievous again. "When you get a thousand points."

"I was afraid that little game would come back to haunt me."

69

"You won't have to wait long. I give you five hundred for tonight."

They went to the living room and changed the Johnny Mathis record which had been making the room more and more misty for half an hour. After substituting Strauss waltzes, he put the sofa cushions on the floor, and they lay holding hands, jiggling their feet in time to the music, the best dance that was ever invented, she said. All the tensions were gone. For the first time in years, he was full of a strange, unreasonable certainty that the future was going to be better than anything in his past.

5

WHEN Ben woke up the next morning, he could hear rain beating on the slate roof of his old house. Glancing at his watch, he saw that it was a little before 8:30. Assuming that Rose always got up early, he telephoned her at her farm.

"Hello," she said sleepily.

"I'm in trouble."

"Ben! What is it?"

"When a man starts loving the way a woman says 'Hello,' he's out of control."

She laughed.

"It's also a very bad sign when a man has to call a woman as soon as he wakes up in the morning. And a worse sign when he counts any hour lost when he does not see her."

"I wish I could see you today, Ben, but I'm in charge of a damn banquet tonight. The manager of the mill is retiring."

"Can I see you tomorrow?"

"Tomorrow is Annie's seventeenth birthday. We're having a little party at six o'clock. Of course you're invited."

"Can we go somewhere afterward?"

"The party will probably last late, Ben. I don't like to leave the kids alone."

"I suspect you're trying to avoid me. What if I promise to stop making bad jokes?"

"I love your jokes! I'll see you Monday or any night next week."

"How about every night? I'm sorry. Fatuousness is yet another symptom."

"Ben, you're good for me. You make me feel as though I were the heroine in some wonderful old movie."

"That is the worst compliment I ever had. Do I flicker when you look at me?"

"I mean it as a fantastic compliment! You're the last of the great romantics."

"That dress of yours did it. All ivory and lace in candlelight."

"There's no lace on that dress."

"All ivory and décolletage in candlelight. Who cares about lace? Rip it off. It doesn't belong there."

"Ben, I'd love to make this a double feature, but I simply have to run. My boss is waiting for me, Saturday or no Saturday. Anyway, from me you get rave reviews!"

"I'll put them in my scrapbook. Can I talk to Ebon?"

"Sure. Thanks for calling, Ben. Your latest hit has just won you one hundred more points. Your total is now nine hundred and ninety-nine!"

She put the receiver down and he heard her walk quickly away. There was a long wait before the sound of heavy footsteps came through to him.

"Hello," Ebon said in his deep voice, the new resonance of which still surprised his father.

"Hi, Eb. Would you like to have lunch with me?"

"I'm going fishing. . . . Would you like to go?"

"It's raining like hell!"

"That's when the fish bite. Anyway, it will stop before long."

"Where are you going?"

"The big falls, for a start."

"Can I have an hour to get ready?"

"Sure, but trout eat early. ... ."

After dressing, Ben went to the third floor of the old house, where long ago he had built a darkroom. Among the photographic equipment on the shelves was an old Leica camera with a leather case containing a variety of lenses and filters. The outside of the camera and case looked worn, but everything was functional Ben found as he checked it. If Annie was serious about learning photography, nothing could give her a better start.

In search of fishing equipment, Ben went up to the attic. The sound of the rain on the roof was loud here. Snapping on a light, he saw the debris of his past piled like jackstraws all around him. A plywood dollhouse he had built for his daughter Laura for a long ago Christmas sagged against a steamer trunk that he had bought for Heidi's and his first trip to Europe. A double-barreled 12-gauge shotgun and a Marlin .30-caliber rifle which he had inherited from his father hung in cracked leather cases from pegs on the wall. On an old bureau was a box of polished mahogany. Opening it, Ben took out the snub-nosed .38-caliber revolver which his father had kept in the drawer of his desk at his office. Almost every Saturday afternoon, Stephen Winslow had blasted away with rifle and pistol teams at the Fish and Game Club, or had shot skeet.

"I'm in a business that often gets people mad at me," Stephen had said to his son. "There are a lot of rough people in these hills, but so far I've had no big trouble. Maybe one reason is that it does no harm to have people know I'm good at handling a gun."

Even as a boy, Ben had thought his father's preoccupation with guns melodramatic, but now he wondered. In the dry Adirondack air, the pistol had not rusted. Its wicked little barrel was still smooth to the touch, and it smelled faintly of oil.

Ben's fishing equipment was piled in a corner near a small window. The waders and canvas case with his fly rod were there with his creel and foul-weather gear, but his tackle box was missing. After searching for it without luck, he carried

73

his gear downstairs and put it in the jeep with the Leica camera.

Before driving to the farm, Ben made himself a cup of tea and toast. Onrushing middle age is a hell of a thing, he thought. Just getting ready to go fishing made him tired.

The rain pelted the canvas roof of the jeep as Ben splashed through puddles on the road to the farm. Ebon, already dressed for fishing, let him in.

"Here's the camera for Annie," Ben said, handing him the case wrapped in newspapers.

"Thanks, Dad. I'll be right back."

While Ebon took the camera to his room, Ben went to the kitchen. Ann and her grandmother were making a green dress on the big round table. Ann's mouth was full of pins, but she waved cheerily to him.

"You going fishing in this weather?" grammie asked.

"We're going to try it."

"Thought you was old enough to have more sense."

"I'm afraid that wisdom does not always come with age, grammie," he replied with a smile.

When Ebon entered the room a few moments later, he stuffed an apple into his pocket.

"I'm going now," he said gruffly to Annie.

She took the pins from her mouth. "Have fun." Her voice was flat.

Ebon seemed about to say more, but turned suddenly and strode from the room. Obviously there was some tension between them. There was no reason to be surprised, Ben told himself. Only the forgetful old think that young love is usually more music than discord.

When Ebon carried his equipment to the jeep, Ben saw that it included his missing tackle box. There was nothing of real value in it and he knew he should ignore it, but he heard himself say, "You've got a pretty good tackle box there, son."

"Muth said I could take it."

74

"Well, there's no harm in that."

The fact that he had not been thanked for the box rankled Ben and he was annoyed at himself for letting such a small matter disturb the beginning of what should be a good day with his son. As they drove away from the farm, the rain seemed to be letting up a little.

Ben drove up to the mountain road which paralleled the river. After parking on the edge of the grove of big pines, they walked through the woods to the pool at the foot of the falls. The noise of the rushing water was so loud that they had to shout at each other as they pulled on their wading boots. Ready in almost no time, Ebon stepped into the pool, skillfully flicking his tapered line toward the deepest spots. The wrist action with which he handled his long, limber pole was expert, and Ben found it odd to remember a day only seven years ago when he had almost given up trying to teach his ten-year-old son how to cast a fly because his line kept getting tangled in the branches.

After readying his own pole, Ben waded tentatively into the pool. The rocks under his feet felt slippery, and the chill of icy water bit through his rubber boots. He cast toward the foot of the falls, reeling in rapidly when he saw that he had just missed a sunken branch. Rain dripped from the brim of his hat to his nose, and his hands were cold.

"I'm going upstream," Ebon said.

Jumping agilely from rock to rock, the young man climbed around the falls. Doggedly Ben forced himself to follow, choosing easier but longer routes. When he reached a point within sight of the rapids above, Ben leaned against a tree, watching his son stride through the shallow stream as though he had found the secret of walking on water. Since Ebon had been brought up in the Adirondacks and since Ephram, as well as Ben, had been his tutor, it was not surprising to see that he was a highly skilled woodsman and fisherman, but there was a kind of grace in the boy's movements which could never have been learned. On his son's face Ben saw a look of pure joy as the young man stood there in the rushing water with the gleaming pole in his hand.

Walking in the waders was not easy. Ben's hip started to ache and he sat down at the base of a big pine tree, against which he leaned his pole. The rain in the pine needles and the damp resin smell of the forest reminded him of camping trips on which his own father had taken him long ago.

"Hey dad, I got one!" Ebon called.

Ben climbed wearily toward a pool above the rapids. His son was triumphantly holding up a rainbow trout that was a good foot long.

"That's great!" he said.

"Try it here!"

A cloud of black flies descended on Ben. Slapping his face, he made his way over loose rocks to the edge of the pool. Attempting to ignore his aching hip, he tried to cast, but the line snagged in a maple branch overhead.

"Damn!" Ben said, pulling on the line.

"Wait a minute, dad, I'll get it!"

Slipping out of his boots, Ebon climbed the maple tree hand over hand, far enough out on the offending branch to bring the end of it within Ben's reach. After Ben had detached his hook, Ebon let himself drop lightly to the ground.

"I can remember when you used to unsnag my lines," he said with a grin.

"I'm sure I never did it so gracefully."

This reversal of roles bothered Ben more than was reasonable. Here in the woods, it seemed, he was already getting on to being an old man, while Ebon was in his absolute prime. He couldn't wait to get back to the town, where his own competency lasted longer, and where youth still had something to learn.

The rain stopped, but it was still cold. As though attracted only to youth, the trout bit only Ebon's line. Bored with casting, and cold, Ben decided to build a fire, but the matches in his pockets were wet and he had no paper.

"I've got some matches," Ebon said, taking a waterproof box from his pocket. "I'll get a fire started."

With a sharp Buck knife Ben had given him long ago, Ebon pared dry shavings from a dead branch of a pine tree. There was nothing mysterious in his efficiency—Ben himself had taught him always to carry a waterproof box of matches and a sharp knife in the woods. In point of fact, the waterproof box came from his own tackle box. Even so, Ben felt like an elderly city tenderfoot under the care of an Indian guide as his son built the fire and toasted two of the trout over it.

Ben's ankle, which had not been bothering him at all lately, began to hurt worse than his hip as they walked back to the car.

"Do you want me to drive?" Ebon asked.

"Damn it, that's one thing I can still do!" Ben said, and laughed.

On the way home, they stopped at a roadhouse and drank beer. They talked about nothing Ben recalled, but the memory of sitting in damp clothes before an open fire with his son endured. When he glanced at the sharp angle of Ebon's jaw and the lean shoulders, he was almost shocked by the strength and beauty of his son. For an hour or so, at least, he could feel pride and love. With hardly a trace of envy.

6

THE next morning Ben was awakened by the sound of church bells. For a town of only about 5,000 people, many of them irreverent, Livingston had an awful lot of churches, Ben's father had observed. The Catholic cathedral would have done justice to a fair-sized city and a dozen Protestant faiths were represented. One reason there were so many churches, most of them more than half empty, old Stephen Winslow had said, was that everybody in Livingston wanted to be a deacon, a moderator or religious leader of some sort. When defeated in a church election, the obvious thing to do was to start up a branch of Christianity new to the town.

Ben's father had also been amused by what he referred to as "the battle of the bells." The parents of Mary Costello, who ran Mary's Bar, had bought a beautiful set of Italian bells for the Catholic church shortly after the First World War. These mellow, deep-throated chimes had made the bells of all the other churches sound little better than bicycle bells. Ben's grandfather had been so disturbed by this that he had purchased an enormous German bell for the Lutheran church, of which he was the lay leader. The German bell sounded dismayingly like a giant locomotive, but it was louder than the Italian chimes. Not to be outdone, the Episcopalians sent to England for a bell almost as big as a barrel, and all the other

78

denominations took up special collections to make their voices heard.

The final result was a wonderful "tintinnabulation of the bells, bells, bells," as the poet had it, every Sunday morning in Livingston. Even though the bells were competitive, they by chance (or by the will of God, some said) were not discordant, and seemed almost to have been chosen by a master of harmony. The church bells were a pleasant part of Ben's memories of his youth, and it was good to hear them again, as unchanged as the sound of rain on the roof.

It was a little after nine o'clock and Ben was making coffee when the telephone rang.

It was Pete. "Did I wake you up, Ben boy?" he asked.

"Nope."

"I'm sorry to bother you so early, but I know you want a decision on this thing about the *Recorder*. I talked to Howie about it, and he wants to get together."

"That's nice."

"Howie's sort of busy these days, Ben. Tomorrow he's got to go to Albany for about a week. Today he's going to church at ten-thirty and he's got a golf date at one. He would like to have a drink with you at noon at the country club."

"It's sort of like getting to see the President of the United States, isn't it?"

"Now don't be so snide about Howie, Ben. He's the one man who's trying to do anything for this town."

Ben let it go. "Sure, I'll have a drink with him. Noon at the club."

Only a few minutes after Ben had hung up, the telephone rang again.

"Good morning!" Rose said. "Did I wake you up?"

"Nope. I was thinking of calling you, but I thought you'd be in church."

"The pope and I had a falling out some time ago. We respect each other, but he went his way and I went mine. . . . Would you like to come over here for brunch? I have an ul-

79

terior motive. Eb gave that fantastic camera to Annie, and she's dying to have you show her how to use it. She's too shy to ask."

"I'd love to this afternoon. I have a date with Howie Hewat at noon. We're going to have a drink at the country club."

"Did he set that up?"

"Pete did. I take it that they're going to tell me that there's no place on the *Recorder* for me."

"Don't tell them we're thinking of starting a paper of our own."

"Why?"

"That would just give them time to line the advertisers up against us. My father says a man should never telegraph his punch."

"Rosie, I think you sort of like this kind of fighting!"

"I think it has to be done and it's fun to fight the devil. Of course Howie may not be a devil, as you said, but he'll sure do until the real thing comes along."

"Why are you so sore at Howie? I don't mean to pry, but I sense an awful lot of steam in your feeling about him. Want to tell me before I see him?"

"Someday I'll tell you, but you'll just think I'm melo-dramatic. Would you like to have lunch with us at a little after one?"

"I'll be there. Rosie?"

"Yes."

"You said I was a romantic and I guess I am. I still think all women are a mystery ... or I want to ... but you're sort of tops in that department for me. There's something about you, lady, that I just can't put my finger on." There was a well-timed pause before he added, "Of course I'd love to try."

"Ben, you're all poet."

"I'm sorry, I didn't mean to make a dumb joke of it ... but damn it there *are* so many questions about you that I'd love to have you answer, say in the next few years. You're like a book I've just started and can't put down—"

"Now come on, Ben, cut it out. . . . Look, I'm trying to be casual! Can you bring some film for Annie's camera?"

"I've already got some wrapped as my present to her. Rosie, if you're as good and wonderful as I think you are, you're going to louse up my well-cultivated cynicism. Do something rotten today!"

"Like what?"

"Try to borrow huge sums of money. Tell me in detail about all your old lovers. Hock the family jewels."

She laughed. "Ah, Ben, you do keep me laughing."

"I've heard that the comedian never gets the girl."

"Nonsense. If you can keep me laughing, mister, I'm yours forever. Things have been grim around here too long. *Too long . . .*"

In the small suitcase which he had brought from California there was only one change of clothes. Remembering that some of his old things were stored in a closet on the third floor, he found a white linen suit which Heidi had given him long ago and which he had disliked because she got upset whenever he got a spot on it, a disaster he was rarely able to avoid throughout an evening. Now the idea of looking as elegant as possible when he confronted Howie, and later when he attended Annie's birthday party, appealed to him, and he was gratified to find that the waist was only a little too tight. Rummaging on the floor of the closet, he found some white shoes, in the toes of which he had sloppily but fortunately left some white socks. After washing these in the sink and throwing them in the dryer, he ironed the suit and from his suitcase he took a bright red tie with a floral pattern which a woman in Santa Barbara had given to him.

It was a bright May morning with the sun a warm promise of summer as he left his house at noon. Two hummingbirds hovered by the lilac blossoms and a bright red cardinal was perched on the hood of his jeep, flashing away as Ben approached. After carefully brushing the driver's seat with a whiskbroom to avoid marring the seat of his immaculate pants, Ben picked a red rosebud from a nearby bush and put it in his buttonhole. When a man feels very important, it may be wise to keep him waiting a little, he thought, and took pleasure in driving slowly toward the country club. Although the mill usually ran seven days a week, it apparently had been shut down today. No acrid stench marred the sunlit symphony of spring aromas—the fragrance of apple orchards, lilacs, newly cut grass and the gardens which were coming into bloom behind even the meanest shack. The last of the fall leaves were being raked up and burned on the lawn of the country club, adding a further spice to the air.

It was sixteen minutes after twelve when Ben entered the bar of the club. Howie, dressed in a tentlike leisure suit of pale blue, and Pete in his usual banker's attire were waiting. When they saw Ben they looked surprised by his white suit and annoyed by his lateness.

"Good morning, gentlemen," Ben said with a smile. "Isn't it a beautiful day?"

"You going to a wedding?" Pete asked.

"I am going to spend the afternoon with two beautiful young women, but first, what can I do for you?"

"We better go into my office and talk," Howie said. "I don't mean to be abrupt, Ben, but I don't have much time. Order a drink and take it with you."

"I don't need one."

Howie, who was president of the country club, led the way to a large room which was paneled with knotty pine. Ben and Pete sat in leather chairs while Howie half reclined on a big couch. No one went near a desk in the corner.

"I understand you want to move back and take over the *Recorder*," Howie said after taking a sip from his highball glass.

"I'm looking into it."

"Naturally," Howie said, "we are pleased that one of our

82

most distinguished citizens wants to come home again. There are, however, certain difficulties. . . ."

"We gave Fitzgerald a two-year contract," Pete said.

"And we don't think it's fair for you to ask Pete to give up the publisher's job after he's done it so well, so long," Howie continued.

"Just to set the record straight, Pete, you've done the job very badly," Ben said, keeping his voice soft. "The *Recorder* really isn't a newspaper anymore. There's no news in it. That's a disservice to the town."

"We make money!"

"Now wait a minute," Howie said. "Journalistic excellence is a matter of opinion. We've had few complaints."

Ben said nothing. They both glanced at him nervously.

"Anyway, we don't want you at the *Recorder*," Pete said. "It belongs to the trust and we control the trust. So there's not much you can do about it."

Again Ben did not reply. Pete cracked his knuckles uncomfortably.

"I'm sick of this prodigal son act of yours," he said. "Every few years you come back here and expect us to kill the fatted calf. Well, we're all out of fatted calves today."

Ben smiled, said nothing.

"Another thing," Pete continued, "we want you to move out of that house that you call yours. It's not yours, it belongs to the trust. Mother wanted Heidi to use it as long as she wished, but now that Heidi's gone, we should put it to use—"

"I thought mother gave us each the use of a house for as long as we wanted it," Ben said in surprise.

"You're never in the place. I have to take care of it."

"If I came back to town, I might use it."

"There's no job for you here. What would you do?"

"Collect butterflies? There are a lot of them out there."

Pete ignored this.

"The thing is, we have a buyer for the house," Howie said.

83

"The new manager of the mill wants it. That would add quite a bit to the capital of the trust. With inflation and medical costs, your mother could use it."

Again Ben said nothing. It was the first time he'd argued with silence.

"Well, that's it," Pete said. "Stay away from the paper—I don't want you getting Scotty all upset. And get your stuff out of the house as soon as you can."

"There's no great hurry," Howie added smoothly. "We're not trying to be tough on you, Ben. It's just that we have a responsibility to the trust. It's a legal matter, really."

Ben smiled.

"Well, what do you think?" Pete asked.

"I think that you two very much want me to leave town, and there must be a reason beyond bad breath."

"That's not true, Ben," Howie said. "Gosh, a fellow like you with a Pulitzer prize and a national reputation as a photographer—gosh, I'd like to have you in town, even if we weren't old high school buddies."

"Remember when you threw the football helmet full of toilet water at me, Howie? I was all dressed up for a date, as I recall."

"Hell, Ben, I don't remember crap like that." And snuck in a smile at his own inadvertent joke.

"I remember it," Pete said. "God, I should think you'd be ashamed to bring that up, Ben."

"Why? I retaliated. I emptied two quart bottles of ink into a wastepaper basket, Howie. I waited until you got dressed up for a dance before I let you have it."

"I remember," Howie replied, reddening. After a moment he added, "I think that's the incident that helped me to be class president. If you remember, I called off our war. I apologized for my part in it and shook hands."

"You always were a big man, Howie, and a quick learner," Ben said.

"Well, I really enjoy all this nostalgia," Howie replied,

glancing at his heavy gold wristwatch, "but I've got a golf date."

"Ben, Ephram is busy with mother's garden, but I'd be glad to have Winters drive you to the airport at any time," Pete put in.

"I bet you might even drive me yourself."

"Ben, there's no point in hard feelings," Howie said. "If you wanted to move back here and just work as a photographer for the paper, that would be fine. Course there wouldn't be much money in it."

"That's very generous of you."

"And there's plenty of places you could find to live around here," Howie continued. "I'll have some of my real estate people help you to look if you want. I don't want you to get the idea that I wouldn't make you welcome."

"Howie, I know that you speak from the heart."

Patting him heartily on the back, Howie walked briskly from the room.

"Pete, what do you suppose happened with us?" Ben asked suddenly.

"What does that mean?"

"Why can't we work together instead of against each other?"

"So now you get sentimental! You never gave a damn about me ever since I can remember."

"Maybe I deserve that. But did you ever give a damn about me?"

"I *used* to think you were God. No more. I just want you to stay the hell out of my life, out of Livingston."

"It's my hometown too."

"Your beat, as I believe you people call it, is the world. You said that once."

"When I was very young. I don't know why, but I can't get this town out of my blood—"

"It sounds to me like you're broke and expect mother to bail you out."

85

"No, I'm not broke. I'm not building any swimming pools, but I'm not broke."

"What are you going to do?"

"Think. And maybe it's time for you to think, too. I have an idea that Howie could get you into a lot of trouble."

"Now don't tell me how to run my life! Here you blow into town, shack up with that crazy Kelly broad, and..."

Ben tweaked his nose.

"What the *hell* do you think you're doing—"

"It was better than hitting you. I like Rose Kelly and I like her sister Annie. If you say anything more unpleasant about them, I'll maybe have to box your ears."

"You son of a bitch," Pete said, and stormed out of the room, slamming the door behind him.

Ben stood looking out a window, where he could see Howie climbing into an electric golf cart. The bottom line of their exchange was that he had lost a job and a house. Despite its beauty, the house really didn't cause him much regret—too many unhappy years had been spent in it. The loss of the paper at least didn't surprise him any more than Howie's opposition did. The hostility of his brother should be familiar by now, but when Ben was away from Livingston, his memory softened it. Now here it was again, harsh as an Adirondack blizzard, and the worst part of it was the suspicion that in this lousy relationship, he himself was not entirely innocent. As always, Pete made him feel guilty and depressed.

On the way out of the country club, which his grandfather had founded, Ben started to get a drink, then remembered that he was no longer a member. He hurried to his jeep and drove rapidly toward the Kelly farm. Rose opened the front door when he knocked. In celebration of her sister's birthday and the first warm day of spring, she was wearing a summer dress with a pattern of brown and orange.

"Ben!" she said when she saw the white suit. "You look so *splendid*." She gave him an enthusiastic hug, darting back with a laugh before he could fully return it.

"And you, lady, look like a sunflower."

"Did you see Howie? I'm dying to know what happened."

From the living room came the sound of rock and roll music.

"I saw him," he said.

"Let's talk outside. I was crazy enough to give Annie records."

They sat on a bench on the front porch, surrounded by piles of firewood. In a small garden ahead of them, tulips were already beginning to bloom, bright blades of yellow and red. The wind ruffled the grass in the surrounding fields.

"I love this place," he said as he sat down.

"What happened?"

"In a nutshell, I can't get the *Recorder* back and they want to sell the house out from under me."

"Can't you stop them?"

"I'm not sure I'd want to if I could. I've never been happy in that damn house, not for long. First it was mother's and then it was Heidi's. The echoes of divorce are still there."

"What are you going to do?"

"I can stay in California. I'm making a fairly good living there, even if the work is dull."

"Yes, you could do that," she said quietly.

"Have you ever thought of moving to California?"

"Me?" she asked in astonishment.

"You could stay in my house out there for a few days to see if you like it."

"What would happen to Annie and grammie?"

"Isn't Annie old enough to take care of grammie for a while?"

"Oh, Ben, that would never work! What are you doing?"

"I'm trying to give you some options to think about. A lot of people want to get the hell out of this town the first chance they get."

"Not me. Have you given up on the whole town?"

He sat watching a flock of red-winged blackbirds which

were skimming just over the waves of grass, like black sea-gulls. "I love this town," he said. "That's unreasonable, but I'm stuck with it. No matter where I live, this is always home, damn it."

"Thank god," she said. "I thought I'd lost you there for a minute."

"I'll tell you something else. We haven't known each other anywhere near long enough to make this reasonable either, but I think I'm in terrible danger, as they say, of falling in love with you."

"Oh, you'll weather it," she said, blushing.

"Wait a minute." He took her hand. "I'm too old to go blundering around, wrecking your life and mine. What if I start a newspaper here? What if I do that mostly to be with you, whether I admit it to myself or not? What if I get you to quit your job at the mill to work with me? Then what if you find that you've been pushed too fast into something that you really don't want?"

"That would be pretty bad," she said, looking down.

"It could happen, too. I've been lonely a long time, and I guess that you have. We're both bored with our work. We at least seem to offer each other a solution to a lot of problems. But you know as well as I do that a person you've known only a few days can turn out to be something quite different from anything you expected."

"It's happened," she said.

"So I don't know what to do," he said. "I can go out to California, sell my house, sell my studio, and come back to start a business which in part, at least, is just an attempt to attract you."

"Ben, would it help to know you can have me without starting a newspaper? That's the most complicated way of seducing a girl I've ever heard."

He kissed her, a hungry kiss.

"I wasn't trying to lead up to this," he said finally.

88

"God, if you weren't trying, I pity the girls when you do try!"

He laughed uncertainly. "Damn it, I wish we'd known each other longer. I'm not sure what—"

"What do you want?"

"About two days in Vermont alone together. Then I'd like to go to California, cash in my chips there, and come back to take whatever chances are necessary with the paper."

"All right. If you want. But it might be better if you went to California first."

"Why?"

"When you get back there, you may find you don't want to leave. Maybe you shouldn't feel you're committed to anyone here."

"I don't think that could happen."

"Talking about pulling up stakes and actually doing it are two different things for anyone. And maybe we'll both feel better if we can look back and know we took more time to think. It seems impossible, Ben, but it's true, we've only known each other four days."

"If we wait another twenty-four hours, would we be more respectable?"

"About twenty percent. Ben, do you have a girl out in California?"

"Not really."

"I think that means yes."

"I'm not in love with anyone out there and no one is in love with me. I was traveling in a set where talk of love was not exactly fashionable."

"But you have a lady who doesn't talk about love."

"She's a good friend, but I guarantee she won't weep when I go."

"I'm going to be scared to death the whole time you're gone."

He kissed her, finding it almost impossible to stop, despite

89

the fact that a wooden bench between two piles of logs was not the most comfortable situation. She pushed him away gently.

"I'm going to be honest with you," she said. "I am a shrewd and calculating woman who has lived by her wits since the age of fifteen. I want you to plan our weekend in Vermont. I want you to find an elegant inn with a huge double bed, a fireplace and gourmet meals delivered to the door. I'm going to get myself a black lace nightgown, something I've wanted all my life, and I'm going to prove to you and myself that I'm not exactly the iron maiden or the frigid spinster that people around here call me."

"Who calls you that?"

"All the guys at the mill who get mad when I won't go to a motel with them. Anyway, on our weekend, I'm going to cut loose. I'm going to go braless and I'm going to drink champagne if you can afford it, and say perfectly shocking things whenever I feel like it."

"I can hardly wait."

"But you're going to have to. It kills me to send you to California first, but I'm smart enough to figure that the anticipation of our weekend is more likely to bring you back than the memory of it."

He laughed.

"I shouldn't have told you. Now you know what a cynical bitch I am."

"Also, I'm sure, too modest." He kissed her, lightly this time, which was fortunate because Ebon interrupted them.

"Hey, dad," Ebon said. "Oh, sorry . . ."

"It's all right, Eb," he replied. "I guess spring got the best of us."

"I was powerless against your father's white suit, Eb. Isn't it gorgeous?"

"Yeah. Sorry to barge in, but we saw your jeep, dad, and Annie has been waiting all day to try out the camera."

90

"Tell her to meet me in the kitchen," Ben said, and got the package he had left in the jeep.

Annie was wearing a candy-striped skirt and a white blouse which her sister had made for her birthday. The camera case lay open on the kitchen table. Ebon was opening a window.

"Happy birthday, Annie!" Ben said, and gave her his package.

Ebon paused to watch while she opened it, finding a dozen rolls of film and some flash bulbs.

"*Thank* you!" Annie said. Thank you for all this and the *fantastic camera!* I mean, Ebon gave it to me, but I know it really came from you—"

"It was my idea," Ebon said.

"Of course it was," Ben added. "Now, do you want to start going into photography seriously, Annie, or do you just want to learn how to take a few snapshots?"

"I want to learn everything I can."

"Well, I'll show you how the camera and all the equipment work. When you've got the mechanics of it down, take as many pictures as you can, but never snap the shutter without noting the camera settings and the reading of the light meter in a notebook. Then you'll know why you succeeded or failed."

She already understood the basics, he discovered, and was quick to learn the intricate mechanisms of the old Leica. She had beautifully tapered fingers, but her nails were bitten to the quick, he noted with compassion. Usually she kept her hands doubled up to hide them, but as she touched the camera, she overcame her self-consciousness. He liked the way she handled the Leica, precisely but almost tenderly. After years of teaching photography to high school and college students, which he often did for the fun of it, he felt he could almost gauge someone's talent for photography by the way they handled a camera. When he told Annie that she passed this test with flying colors, she blushed. He had seen more blushes in the Kelly family, he thought, than he had seen in the past decade.

After loading the camera, Ben and Ann decided to take some pictures outdoors.

"You want to come, Eb?" Ben asked.

"No, you go ahead."

"How about you, Rosie?" Ben called. "Want to take some pictures with us?"

"I've got to start getting dinner," Rose said, coming from the living room.

The sun was still bright, but it had set enough to cause the trees to cast shadows.

"I don't know why Eb doesn't like to take pictures," Ann said. "You'd think as your son—"

"Maybe that's why. I tried to teach him but he always got so frustrated . . ."

"I don't see anything frustrating about it. Can I take a picture of you?"

"Sure, but I think that inanimate objects are better at first. The main thing when you take people is the ability to bring out a good expression. Right now we're interested more in just getting the right exposure."

She began taking pictures of the farmhouse, carefully writing the details of each in her notebook. The angles she chose were interesting, and the prolonged concentration with which she worked was unusual for a novice. His daughter Laura had never been able to treat a camera as anything more than a toy, and Heidi had infuriated him by acting as though photography were so easy that it demanded no real effort. Annie was the first member of his family . . . or first friend . . . who gave promise of being a serious apprentice. He found her a delight.

"Can I take animals?" Annie asked.

"They're real tough, but you can try."

Running, she headed toward the sheep pen. The lambs came

running to meet her, and for half an hour she photographed them.

"Oh, I'm dying to see these shots," she said. "How long will it take to develop them?"

"In the darkroom at my place I can get you contact prints in just a few minutes," Ben replied.

"Oh, I'd love to see you do that! Can we go there?"

"You better see if Ebon and Rosie want to go. I'll meet you in the car."

Running ahead of him, Annie went in the back door of the farm. Coming out again almost immediately, she joined him as he approached the jeep. "Sis is cooking dinner and Eb's being awful," she said. "I'm not going to worry about him."

"How is he being awful?"

"Oh, he just gets grumpy sometimes. Do you have an enlarger and everything?"

As Ben parked in front of the old house, he saw Ephram cutting the lawn, perhaps in preparation for selling the place.

"Afternoon, Bens," Ephram said and watched with open admiration as Ann got out of the jeep, showing a fine flash of tanned leg in a swirl of candy-striped skirt. He leaned on the handle of his power mower, watching while Ben led the girl into the house. The gossip he would spread at Joe's bar would be admiring, but bad for the girl, Ben thought. Still, since there was nothing he could do about it, he dismissed the thought from his mind.

The lilacs which had been put in the vases were wilted now. Ben was pleased to note that Ann was so eager to see the darkroom that she didn't pause to admire the other rooms in the stately old house. He got himself a drink before climbing the stairs to the third floor. It was hot there now, and he had a sudden flash of memory, of a hot summer afternoon when he and Heidi had run to the third floor to find a moment of privacy while her relatives and the children were talking endlessly in the living room. . . . Well, for a few years it *had* been a good marriage, and that in a sense was more scary than the memory of a marriage which had been bad from the start. If gold can turn to lead, what miser can be safe?

"I've never seen so much equipment," Ann said as he opened the door to the darkroom. "Will you show me how *all* of it works?"

They became engrossed in developing her films and discussing the reasons why each turned out as it did. As they bent over the sheets of prints, her hair brushed his forehead. It was so soft that he could hardly feel it, and had the same clean fragrance that Rosie's did—probably the two sisters used the same kind of shampoo, but there seemed more mystery than that to this identical scent which made him remember one when he was with the other. In the red light of the darkroom, Annie's lips looked lavender and her teeth very white. The pearl buttons on her blouse glowed. To find relief from the heat of the windowless room, she had unbuttoned the top two. He could see just the beginning of her cleavage, over which a gold cross was suspended by an almost invisible chain, but the red light lent it all a faintly lurid effect. This, with the admiring tones in which she talked to him, caused fantasies to come to his mind which rather astonished him.

"Come on," he said, "it's after five. We better go."

"You haven't showed me how the enlarger works yet."

"We'll have plenty of time."

"Rose says you'll be going back to California."

"I'll be back."

"To *stay?*"

"I think so."

To his surprise, she gave him a quick hug. "Oh, I'll be so glad, and Rosie will too!"

Ben could not remember when in his whole life he had felt so *welcome*. It made him feel ebullient, and he took the down stairs two at a time. No sweat. No pain.

Although it was past quitting time, Ephram was still mowing the lawn when they left the house. Probably he had timed their stay—a good detail for his story.

"We were developing pictures," Ben said as they passed the old man. "Annie here got a new camera for her birthday."

He gestured toward the camera hanging around Annie's neck, but that of course would not help. He wished that the girl had buttoned her blouse back up to her throat.

"Well, hope things came out good," Ephram said with his sly smile. "Happy birthday, miss, and many of them!"

When they got back to the house, they found that Ebon too was mowing a lawn. Dressed only in dungarees, he was muscling a heavy hand machine through thick weeds.

"Most of my pictures came out terrific," Ann shouted.

"Good," Ebon grunted, making the mower lunge ahead.

"Don't you want to see them?"

"Later."

Ben went to the kitchen, where Rose was frosting a birthday cake. If Ebon was disgruntled, he shouldn't be surprised, he realized. Without meaning to, he had appeared on this festive day and had stolen Annie for a whole afternoon. More than that, Annie gave Ben more respect and admiration than he had ever seen her give Ebon.

As if this weren't bad enough, Ben more than suspected that Ebon was troubled by the kiss he'd seen. If he had felt somehow proprietary about both Rose and Annie, he was having a bad day indeed.

The thought that his son might wind up hating him as much as his brother did was, of course, ridiculous. Then why did he have it? . . .

7

Rose offered to drive Ben to the Albany airport the next day, but he worried that neither the pickup truck nor his old jeep was capable of the 200-mile round trip on the turnpike. He asked Ephram whether his mother planned to use her stately old Cadillac.

"Pete says I can't get off, but I don't see why you can't use the car," Ephram said. "Your mother never goes out anymore."

Sure that Pete would object if he could, Ben went to visit his mother, as he had briefly almost every day he had been in town. Some days the old lady seemed to be almost her old energetic self, while on others she seemed completely bewildered. This was one of her bad days.

"Good morning, Petey," she said when she saw Ben. "Where have you been?"

"I'm Ben, mother. How are you feeling?"

"Pretty well. Did you see some horses on Elm Street?"

"No."

"I heard them just a few minutes ago, but my eyes are so bad, I can't see anything. They were galloping right along at a good clip. I often hear them at night. Who do you suppose goes riding in the dark?"

"I don't know," he said, touched by the thought of these echoes from her childhood, when almost every family in Livingston had kept horses.

"What do you want, son?"

"Mother, do you mind if I use the car?" he asked, amused by the classic teenage question.

"Where do you want to go?"

"Albany. I'm not sure my old jeep can make it."

"Will you pay for the gas?"

His mother had always been careless in the management of millions, but careful with pennies, especially with her sons, who were supposed to learn prudence from her parsimony.

"I'll pay for the gas."

"Pete, have you seen Benny lately? I worry about him."

"I'm Ben, mother. Why are you worried?"

"People are talking. People are always talking about you, Benny."

Elizabeth, no doubt, had been keeping her up to date.

"Well, that shows I'm still alive, doesn't it?"

He kissed her soft, wrinkled cheek and hurried down the stairs, eager as always to escape that house, and feeling guilty about it.

At seven the next morning, Ben and Rose drove to Virginia Winslow's garage in the jeep and got into the Cadillac. When she sat on the gray upholstery in the front seat of the high old sedan which, except for its boxlike shape, still looked new, she said, "I feel like a Rockefeller. I wouldn't call the queen me aunt!"

He backed out of the driveway and headed toward the turnpike. The long black hood of the Cadillac gleamed in the sun.

"I keep forgetting that you have money," she said suddenly.

"My mother does. By the time Pete and Howie get through with it, I doubt whether there'll be much left. . . ."

97

"I like you poor. People always get bastardly when they get rich."

He laughed, glancing at her. She was wearing a gray flannel skirt, a black patent leather belt which emphasized her small waistline and a white cashmere sweater which emphasized a good deal else. Slowly they climbed the hill from the top of which he admired the view of the town when entering it a few days ago. When they got to the summit he made a U-turn and stopped in the parking place overlooking the valley.

"We've got time," he said. "I've always loved this place."

"Me too, but I've spent about half my life fighting off men who want to take me here."

He laughed. "Is it a reflex action? Can I expect trouble?"

"All the fight's gone out of me," she replied and came close as he put his arm around her shoulders. The silky cashmere felt warm and good.

"I suppose this car is about twenty years old," he said, "but I bet nobody ever parked it to kiss a pretty girl."

"What a waste!"

Her kisses were surprising, he thought ... they were such a complete gift of herself, yet curiously restrained, a gift sensibly limited by the time and the place. ...

"We better get going," she said finally. "You don't want to miss your plane."

"Wrong. I do—let's go to Vermont instead."

"They only gave me a half-day off from the office. Do you hate me for being practical?"

"Yes."

"Drive the car. I promise I'll be free for a weekend as soon as you get back."

"I'm going to make the fastest trip to California and back in history. I'm going to commandeer a military jet."

He started the car, then added, "Hey, do you want to drive this thing? Since you're going to drive it home, you ought to get used to it while I'm still here."

98

He got out of the car and helped her to slide the front seat forward. When he got in on the other side, she said, "It's just a standard American shift, isn't it?"

"That's right."

After waiting for a truck to pass, she drove smoothly onto the highway. "It's kind of crummy compared to my truck," she said. "No four-wheel drive. Well, I guess it's the best the rich can do."

Ben tended to believe the old saw about people driving the way they live. While middle-aged, his mother had driven slowly but so absentmindedly that she was always bashing fenders or requiring Ephram to drag her from a ditch with a tractor. Heidi, his former wife, had prided herself on being an expert driver, but had been arrested for speeding so many times that her license had been suspended. Rose, he noticed, kept the speedometer right on the limit except when passing, which she did with swift precision. If the old saw remained true, Rose was a lady who knew what she was at, and took pride in doing it well.

"Do you mind talking business?" she asked suddenly.

"Newspaper business?"

"What else? I made a few calls and got some figures. It might not cost as much as you think to start a weekly."

"What's your guess?"

"There's a company up in Elizabethtown that does the printing for about a dozen weeklies around here. Photo-offset of course. It's owned by a guy named Phil Haverstraw. Phil's an old friend of mine. He says that experienced people can get a new weekly off the ground here for about twenty thousand dollars."

"That's less than I thought."

"Some people can do it for a lot less. A guy over in Ticonderoga started one with a total capital of five hundred dollars."

"How?"

99

"He and his wife did all the work. After they got out their first issue, they were able to sell enough advertising to keep going."

"I admire that."

"The basic figures are really interesting," she went on. "A new paper in a town like ours probably would start with a run of two thousand copies, each with fourteen pages. It costs only one eighty to print that. Call it two hundred. For a year, then, your printing bill would be ten thousand four hundred."

"Still less than I thought. I'm used to letterpress."

"I think I know where you could get the basic equipment for making camera-ready copy for about three thousand—secondhand, of course. A little paper went out of business up near Keene some time ago. The three thousand would include desks, typewriters, everything in the office. It's all stored in a barn now."

"How do you get information like this?"

"As a PR girl, I'm in touch with all the newspapers. And as I think I told you, I've always had sort of a crazy dream about starting my own."

"I bet you could do it, and without my help."

"There are lots of catches. You usually have to operate for at least a year before you get in the black and five years before you get your initial investment back. You can figure your expenses almost to a penny, but you can't predict how much advertising you'll get."

"I used to help my father sell advertising. Between us, you and I know a lot of people in Livingston, Rosie. We shouldn't have any trouble—"

"The question is whether Howie can stop us. I'm dead sure he'll try."

"What can the bastard do?"

"I saw him go to work on the radio station—the tower thing was just finishing it off. Advertiser after advertiser was scared away."

"Again, how?"

"The main advertisers are the supermarkets. The managers know that Howie has all kinds of political power. He can have the plumbing or the electric wiring inspected and found defective. He can have the tax assessment raised. If somebody falls and hurts himself in a supermarket, Howie can have a lot to say about whether the claim is pressed or thrown out of court. If you were the manager of a store like that, wouldn't you want to keep Howie happy?"

"I'd want to kill him, I think."

"God knows, I'm not trying to discourage you, Ben. I just feel honor-bound to spell out the dangers while I'm really trying to sell you on this idea."

"I can handle Howie. Of course he'll make trouble, but I can handle him."

"How can you be so sure? Nobody else in town can."

"I don't mean to be arrogant, but it's just a kind of gut feeling I have when I'm with Howie. I can handle him. If he wants to get tough, I think I can get tougher."

"Jesus, I'd love to see you get him," Rose said as she passed a gasoline truck on a long hill. "I've got to admit that I hate the bastard. I suppose that's one thing you ought to take into account if you work with me. I'm not quite rational about the man."

"What happened? Can you tell me now?"

"He's done a lot of things that hurt this town, but that's not my real grudge. . . ."

Haltingly at first, Rose told him about going to work in the public relations department of the mill seven years ago, when she was twenty-three years old. Howie then, as now, was the lawyer for the mill, and was considered almost more important than the manager. He had an impressive office on the top floor of the administration building, and Rose was flattered when he took to asking her up there to help him with speeches and news releases. Perhaps because he was so fat, because he appeared so old to her, and because his wealth seemed to lend respectability, it really never occurred to her that his interest in her could be anything but professional. When he recommended a raise for her, he squeezed her arm while telling her about it. That was the only physical contact they had.

A week later he asked her to accompany him to New York to help him at a convention. There was nothing very unusual about an executive taking a public relations person to a convention, and she went without any real qualms. On the drive to the city in Howie's white Lincoln, he was avuncular and full of questions about Rose's personal life. He sympathized with her about the long illness of her mother, and had heard about some of her father's difficulties in Livingston and his retreat back to Ireland. Warmed by his interest, Rose almost found him charming.

In the Hilton Hotel in New York, Rose found that she and her boss had adjoining rooms. She didn't much like it, but assuming that the door between them was locked, she also didn't think much about it . . . naïve, probably, but in a way she'd always been naïve, assuming that most people were reasonably decent, until proved otherwise. Anyway, soon after they arrived they had dinner in an elegant restaurant, and Howie drank a great deal. He talked a lot about the great future she could have, explaining that he had influence with businesses not only in Livingston, but in Albany and New York.

"If you got a really good job in a city with colleges, you could finish your education. A girl with your brains and your looks could go anywhere...." He squeezed her arm. "I'm good to my friends if my friends are good to me. I never ask anything for nothing. Howie Hewat knows how to express gratitude. Anyone who knows me knows that." He patted her knee, squeezed her thigh.

"I think it's time I turned in," she said nervously. "I'm awfully tired."

"You're right," he said. "It's time we both hit the hay."

He paid the check with the first hundred dollar bill she had ever seen. Riding up on the elevator with her, he kissed her forehead, still avuncular.

"You don't know how much it means to a fellow like me to be with a charming young lady like you," he said, sounding damn near pathetic. "You give me a regular lease on life. I'll do everything I can to make you like me as much as I like you."

"Thank you," she replied with embarrassment. He held her arm as they walked down the hall, and she was relieved when she got to her door.

"Good night, Mr. Hewat," she said. "Thanks a million for a wonderful evening—"

He squeezed her arm again, but didn't try to kiss her, as she had worried he would. Letting herself into her room, she felt shaken, far too tense to sleep. For a long while she stood by the window, staring at the towers of Manhattan and the sea of lights. Later she was profoundly thankful that she had not undressed. She suddenly heard a noise behind her. The door from Howie's room opened, and he walked in. He was wearing red pajamas and a matching bathrobe, a get-up which his great belly made absurd. He was carrying a bottle of champagne in his right hand, two glasses in the other.

"I thought you might like a little nightcap, dear heart," he said. Dear heart!

"I'm sorry, but I can't drink any more—Mr. Hewat."

His face suddenly turned hard. "Look, I didn't bring you all the way down here for nothing. Are we going to have a good time or not?"

"I hope so, Mr. Hewat, but I really have to go to bed. I'm not feeling so well—"

He put the bottle and glasses on a dresser and stepped toward her. She stood paralyzed as he dragged her into a rough but sickeningly soft embrace.

Pulling free, she gasped, "I have to go to the bathroom. . . ."

With the door locked, she stood in that small, white-tiled

compartment, and was sick to her stomach. She could hear him pacing on the other side of the door. "... Why don't you ... go back to your room?" she called out. "I'd like a little privacy while I ... change...."

"Okay. Don't take long!"

When she heard him leave, she grabbed her purse and coat from the closet, and literally ran from her room, down the service stairs and out of the hotel. After paying for her bus ticket, she had less than a dollar, and her anger was increased by hunger as the Greyhound took her back to Livingston.

The worst problem, of course, was her certainty that she would be fired from the mill, the only big employer in the town. She soon found, however, that Howie was too smart for that—he wouldn't take any action that would increase the likelihood of talk. Instead of having her fired, Howie simply blocked every promotion she became eligible for.

"I didn't realize it until the public relations director retired," Rose said. "Me and everyone else had assumed that I was going to get that job, but instead they hired a third-rate newspaper man from Albany. Even *then* I was slow to get the drift until Howie came up to me on the street one day. 'How are you, Rose Kelly?' he asked with his horrible fat smirk. 'Do you finally get the message?' "

"Of course you hate the bastard!" Ben said, furious. "Jesus ..."

"Wait a minute, there's more, much more. I won't bother you with all of it now, but there's one thing I'll never forgive that man for."

This story was short and bitter. An eighteen-year-old secretary by the name of Peggy Martin in Rose's office had been subjected to similar treatment by Howie. This time the trip was to a convention in Boston, not New York, and this time the girl had been scared into submission. She had been Howie's mistress for almost a year, driving to Montreal with him on many weekends. When she got pregnant, Howie explained that he didn't believe in abortion and it would be awkward for her to have the baby in Livingston, where people would talk. He would arrange for her to get a job just like her old one in Bangor, Maine, where World Paper also had a mill.

"She was suddenly just shoved into another world," Rose said. "I was the only person she could talk to, and she wrote me a lot of letters. Can you imagine what it would be like for a girl to be pregnant and alone in a strange town at the age of nineteen? Well, she didn't make it. She fell or jumped, as they say, from the top floor of her office. And meanwhile, Howie was out making speeches about the sin of birth control and Right to Life. The son of a bitch isn't even a Catholic. He just wants what he assumes is the Irish and the Italian vote."

Rose's face was flushed and she was breathing hard.

"Would it help you if I beat up the son of a bitch?" Ben asked, hoping that he still could.

"That's the kind of thing dad does. You'd just end up in jail looking silly. I want some kind of revenge that's a damn sight more substantial than that. . . . It's wrong to want revenge, isn't it?"

"Only for saints. . . . What do you want to do with him?"

"Hit him where it *hurts*. He's planning to run for state senator. For starts, I'd like to make him lose."

"And that's why you want a newspaper!"

"Plus I also want to be Rose Kelly, girl reporter!"

"For a start, how about putting those figures you were talking about on paper while I'm gone? I want as accurate an estimate of costs for the first year as I can get. Put yourself down for eight thousand dollars, and we'll need a secretary, a part-time accountant, and some small guarantee for a space salesman. We might as well figure in my own living expenses. In Livingston I probably can get by on eight thousand a year, the same as you."

She slowed down as a lumbering truck swung out to pass

an even slower one ahead. "Ben, where are you going to live when you come back?"

"Oh, there're plenty places for rent."

"We'd love to have you at the farm. God knows, it's not luxurious, but there's plenty of room. There are whole wings I keep closed."

"Will you let me pay rent? A gentleman should never let a lady give him a free apartment. There might be strings attached."

"Damn right . . . okay, you can pay me fifty a month if it will keep you honest, plus a share of the groceries. There still may be strings attached, though."

"Can you give me a room next to yours with a connecting door?"

"No, but we have an attic with an old bed in it, a hayloft in the barn and all kinds of delightful places. We even have a spring with a pool covered by a little shed. It's a very private place to swim."

After a moment Ben added, his voice suddenly serious, "I'm afraid Eb may resent having me at the farm."

"I've thought of that. He still needs you, Ben. He needs to be reminded that his world holds more than Annie."

Soon she turned onto the exit that led to the airport. Arriving with almost an hour to spare, he made the arrangements for his ticket.

"Would you like to have a drink," he asked, "or would you like to wait in the car?"

"The car, I think."

"Let's wait in the back seat. It's more comfortable."

As soon as they sat down, she came toward him. With her feet curled up, she could lie with her shoulders on his lap. After a deep kiss, he slipped his hand under her sweater.

"People can look in," she said.

He pulled down a gray silk shade at each window. "My mother was always prepared for emergencies."

106

"The rich, they have all the answers," she said, but after a while she sat up abruptly. "This is getting too frustrating," she said. "It's a hell of a way to say goodbye. How about that drink?"

She ordered a Coca-Cola with lime, and to him looked almost like a high school student as she sipped it through a straw.

"I could see what offices are for rent," she said suddenly. "Do you want one on Main Street?"

"Sure, something on the ground floor."

"When do you hope to get out our first edition?"

"The Fourth of July would be good. We should be able to sell a lot of papers to the crowd—"

"I'm sorry to keep asking all these questions. I guess I'm still afraid it's a dream."

"It might turn into a nightmare, but it's well past being a dream."

"Have you really made a decision to do it?"

"Without being quite aware of it, I guess I have. I've even thought of a name for it. What do you think of 'Livingston *Ledger?*'"

She wrinkled her nose. "That's a little stodgy, isn't it? If you want alliteration, how about 'Livingston *Life?*'"

"Much better."

He ordered another Scotch and felt curiously as he had when army leaves came to an end long ago, when he and Heidi had still been in love. There was a desperate need to take his departure on the right note, to do nothing at the last minute which would be regretted in solitude.

"You haven't told me when you're coming back," she said.

"I can't tell exactly. I have to see about selling the house and the studio and shipping all my stuff. Real estate moves very fast out there. It might not take more than a week."

"I'm like a kid waiting for Christmas," she said. "A week seems like a long time."

107

Her face was somber. How many men had she known, other than her father, who couldn't be relied upon? Who had lied to her?

When his flight was announced, she followed him to the gate. Her goodbye kiss was oddly chaste.

"If you find an office that's right, sign the lease," he said. "You can tell me how to make out the check on the phone and I'll mail it from Santa Barbara."

"You're willing to rent an office *now?*"

"We'll have to have someplace to work."

"Oh, Ben, now I really do believe it's all going to happen." She hugged him as though she would never let him go.

When the imminent departure of the plane was announced, she finally pushed him away. "Go!" she said. "Go and get your ass back here, Ben Winslow. I'll be waiting with my suitcase all packed for Vermont."

BEN had left his red Triumph sports car at the airport in Los Angeles. As he drove along the coast to Santa
Barbara, he kept comparing this part of California to the
Adirondacks. No scenery could be more beautiful than the
dun-colored mountains he saw now, with cliffs falling to
beaches and the Pacific surf. Most of the cars on the Freeway
were expensive new models, not the salt-corroded rattletraps
which most people in Livingston drove. Most of the people
in them looked tanned and young. The gnarled old faces
which one saw so often in Livingston were rare on the
Freeway.

When he reached Santa Barbara and turned onto the road
leading to his beach cottage, he was as impressed by the houses
he passed as though he had never before seen them. In that
city, a house which cost $150,000 was considered relatively
inexpensive. Even million-dollar mansions were common
enough to be inconspicuous. The attempts to re-create Span-
ish architecture and the modern structures of glass were
strange to an upstate New Yorker, but with their gardens of
oversized flowers, the palm trees, the tiled terraces and the
blue swimming pools, they offered a lush beauty of their own.

Ben wondered why at heart he was so hostile to this part
of the world, so anxious to leave it. For one thing, he was

without doubt an east-coast snob, a realization which brought him no special pleasure. Perhaps he also resented the fact that he lost his sense of small-town importance here. In Santa Barbara no one gave much of a damn what Ben Winslow thought or did . . . except in a way that wasn't true, because the people of Santa Barbara recognized his talents as a photographer more than his hometown did. And in the two years he had lived here, he had found more witty, attractive drinking companions than he would ever find in Livingston.

Still, he ached to leave. Even if he could bring Rose out here and start a little newspaper somewhere on the west coast, he would long to go back to that impoverished mountain milltown where he had been born.

Hell, I'm just homesick, he thought, a hometown-body, and that was certainly part of it. Yet some mystery remained. The quality of life in this rich, flowered city of beautiful people was not as good as it was in struggling Livingston. A statistic he had discovered while doing a magazine article on Santa Barbara said the city's suicide rate was phenomenally high, as was its divorce rate. The suicide rate in Livingston was minimal, despite the poverty and harsh climate, and few people got divorced, even if only because all that lawyering was so expensive.

Statistics rarely had much impact on Ben, but the one about suicide did because soon after moving to Santa Barbara he had been shocked by the news that the seventeen-year-old son of a neighbor had shot himself on that golden beach. And there had been times, while he tried to wrestle with the loneliness of divorce, when he himself had had recurrent fantasies of swimming out through the surf some dark night. His anguish had seemed all the more grotesque when he had sat on a blanket at beach parties surrounded by handsome people who were laughing, singing and playing guitars. There is no one in the world as lonely, he discovered, as a man who can't find relief even in the midst of the most frenetic gaiety. In the first few months of his divorce he had blundered into one brief love affair after another, hoping to find in sex, at least, some escape from solitude, but even a waterbed, mirrors on the ceiling and the most imaginative interlockings of the flesh had left him as he had started: lonely as hell.

His excesses had also scared him, making him wonder whether he could ever again feel any strong genuine emotions. Retreating into himself, he had spent most of his time in his studio, turning to commercial portraits when he found that he didn't have any compelling ideas for anything else.

It was, of course, wrong to blame a city for his own misery, he reminded himself, as he parked his little sports car on the road near the boardwalk which led along the dunes to his cottage. As he climbed awkwardly out of it, the shiny red toy seemed infinitely inferior to his ancient jeep. The jeep, after all, could go anywhere, while the little roadster was strictly a fair-weather car. Like everything else around here. Before going home, he would sell it. . . .

The cottages on the dune had once been fishing shacks and they were built so close together that they almost touched. Many of them were owned by people who prided themselves on their artistic flair. The roofs were tiled in bright reds and blues, or covered by redwood shingles. Ben's cottage boasted silvered shingles everywhere. Letting himself in the door, he stepped into his spectacular living room, which had been enlarged by extending the house toward the sea on heavy pilings which were awash at high tide. On the east coast, such a structure would have been blown away in the first hurricane, but they didn't have hurricanes here and the beach was protected by the distant Channel Islands. Natural storms, a neighbor of Ben's had once observed wryly, were not allowed in Santa Barbara.

Pulling a cord, Ben opened the curtains which covered an enormous glass wall that faced the sea. In the blinding sunlight, he saw a group of tanned young girls and boys attempting to ride surfboards on glittering waves that were too gentle. His big room was hot and stuffy. Sliding open a glass door, he walked out onto a balcony that projected over the beach.

"Hey there! Welcome home!"

The voice came from the neighboring balcony to his right. Trudy Basom, who had been sunbathing on a rubber mattress, was sitting up, holding the top of her yellow bikini loosely against her.

"Good to see you, Trudy," he said.

"Are you home for good, or will you be off again?"

"I think I've decided, if you can believe it, that home is the place I was born."

"Is she pretty?" Trudy asked with a smile.

He laughed. "She looks awfully pretty to me."

"That's all that counts. Come on over for a dipper, Ben. I've missed you."

Her living room was much like his, except that the walls were in different soft shades of rose, blue, yellow and avocado. Trudy was a successful commercial artist. She put on a lime-colored beach coat and went to an elaborate bar which had been built from the wreck of a fishing boat, preserving the shape of the bow, which projected from the southern corner of the room with eerily glowing running lights. One thing they didn't have in Livingston was expensive bars which looked as though they were about to run you down.

She handed him a Scotch on the rocks and made one for herself. "So you're going back to the boondocks," she said. "Livingston, New York."

"You remember the name."

"It's all you ever talk about when you get a skinful. I bet I could find my way around that burg without a guide."

"Well, I guess you can take the man out of the small town, but ..."

"That may be true for you, but not for me. I wouldn't go back to the goddamn little town I came from for the world."

"A lot of people feel that way."

"What's so great about your Livingston? I know, you've got the change of seasons. What's so marvelous about being violently uncomfortable half the year?"

He laughed. "I don't look at it that way. Now in spring, everything is fresh and new back there. Summer will be as hot as here, great for swimming in the lakes, but for me, fall is the best part of the year. The foliage in the mountains looks like a smokeless forest fire."

"And in winter you freeze your ass off."

"It only goes to forty below."

"And you're right proud of that."

"I guess I like extremes. I love the winter up there. I love fishing through the ice and riding the ridges of the mountains on snowmobiles. Best of all, I like sitting by an open fire at home while a blizzard piles eight-foot drifts against the door."

"That girl of yours must be sensational to make you talk such crap. What has she got that I haven't got? On second thought, don't answer that."

To me she's a whole new life, was the grandiose line that came to Ben's mind, but of course he didn't say it. Instead he said, "We have a lot of interests in common. We're going to start a weekly newspaper—"

"My God! That's as good a way to go broke as any I've heard."

"Your trouble, Trudy, is that you're too optimistic."

She laughed. "Can I put a steak on for you?"

"I had so much junk on the plane that I don't think I want to eat for a week. Can I have another Scotch?"

While she mixed the drink, he heard the mournful shriek of a siren nearby, maybe an ambulance, maybe a fire engine. It reminded him of the great fire which had happened in Santa Barbara soon after he had moved there. On one dry July evening, a forest fire had spread in the adjacent hills, building into a curtain of flame some three miles wide which had swept through the canyons on the outskirts of the city, wiping out some three hundred houses. The police and firemen had kept spectators far away. All the people in the beach cottages had seen was a great glow in the sky and a momentary blackout when electric cables were cut.

During the fire Ben had been sitting just where he was now at a party in Trudy's house. Except to glance out the window at the sky glow every once in a while, no one paid any attention to the fire. Sitting with his arm around Trudy on the couch, Ben had told her about the night the Elks building had burned down in Livingston. He had been a volunteer fireman, as had almost every able-bodied man in the town. He and his friends had fought the fire all night, while the women of the town supplied ice water, coffee, sandwiches and dry clothes. "That's lovely, dear," Trudy had said. "Are you trying to say that we should be up in the canyons holding hoses now?" "No, but don't you sometimes feel ... well, terribly uninvolved here?" "I'm not as involved as I'd like to be," she had replied, stroking his thigh. "Cheer up. Maybe we'll have a major earthquake which will really involve you before long."

That was the night when his oddly tepid affair with Trudy had started. It had ended about a year later, when not especially to his surprise she went off to Hawaii with a vice-president of her agency.... "Darling," she said when she informed him of this, "I'm sorry to disappoint you, but I have my own life to live. I love fun and games with you but I'm too old to get really *involved* with anyone...."

Trudy was not much older than Rose, but he couldn't imagine Rose saying that she was too old to get really involved with anyone. Matter of fact, who could actually go through life without being involved? Well, Trudy was for some reason trying, but he wondered whether she was succeeding. Her face, weathered by too much sun, shone with the oil she had put on it and looked a little like a polished mask. Although she talked a lot about sex and appeared to be proud of the role of a happily promiscuous woman, her breasts were shapeless and her waist was thickening. While her eyes and lips kept dropping invitations, her body appeared to be denying them, dampening all interest. As he watched her cooking her steak, he suddenly felt very sorry for her. With all her friends, she was fundamentally alone, and the sexuality which had brought her the only closeness she knew was slipping away. In five or ten more years she would be regarded as an old woman by the beach crowd she admired so much. Where do old beach girls go?

"Are you going to sell your house?" Trudy suddenly asked.

"I guess so."

"Try Nathan Guest—he's honest, as real estate agents go. You should make a mint. Beach property has gone out of sight. When I bought this place I thought it was a sinful luxury, but it turns out to be the best investment I ever made."

"I think I'll give him a call right now," Ben said. "Now that I've decided to do this—"

"I envy the girl that can make you sell that house. Have you got a picture of her?"

Ben did have one which he had taken while showing Ann how to use her camera. It was a contact print, too small to show much detail. In it Rose did not look like anything very special, he realized as he saw it through Trudy's eyes. She appeared as just a slender woman with short brown hair, a rather wry smile and a figure too meager to rival the outsized beauties on the Santa Barbara beach.

"Very nice," Trudy said, handing back the photograph. "I hope you two will be very happy delivering newspapers hand in hand in the blizzards."

Nathan Guest was a tall man so handsome that he looked as though he should have been a movie star, not a real estate agent, and in fact he *had* tried for years to get into the movies. He maintained his home and office, it turned out, near the end of the row of beach cottages where Ben's place stood.

Although he was in the midst of his cocktail hour, he strolled over when Ben called. In white ducks, blue blazer and yachting cap, he looked both elegant and phony.

"This is a nice place," he said as he casually walked into the living room. "You bought it two years ago for forty-eight thousand. Right?"

"I see you know your beach property."

"It's my bread and butter, my cake and frosting. I can get you a hundred grand for it, maybe a little more."

"That's fantastic!"

"Some of this beach stuff doubles every year."

"How long will it take to get a sale?"

"Not long. I have a waiting list of people who want beach cottages. Of course, you won't know exactly what you can get until a few offers come in. I'd ask a hundred and twenty-five thousand."

"What are the chances of a sale inside of a week?"

"You don't want to let anyone know you're in a hurry. Give me two weeks. I should have a deal sewed up before then."

Ben was delighted, the money appeared to make the job of financing his newspaper easy. He was anxious to call Rose, but it was only a little after two o'clock, five in Livingston, and she would still be at work. Sitting down by the glass wall, he stared out at the ocean, which reflected the last gleam of twilight. Some youngsters were building a fire just beyond reach of the surf and the flames leaped up as they piled on cardboard beer cartons. Two weeks suddenly seemed a long time to wait before going home, and he wished he were not so morbidly susceptible to loneliness. A phonograph in Trudy's house blared loud rock music. She was always proud of keeping up with the latest in kid music. Even with all the windows open, his living room was hot.

Restlessly Ben walked to the bedroom downstairs, where he changed his gray flannel trousers and tweed jacket for lighter clothes. He had furnished the place with care himself during his first days of trying to learn how to be a bachelor, and he was surprised to find that he did not feel a tinge of regret about selling all these teakwood chairs and tables to the highest bidder. The huge waterbed seemed vulgar and the big photographs of Laura and Ebon as children of ten and thirteen gave loud testimony to the fact that his fatherhood had become almost abstract.

At nine o'clock his time, Ben lay down on the bed and dialed Rose's house. He was surprised by the speed with which the call was completed.

"Hello!" Rose said.

"It's a very bad sign when a man finds himself dotty over the way a woman says hello."

"Ben! Are you in Santa Barbara? You sound next door!"

"I had a good enough trip and like the old joke, I have good and bad news."

"What's the bad news?" She sounded scared.

"It looks as though it's going to take about two weeks to sell this house. I'd hoped to do it in one."

"Well, when you come to think of it, it often takes a year or more to sell a house around here."

"Santa Barbara has its faults, but it's a real estate man's dream."

"What's the good news?" she asked eagerly.

"I'm told that I can get a whopping good price. We'll have plenty of money for starting the paper."

"Wow! I've never had plenty of money for *anything!*"

There was a pause. He had been brought up never to discuss figures with anyone, sometimes not even with his wife, but the nature of the intimacy he was trying to build with Rose made secrecy out of order.

"The agent says I can get a hundred grand, maybe even more," he said. "I only paid forty-eight thousand for it. I have a mortgage of about twenty thousand. There will be a

117

commission and capital gains to pay, of course, but we're still in the chips."

"I'll say! Ben, if we can't start a paper with all that, we're both nuts! I've been checking around, and a good weekly can net about fifty thousand a year easy, once it's established."

"We'll have to work our tails off, but we should do all right. Did you find an office?"

"There's a great one available on the ground floor, just two doors down Main Street from the *Recorder*. Wouldn't it be good to be in a place where people coming in to buy advertising at the *Recorder* would see us first?"

"Ah, you're a sly one!"

"I didn't sign a lease because they want to know what I'm going to do with the place. Are we still a top secret operation?"

"The word will get out anyway as we go along. How much time can you spare for this stuff?"

"I love stealing time from the mill!"

"You can give them notice, if you want. I can start you on the payroll any time."

He heard the sharp intake of her breath.

"God, do you know what it means to know I can walk out of there any damn time I want?" she said.

"I can guess."

"Let me stay and milk the damn mill a little longer. You might as well save your money as long as you can."

"Okay, but I have to ask you to do two things. See a lawyer named Vardi in Ticonderoga, and get Livingston *Life* incorporated. I know it's a long drive, but I don't know any lawyer in Livingston who's not tied up with Howie."

"I'll go tomorrow."

"Also, I want you to buy a van in the paper's name. We'll need a delivery truck, and we need a car of our own for long trips."

"Do you want something new or secondhand?"

"New. I want it to look good when we put the name of the paper on it in big gold letters."

"Do you want a Ford, a Dodge, or what?"

"I don't much care. Why don't we let Ebon check it out? He likes cars, and we ought to give him a part to play in this."

"Eb took grammie and Annie to a bingo game."

"Well, just tell him that I want him to get us the best van he can for the best price. Let's see what he does with it."

"How do you want to finance it?"

"Cash. I can mail it, but I think most of the local dealers know me well enough to wait until I get home. Whatever they want. When you get the paper incorporated, ask the lawyer about car insurance."

"What color do you want the van?"

"Black might look good with gold letters. What do you think?"

"Too hearselike. How about mountain green for the Adirondacks?"

"You're right." There was a pause before he added, "The hell with all this business. God, I miss you!"

"Aren't all the California beach girls welcoming you back with native dances?"

"Not exactly. Rosie, I ache for you."

"Have you tried bicarbonate of soda?"

There was a moment of silence before he said, "What would you think if I flew into Burlington instead of Albany when I come home? You could meet me there in the new van, and we could have our weekend in Vermont before going back to your farm."

"You do have an ingenious mind, don't you?"

"I try, when important issues are at stake."

"Well, don't be mad at me, Ben, but I've been thinking about it, and that weekend idea worries me."

"Why?"

"How can we possibly keep it a secret from the kids? Here

I've done everything possible to keep Annie . . . intact, but the first chance I get, I slope off for a weekend with you. How the hell would that look?"

"Like it looks. We have to have a life of our own."

"Would you settle for a day in Vermont, a long day and maybe an evening? That wouldn't be so blatant—"

"I was sort of counting on a long, leisurely weekend," he said.

"Come on, Ben. Is there anything we can do in bed that can't be done in a day? Just what do you have in mind?"

"You win," he said. "I guess . . ."

"I'm sorry, but I want everything to be right for us and it wouldn't be right if I were worrying all the time about what we were doing to the kids."

"One reason I love you is you're so responsible, if not exactly consistent."

"One reason I love you is that you make me feel so dangerous. For a long while there, I thought I was just a jerk."

He laughed. "Look, do you mind if I talk business again?"

"To me the paper isn't business. It's just another part of our love—"

"Don't tell that to our accountant. Look, how do you want to divide up the work? What do you do and what do I do?"

"I assumed that you'd do most of the writing and the photography. I can take care of the printing because I've done that at the mill for years. I think I can sell advertising—when I was an Avon girl, they once told me I could sell anything. And I'll be your girl Friday. Isn't that the general pitch?"

"What should we do about titles?"

"You'll be the editor and publisher, I assume. Can I be assistant to the publisher?"

"That's not a title that would get you through many doors when you were selling advertising. They always want to deal with the top dog."

"Do you want to make me advertising director?"

"How about publisher?"

"Me?"

"Why not? If I'm the editor and publisher, we'll have just one bigshot in the office. If I'm just the editor, my importance won't be diminished, but we'll have two bigshots to impress people with."

"Rose Kelly, publisher? Would anyone take me seriously?"

"It wouldn't be sham. Years of PR work aren't bad preparation for it, and god knows you exude efficiency."

"And here I was trying to exude sex. Ben, I'm sorry to be childish, but I can't help thinking about how all my friends, and enemies, will react when they hear the news. They'll drop dead!"

"The pleasures of success."

"I think I can do a good job for you. I'll work night and day, but I would have done that without the title. Ben, why are you doing this? You don't have to give me a fancy title just to get laid."

"Damn it, I thought I did. Would you consent to a whole weekend in Vermont if I dubbed you Commander in Chief?"

"I'll spend the whole weekend with you if you're still able to function after I get through with you the first day. Are publishers allowed to talk like that?"

"Only when talking to the editor."

"Ben, I haven't even thanked you . . . all my life, people, especially people at the mill, have taken as much of me as they could get, and given as little as possible. You give much more than you have to give and take much less than you could get—"

"Just how much more can I get?"

She laughed, and then he realized that she was crying. "I don't do this often," she said. "You don't know how hopeless I was feeling when you came along. Everything was going wrong—with the damn zoning, I couldn't even sell the farm.

I was stuck, mothering people and working at an impossible job. And now all of a sudden I have a wonderful job and a wonderful man. Do you mind my saying I have you?"

"You got me. And in all seriousness, do you know what it does for me to know that I can make you happy? It's a sad thing to admit, I guess, but I can't remember my mother, or my wife, or my daughter ever telling me that."

"But plenty of other women must have."

"Night words. That's not what I meant. Rosie, you make me happy in other ways, too. I'm a little old to be finding a woman as young and honest as you are who really gives a damn about me. In some sense I think I've been looking for you for almost thirty years—the old romantic again—ever since I was Ebon's age. When I came back to Livingston to rescue Eb, as I thought, I'd just about given up hope for being anything but the middle-aged man who sits at the edge of the firelight during beach parties. I don't altogether understand, don't need to, but almost as soon as I saw you, I found myself starting to hope."

"What a hell of a thing to be three thousand miles apart when we feel like this," she said. "Hurry home, Ben. Among other things, I'm cleaning out a whole wing for you, and believe it or not, it does have a sort of secret door to my room."

"How did you arrange that?"

She laughed. "You'll have to see it. I hope you're good at climbing ladders. Your room is in a part of the house that used to be a hayloft, maybe a hundred years ago. It still has a door that was for loading the hay. You go out that, crawl along the top of the roof about twenty feet, and come in my dormer window—"

"Sounds marvelous, but I hope we can make some other arrangement before winter . . . on second thought, blizzards won't stop me."

"It can work both ways. I can come to your room too. We can rig a safety rope of some kind. We often do when we shovel the snow off the roof. I'll be in a black lace nightgown and I'll get you a gold bathrobe."

"I hope I dream about that tonight. Thank you, love. I'll call you tomorrow about this time."

"One more thing—*thank you* . . . for living."

"Same from me, Rosie, the very same."

9

BEN's house was sold for $118,000 after only eight days, but technicalities delayed the closing for about three weeks. Since he had sold most of his furniture and his car, and since he had also sold his share of his studio to another photographer who had been working with him, he had little to do but walk on the beach or pace in the empty house. The days passed with maddening slowness. To further their plans of getting the first issue of Livingston *Life* out on the Fourth of July, Rose rented the office near the *Recorder* and bought the equipment which had been stored by a defunct newspaper near Keene. She got the legalities of the birth of the newspaper straightened out, and after many days of comparative shopping, Ebon bought a new Ford van. Finally Rose gave notice at the mill. That night she telephoned Ben.

"I love stealing time from the bastards and I ached to tell them all to go to hell instead of giving them two weeks notice, but then I realized that we'll have to do business with them," she said on the telephone. "The mill advertises a lot in the *Recorder* and they might decide to split their local schedule with us, just for good PR. So I'm going around being sweet as pie with everyone."

"That's smart," Ben said.

"The word's out, and everyone is talking about our paper," she continued. "I'm afraid I told Annie about being publisher, and she told everyone at school. Now I'm famous!"

"Don't let it go to your head."

"I love every minute of it! Even Howie Hewat congratulated me. What he was really doing was pumping me for all the information he could get, but he started with congratulations and a big sloppy smile."

"What did you tell him?"

"I just smiled back and said that all details were top secret until the paper hit the street. Then he squeezed my arm and left. Howie the squeezer."

Ben was so impatient to get home that he almost departed before the closing, but the agent assured him that more delays would be caused by this. After packing almost all his clothes and personal effects in cardboard cartons, he shipped them to Livingston. His cameras and equipment filled two heavy leather cases which were too fragile to ship, and which he knew the airline would let him keep in the passenger compartment.

Finally the title was cleared, the mortgage was arranged, and the closing was set for the next day. After checking airline schedules, Ben jubilantly telephoned Rose.

"Are you doing anything the day after tomorrow?" he asked.

"I was going up to see the printer again. Why?"

"I'm going to get into Burlington at nine thirty-two in the morning. I thought that if you weren't doing anything, we could spend a day in Vermont together, tapping maple trees or something."

"Ben! I can't believe it's happening!"

"Can you drive the new van over?"

"Sure. It goes like a sports car."

"Tell the kids we're going to check on printing plants in Burlington, and plan to take in a movie there. We should be home at about one o'clock."

125

"Thanks, Ben. Much easier than trying to explain away a weekend."

"Let's try to forget everything for that one day. I won't even talk about the paper."

"I can't guarantee that I won't do that, but I'll try. Goodbye! I'm going to get my hair done and buy a new dress and make myself over entirely—"

"I sort of liked the old model. See you."

Ben next placed a call to the Elmsford Inn near Shelburne, Vermont, and reserved a bedroom suite for the day, complete with a fireplace and plenty of flowers. A lobster luncheon with the appropriate wines was to be served at one in the afternoon.

Ben's next preparation for his return home was a visit to a jeweler in Santa Barbara. He and Rose had not known each other long enough to make engagement or marriage a sensible topic, but he felt so grateful for the way she had given him a new hold on life that he wanted to buy her something expensive and beautiful. Never in his life had he bought diamonds or any expensive jewelry for a woman, except an engagement ring. This was perhaps the time to change that pattern. Reminding himself that Rose would not want to be ostentatious in Livingston, he bought a dainty ring with three small diamonds, the biggest only about a carat. It could be considered either a dinner or an engagement ring, the jeweler said, according to how it was worn. The price tag of $3,880 rather shocked him, but now, he felt, was a time for a real gesture. As soon as he got the little leather velvet-lined box in his hand, he could hardly wait for the moment when he could give it to Rose.

On the flight to Boston, where he was to change planes for Burlington, Ben was careful not to drink; one of the disgusting discoveries he had made was that at forty-five, love and liquor do not go well together. Too restless to sleep, he sat talking with a film distributor who kept telling him that people were animals.

"I know you think that's a terrible thing to say," the short, rotund man continued, "but if you had to deal with the owners of movie houses, you'd know what I mean. The only thing worse than them is the people in the movie houses, the customers. They smear bubble gum over everything, they throw up, they fight and they screw right in the theater! I tell you, the world is a zoo!" Hooray for Hollywood.

The plane which took him from Boston to Burlington was small enough to react violently to the updrafts of a hot June day, and to make Ben fear that he was going to arrive for this much longed for tryst in a state of acute nausea. As the plane touched down on the runway, however, his stomach quieted down. Although he usually waited until everyone else was out when he carried cumbersome camera cases, he was first in line when the plane halted by the gate of the airport. The wait for the door to be opened seemed endless. Nervously swallowing until his throat was dry, he longed for a drink. Finally the door swung open. On the other side of a rope barrier Rose stood, a slender woman in a silk sundress, a red and blue print, low-necked with spaghetti straps. The wind was blowing her brown hair, and she was shielding her eyes from the sun with her right hand as she tried to see him clearly. Realizing that it was he, she skipped effortlessly over the rope barrier, and came running toward him, arms out like an eager child. Setting down his camera cases, he picked her up, astonished by her lightness, and whirled her around. When he put her down, she put both arms around his neck and gave him a kiss which caused some college students in the surrounding crowd to cheer.

"I guess we better get out of here," Ben said. "Where's the van?"

"I couldn't park it anywhere near here. It's on the far side of the lot on the other side of the building."

"That's okay."

127

She insisted on carrying one of the heavy camera cases, and would not put it down, no matter how much he protested. Listing under the weight like a freighter with too much cargo, she struggled rapidly through the building, up some stairs and across a parking lot, where the asphalt was already hot in the morning sun. Suddenly she paused, put the bag down, and stood with her right hand gripping her forehead.

"What's the matter?" he asked in alarm.

"It's the heat, I guess. I feel a little light-headed."

"Let me help you to the car. You should sit down."

"No, I'm fine. I guess you were right about the bag, though. It's too heavy for me."

Carrying both bags, he followed her to a big green van. On the side, in gold letters a foot tall, were the words LIVINGSTON LIFE.

"That kind of makes it official, doesn't it?" she asked, obviously pleased.

"It sure does. How are you feeling now?"

"Great. I get these little dizzy spells every once in a while. They're nothing to worry about."

He climbed into the van, which still smelled new, and admired the space in which thousands of newspapers could be carried from the printer, or, Rose pointed out, in which they could camp.

"I almost brought a big mattress," she said. "But I thought you might think that a little forward."

"I have better plans than a mattress in the back of a truck," he replied. "I hear that the Elmsford Inn is the best this side of Boston or New York. I've reserved a suite there."

"You do go first class!"

"That's why I'm with you."

The Vermont countryside through which they drove was a patchwork quilt of varicolored fields, the rich blacks and browns of newly ploughed earth next to the fresh, mint green of newly sprouted corn and the yellower green of pastures. Many of the farms looked as though they had been designed and built by Currier and Ives, except for new aluminum silos, which gleamed in the sun like flashlights fifty feet tall.

"Nothing turns out the way you expect it to," she said suddenly.

"That has the ring of truth."

"For weeks I've been dreaming of nothing but escaping Livingston for at least one day with you, and reverting to my basic wild self. You wouldn't believe what that town has done to me! I wanted to buy a shocking black lace nightgown, but I knew that Helen DeRosia at Fashion Frocks would tell everybody. Even Howie Hewat would know it before long."

Ben laughed.

"It's no laughing matter. The hell of it is, I drove all the way to Ticonderoga to buy a shocking black nightgown, and frankly, I look awful in it. I'm just not the type."

"I much prefer a sexy girl to a sexy nightgown."

"But what's the matter with me? I've always secretly envied the girls, summer people mostly, who just flop around town without bras. What freedom! How great just to flaunt your body, without fear of causing talk. This morning I put on this dress without a bra, and guess what? Nobody can tell the difference! I look just the same as I always do."

"Most women wouldn't mind having a figure that looks the same without a bra as with one. And anyway I immediately diagnosed the situation the first glimpse I had of you."

"Did you?" she asked, blushing.

"Some things these tired old eyes just don't miss."

"I had more crazy ideas," she continued. "I bought some fancy cigarettes. I never smoke, but the idea of these perfumed cigarettes seemed part of a day without rules. On the way over here I tried one, and almost choked to death. I was also going to buy a cold bottle of champagne we could drink on this drive, but then I started worrying about cops stopping us, and it seemed like a lousy idea. No matter what I do, I'm just not the temptress type."

129

He stopped the car by the side of the road near a field where a man on an enormous yellow tractor was spreading fertilizer, a sharp smell which was not at all unpleasant in the moist spring air. The widely spaced bucket seats in the van made an embrace difficult, but they managed.

"You'll learn that I'm too old to care about anything but the basics," he said. "You love me or allow me to hope that you do, and I assure that there's nothing in the world sexier than that. You're young, you're pretty, and you're a person I respect in a thousand ways, as well as love. For me that's very sexy. So you've got it all. You're a cake that doesn't need icing."

She sighed. "Why do you think I keep putting myself down? I love to have you build me up like that. I need your compliments, Ben. You've got me hooked on them. I don't want to know myself the way I seem to me. Your version is so much better."

After they drove another fifteen miles, they saw a billboard with the profile of a colonial soldier. He was holding a big sign which said THE ELMSFORD GREEN MOUNTAIN INN—AC-COMMODATIONS AND DINING FOR PARTICULAR PEOPLE.

"Oh my! Rose said. "What would happen if we just breezed in and asked if we could rent a bed for an hour?"

"Probably they would give you a very good bed for a very high price. I'm told that this is a favorite retreat for Bostonians."

"This is where the Puritans go for dirty weekends?"

"I don't think respectable married folk are barred entirely. Say, it's a pretty place."

The inn was an ancient colonial hostelry, a big white building beside a pond. Weeping willows on the shores bent over the still dark water, on which two swans swam, followed by three cygnets. As soon as Ben parked the van, Rose jumped out and ran to get a closer look at the family of birds as they swam beside their reflections. Near a garden of yellow daffodils on the bank of pond, she stepped into soft mud. Ben, who had been following her, stumbled into it before he could stop.

"Damn!" she said as she raised one new black slipper which was now dripping with muck.

"I got it too," Ben said. "I think I saw a newspaper in the van. We can wipe this stuff off."

"I never do things right," Rose grumbled. "Here you take me to the most expensive, fashionable passion pit around, and all I do is chase swans like a kid and get caught in the mud. We'll look terrible when we walk in!"

While they were scrubbing their shoes with paper, she added, "Are you going to register us under a false name?"

"I hadn't thought. We can do 'Mr. and Mrs. Winslow' if you want, or 'Mr. and Mrs. Smith.' Whatever."

"Do you mind if I screw under my own name?"

"Feel free," he said with a laugh.

"I mean, I hate deception. I'm very proud to be here with you, so I want to sign my own name."

There was an intimidating quality about the big lobby of the inn, which looked as though it were doubling as an expensive antique store. Most of the employees were in early-American costumes, and Rose felt quite out of place in her sundress. Carrying only her tiny overnight suitcase, she didn't think any of the colonial soldiers doubted the purpose of her visit. Striding up to the desk with a fine show of self-confidence, Ben boomed, "I'm Ben Winslow. I have a reservation."

The tall, thin manager was dressed like Ethan Allen, the leader of the famed Green Mountain Boys, but he had a prissy face and effeminate manners. Good heavens, Rose thought, I didn't know the Green Mountain Boys had that problem. She was embarrassed by a nervous need to laugh, which she disguised by taking a tissue from her purse and blowing her nose repeatedly. Looking behind to check, she was relieved to see no muddy footprints on the wide floorboards.

"Yes indeed, we have your reservation," Ethan Allen said. "I have you down for luncheon in the Fort Ticonderoga suite at one o'clock. Frankly, I didn't expect you so early."

"I'm sorry I didn't make that clear," Ben replied.

"No harm, no harm at all! Perhaps you'd care to step into our lounge for a cup of coffee or a Bloody Mary. We'll have everything ready in a few minutes!"

He pushed a registration form toward Ben. Rose stepped forward, and after Ben signed, she added her name and address in a firm hand. Without appearing to glance at it, Ethan Allen swept it under the counter.

"We're glad to have you with us, Mr. Winslow and Miss Kelly," he said crisply. "We have a Ping-Pong room, a billiard room and a small library. The library is open, but if you want the other rooms, please ask for a key at this desk."

"I guess we'll let that go for now," Ben said, and walked toward the lounge.

"I think he was laughing at us," Rose whispered.

"I doubt it. Anyway, what difference does it make?"

"What did they do to adulterers in Ethan Allen's time?"

"We're not adulterers. Neither of us is married."

"Then we're fornicators, and that sounds even *worse!*"

The cavernous lounge was deserted at this time of the morning, except for one burly colonial sergeant, who took their order for coffee. The walls around their table were covered with murals depicting soldiers in the act of shooting cannon and bayoneting redcoats without mercy.

"I think they put them in the stocks or flogged them to death," Rose continued.

"Who?" Ben asked absentmindedly as he tried to get the drift of the battle that was going on in the murals.

"Fornicators! They were very strict with them in Ethan Allen's time."

"Rosie, are you just joking, or do you really feel guilty about all this?"

132

"How could a modern liberated newspaper publisher like me feel guilty?"

"Damned if I know."

"I don't feel any guilt at all, but maybe I am nervous, a little scared. Damn, I wish we had made love when we felt like it, that night we had dinner in your house. This way is so deliberate, so contrived. Aren't you at all nervous, or do you do this sort of things all the time?"

"Only on Tuesdays. Never on Wednesdays."

"Stop it. You are nervous! Do you know how I can tell?"

"How?"

"You keep smoothing your hair back. If you keep on doing that, you're going to rub it all away."

"Okay, I do feel a few butterflies."

"Why?"

"I don't like to discuss fears. You never know whether talk will make them better, or just spread them."

"Thanks for using that word *fear*. God, I'm scared to death. We've pinned so much on this, you and I. What's going to happen if you decide I'm just plain lousy in bed? God! How can I come up to California standards?"

"Honey, you're not auditioning for a part and neither am I. If things don't work out, we'll laugh and wait till next time."

"That makes me feel better," she said, and took his hand.

"And if we have real sense, we should not try to make love when we go up to that room. We should just talk and know it's okay to go home without anything much happening. The bed is just there for emergencies, in case we can't help jumping into it."

"You wouldn't feel frustrated at all if I just got cold feet?"

"I'd be nice. I'd fake it."

She laughed. "I'm sorry to be so difficult. I don't know why I make everything so complicated."

The colonial soldier brought their coffee and hovered over

133

them, arranging paper mats, sugar and cream. Ben felt Rose grip his right ankle between her two feet under the table, an oddly touching little embrace. When the waiter left, she said, "The last thing I want is this damn coffee. When do you suppose the room is going to be ready?"

Only a few minutes later, a drummerboy appeared to announce that they could go to their rooms. Carrying Rose's little suitcase, he led the way up a broad set of stairs and down a wide hall. The Fort Ticonderoga suite turned out to be a long living room with more military murals on the walls, a fireplace with white birch logs which were unlit, and a bedroom with a canopied four-poster. All the furniture was antique, and there were vases of daffodils and other spring flowers everywhere. There was only one thing wrong with the place, Ben realized as soon as he stepped into it: the rooms were impossibly stuffy and hot.

"Can you open a window?" he asked the drummerboy.

"I'll see. They hardly ever are opened, and the storm windows are still on. In the summer we have air-conditioning here."

As he spoke, the drummerboy tried to force up sash after sash without budging any of them.

"Can you turn on the air-conditioning?" Ben asked.

"The machines are down in the basement. I'll ask the manager if he can have one put in."

"Well, tell him that no one can stay in this room now. I can't imagine what kind of particular people want to be roasted to death."

The boy disappeared and Rose sank onto the couch, laughing helplessly and pounding a pillow with her fists.

"We're doomed!" she said. "Everything was so great when we came in here, and then we step into a damn oven. Do you love your women hot and sweaty?"

"It's not funny. I'm about ready to tear this whole bloody army apart. I'm declaring war on Ethan Allen and every bloody Green Mountain Boy he's got!"

"Can't we just go to one of your basic motels?"

"I have this great luncheon planned. I had this whole fantasy of the flowers and the open fire."

"Go ahead and light it!"

He knelt by the couch and they kissed, both their faces beaded with sweat. He was just concluding that the heat wasn't all that important when the manager appeared, accompanied by a carpenter with a full box of tools.

"I'm sorry about this," Ethan Allan said. "We've had so much cold weather recently that I didn't take the storm sash off. It will only take a few minutes."

This was not accurate. The inn had recently been painted and everything stuck. A man on a ladder suddenly appeared outside the window, and there was a great rending of wood and metal. When the job was finally done, a chambermaid dressed like Martha Washington had to vacuum the paint chips from the rag rugs.

"You've been very kind about this," the manager said to Ben and Rose, who had mutely sat on the couch throughout the performance. "I'd like to send up a bottle of champagne on the house."

With the windows open, a cool breeze flooded the room, and Ben was able to complete his fantasy by lighting the fire. Just as he started to take Rose into his arms, there was a knock on the door, and a soldier brought in an ice bucket with a quart of champagne. He took a long time to serve it, cooling the glasses with lumps of ice, but finally he withdrew.

Rose took a sip of the wine and put her glass down. "The hell with this!" she said. "Where were we? For god's sake, let's make love."

135

10

Hᴇ took her suddenly, much more suddenly than he had intended, as though he feared another interruption at any moment. Afraid that he had been too fast for her, he stood up and was astonished to see that she lay as though asleep, her right arm on her left breast.

"Are you all right?" he asked.

"Fine," she replied, sitting up and shaking her head. "I get a little dizzy sometimes, I told you that. This time I guess it's a sort of compliment to you. Could you hand me my bag and a glass of water? No, make it champagne. I rather like the idea of washing down pills with champagne!"

After she had swallowed the pills, she stood, picked up her little suitcase, and walked into the bathroom. He had admired her figure, but was unprepared for her beauty as a nude, a slender woman with thighs about half the size of those he was used to seeing, compact buttocks, a lovely line leading from broad little shoulders to the narrow waist, and fleshy round little breasts, like those of a well-developed teenager. She was thirty years old, but her body had apparently declined to age. Only her face, which was often pale and a little haggard, showed the abrasions of the years.

She stayed in the bathroom a long time. When she came out, her hair had been freshly brushed, she had applied new makeup, and she was wearing a short white cotton bathrobe which was fastened around her waist with a yellow sash. She looked tired but relaxed. Standing on her toes, she kissed him.

"You surely passed your examination," she said. "Did I mine?"

"Marry me."

She laughed.

"What's so funny about marriage?"

"If you ask me in six months, I'll say yes."

"Seriously?"

"*Seriously*. Can I have some more champagne?"

He poured a glass for her and handed it to her after she sat in a small armchair by the fire. "I have never felt so content," she said as she stared dreamily into the flames. "I have a marvelous job, a marvelous man and I've just been well laid. What more could a girl want?"

"A lot of women would say marriage."

"Marriage is like a great cathedral, my mother said. It must be carefully planned and built. She should know, because her cathedral got built in about two weeks and started crumbling almost immediately."

"How can you really plan a thing like marriage? Doesn't it work or not work according to laws pretty much beyond control?"

"To tell you the truth, I'm not sure," she replied thoughtfully. "I just try to go along carefully. It seems silly to get married when we haven't known each other at least six months. If we've got something good, it will keep. If not..."

"The trouble is, damn it, you're right, of course. How can such a spontaneous, passionate woman have so much common sense?"

"Maybe by observing too many people who have none," she replied with a grin.

"I guess I'm your opposite," Ben said, sitting in a chair opposite her. "My people were all so sensible that nobody had any fun."

137

As Ben talked, he was fascinated by Rose's feet. They were small, high-arched, with pink toes and carefully tended but unpainted toenails. The insteps were whiter than the balls of the feet and the heels. Sitting cross-legged, she waved one foot as she talked. To his astonishment, he was full of a desire to kneel ... yes, kneel ... and kiss her feet. He'd certainly never had a foot fetish or anything like it, but the desire to press his lips against those delicate insteps and those pink toes was damn near overpowering. It was difficult to get *this* fantasy sufficiently out of his head to make conversation. He found himself swallowing hard.

"Are you all right?" Rose asked.

"Sure. Except I think I'm going crazy."

"How?"

"I don't think I know you well enough to tell you."

"If we don't talk, how will you know me better?"

"I'm embarrassed. I have this crazy desire. I've never had anything like it in my life."

"If it's whips, forget it," she said with a smile.

"No, it's not that."

"What then? I'll tell you a crazy desire I have if you tell me one of yours."

"You go first."

"Hey, you brought this thing up. What do you want to do?"

"I have this strange desire to kiss your feet."

"So kiss them. But let me wash them first."

"Always practical," he said with a laugh as she went to the bathroom.

He heard the water run in the bathtub. A few minutes later, she returned and sat on the rug in front of the fire. He lay at her feet, feeling both grotesque and passionate. Timidly he kissed her ankle. He was afraid that she would collapse into childish giggles, but she did not. Abandoning himself to realizing his fantasy, he showered both her feet with intense kisses, concentrating on the delicate insteps, then the toes. He felt her muscles tighten.

"Do you mind this?" he asked.

"Hell, I love it! Do it enough, and there's no telling what will happen."

They were interrupted by a knock on the door. Rather shamefacedly getting to his feet, Ben opened it. A soldier stood there with a wheeled table holding their luncheon.

"Cherrystone clams!" Rose marveled as the covers were removed. "Lobsters! Chablis! What's this, the economy lunch?"

The table was formally set with Wedgwood china and Wexford glass. After twirling the bottle of wine in the ice bucket, the waiter withdrew. Rose and Ben sat at opposite ends of the table. As she dipped her first clam, Rose spilled some of the red sauce on the lapel of her white bathrobe.

"Damn!" she said, rubbing the spot with her napkin and making it worse.

"It doesn't matter," he said.

"The hell it doesn't. That's one of my hang-ups. I can't stand dirty clothes."

Taking the bathrobe off, she threw it on the couch. "Nudity is another one of my hang-ups," she said. "I like it. Does it bother you?"

"Not in your case."

She sat down at the table again, placing a napkin primly on her lap. "To tell the truth, I've often dreamed of sitting in an elegant dining room completely nude. It's marvelous! Now I can dribble all the sauce and melted butter I want without worrying about the cleaning bills."

She was, he realized as the meal continued, an accomplished tease of the best kind, the sort who tantalizes only when there can be fulfillment. With a mischievous grin she put on the paper bib with the red lobster printed on it, first folding it so that one breast projected on each side of it, then putting a hole in the center for her right breast. Suddenly embarrassed, she took it off.

"You must think I'm crazy," she said with a blush.

"Don't get cured."

"When you take out a lonely small-town spinster, you can't tell what will happen. The dam's burst!"

"When you go out with a middle-aged photographer, there can also be some surprises. I have a little gift I bought for you in Santa Barbara. So much has been going on that I haven't had a chance to give it to you."

He took the small, fancily wrapped box from his pocket and handed it to her.

"What is it?" she asked, her eyes sparkling.

"Maybe a thimble?"

"I could use a thimble," she said, unwrapping it carefully to avoid tearing the gold paper. When she saw the leather-covered box, she said, "The box alone is worth a fortune!"

She was, Ben saw, a master at the art of savoring a moment. Instead of opening the box immediately, she pressed it to her lips, then against her cheek. Then she opened it such a little way that she couldn't see inside. Finally she pulled the top all the way back. The ring with three diamonds gleamed brightly on its black velvet cushion.

"My god! I don't believe it! And I bet they're real, too! You wouldn't give any other kind."

"Small but real. The biggest is just about a carat."

"It must have cost a fortune! Why did you do this, Ben?"

"Sometimes words aren't enough."

"Do you want it to be an engagement ring?"

"Yes, but I respect your thing about six months—"

"If I put it on my right hand, is it a mistress ring? That's marvelous! After six months of enjoying that, I can put it on my left hand and have the best of both worlds." She tried the ring on the fingers of her right hand, finding it fit the middle one well. Holding it up to the window, she turned it in the sun, watching the diamonds sparkle.

"Of course you know," she said, "that when I wear this, everyone in Livingston will know that I'm your mistress. Will you mind that?"

"They knew that even before it happened."

She laughed, and running to him threw both arms around his neck. "It's not so much the thought, Ben, it's the sheer *value* of this gift that I love. I mean, anybody can bring you a cheesy gift full of thought, but you wouldn't spend that kind of dough unless you really wanted me—"

He kissed her, running his hands over her back.

"I shouldn't expect twice in the same day," she said.

"You're damn right, but today is an exception."

Picking her up, he carried her to the four-poster bed. This time he tried his best not to hurry, but the pace she set was not slow. Suddenly he heard her gasp. The harshness of the sound scared him, but he told himself that it wasn't unusual at such a time. Then he pulled away from her enough to look at her face and terror struck. She was gasping for air in a way that had nothing to do with passion, and her agony showed in her eyes.

"*What is it?*" he asked as he jumped to the floor, but obviously she could not speak. Her struggle for air increasing, she sat up. Her mouth was open and to his horror he saw a delicate froth forming on her lips. It was flecked with blood.

He ran to the telephone and as soon as he got the manager said, "Emergency! Doctor! Ambulance! Rush! Probably heart attack!"

Ben blessed the town of Sherburne for the fact that he heard an ambulance siren almost immediately, and within minutes a stout white-haired man with an old-fashioned black doctor's bag appeared at his door, so winded by his hurry that he looked as though he might have a heart attack himself. Ben showed him to Rose, who was still sitting up in bed, desperately trying to breathe and unable to speak.

141

"Wait for me out there," the doctor said, going to his bag. "Tell the ambulance we'll take her to Burlington."

Rose was breathing more easily as the ambulance attendants lifted her onto a stretcher, where she lay covered by white sheets, looking shockingly pale. She stared at Ben with frightened eyes, still lacking the air to speak, but when he took her hand, she squeezed his hard. He had time to say only, "You're going to be all right, love," before the attendants rushed her on the stretcher to the ambulance.

The doctor was washing his hands in the bathroom. "*Is* she going to be all right?" Ben asked.

"She's got a good chance. If she gets over this attack she'll be in the clear for a while. You better get down to the Mary Fletcher Hospital and check her in."

Ben ran for the van and soon caught up with the ambulance. During the three quarters of an hour that he followed it into Burlington, he tried not to think of anything except the immediate job of keeping the speeding car on the road.

When the ambulance stopped at the emergency entrance of the hospital, Ben tried to park the van in a crowded lot, abandoning it at the side of one of the lanes when he could find no space. He got to the emergency entrance just in time to see Rose being pushed on a wheeled table toward an elevator. This time she was able to manage a smile as well as a squeeze of the hand. The elevator doors closed.

"Where are they taking her?" Ben asked a young man in a white coat who had accompanied her to the elevator.

"Intensive Care. Tomorrow morning she should be better. I wouldn't try to see her until then."

"What's the matter with her?" Ben asked.

The doctor glanced at a clipboard in his hand. "Congestive heart failure. Pulmonary edema. We won't have details until we get some tests."

"She's only thirty years old! *Why* does she have this?"

"Rheumatic heart condition, probably. Sometime when she

was a kid she must have had a strep throat that wasn't treated right."

"What's going to happen now?"

"If she comes through this, which she seems to be doing, she'll be all right for some period of time, maybe quite a while. You'll have to wait for the results of the tests."

"And if she has another attack?"

"I'd say her chances would be poor, very poor indeed. That's why, when we get the tests, you ought to give a lot of thought to the alternative."

"What's that?"

"Open-heart surgery. It's always a calculated risk, of course, but in some hospitals it's become a highly developed art."

"This one?"

"We do it, but we're not really big enough. If you go that route, take her to Boston or Dallas, and don't tell anyone I said so."

Clapping Ben on the shoulder, he walked down the hall.

"Thanks!" Ben called after him.

Without looking around, the young doctor waved.

Ben stood in the middle of the hospital corridor, confused by the many things he felt he should do. First he should sign Rose into the hospital. Then he should find a legitimate parking place for the van. Next he should call Annie and Grammie and Ebon with the news. Then he could have a drink, or maybe he should have the drink before calling home.

The woman at the receiving desk of the hospital asked him a whole battery of questions, the answers to which she typed on a form in an IBM typewriter with an especially long carriage. Her manner was so impersonal that Ben began imagining her to be part of her machine, a new attachment provided at small extra cost by the wonders of IBM research.

"What is your relationship to the patient?" the plastic woman asked.

"Employer," he replied after a moment of hesitation.

143

"What kind of health insurance does she have?"

"Well, none, I'm afraid. She just quit the World Paper Company...."

"You don't carry health insurance for your employees?"

"It's just a brand new company, not even on its feet yet."

"Does she have Blue Cross?"

"I doubt it. With the paper company she would have had group...."

"Will she be able to pay substantial hospital costs independently?"

"Yes. I'll guarantee that."

"Who is her closest relative?"

"She has a grandmother and a sister, the sister's still a minor. She also has a father, but he's in Ireland."

"Would he take financial responsibility for her?"

"What happened, did a wheel slip? I told you that I'll do that."

"Who is your employer?" she asked, her flat voice a reproof to his display of temper.

"I am self-employed. No, I'm employed by Livingston *Life*, a newspaper."

This grilling would last forever, he was sure, but finally she gave him her mechanical smile and said, "Thank you. That will be all."

He should not find fault with an institution which was trying its best to save Rose's life, he told himself, and went to his van which, of course, was ticketed. Cramming the notice in his pocket, he drove to the nearest motel, where he had two shots of vodka at the bar. Although he rarely smoked cigars, he bought two Dutch Masters, and nervously puffed one as he entered a telephone booth.

Ann answered. "Hi!" she said cheerfully the moment she heard his voice. "Was your plane on time? Did Rosie meet you all right."

"Yes. Annie, I've got some sort of bad news—"

"Oh, god! Did Rosie have a heart attack?"

"Yes. She's in the intensive care unit here in Burlington."

"She never needed that before. She just got dizzy spells sort of. Is she going to be all right?"

"They seem to think so."

"Look, I'm coming right down. Eb will drive me, and grammie will want to come. You can't keep her away when people are sick."

"We can't see her at all until tomorrow."

"If Rosie's sick, Ben, we're going to be there. I don't care if we have to camp for a month in the hospital lobby."

Ben had another drink at the bar. Suddenly he realized that he was exhausted. He felt as though he had lived a thousand years since he had taken a last ceremonial swim in the Pacific Ocean in front of the cottage that was no longer his in Santa Barbara that very morning. After renting a room in the motel and telephoning the hospital to give his location, he called home again. This time Ebon answered.

"Is Rose all right?" he asked immediately.

"I think so. Look, you better drive to the Champlain Motel on Fifth Street. I'm going to bed down here and we'll get rooms for everybody. Rosie can't have visitors until tomorrow."

"I got to wait a few minutes. Grammie and Annie are pretty broken up. Do you know this is the way Rosie's mother died?"

"No. I just knew she died young and was sick a long time."

"Are heart attacks hereditary, for god's sake?"

"I don't know. I guess most families are predisposed toward one disease or another. Anyway, they can treat most heart conditions a hell of a lot better now than they could twenty or thirty years ago. Tell Grammie and Annie that."

Ben felt so tense that he needed another double vodka before he could make his exhausted body lie down. He immediately fell into a deep sleep, which was interrupted a few hours later by the arrival of Ebon in the dilapidated pickup truck with grammie and Annie. They too were tired and did not object when Ben staggered back to bed after signing them in.

At seven Ben awoke with a pounding headache. Hurriedly he dressed to go to the hospital and was surprised to find Ebon, Ann and grammie already eating breakfast. After Ebon loaded grammie's wheelchair into the back of the van, they drove to the parking lot near the emergency entrance. Soon the four of them presented themselves to the receptionist in the waiting room, who called to find if Rose could have visitors.

"Dr. Knight will be down to see you in a few moments," the receptionist said.

"Who's Dr. Knight?" Ben asked.

"A heart specialist, the chief of our cardiac section. Won't you please sit down?"

This development somehow seemed ominous. Ben sank into an armchair, picked up the first magazine at hand, and glanced at some photographs of fleshy, leering nudes which suddenly seemed disgusting. He tossed the magazine aside, and studied the faces of the men and women in the big waiting room. Most of them were old people, their faces frozen into a kind of granite dignity as they waited, waited as he was waiting for intimations of life or death. He had never realized that courage is probably more common in civilian life than it is in the military.

"Now who is going to see Miss Rose Kelly?" a tall, bald man in a white coat asked.

Grammie pushed her wheelchair eagerly forward while Ann, Ebon and Ben stood up.

"I'm afraid she can just have one visitor today, and then for just a few minutes," the doctor said. "She's recovering, but she still needs rest."

"Ben, she'd rather see you!" grammie said in her loud, gravelly voice. "You go on up and bring us a report."

The others nodded. Ben followed the physician, who led

146

the way to a small office, not the elevator. Sitting behind a metal desk, he motioned Ben toward a folding chair.

"I've had quite a talk with your little lady," he said in a dry, nasal voice. "I can't tell you a great deal about her heart until we take tests. That generally takes about two weeks. She has, however, another problem: she's scared nearly out of her wits."

"Who wouldn't be? Apparently she watched her mother die this way."

"She told me that. Despite it, she seems hopeful about her chances for survival. What worries her is the thought that she won't be able to do much work for a long while. She feels she has no right to try to hang on to her job and frankly, no right to try to hang on to you. She's very much embarrassed about having no money and no health insurance at a time like this. She feels she has no right to depend on you."

"I see," Ben said, glancing down.

"She also worries about her sister and grandmother, both of whom are apparently dependent upon her. She says she can't take a salary if she can't work, and then there will be no money. She's talking rather wildly about selling her farm. I tell you, she's one scared little lady."

"I'll offer help of course," Ben said. "The problem is whether she'll take it. She's always been so proudly self-sufficient."

"Just reassure her all you can," the doctor concluded. "This isn't a time for any big emotional fireworks. Just be calm and loving. She says you're just her employer, but she never talks about anyone else."

With a smile which made him look younger, the doctor led the way to the intensive care ward, a large room full of gray people on beds with rails, many of them surrounded by ominous white curtains. Rose was in a corner by the window. Her bed had been cranked up, and she sat in a normal position, a sheet up to her chin to cover her gray hospital gown. Her hair had just been brushed, and she had applied fresh makeup. When she smiled, Ben had the startling sensation that the whole ghastly business about her gasping for breath might have been nothing but a nightmare. She said nothing as he walked toward her bed. Leaning over, he kissed her chastely on the lips. "I love you," he said.

"Don't." Her voice was little above a whisper.

He took her hand, finding it listless for the first time. "All right," he said, "let's look at it straight. You're going to be sick for a few weeks, but believe it or not, I can get out a newspaper without a publisher for a month or so. Publishers are always exaggerating their own importance."

She squeezed his hand.

"And like anybody else when you're sick, you're going to need money. As it happens, God's been good, and I'm fairly well loaded. Your salary will continue and your hospital bills will be paid. What's to worry?"

"Because there's no point in your doing this," she whispered. "If you're smart, you'll head right back to California. Cut your losses. You're still not in too deep."

"I've always been something of a bastard, Rosie. No doubt I would do that if I thought I'd be happier that way."

"I have nothing to give you but sickbeds and bills."

"Let's at least stick to facts. Regardless of sickbeds and bills, I'm happy only when I'm with you. All the rest of the time, I'm just waiting, whether you're sick or well."

"*Why?*"

"I don't know. Maybe it's because you're such a marvelous lay."

She smiled for the first time, and the sheet quivered with her low laugh.

"And you're also pretty funny," he continued, "and sensible at all the right times. I've also fallen in love with your sister and your grandmother, never mind you. I've even fallen in love with your farm, and can't wait to crawl over the rooftop to your room. Now why on earth would I go back to California?"

"You're better at blarney even than dad."

"This is a good deal more than blarney. Say, I just got a wonderful idea. I know how you can get Blue Cross coverage fast."

"How?"

"Marry me. Then you'd come under my family plan. You may think it's silly to marry a man for his Blue Cross, but people have got hitched for worse reasons. How about it?"

Two tears appeared on her cheeks. "I'll say yes if you ask me in six months."

"You said that yesterday. Now I only have six months minus one day to wait."

"You want to know something?" she asked softly. "I feel engaged to you. I have ever since you gave me that beautiful ring, no matter what finger I wear it on, no matter what I say. I tried to stop the nurse from taking it off. I know they have to, but hell, I'd just had it about two hours. And now I can't even wear it because of some damn regulations."

A nurse gestured to him, pointing to her watch.

"Do you mind a corny gesture?" he asked Rose, taking a cigar from his pocket.

"It sure will be corny if you try to light that thing here."

"No," he said, and slipping the paper band off the cigar, he put it on the proper finger of her left hand. "With this ring I thee wed," he said, brushing her lips with his. "Rest and get better. My world is nothing without you. We need you at home. You have no idea how much cleaning ladies charge."

The sound of her chuckle was short and faint, but she squeezed his hand hard before pressing it to her cheek, which felt dry. He walked between rows of desperately ill people toward the hall. Ducking into the first men's room he saw, he put cold water on his face. Shaking with more emotion than he could control, he went into one of the booths and cried, holding his face buried in his hands. Rosie had looked so weak and so awfully fragile. Whether his reassurance and forced gaiety had helped, he didn't know, but her voice had seemed

149

to be calling from someplace far away and there had been a look of fear in those usually sparkling eyes that resembled what he'd seen in the eyes of mortally wounded soldiers he'd photographed on battlefields. They too had been so passive, so curiously accepting, as they drifted into the night . . . Shaking his head to clear it, he splashed more cold water on his face before he went downstairs to Ann, grammie and Ebon.

"Did you see her?" Ann asked as he approached.

"I saw her and she's fine. A little tired, of course, but it won't be long before she's fit as a fiddle."

11

"Can I drive home in the van with you?" Ann asked Ben as they emerged from the hospital.

Ebon, who had to drive the old pickup truck, was obviously miffed. "Come on, Annie," he said, "what did I ever do to you?"

"I'll keep you company, Eb," grammie said, "but anyone would rather ride in a new car than an old one."

"You go on with dad, too," Ebon grumbled.

As soon as Ann got into the van she saw the two big leather cases of camera equipment in the back and asked what they were. When Ben told her, she said, "Wow! Will you show it all to me and teach me how it all works?"

"Soon as we get a chance."

Because Ben was afraid that the dilapidated pickup truck would break down, he followed Ebon out of Burlington with the van. He expected that the truck would be annoyingly slow on the open roads, but as soon as Ebon escaped city traffic, he picked up speed alarmingly, and soon was careening around curves so fast that the new van was hard to keep on the pavement. Going down a long hill, Ben realized that his son was driving the ancient truck more than seventy-five miles an hour. This display of recklessness infuriated him. What if a wheel came off the rusty chassis, what if a tire went? Wasn't it enough to have one person in the hospital?

Ben's anger grew as he realized that his son was a reckless driver in several ways. The boy passed in places where there was barely room, he tailgated other speeding vehicles, and he kept veering over the center line, almost as though he were drunk.

"What's the matter with Ebon?" Ben asked Ann. "Does he usually drive like that?"

"He's all upset. You know how he is about Rosie. He started to drink last night, and even this morning while we were waiting to go to the hospital."

"Does he go on the booze much, Annie?"

"Only when things really get to him."

On a level stretch of highway, Ebon wove in and out of traffic with such abandon that Ben was afraid to follow him closely. "Can you drive, Annie?" he asked her.

"She drives good when Ebon lets her," grammie said. "She ain't crazy, anyway."

Ben's concern for his son grew. When the highway went up a steep mountain which slowed the old truck, he passed Ebon, honking his horn repeatedly, and stopped at the side of the road a few hundred feet ahead. Getting out, he waved his arms, motioning for Ebon to stop. For a moment he thought his son was just going to leave him there, but then the truck slowed suddenly and skidded to a stop on the shoulder ahead. Ebon got out, looking very tall. He had not brought shaving gear with him, and his dark stubble of beard made him look considerably older than seventeen. He was holding a beer bottle in his right hand, and as he approached Ben, he tossed it away. In his left hand, the stub of a cigarette smoldered.

"What do you want, old dad?"

"Are you on pot, booze or both?" Ben demanded.

"A little of each and not enough of either," Ebon replied.

"What the hell would you do if I were a cop?"

152

"Fortunately," he said, "fortunately you're not. You're a lot of damn things, old dad, but you're not a cop."

"The way you've been driving, you're lucky you didn't kill yourself and about ten other people. Do you think Rosie would be helped by another disaster?"

Ebon looked confused. "I'm *sorry*," he said. "Can't stand to think about all this sometimes."

"I know. Just don't drive. Annie will take the pickup home. You better come in the van."

"Annie can drive if you want, but I'm going with her."

"No," Ben said. "Not when you're wild like this. Get in the van."

"Can you make me, old dad? You seem to make everybody else do everything."

"I can handle him," Annie said, getting from the van.

"He's not going to ride with you," Ben said grimly. "Eb, cut the crap and get in the van."

"You wreck everything and everyone," Ebon said. "Now at least leave Annie and me *alone*."

"If you don't get in the van and calm down," Ben said, "you'll find yourself in the embarrassing position of having to beat up an old man who happens to be your father—"

"You never lose, do you, dad? Even with Rosie, you never lose!"

"What the hell does that mean?"

"She was all right till you got here and got her all fussed up—"

"Stop it," Ann said, rushing to him and giving him a sharp push.

"Don't talk rubbish, Eb," grammie said. "Get in here."

"I'm going to get myself another beer. If I'm not driving, it can't matter, can it, old dad?"

With an odd kind of dignity he walked back to the truck, refusing to talk to Annie, who trotted by his side. Soon he came back with two bottles of beer and jack-knifed his tall frame onto a pillow in the rear of the van. Glancing ahead,

Ben saw Ann start the truck. After waiting for a break in the traffic, she signaled and pulled onto the pavement. She drove no more than fifty miles an hour all the way home.

In the back of the van Ebon sipped his beer and said nothing.

"I understand you're upset about Rosie," Ben began. "We all are . . ."

Still Ebon was mute. After a while he stretched out on the rug which covered the bottom of the van and slept with his head on the pillow. The two empty beer bottles rolled noisily around him until Ben stopped and got rid of them.

After leaving Ebon and grammie at the farm, Ben decided to start by inspecting the newspaper office which Rose had rented and furnished.

"Let me go with you," Ann said. "I helped Rosie work out a surprise for you. I want to be there when you see it."

The office was located in a building on Main Street which was affectionately familiar to Ben. The long, low structure had once been occupied by an army-navy store, where he had bought camping equipment for himself when he was a boy, and for Ebon later. The surprise was that the entire storefront window was now covered by a photographic mural, a blowup of an aerial photograph which showed the entire town of Livingston in more detail than a map ever could. In the center of the window a beautifully hand-lettered placard said THIS IS THE TOWN OF LIVINGSTON. A NEW WEEKLY NEWSPAPER TO BE CALLED LIVINGSTON LIFE WILL BE PUBLISHED HERE, STARTING JULY 4. EDITOR: BEN-JAMIN LIVINGSTON WINSLOW. PUBLISHER: ROSE M. KELLY.

A knot of people was studying it now, and this part of the sidewalk was rarely deserted, Ann said.

"It's a marvelous idea," Ben said. "Where on earth did you get the aerial?"

"Rose knew that the park agency had photographed this whole area. She's given them hell so many times that they were glad to do her a favor. They helped her to arrange for the blowup. It didn't cost much."

"In our first issue, we'll give it a full page. People will want to frame it."

Taking a key from her pocket, Ann let him into a good-sized room with five desks, typewriters and chairs, all worn but serviceable. In the back were two small rooms which had been used for storage. They were empty, but had been freshly painted, a pleasing shade of light beige.

"Ebon cleaned out a lot of junk that was here and did the painting," Ann said. "How about a darkroom in one of these?"

"Fine . . . I'm sorry I gave Eb such a hard time. I was afraid he'd mess up his whole life."

"He'll come out of it. You know, Eb loves me, I guess, but he worships Rosie."

"I've been stupid . . . I never fully realized that—"

"Everybody goes ape over Rosie," Ann continued in a matter-of-fact voice. "I hope you do too, because I think she's gone ape over you, and that's funny. She usually plays it real cool."

"Well, I think it's fair to say that I've gone ape over your sister. Can you keep a secret?"

"No," Annie said, her eyes sparkling with anticipation.

"I've asked Rose to marry me."

"That's no secret. Everybody in town knows that."

"Well, I just did it yesterday!"

"Everybody knows you wouldn't make her publisher of your paper if something wasn't going hot and heavy. And everybody knows that Rosie doesn't just shack up. So there was only one answer."

"That kind of reasoning isn't always accurate. She said she'd say yes if I asked her in six months."

"Rosie always told me never to marry a man I hadn't known for at least six months, no matter what. And she always follows her own rules."

155

"Has she had a lot of trouble with her heart before this, Annie?"

"Some. She never talked about it. She didn't like to worry us, but we knew there was something. . . . I guess I always tried not to think about it. That's the way she felt, I think—if you don't talk about it, maybe it will go away."

Sitting down at one of the desks, Ben tried out the typewriter. He was suddenly conscious of the fact that he had an enormous amount of work to do if he actually expected to produce a newspaper on July 4.

"Ben?" Ann suddenly asked. "Can I work for the paper? I took typing in school and I'm pretty good. I already take some pretty good pictures, and I'll get better. I can keep the office clean, and maybe I can sell advertising. I can drive the van. I wouldn't expect any pay—"

"Good lord, I think that's the best offer I've ever had!"

"Don't laugh at me."

"Who's laughing? We'll start you at the minimum wage, whatever it is these days. When do you get out of school?"

"I finish my junior year in two weeks. Ebon's a year ahead of me. He's lucky. He's all through this year."

"Well, you've got a summer job, anyway." He rubbed his eyes with his hand. On the corner of the desk, he noticed several slips of paper. Picking them up, he said, "What are these?"

"Ever since we opened this office, people have been coming in, looking for jobs. There was one woman who said she helped her husband to get out a paper like this for twenty years. Her name is Lillian Fletcher. Rosie thought you might be interested."

"Is this telephone connected?" Ben asked.

"Rose just had it done."

Lillian Fletcher turned out to be a brisk woman about forty-five years old who long had summered nearby on Lost Lake. Before his recent death, her husband had published a country weekly not far from Albany, and she frankly said she would like nothing more than to work for a similar publication, even if the beginning pay was low. A plump, vigorous woman, she talked as though she knew the business, and Ben liked her looks, despite the fact that her hair was dyed an improbable shade of yellow. Too much in a hurry to check her references right away, he hired her on the spot.

"We need an advance copy of our first edition to sell advertising with," he said. "Just a front and back page will do, and the back page will be the aerial photograph in the window. How many days will you need?"

"If you have all the basic equipment and a good printer, give me about four days. As my Tom used to say, no sweat."

When Ben got back to the farm that night, he found that his son had been waiting for him. Dressed in clean bluejeans and a spotless white shirt, the tall young man came out the door almost as soon as Ben climbed down from the van. Ebon had shaved, but with his deep-set eyes, prominent nose and chin, he still looked much older than seventeen, his father thought.

"Can I talk to you a minute, dad?" Ebon asked in his deep voice.

"Get in the car," Ben replied, and returned to the seat behind the wheel.

"First of all, I'm sorry," Ebon began. "I'm really sorry about driving badly and about giving you a hard time."

"Well, thank you," Ben said. "Anybody who drives recklessly damn well should be sorry. On the other hand, if you had a dollar for every time I've been drunk in my life, you probably could retire now. And I got drunk after I took Rose to the hospital. So we're about even."

There was an awkward silence. Perhaps everything had been said which should be said. The throb of the spring peepers was unusually loud.

"I know how you admire Rose," Ben added suddenly. "I'm

157

in love with her. I can see how that could upset you too."

"How can you just barge in here, know her for three or four days, roar out to California, come back and say you love her? If I did anything like that, you'd call me a crazy kid!"

"You're right. I'm not sure I have an answer to that. Sometimes, though, that's the way it happens. Even to an old dad. Anyway, we're not going to get married for at least six months."

"But you've got a thing going. . . . I wondered when she said the two of you were to spend a whole day checking printers in Vermont before you even came home from Burlington."

Ben paused. "Don't you think this is an odd kind of reversal? Is this a world now where the son lectures the father on morality and keeps checking on his whereabouts?"

"I'm trying, like they say, to *communicate*. If you've told me once, you've told me a million times, a father and son should be able to *communicate*."

"So they should. Now let me have at it. I came back here about a month ago feeling a thousand years old. I met Rosie and fell in love almost immediately. I know that it's almost impossible for a person your age to believe that a man my age can actually fall in love, sometimes on short notice, but it's not an unheard-of phenomenon."

"And I suppose that Rosie fell in love with you," Ebon said tightly. "I wish I had your secret, dad. God, you don't look like so much, if you'll pardon my frankness, but first mother goes crazy over you, and then when she finally pulls out you have girls all over the world before you finally settle on Rosie. What the hell is your secret?"

"I think I'll give you a serious answer to a sarcastic question. I am not self-obsessed. When you can say the same, you may have better luck."

There was another painful silence. The first fireflies of the season were flashing their signal lights at each other as the twilight deepened. The air was sweet with the perfume of rambling roses on a nearby trellis.

"But Rose still almost died with a heart attack," Ebon said, his voice flat.

"*She* doesn't blame me for that. The *doctors* don't. Annie and grammie don't. Why do you automatically blame me because a woman I love has a heart attack?"

"What were you doing with her?"

"I think you're implying that we were in bed and that sex causes heart attacks. Well, you're supposed to be part of a liberated generation. Rose is thirty and I'm forty-five. Neither of us is married. If and when we decide to go to bed, I don't think we have to apologize to my son or anyone else. And sex doesn't cause heart attacks. Disease does. I didn't cause the disease, damn it. I wouldn't bother to spell all this out but I don't want you to live the rest of your life imagining that I gave Rose her heart attack. Damn it, I'm dying of guilt all on my own, even though I know it's not reasonable. I don't need you to make me feel worse—"

"I'm sorry," Ebon said gruffly. "Of course I know it isn't your fault but—"

"Rosie and I . . . more than anything else, she wanted to start a newspaper. I helped her to do that and made her the publisher. I proposed to her. Now do you think I've really been dishonorable? Do you think I've been taking advantage of her?"

"No."

"You think Rose is wonderful, but do you know what a bind she's been in? She had a job she hated, which offered no promotions and which paid damn little. She has a younger sister to put through college and an old grandmother who will need hospitalization any year. She has a bunch of land she can't sell because of the Park Agency zoning. I think she knew she was sick, though probably not how serious it was. Now what the hell did she think of when she woke up in the

159

middle of the night? Can you see that she might have liked me when she realized that she could rely on me, and that I was capable enough to help?"

"Yeah," Ebon said. "I guess all I did was eat her food and worry her by horsing around with Annie."

"No, don't go overboard...she said you were great in many ways....Look, this whole situation isn't going to be helped if we just sit here indulging in orgies of self-recrimination. You've done fine. I've done okay. God knows, the women are doing their best. God or whatever has served up something like a knockout blow, but not quite. We can help Rosie to get better."

"Yes," Ebon said, swallowing.

"Now I'm *sure* she'll want me to get that paper out. I'm going to do that. You finish your school year and get into a good college. Keep Annie happy—she needs somebody she can rely on."

"Yes," he repeated.

Ben took hold of his son's arm, wishing he could finish the conversation with a hug, but Ebon's big body felt stiff.

The boy looked at his father's hand. "Thanks, dad. I'll do everything I can." He walked toward the barn, his tall frame silhouetted against the glowing sky.

With a sigh Ben went into the house.

12

AFTER helping Lillian to start the advance copy the next day, Ben took a prospectus of the paper which Rose had written and decided to call on the major advertisers in the village personally to see how much support was available. He was hurt but not much surprised to find that the answer was none. The managers of the two supermarkets were too busy to see him, despite the fact that he had known them as a customer for years. The owner of the Iron Mountain Motel, the closest thing to a summer resort in town, said his advertising budget had already been committed and the woman who ran the biggest real estate and insurance agency in the county said she wasn't going to do much advertising this year and could make no promises. These reasonably polite evasions continued until Ben came to Paul Trudeau, who owned the only big local hardware store and lumber yard. He had recently built an impressive new center for farm machinery on the outskirts of town. Paul and Ben had never been close friends, but they had served in the army together in Korea ages ago, and Ben hoped that some trace of a bond remained.

It was about noon when Ben drove his jeep to the lot on which rows of new yellow tractors and their complex attachments gleamed. Paul, a small trim man who usually dressed like a farmer, was in his office dictating a letter to an elderly secretary. Whether it was true or not, he had the reputation of being a miser and the richest man in town, after Ed Pace, the undertaker, the doctors and Howie Hewat. In the army he had been a company clerk, and even in Korea, he had made money in all sorts of ways, some of them legal.

"Morning, Ben" he said with a smile that was surprisingly humorous. "You lookin' to take up the farmin' life for a change?"

"Not today," Ben replied with a grin. When the secretary withdrew, Paul offered him her chair. Sitting down, Ben added, "I guess you heard about the newspaper I'm starting."

"I saw your office. That's a great picture you got in the window. I'd like to have a copy."

"We're going to print one in our first issue. How would you like to have an ad on the back of it?"

Paul took a toothpick from the drawer of his desk and seemed to smoke it like a cigarette. "I'd like that fine," he said. "We need two papers in town, or at least one real one. I sure wish I could help you."

"Why can't you?"

"Hell, Ben, you ain't wet behind the ears. You been away a lot, but you ain't some city feller who thinks there's nothing around here but us honest hicks and lovely scenery."

"No."

"You got to remember that I got a lot of valuable machinery out in that lot night and day. Over at the other yard, I have thousands of dollars worth of lumber stacked right out in the open. If the cops didn't patrol my property around the clock, I'd be stole blind, or I'd have to hire private guards, a damn expensive deal."

"And Howie could pull the cops off with one telephone call. Right?"

"Well, I wouldn't say you were a thousand percent wrong."

"Did he threaten to do that?"

"The other day he dropped in to look at a garden tractor.

162

Didn't buy, just looked. We chatted. I don't remember exactly what we said. He asked if I knew you, and when I said yes, he asked what I thought of your idea for a new paper. When I said it sounded pretty good, he said he liked you and he used to like your father, but you were both reformers at heart. And that's fine, he said, but reformers always want better schools, a better hospital and better police service. So inevitably they're working for higher taxes. He said people around here can't afford higher taxes, and to save money, they might have to cut down on things, like the police patrolling private property. He said he wasn't worried about your paper because he doubted that any *real* friend of his would advertise in it. Then he left."

"That's very interesting," Ben said. "Did anyone else hear him say all that?"

"Howie's too smart for that. I wish I'd taped it. Howie tapes stuff all the time in every office he has. He's a regular Nixon."

"Would you testify to what he said if I got Howie into court?"

"Want a beer?" Paul asked blandly.

"It wouldn't hurt."

Going to a Coca-Cola machine in the corner, Paul pressed a lever and returned with two cold Genesee beer cans. "Ain't supposed to put beer in them machines," he said. "If you're going to get me to fighting with Howie, I guess I'll have to stop."

"Would you testify?"

"Christ, we're both ex-soldiers, Ben. I don't want to fight no battles I can't win. Look, I hate the bastard. I don't like being pushed around and threatened and manipulated, the way he's been doing to people since he was in high school. But I got to live here. I'd take a real hiding if I had to sell out this business and move."

"I think we could take him. It would mean digging and work but Howie can be taken."

163

"Christ, he's vulnerable as a hot-air balloon if you know how to dig for facts and use them," Paul said. "Take any organization he's been running, whether it's the country club, the hospital, the school board or the town council. Howie's a lawyer, but he's so stuck on himself that he thinks he can do anything he wants. Investigation is the last think he's sucking for. Why do you think he's going to so much trouble to sink your paper before it even starts?"

For about an hour Paul discussed all the facts and rumors he remembered about Howie Hewat, giving Ben a picture of a small-town dictator to enlarge Ben's already considerable personal anger. Suddenly Ben stood up. "That's enough," he said. "I've got a job to do right now."

"Where are you going?"

"I'm going to pay Howie a visit."

"Jesus, not now! Don't go off half-cocked! You've got to build a case."

"That will take time. If I don't do something right now, I'm not going to have any newspaper to print a case in. How long do you think I can go without advertising?"

"I don't know, but Howie will chop you if you come at him like an amateur—"

"Look, I've been through five wars and he's sat out every—"

"This is a different kind of battle, Ben. You know that."

"I can still duck good when somebody aims a roundhouse right at me, which he's just done. Don't worry, Paul. I won't get you in trouble, not today at least."

On a bright June day like this, Ben guessed, Howie would be having lunch at the country club. As he drove there, he was surprised by the intensity of the anger which continued to build in him. The worry about Rose had rubbed his nerves too thin, perhaps, to handle a new threat to the idea of the newspaper they were going to run together. If Howie succeeded in scaring all the major advertisers away, Livingston

Life would die before it was born and Rose would have one more colossal disappointment. And with the medical bills he was going to have, he would soon go broke if he had to support a profitless newspaper. Suddenly the inflated figure of Howie Hewat seemed to stand between Ben and everything important in his life.

Howie's white Lincoln Continental was parked in front of the country club. Ben made himself breathe hard to reduce tension as he approached the front door, but his heart was still beating fast. The moment he got into action, he would feel calm, he had learned from experience, but this preliminary stage was agony, like crawling up a hill, waiting for the machine-gun fire to cut loose.

He found Howie sitting in a corner of the dining room with Pete. A bulging brown briefcase leaned against Howie's chair and he was reading a legal document in his left hand while he ate beef goulash with his right. Pete was writing with a pencil on a yellow pad. They were both so preoccupied that they didn't even see Ben approach. When Ben was within ten feet of them, his heart slowed suddenly and his crippling tension vanished.

"Good morning, Howie," he said, making his voice cheery. "Top of the day, brother Pete."

"Morning," Howie grunted. "What do you want, Ben?"

"A few minutes of your valuable time for a little chat—"

"Sorry, but we're busy right now," Howie said.

"We have an important matter here that won't wait," Pete ratified.

"I'm afraid that my matter is more important," Ben said. "Life or death, you might even say, for me and maybe for you, too."

"Oh, for Christ's sake, Ben," Pete said with disgust.

"What are you getting at?" Howie asked, wiping his big lips with a napkin.

"I think we ought to have an emergency session on the golf course away from all these people."

165

"How about my office?" Howie snapped.

"Oh, I prefer those open slopes of greensward for confidential conversations."

"Well, I don't know what this is all about," Howie grumbled. "Can't we even finish our lunch?"

"Eating when under tension is very bad for you. Fine way to get ulcers. You're in enough trouble as it is."

"What kind of trouble?"

"Follow me."

Ben led the way to a two-man electric golf cart which was parked in a row of similar vehicles. "Get in," he said to Howie.

"How about me?" Pete asked.

"I don't want to hurt your feelings, but I think I prefer a kind of one-to-one relationship with Howie at the moment, Pete. Why don't you try croquet?"

"Humor him," Howie said. "I'll meet you at the bar, Pete. I'll get this over with fast."

Howie was so large that he left little room for Ben behind the steering lever. A blue and white canopy over the cart fluttered as Ben sped up a slope.

"Where the hell are you going?"

"High on a windy hill, Howie—just you and me together."

Abruptly he stopped on a knoll. "Now Howie, I want you to sit right there and shut up until—"

"For Christ's sake, do you think I'm intimidated by you?"

"Facts, Howie. Point one. You've been running all over town trying to scare advertisers away from my paper. That is illegal and it also is going for my jugular vein. Before you go for a man's jugular, How boy, you better make sure that he can't fight back—"

"I wouldn't bother with your damn paper and you have no proof whatsoever."

"You hope. I can build a pretty good case against you, How boy. You're the lawyer. Will they call it restraint of trade, intimidation, misuse of official position, or *what?*"

"You're bluffing."

"If so, how long will it take you to prove it? I understand you're running for the state senate. The case will make good copy right up to November if I play it right."

"Blackmail," Howie said, his face reddening.

"Oh no. I'm not asking for anything. I'm just an honest newsman exposing a crooked politician."

"Without evidence you'd be laughed out of court."

"Obviously I wouldn't undertake such a crusade without evidence. Now, that's just number one, Howie. Do you want a preview of some of the rest of the ammunition that can make mincemeat out of you if you go for my jugular?"

"I've never been afraid of threats."

"Okay. Then I won't show you any more of my ammunition," Ben said, starting the golf cart. "Let's go home."

"All right . . . might as well know what you've got on your mind."

Ben stopped. "You shouldn't attack me, Howie, because you are too vulnerable, vulnerable as a hot-air balloon, as a man who knows you well said. Men who live in hot-air balloons shouldn't throw darts."

"Do I have to get all this horseshit with whatever you've got on your chest?"

"Sorry. Point one was the fact that I can formally accuse you of intimidating my customers, and I may be able to make the charge stick. Point two is a charge I'm sure I can prove: You are president of the town council and the lawyer for the mill at the same time. Our tax assessor is also an employee of the mill. Damn near every town official is, and that's conflict of interest, as I'm sure you know. No wonder the mill pays so little in taxes and never gets hit for pollution. You rig the town for them."

"It's always been that way here, it is in most mill towns—"

"And slavery used to be legal."

"I don't think you'll get anywhere with that charge," Howie said, but he was sweating despite the cool breeze.

"Of course I can always charge conflict of interest during your campaign. The piece will make good copy. Are you ready for number three?"

"What kind of crap—"

"I can inquire why you usually hire out-of-town firms to paint and carpet the hospital and the country club. I can also inquire why your house always seems to be carpeted and painted at the same time by the same people."

"I pay for that."

"But how much? I bring up this small matter only as an example. If I have accountants and outside lawyers go over the books of every operation you've supervised, we might get some more interesting information."

"That's a fishing expedition—"

"In troubled waters. I'd be interested to know how much you paid for your Lincoln. Was it sold to you for a very low price by a doctor, maybe an incompetent radiologist you got a part-time job for at the hospital that pays forty-five thousand dollars a year?"

"The car's engine was shot, I had to have it rebuilt—"

"Explain it to the IRS, not me. I'm dumb about the nuances of kickbacks in all their infinite variations."

"Christ, Ben, you're making me out as some kind of a thief. Did you ever think of the man-hours I donate to the hospital, the school board and the town council?"

"I know, you even make some good things happen in this town. But what I'm *telling* you is, get your goddamn knife away from *my* throat...."

"I never meant to knife you. I have an interest in the *Recorder*, after all. Naturally we'll compete for advertising." Howie at least knew how to beat a retreat, even if only strategic.

"But not the way you competed with the radio station. First you dried up their advertising and then you knocked over their tower. Thank god I don't have a tower vulnerable to blizzards—"

168

"Now you're really just going by rumor—"

"There's one big difficulty, Howie, in dealing with thugs that you spring from jail. They are grateful, I know, but they drink in bars, and they often talk—even boast."

"You can't believe drunks! No one would, goddamn it, anybody can say anything—"

"Like 'Don't buy space in Ben's new paper. I'll get you if you do.' "

"If you can prove I ever said that, I'll retract it!"

"I hope you'll retract it without my pushing this much further. Do you want to hear my point four? It's the biggie."

"Rave on."

"I think there's a good story in your life-style, How boy. On the one hand, you're a deacon of the Episcopal church, but when you give speeches against birth control and abortion, you're more Roman than the pope. No law against that, of course—you're just a moral, conservative, God-fearing man."

"Damn right," Howie said, patting his face with a handkerchief.

"You're active with the Boy Scouts, a thirty-second-degree Mason, *and* a candidate for the state senate next fall. Now that sounds like a very moral, upstanding citizen, doesn't it?"

"You said it. Modesty prevents—"

"Then how come you can't control this urge you have to seduce young girls?" Ben asked mildly.

"What the *hell* are you saying?"

"Come on, Howie. Everybody in town has known it for ages. I could forgive you for a compulsion to lay hands on young girls at parties or for trying to make them like you, but when you use deception and intimidation, well, you make me a tad upset—"

"I have *never* done that—"

"You've never asked a young woman to go to New York with you on business? You've never tried to force yourself on her at night in a lonely hotel room? You never denied her promotions because she ran instead of cooperating?"

"I don't know what the hell you're talking about. I wouldn't let them make Rose Kelly head of the PR department because she's incompetent. I suppose that's the kind of rumor she's circulating—"

"I wonder which one of you a jury would believe? I also wonder what a judge would think about the story of a nineteen-year-old girl you had transferred to the mill in Bangor. She was alone there and pregnant, I understand. Wasn't it a shame how she died?"

"I heard about that, it had nothing to do with me, except she wanted a transfer to get away from home and I arranged one for her. I don't know who knocked her up—"

"She didn't seem in much doubt."

"How do you know what she thought?"

"What do you suppose a lonely pregnant girl does in a strange city? She writes letters to a friend at home."

"And you have the letters?"

"I know where they are."

"She might have been trying to get even. She was a promiscuous little thing. When those girls get pregnant, they always try to pin it on the richest guy in sight—"

"Maybe you can squirm off that hook, Howie, but I'm fairly sure I can find a way to write all this up without getting involved in libel. I don't like yellow journalism, but if I need it to keep my paper alive, I'll turn yellow as a drugstore tabloid."

"I think we've let this get all out of proportion," Howie replied carefully. "It's all nothing but a misunderstanding. I don't know where you picked up the rumor that I'm trying to block your advertising. I'll make a few calls as soon as I get back to the office and clear that up. Your advertising will start coming in."

"I would indeed be grateful for that."

"Hell, I'll take out an ad in your first edition myself—a 'Good luck on your new enterprise' sort of thing—"

"Should make you a lot of friends, Howie. Look, I don't want to mislead you . . . you're not buying immunity, you're just calling off a war in which I'd nail your hide to the wall."

"Well," Howie said with a Howie grin, "no point in being enemies, Ben. Hell, we're old friends! Let's shake."

When they got back to the country club, Pete looked as though he had not much enjoyed his wait at the bar.

"What happened?" he asked suspiciously.

"Ben and I just had a heart-to-heart, is all. We're going to help him launch his new paper . . . it's good for the town."

Pete stared hard before taking a gulp from his glass.

"Have a drink, Ben?" Howie asked.

Ben glanced at the golfers and their wives who surrounded them. "Howie, I'll buy you champagne for a real toast," he said.

The bartender opened a small bottle and filled three goblets. Picking his up, Ben said, "I don't mean to be theatrical, but when we were talking a while back, I neglected to mention a rather important item. As I'm sure you've heard, Rose Kelly is the publisher of Livingston *Life*. She is also my intended, to use an old-fashioned word. And she is also very ill right now in the Burlington Hospital. I propose this: Dear God, please make Rose well, we *all* need her."

"Amen," Howie said piously and drained his champagne, as did Pete. When Ben made the grand gesture of breaking his glass on the floor, Howie followed suit, though he looked surprised, and Pete appeared to simply drop his in astonishment. Leaving a ten-dollar bill on the bar, Ben gave them a wave and left.

Feeling the need to tell someone of his triumph, Ben hurried back to Paul Trudeau's farm-machinery center, where he found Paul alone in his office.

171

"Well, you can't lose 'em all," Ben began. "I used the information you gave me without naming you, and I guess I implied I was closer to proof than I am. It worked, though. Howie said it was all a misunderstanding, he's going to call off his dogs."

"Don't get too cocky," Paul said.

"You think he'll try to block the advertising again?"

"He probably won't try the same tactic twice, but I don't imagine you made Howie a pal for life, Ben. He wants your jugular now just the way you wanted his a few hours ago. You've got yourself a war going. You maybe won the first battle, but that's about all. Howie has a long memory."

13

At a little after four, Ben drove back to the farm. Ebon and Ann were studying for examinations at the kitchen table while grammie made tea.

"How many for Burlington?" Ben asked.

"Rosie got a nurse to call us," Ann said. "She still can't see more than one of us, but she has business she has to discuss with you."

Ebon did not look up from his geometry book, but as Ben started for the car he called, "Wait," and took a bouquet of red roses wrapped in a newspaper from the refrigerator. "Tell her they're from the bushes we planted last year."

"She'll be very pleased, I know. Thanks, Eb."

"They're from all of us," he added with a curious little shrug.

The fifty-mile trip to Burlington took Ben down the Champlain Valley and across the iron bridge at Crown Point. It was a trip he had always loved, but now he was so worried about Rose that he hardly noticed the scenery. If a nurse had called for her, she might still be in the intensive care ward. The doctor had told him she probably would be moved to her own room this morning, and that then she could see her relatives. Had she had a setback?

He drove as fast as he thought he could get away with, and was stopped by a Vermont state trooper who surprised him by letting him go with a warning after he had explained where he was going. The woman at the reception desk in the hospital kept him waiting for what seemed an eternity while she tried to locate Rose, who had just been moved to a semi-private room on the third floor. This turned out to be so small that there was room for only one wooden chair between two beds, one of which was occupied by an elderly woman with tubes in her nose. Rose was in the bed nearest the door. Again she had mustered the strength to brush her hair and apply makeup for his visit. She looked alert and somehow childlike as she smiled and wordlessly held her arms out to him. As he embraced her, he wondered if ever in his life he had caused a woman's face to light up that way, and he felt profoundly grateful for it.

"Thanks for coming, darling."

"I hope you'll always be so glad to see me."

"I will if you keep me locked in a room with horrible food and people who keep doing disagreeable things to me."

Her voice sounded much stronger, and he had a wonderful feeling, a near certainty that she was going to get better. He gave her the roses from the bushes she and Ebon had planted.

While she admired them, he said, "I have things to tell you, but I want your news first. Has the doctor talked to you?"

"I'm stuck here for two weeks of tests and when I get home, I'm going to have to rest for a long while. He seemed shocked when I asked him when I can make love. Oh, it's all so awful!"

"Why?"

"He said it will depend on the tests. Can you imagine taking a bunch of complicated medical tests to find when you can make out?"

"We better go by the rules."

"Well, that's my wonderful news. What's yours?"

"I told off our old buddy Howie Hewat."

Rose's eyes gleamed as he briefly recounted the story. When he got to the part about drinking a toast to her with Howie and breaking the glasses, she burst into laughter, which she tried to keep low because of the old lady with tubes in her nose.

"If you actually got Howie Hewat to drink a toast to me, you can do *anything*. Do you think you've really beaten him?"

"Short run, yes. Long run, we'll see."

Rose paused, obviously relishing the moment. "You know, I don't really have any letters from that girl he sent to Bangor."

"As long as they exist in his imagination, they can help us."

She smiled and nodded. "God, I wish I had been there."

"We'll have other go-rounds with Howie, I've no doubt. . . . Now, I hear *you* have some business to discuss. . . ."

"Just lying here, I keep getting ideas for features for our first edition. For instance, you ought to print a rattlesnake map."

"What?"

"There are lots of rattlesnakes in the mountains around town, but they stick to certain spots. Get Ebon to ask a forest ranger where they are and print a map showing the danger areas. The summer people will appreciate it."

"Hey, that's a good idea!"

"The rangers could also help you draw a map showing where some big caves are. They could make a good feature."

She went on spouting ideas, but her voice was fading, and she seemed almost too animated.

"I think you better slow down," he said. "I've enough for a dozen editions. . . ."

"Then one more thing." She took his hand and squeezed it tightly. "I don't want you to come here anymore, at least not very often."

"Why?"

"You have a paper to get out. A hundred miles is a long

way to drive to see an invalid—it's hard on me, too, Ben. I know I look awful. I get so tense waiting for you. I keep imagining an accident. . . . You'll get exhausted if you do all that driving on top of a full day's work. . . . No. I can't stand the pressure. Come once a week. If I'm going to be ugly and sick, I'd rather do it alone."

He put his cheek beside hers, bending awkwardly. "I'm not going to argue with you," he said. "You know how I feel."

"Bored out of your skull if you have any sense. Tomorrow I'll have a telephone. Call me up a lot."

"I will."

"At least on the phone I can talk sex and flirt. Even if I look awful, you won't know it."

He was sitting on the edge of the bed, kissing her goodbye, when the nurse knocked to tell him that his visit should end. In the next bed the aged woman continued to lie immobile.

"Rosie, even here you cheer me up," he said.

"Wait till I get home," she said with her elfin grin. "You'll find I'm even better at making you miserable."

It was true that he felt cheerful when he was with her in the hospital, but a crying jag threatened to hit him every time he left her, and he felt a strong temptation to get drunk. Feeling like a man constructed of wood, Ben climbed into the van. He had work to do, and the best thing he could do for Rosie —for himself—was to get at it.

Although advertising rolled in, the job of producing the first edition of Livingston *Life* soon became an exercise in exasperation. Some of their secondhand equipment for ready-ing copy for the photo-offset process broke down. Lillian Fletcher was admirably efficient, but soon appeared to want to run the paper entirely by herself. Ben couldn't guess whether her husband had given her complete authority or whether he had given her so little that she wanted nothing else. At any rate, this plump woman with the brass-blonde hair went pale when Ben decided to change the layout of the front page of his own paper. For the rest of the day she shut the drawers of the filing cabinet with such dramatic force that one came off its track.

The problem of having a temperamental assistant editor was complicated by Ebon and Ann, both of whom came to work on the paper as soon as school was out. Ben was pleased by their desire to do this and enjoyed the idea of having a family enterprise, but complications set in. First of all, Lillian apparently felt that it was her responsibility to train these young people and she ordered them about as though they were army recruits. Ann accepted corrections of her typing, emptied wastepaper baskets and ran out for coffee without complaint, but Ebon's deep-set eyes started to smolder when Lillian ridiculed his first attempts to write copy.

"Do we really need that damn woman around here?" Ebon asked Ben one day when she'd stepped out for lunch.

"I know she's difficult, but she's a pro. Who else can I find around here who can do the job?"

Grumbling, Ebon put a pad in his pocket and went to the police station. The *Recorder* had long avoided publishing news of arrests and convictions ... Ben's father had once said that he published all the news that was fit to print, except what would get him shot, which didn't seem funny when a beer bottle was shot out of Stephen's hand while he was camping with his son in the woods after printing an article about a local hotel owner who'd been charged with arson following fires in two of his Depression-emptied inns. Now that he was starting his own paper, Ben suspected that many people would buy it rather than the *Recorder* just because they wanted police news. Every arrest caused gossip, and it would be a luxury for people to find the truth. If some danger were involved, that would just be part of the business, like battles in war.

It was all very well to decide this in the abstract, but something else when Ebon came running back from the police station about a week later with "a real story!"

177

Both Lillian and Ann listened while Ebon started to give them the information the police had allowed him to copy from their records.

"Have you ever heard of a family called Radeau up on Chasson Hill?"

"Lord, yes."

"Do you know anything about them?"

"There've been Radeaus around here ever since the French and Indian wars, they claim. My father said that when the English chased the French out of these hills, the Radeaus were too drunk to go. They've been raising hell ever since."

"Well, last night they raised a special variety of it. Five brothers, and I can't figure out yet how many cousins and sons, pulled a one-family riot up at Roger Radeau's farm. Three of them are in the hospital, one critical."

"Does anybody know what caused it?"

"Amy Jo Radeau. She's fifteen years old."

"What did she do?" Ann asked.

"She accused her father of incest, forcing her into it. They were all drunk and he was trying to drag her upstairs ... that's when the free-for-all began."

"Is the girl making a formal charge now?" Ben asked.

"Yes, and her mother is backing her up."

"Oh, lord," Ben groaned. "Spring comes to the Adirondacks."

"Well, it's a hell of a story, isn't it?" Ebon asked. "I bet the wire services pick it up."

"Possibly," Ben said, rubbing his face with his hand. "Are the cops keeping any Radeaus in jail?"

"They locked up five of them last night, but one of Howie Hewat's flunkies came down this morning and bailed them out. The cops said they were all cocky as hell but mad because they're keeping the girl and her mother in protective custody."

"I wouldn't touch that story with a ten-foot pole," Lillian said.

"Why not?" Ebon demanded. "It's legitimate news, isn't it? Shouldn't the people in this town know what's going on?"

"I thought we were running a family newspaper," Lillian said. "This isn't supposed to be a penny-dreadful tabloid! My Tom would have died before he touched such garbage—"

"What do you think, dad?" Ebon and Ann looked at Ben.

"Well, I guess a story like that would build circulation. Handled wrong, it could also get us a bad reputation. This is a very conservative little town—"

"So we'll handle it right," Ebon said.

"There's also that the Radeaus may take some sort of action —barn-burning, rocks through windows, worse—"

"Are you going to let them scare us off?"

"Have any formal charges been made against them?" Ben asked.

"So far the five of them are charged with simple assault. The girl and her mother are both bruised all over, and as I said, three men are in the hospital. There may be more charges. The cops, the DA and a whole bunch of lawyers are having conferences."

"Well, keep track of it," Ben said. "I want every fact triple checked."

"You're going to run it, then?" Ebon asked.

"I really don't want to," Ben said. "Did you ever stop to think that Rosie will be coming back from the hospital at just about the time this hits the street? Do we really want her to step right from the hospital into the middle of a big blowup?"

"She'd want you to run it," Ann said. "Everybody knows there's a lot of forced incest around here. There was a girl in my class who kept complaining to the cops about it but they sent her right back to her family because they didn't know what else to do with her. The girl finally got pregnant by her own father. Rosie was furious when I told her. She'd *want* you to nail anyone who did that."

"What happened to the girl?" Ebon asked.

179

"She had the baby and raised it as a sister."

Ben shook his head. "Small town, small matter . . . or is it?"

"I think the whole subject is *very* distasteful," Lillian said. "Do you realize what the chamber of commerce and the businessmen's association will think if you make out this town to be some sort of Tobacco Road? You may gain circulation, but you'll for sure lose advertising—"

"Rosie will be furious if she hears you buried a story like this for her sake," Ann said. "You know her. She's been a fighter all her life."

"You could get pictures of the guys when they're arraigned on charges," Ebon said. "The girl wouldn't mind having her picture taken now. I talked to her."

"Eb, she's a minor. We can't even use her name, and shouldn't anyway. Do you want to publicize the tragedy of a fifteen-year-old girl?"

"I think she wants revenge. I talked to her. I'm afraid she doesn't seem very bright—"

"Lovely," Lillian snapped. "What we have here is a real story for the family hour. If she's not very bright, how do you know she didn't make up the whole thing?"

"The courts have to decide that," Ben said. "Keep me updated, Ebon, right up to an hour before our deadline."

"You're going to run it, then?" Ann asked.

"Let's see how it develops. What we probably should do is to avoid sensational headlines and photographs but print a brief statement of the facts of the case on an inside page."

"Chicken," Ebon said, and Ann looked unhappy, as did Lillian.

"I see I've disappointed everyone," Ben said with a wry grin. "Well, I must be doing something right."

When William Radeau died of a fractured skull in the hospital two days later and Roger Radeau, his father, was arraigned for murder, Ben realized that he could not possibly play down the story. The breaking of a sensational case just in time for the first edition of his paper was, in a sense, a break, no doubt, but he was still worried about its consequences. Maybe he was becoming paranoid, but among other things, the Radeau case could give Howie Hewat an opportunity to hit back at Ben with very little danger to himself. All he would have to do would be to encourage the Radeaus to hit for him. If the Radeaus were caught while trying to punish Ben in one way or another, who could blame Howie? The Radeaus, more than anyone else Howie could hire, would have real motives of their own. . . .

Melodrama? Reality? Ben tried to keep his mind on other matters. A negative story in a small-town weekly, he decided, should be balanced by a positive one. The left-hand side of his front page would have to carry the saga of incest and family murder. On the right side he prepared headlines proclaiming that recent tests proved the air and water of Livingston to be purer than most other parts of the Adirondacks.

The chamber of commerce would be one and one.

During the last week before Rose came home from the hospital it wasn't the Radeau business that had depressed Ben and made him short-tempered. As the tests of Rose's condition were completed, Dr. Knight still did not give the reassurance which Ben had somehow expected, longed for, actually. Instead he talked somberly about diseased valves and the need for Rose to avoid all exertion for an indefinite period of time.

Worse: "I think it's imperative that she undergo open-heart surgery as soon as she gets her strength back, certainly within a few months," the doctor said. "She just survived that last attack. Her heart was badly damaged, Ben. One more attack very probably will be her last."

"What's the . . . probability of another one?"

"Very high, if she does nothing. With open-heart surgery her chances are good. It's not such a big deal in top hospitals

181

these days. I can't put it into percentages for you, but the odds would certainly be in her favor."

"What does Rose think of that?"

"Well, there's the unfortunate circumstance that her mother died while undergoing such surgery. I think she understands that it was much more chancy then, but it's an emotional thing with her. I hope you can help her work it out. Frankly, I think this fear of hers is the biggest obstacle she faces."

The tone of the doctor's voice, as much as his words, left Ben with a sinking feeling. Rose's life might be short, as her mother's had been. He'd better stop trying to measure his own life only in years. Overweight at forty-five, hard-drinking most of his life . . . oh, come on, for god's sake, you're not going to be much use to Rose or yourself this way. The thing to do, obviously—as it was for anybody—was to make every day as good as possible, for Rose and for himself. And the greatest guarantee of a longer life for her would be to learn how to *enjoy* a short one. Happiness, the doctor had said during one conversation, was powerful medicine.

Get down to it, he told himself. Start with the possible . . . for example, something as mundane as installing air-conditioning in her room at the farm. During the summer months damn few breezes blew in the valley, but for the sake of warmth in winter the windows in the old building were small. Still, Rose would never stay in her bedroom. Ben was trying to figure out whether he could air-condition the entire bottom floor when he remembered his mother's summer place, Cliff House, on Lost Lake, which she no longer used.

Of course Pete would raise hell and carry on about the Trust. . . . That evening he drove to Pete's house at about nine o'clock. Winters, the black houseman, let him in and led the way to the living room upstairs, where to Ben's surprise he found Pete and his stout wife Lucy playing bridge with Howie Hewat and his wife Carol, a high school beauty who had turned into a middle-aged woman with a sallow face and

182

a wig of bronze-colored curls. Obviously she too had had problems with her health—and he thought how easy it was to imagine that one had a corner on the market. Having felt such hostility toward both his brother and Howie, it was sort of a shock to come on them in this way . . . as ordinary people, caught in the act of nothing more shocking than playing bridge with their wives. Villainy seemed to have fled them . . . for the moment, anyway.

"Hi, Ben," Pete said. "Have a drink?"

"I don't want to interrupt your game. I just came to talk to you about using Cliff House this summer. Rose is coming home from the hospital soon, and that farm is awfully hot. . . ."

There was a pause. Pete glanced at Howie, and Howie lit a cigar.

"I'm sure that your mother would be happy to have you use the place," Howie said.

"She's forgotten that it exists," Pete added. "I asked her about it the other day, and she didn't know what I was talking about."

"I think she forgets places she doesn't like," Ben said. "Remember how often she told us that she hated Cliff House when she was a little girl because there were no children to play with there?"

"Her father died there, too."

A moment of silence before Ben said, "I guess I will have that drink."

"Get it yourself, if you don't mind," Pete said affably. "By the way, could you get your stuff out of the other house as soon as you can? We've actually sold the place, or got a deposit on it."

"I'll see to it right away."

"How's Rose?" Carol asked suddenly, her voice nearly as frail as her appearance.

"Well, she has a bad heart, no doubt about that. She's going to have to take it pretty easy for a long while."

"I'm sorry, I always liked her...such a vital young woman!"

"Yes, indeed," Howie added, taking a sip from his highball.

"I met her at the school," Lucy said. "I remember she was angry about the way they teach English, and she was right, too—we graduate class after class of illiterates."

"Pregnant illiterates," Pete grunted. "Last year damn near half the graduating class was pregnant. Christ, they'd got me to give the commencement address. I'd written a long speech about the opportunities young people have in law, science and all the rest. I felt like a damn fool."

"Well, give Rose my best," Carol said. "Tell her we're all thinking of her."

Feeling perilously close to tears, Ben left, thinking that it was best never to see your enemies playing bridge with their wives. It ruined the whole picture, could even make you think they were human. Oh, God, stop dramatizing, he told himself, and realized that he'd probably never succeed at *that* ... it was, always had been, his best defense.

In the five days before Rose came home Ben was especially grateful to Ebon and Ann. While he finished the first edition of the paper with Lillian, they trucked all his possessions out of the house that had been sold, and moved the entire family into Cliff House for the summer. After Ann inspected the Victorian cottage with its enormous flagstone terrace built to the edge of a cliff a hundred feet above the lake, Ben said, "Do you think Rosie will like it? Maybe it's wrong to try to surprise her."

"She'll adore it! Besides, she always hated the farm in the summer. She used to call her room the sweatbox."

"Dad," Ebon said, running to the terrace. "I was down looking in the boathouse. I don't know when the old *Indian Princess* was last used, but she looks in pretty good shape. Do you mind if I give her a coat of paint? Riding around the lake is one thing Rosie should be able to do. And I need something to keep me busy."

184

"A great idea." Ben knew his son was worried because he hadn't yet heard whether he'd been admitted to any of the three colleges of his choice, despite the fact that most of his friends had received word. Ebon also shared his worry about Rose, of course, and he was clearly feeling some mysterious tension with Annie, who seemed aloof, even when she was working with him. The joys of youth were somehow not very evident between them, Ben thought. He had the paper ... painting the ancient cruiser might at least help take the boy's mind off *his* troubles. . . .

The day before Rose was to be released from the hospital Cliff House was ready for her, clean and full of hydrangeas, roses and tiger lilies, which grew profusely in the surrounding woods. In her room there was even a large wooden cage containing a pair of albino cockatiels, which Ann had been given by a school friend who was going away for the summer. The pale green birds with bright red spots the size of a dime on their cheeks made cheerful noises to each other.

"She always has adored birds," Ann said, "and if she has to stay in bed they'll be fun to watch. . . . Except let's *not* tell her their names."

"Which are?"

"Jim Dear and Yes Darling. I'm afraid she'd throw up."

At first the entire family planned to bring Rose home in the van, but grammie said that would be too strenuous and asked Ben to go alone. So at nine on the morning of Friday, July 1, he drove to Burlington. Because he had realized that for many reasons she had not wanted him to visit her often in the hospital, he had not seen her in five days, though he had talked to her on the telephone every afternoon. The last time he had seen her he had been shocked by her loss of weight, which had changed her appearance, rather than damaging it. After losing twenty pounds (she'd weighed only 117 when taken ill), Rose's figure had been rendered almost childlike, her cheekbones had become more pro-

185

nounced, and her eyes had appeared to be enormous. She was the only person in Ben's experience whose illness had somehow made her young, an illusion fostered by her hair, which she usually curled slightly but which had started to hang as straight as a young teenager's.

When Ben now went to her room, he found her standing by her bed in a green jersey dress. Somehow she had contrived to curl her hair, and he thought she looked wondrous. As he entered the room, she walked toward him, forcing herself not to run. He could not believe how good she felt in his arms.

"How do I look?" she asked.

"Fantastic!"

"Well, don't get your hopes up. I'm wearing falsies. I couldn't stand looking flat as a board."

"Always keep 'em laughing," he said, his throat tight.

"Actually, this hasn't been exactly a fun place." She gestured toward the other bed in the room, which now was empty. "The whole time she was here, Ben, she never said a word."

"Come on, let's get out of here."

As she did everywhere, Rose had made many friends in the hospital. Ambulatory patients, interns, nurses, cleaning women, came up to wish her well as she climbed into a wheelchair and allowed Ben to push her toward the elevators.

"I'm all signed out," she said. "I'll wait by the door downstairs while you get the car."

In the back of the van Ebon had put a mattress, blankets and pillows, in case she wanted to lie down, but she said she wanted to sit in the front seat. When she was settled, he drove to the middle of the parking lot and stopped.

"I have two big surprises for you," he said. "One's at home and one I can give you here."

Her eyes widened and her face lost some of its pallor. "What is it?"

"I don't want a surprise to be a shock. This is something

that you and I have worked on for a long time, something that never would have happened without you."

"You flunked your Wassermann?"

"Not exactly. Okay, comic, I've got a real live newspaper to give to you, the first edition of Livingston *Life*, hot, if you please, off the press." Whereupon he grandly took the crisply folded newspaper from beneath the mattress, where he had hidden it, and offered it up to her.

"Ben! Oh god, you made it happen—"

"I had lots of help, most of all your encouragement. What do you think of the two lead stories?"

As she read them, he tried to see them through her eyes. The headline on the lefthand side of the front page was:

Charges of Murder and Incest
Make Strange Home Brew Here

The righthand headline said:

Livingston Water and Air
Purest in State, Tests Say

Rose laughed. "Boy, you really got it coming and going. It's a *terrific* front page."

"Look at the bottom half."

She turned to a map about six inches square, which was headed with the line FOR GOODNESS SAKES, LOOK OUT FOR SNAKES!

"You used it," she said, clearly delighted.

"And now look at the masthead. Page three."

The masthead listed her as publisher at the top of a column naming Ben, Lillian Fletcher, the assistant editor, and Ebon and Ann, who were listed as assistants to the publisher.

"Why the hell didn't you put my name in bigger letters?" Rose said before dropping the paper and taking his arm. "Oh, Ben, I don't deserve it, I didn't *do* anything. . . ."

"I never got out a paper before I met you. That's something."

"Just because I got you off your ass doesn't mean I deserve to be called publisher. Is Lillian Fletcher nice?"

187

"No, but she's efficient."

"Is she pretty?"

"If you like fat dominating women with brass hair."

"Is she . . . waiting to be publisher?"

"She's an editorial type. If she ever talked to advertisers, she'd set us back to hand-set type."

"I'm glad. I'm sorry to be so bitchy, but I'm afraid I do love my title. I want it on my tombstone: HERE LIES A PUBLISHER."

She was smiling unself-consciously when she said it, but he felt a shiver up his back. "I guess we better be going," he said. "I have another surprise for you at home."

"This time I won't try to guess," she said. "I hate this car."

"Why?"

"These seats are so far apart. If we were in my truck, we could sit close together, maybe even do a little fooling around."

"The doctor gave me quite a lecture about that."

"I don't doubt it . . . Well, he told me I can't have, as they say, sexual intercourse for ages and ages, but he didn't say anything about a little fooling around. . . . Oh, Ben, I want to *hold* you. All I did in that damn hospital while that poor woman lay dying beside me was think about you holding me. I got to imagining it so well that I could almost feel your arms, all tweedy and scratchy, and sometimes I could actually smell your tobacco and the shaving lotion and manage a light whiff of Cutty Sark. Can't we park somewhere and just love it up for a few minutes?"

"Don't you think we should wait till we get home?"

"The whole family will be all over us. Ben, I need a few minutes alone with *you*."

"I don't know what the doctor would think of it—"

"He didn't say a word about *hugging*, for god's sake."

"Okay." He soon turned onto a leafy lane, and after

driving a mile from the highway parked under a maple tree by a pasture full of Holsteins. Rose was already lying on the mattress. When he joined her, she took hold of him in a tight embrace and kissed him hard.

"Rose, this is wrong," he said finally. "We've got to learn all over again how to exercise some control—"

"I don't want to exercise *control*."

"You want to get better, don't you?"

"If I can. Oh Ben, I waited damn near fifteen years for you. Then after one day, I have to exercise *control?*"

"Yes, Rosie, because I'm a very selfish man." He looked directly at her and he was not smiling. "Listen to me, and listen good. I do not want to live without you."

Her answer was to kiss him again, this time gently, and, unbuttoning his shirt, massage his shoulder and chest.

"Are you getting horny?" she whispered.

"I'm trying not to think about that."

He felt her touch his groin. "But you are," she said. "You can't fake that. Or *control* it."

"I'm sorry, don't worry about it."

"Who's worrying about it? I couldn't be happier. At least you still think I'm sexy! I was so afraid . . ."

The dancing leaves of the maple tree overhead made the sunlight flicker inside the van. Some of the cows wore oddly leaden sounding bells, and the aroma of fertilizer was sharp. On the nearby highway trucks growled in low gear as they started up a long hill.

"I love you, Ben," Rose said, and promptly broke the spell by giving his ear a sharp little bite.

"Rosie, for god's sake—"

"The doctor never said I couldn't bite your ear. Matter of fact, he never mentioned it."

"Rosie, this is no joke," Ben said, pulling away.

"Believe it or not, I do know what I'm doing, Ben. I'm a very learned woman. I had a long talk with the doctor last

189

night. It embarrassed the hell out of him ... myself a little, too, I guess ... but I finally got him to tell me what I wanted to know."

"Which is what?"

"How I can live with a man I adore without *doing* anything for him."

"Rosie, you don't have to worry about me—"

"I guess mostly I'm worried about me. Anyway, the doctor left me a ray of hope after he got over his shock. Whatever my so-called condition, I don't really have to live like a nun."

"Rosie, you make me feel more by holding hands than anyone else could by running through all the oriental positions—"

"That's sweet of you, Ben, but I can do more than that for you. I can, in fact, do anything that doesn't get *me* all excited. It's *my* heart I have to watch, and I do watch it. If I can give you pleasure without getting myself all worked up, even the doctor says it's okay."

"Rosie, just the thought of one-way sex with you makes me feel embarrassed, ashamed. If you have to be celibate, I'll stay celibate, too. We'll be equals, in everything."

"It wouldn't be one way if I enjoyed doing it, not in a way that would make my heart go crazy but because, my darling, I ache to do whatever I can for you. And that's a fact." No smile, very serious.

"Darling, I'm sure we'll work it out, but not the first day. Please. Think of *my* heart. Let's get you home and into your bed—"

"Damn!" she said. "I had visions of really turning you on today. I have the most selfish motives, Ben. I want to keep you. I want to deserve at least a little of all you give, and I don't really have anything else to offer—"

"Nonsense ... you have your *life* to offer—"

"But also a little fun? The men's magazines at the hospital had a serious student in yours truly, I guarantee you. Massage parlors, Japanese pleasure houses ... While the other ladies in the sunroom read *Women's Day*, I studied up on the skin magazines.... You have no idea, you lucky fellow, how much I learned ... for example, one article said that the girls in the massage parlors feel hardly any emotion when they do their bit. Well, that's when I thought their techniques might be good for a heart patient. You should have seen Dr. Knight's face when I told him my idea should be in a medical textbook."

"Rosie," Ben said, starting the engine, "I'm going to ask you to give me two solemn promises. Never tempt me into anything that subjects you to the slightest risk, and never do anything for *me* that might be distasteful to *you*."

"That's easy," she said. "I don't plan to take any risk, and I can't really think of anything distasteful that involves you. See what you get for giving me a diamond ring?"

He turned around in a barnyard and sped back to the highway. Rose lay down on the mattress, and for the rest of the journey slept.

God, how he loved this woman.

Rose appeared almost stunned by Cliff House. She stood on the flagstone terrace overlooking the lake and mountains and inspected her commodious master bedroom with its huge spool bed, hooked rugs, the fieldstone fireplace and the huge windows overlooking the water.

"Are you going to stay here with me?" she asked Ben.

"I thought that might upset the others. I'm right next door."

Rose climbed onto the bed and pulled a silk-covered puff over her lap. "What the hell, Ben! First I get sick, then I end up living like a queen. Keep this up and you'll have me an invalid for life."

14

AT eight the next morning, Ebon and Ben filled the back of the van with copies of Livingston *Life* and personally took them to every store in the area where newspapers were sold. It was Saturday, July 2, and they wanted to take advantage of the weekend crowd. The village was humming with rumors about the Radeau case. When someone in Bert's Country Store said, "Hey, it's all right here in this new newspaper," fifty copies were sold in not much more than fifteen minutes. Ben was glad that following his intuition he had increased his print order from two to four thousand copies and wished he'd gone to five. When the big crowd arrived for the Fourth of July parade, there would be a run on every newsstand.

At 10:08, the telephone rang in the office of Livingston *Life*. Ebon and Ben were still out touring the newsstands. Lillian Fletcher answered, her voice crisp and businesslike as always.

"Is this the new newspaper?" a harsh, rasping voice asked.

"Indeed it is."

"That story you got on your front page about the Radeaus, it don't make some people very happy."

"I'm sorry," Lillian replied briskly.

"Your big boy there? I want to talk to him."

192

"Mr. Winslow is not in at the moment."

"Well, you give him this message. He's loaded a pile of crap on us. There are still a lot of us, and for two hundred years we've never taken crap from the likes of you or anybody else without—"

"Who is this?" Lillian demanded as though she expected an answer.

"The superintendent of schools, girlie," the voice said. There was a sharp click as the connection was broken.

At 10:40 Lillian reported the threatening call to the police. Big Duke, the ranking sergeant, answered, took down the details and said, "It would be hard to prove anything. It's probably one of the Radeaus, but it could be any nut. Tell me if he calls again."

At 11:15, Ben and Ebon returned to the office and learned about the call.

"I'm not surprised," Ben said wearily. "Dad used to get dozens of calls like that. Usually nothing happens. Just making a call gives these nuts a chance to let off steam."

"I still think we ought to avoid stories like this," Lillian said.

"We better watch out or we'll get X-rated—too much sex and violence," Ebon said.

"That's not funny," Lillian snapped.

Ben smiled. "Maybe the whole of Livingston County should be X-rated, with no kids allowed in."

At 12:18, there was a long-distance call for Ben from Albany. It turned out to be from Bill Crawford, editor of the Albany *Star*, whom Ben had known several years before when they were both covering the conflict in Northern Ireland.

"What the hell are you doing up there in the sticks, Ben?" Crawford asked.

"Enjoying the peaceful mountain air."

"Well, I hear you've got a new weekly, and have come up with a hell of a story."

193

"News always travels fast, especially when I don't get paid for it. You don't waste time, do you, Bill? We've only been on the street a few hours."

"I've got a stringer up there who had the sense to call me and read me your piece, but when I asked her to get me more details, she said she wouldn't touch it. She's strictly funerals and weddings."

"That's a smart lady."

"Let's make a deal, Ben. You be our stringer and we'll buy first refusal on anything you print."

"For how much?"

"I'll have our business people get in touch. Meanwhile, we want everything about this crazy Radeau case we can get. What the hell happened? Did the guy actually rape his daughter and kill his son?"

"Everyone has a bad day now and then."

"I know. Nobody's perfect. But why did he kill the boy?"

"He tried to rescue his sister, or so his mother says."

"Sounds reasonable."

"Apparently they had sort of a triangle going. Just your basic family plot: brother with sister, father with daughter, father versus son—upshot, murder."

"Good god, I thought that kind of thing just happened down south."

"This is sort of your southern Adirondacks."

"Well, we want more details on it, anyway, Ben. And we want pictures. Our stringer said there were no pictures in your paper. How come?"

"To tell the truth, I've been trying to play this down a little. For the people down here, it's a shock to see any part of a story like this in print. I didn't want my first edition to look like the *National Enquirer*."

"Well, I'll pay for those pictures. We need them yesterday. When can you put them on a bus for us?"

"As soon as I get them, but in my own time. Now damn it,

Bill, don't start pushing me as though I were working for *you*. Your deadlines are your problem, not mine."

"Same old good-natured Ben."

"The same. I'll get you your pictures as soon as I can."

As he put down the telephone, Ben took a 35-mm. camera from the top drawer of his desk.

"Where're you going?" Ebon asked him.

"The jail, for some shots of the old man. Then the Radeau farm."

"Can I go with you?"

"The jail, okay. Let's think about the rest."

The jail was at the rear of the county courthouse, an imposing structure of red brick surrounded by maple trees and a few surviving elms. Big Duke led them from the police station to the single row of cells, in the first of which Roger Radeau sat on the edge of a cot. After the stories he'd heard about him, Ben found the prisoner to be an astonishingly innocuous-looking man. In only his early forties, Radeau was short, thin and oddly ascetic-looking, the center of his head bald in a rather monkish way. This impression, though, was denied by his eyes, which were ice-cold, and by large, heavy lips which covered the stubs of his teeth.

"What the hell do you want?" he asked in a guttural voice that sounded as though it came from a much bigger man. He stood up, walking slowly toward the front of his cell.

Ben took his picture immediately and without warning, after which the man tried to cover his face with his hands.

"You bastard, come in here, catch me in a damn cell, and take your damn pictures to make fun of me in the newspapers. You ought to be ashamed of yourself! If I ever get out of here . . ."

Radeau raised his fist, and Ben got a picture of that too. "All right, let's go," Ben said abruptly, and went out of the jail, trailed by Big Duke and Ebon, and the obscenities of Roger Radeau.

195

"I think you got the old boy a tad upset," Big Duke said. "You better start hoping we get a conviction. Them Radeaus can be bad people."

Ben nodded, not feeling especially proud of himself. It was a job, but Radeau did have a point. "You know how many are up at their farm now? I have to take some pictures of the place."

"Must all be there. The ones we booked on assault are out on bail. You be careful, hear? Do you want me to come with you?"

"No thanks, Duke. But like the man said, if I don't come back in an hour, send out the posse." Some joke, he thought.

Ebon followed Ben to the van. "Why didn't you want Duke to come with us?"

"Those folks wouldn't even open the door if they saw a cop."

"Aren't you afraid to go to that place alone?"

"Sure."

"Can I go with you?"

"They could take the two of us about as easily as one. If you stay in the car, you can at least go for help if there's trouble."

"I guess that makes sense," Ebon replied moodily. After a moment he added, "You know, it's kind of strange . . . we go to see a man who's raped his daughter and killed his son, and he says to you, 'You ought to be ashamed of yourself,' and damned if I don't wind up feeling guilty as hell."

Ben looked at his son. "Not really so strange, Eb. I'd worry if you didn't feel a little that way."

The road to Chasson Hill snaked up through granite ridges and abandoned farms, where the pastures were already filled by advancing young trees. The Radeau place was a collection of ramshackle houses, barns and trailers near the bottom of a gully, through which ran a wide but shallow brook. Abandoned cars, snowmobiles and a rusty tractor littered the front yard. On the hardpacked earth near a well, a grizzled German shepherd that looked mean as the proverbial junkyard dog lay with his foot tangled in a chain that led to a nearby tree. The dog looked up when Ben parked his car nearby, but dozed again when no one got out of it immediately. Nobody was in sight. There was no sound, not even birds.

"Are you sure it's not crazy to go in there?" Ebon asked. "That dog alone—"

"It's chained."

"These people are pretty sore at you."

"Ninety-nine out of a hundred, nothing ever happens. This is my business, Eb. It's a job."

As Ben, camera in hand, approached the dog, the fear he'd been trying to hide from his son ebbed, and he got that old calm feeling which occasionally made danger almost attractive. The dog watched him for a moment, ears tilted forward, before jumping to its feet and springing forward. The chain was longer than Ben had thought and the possibility that it might be broken crossed his mind. Stepping backward, he caught his foot on an abandoned stove grating and went sprawling, still hanging on to his camera. The dog was brought up by its chain only about two feet away. A door at the front of the biggest farmhouse slammed, and two bearded Radeau brothers came running out, one carrying a baseball bat, the other an ax. They were much heavier than the elder Radeau, and from Ben's perspective on the ground they looked almost gigantic.

"Who the *hell* are you?" It was the one with a black beard.

Before Ben could answer he heard a scramble of feet behind him and spotted Ebon running to his rescue, or to share his demise. Glaring hard at the two men, Ebon was saying, "The police will be here any minute . . ."

"Good," the man with a brownish beard said. "They can arrest a couple of damn trespassers."

Struggling to his feet with Ebon's help and backing farther away from the furiously barking dog, Ben said, "I'm just here to try to clear up a misunderstanding. Can we talk somewhere without the dog?"

"What misunderstanding?" the black-bearded man asked. He stroked the dog to quiet it.

"Well, you know, there has been some talk about whatever happened here the other night. The trouble is, no reporter ever got your side of it. Everything heard or read was based on the police reports. The Albany *Post* wants to know what *you* and the other members of your family have to say."

"You better come in and talk to ma." The black-bearded one again.

Ma was the bitter, ravaged woman who had publicly charged her husband with murder and incest, but now she was telling a different story. There'd just been a party, a little drinking, and poor Seth had been killed by pure accident . . . fell down the stairs, God rest his soul. As for incest, she didn't know anything about that, but frankly she suspected that her daughter had got pregnant at school and was trying to put the blame on somebody else. Never did much care for her father . . .

While Ebon took notes, Ben took pictures of the people, the interior and the surrounding yard, including the dog. Nobody seemed to mind.

"Would you like a beer?" the Radeau who had carried an ax asked.

"Sure."

The beer came in a Genesee bottle, but it had the slightly sweet taste of home brew. Remembering his headline, Ben wondered whether this was just a prelude to more trouble, but the mother had become incredibly friendly. Like a good suburban matron, she said she was delighted to have him take pictures of "my family and my home," and asked for copies.

The man with the black beard silently escorted them to their van.

198

"What's going to happen when they read what you'll print about them?" Ebon asked.

"I don't know. They seem rather unpredictable. Well, one thing about the newspaper business—you meet such interesting people...."

"I know this sounds a little nuts, but I can't help feeling sorry for them."

"And I still say that's good," Ben told him. "And I also want to thank you for coming to my rescue when I was about to be attacked by a dog, a man with an ax and a man with a baseball bat."

Ebon couldn't entirely suppress a smile of pleasure. "Just instinct, I guess. I didn't have time to be scared or brave or anything—"

"Someone else might have had an instinct to get the hell out of here."

The two of them, father and son, exchanged brief looks, and Ben thought he had never in his life felt so close to his son.

AT a little after four-thirty that day, Ben put his photographs of the Radeaus on the bus to Albany. The next day they would appear in the *Star*, quite a few copies of which were sold in Livingston and there might be more trouble from the family in Chasson Hill, but he was just too tired to worry about it as he hurried home to Cliff House. He found Rose sitting on a chaise longue on the terrace. She was wearing a sleeveless summer dress, a print that he particularly liked. It revealed her arms as too thin, but her smile was so vital, and her eyes so full of life that it was—thank god—difficult to think of her as an invalid.

"Ben," she said, "this is a gorgeous place, but not much fun without you. Thank god you're home."

Leaning over, he kissed her forehead lightly.

"Hey," she said, "I'm not sure whether I've been kissed or blessed. Can't you do better than that?"

Sitting on the edge of the chaise, he gently kissed her lips.

"I'm so bad," she said. "I've been sitting out here all day, so restless I could take off like a rocket."

"I know the feeling."

"I've been watching the hummingbirds around that peony bush over there, and they make me feel even worse."

"What have you got against hummingbirds?"

"They're smaller than my finger and weigh less than an ounce, but they fly all the way to Mexico and points south every fall and back here every spring—I'm not even supposed to walk upstairs. Damn it, I don't mean to complain—"

"When you have your operation, Rosie, *we* can fly to Mexico."

"Oh god, the parallels! Mexico! That's where my mother planned to go after her operation!"

"The doctors didn't know anywhere near as much then . . ."

"I know. Ben, let's go up to my room. I need to be alone with you. Just alone . . . I need you to hold me, Ben."

He lay on the bed beside her, cradling her in his arms while she buried her face under his chin. There was that scent, that musky but clean fragrance that was so peculiar to her and to Annie. The skin of her shoulder was satiny. From far away a crow called some alarm, and was answered by its brothers.

"Oh, god, Ben, I love you so much." She took his hand and pressed it against her breast, holding it there tightly.

He tried to kiss her only lightly, but her lips were parted. Separating himself from her, he lay there, stroking her forehead and hair. He felt her gently caressing his thigh. "Rosie, it's going to be easier if we just don't let ourselves get started. And I'm as responsible as you. We can't afford games—"

"I'm sorry," she said, her eyes widening. "I wasn't playing a game—"

"I know. Rosie, I'm scared to death."

"I'm not. Let me be in charge, leave it up to me. Okay? . . ."

"I don't know. I'm not sure I can trust you, or myself."

"Look, damn it, I am not suicidal—"

"I know," he said, holding her hand. "But I worry. I can't help that."

"Ben, my attack must have been pretty awful to watch, I realize, but now you keep expecting it to happen again—"

"No, I know it's not going to happen again—"

"Poor Ben. I think you're even more scared than I am."

201

"I love you, Rosie. If your life goes, so does mine."

She didn't answer that, and he was grateful for the moment of silence.

Finally, "You know, Ben, I think I'm more mature about sex than you are."

"Probably. I'm just older, not wiser."

"Well, for a little while, just let *me* be in charge of our sex life, will you? Let me say go when I feel strong enough. Let me figure out the things I can do without getting into trouble, and let me say stop when I have to. Is that all right?"

"If you're really careful, if you promise not to—"

"There you go again. The deal is, don't tell me what I can do and what I can't do. Besides, an argument, getting upset, hurts me as much as anything else we can do."

"Well, all right, I am at your command, but I'm also one scared soldier."

"*Relax,*" she said.

She was massaging his chest when Ann knocked at the door to announce dinner. It was a welcome, and annoying, interruption.

Ann cooked dinner on the terrace that night. She was wearing a white bikini, and a cheery smile as she served her ancient grandmother and older sister. The contrast between the sisters fascinated Ben. Ann, tanned and statuesque; poor Rosie, pale and thin, and yet Ann somehow still seemed the more vulnerable. There was a natural timidity and gentleness in her face, while Rose's fragile features still reflected a will, a capacity for anger at any injustice, all softened by humor and the affection she felt especially for those around her now. And although Annie in her bikini was enough to tempt any man, her rather placid face somehow promised much less than the fire which appeared to be at the core of her sister.

Fascinated . . . yes, but also annoyed at himself for indulging in such comparisons, Ben, sitting on the low stone wall at the end of the terrace, shook them off and attacked his steak.

"Where's Eb?" Rose asked.

"When he left the office he said he was going to work on the boat for a while," Ben told her, and then gave a blow-by-blow of how Ebon had come rushing to his rescue at the Radeaus'.

"We ought to award him a medal of honor," Rose said.

"Or have his head examined," Ann put in.

A joke of course, said lightly, but it made Ben wonder, as he often had, about the real nature of the relationship between his son and Ann. He never had heard Ann actually compliment Ebon, as he was always complimenting her. From what he could remember of teenage love affairs, theirs seemed oddly docile, enlivened mostly by angry little spats. Perhaps he should be grateful, he thought, for the fact that they didn't go about with their arms forever draped around each other or come blushing from secluded spots. Perhaps wrongly, he had assumed that they were having a full physical relationship, but there was something about Annie's casual manner toward his son that made Ben doubt it. Could poor Eb be caught up in an adolescent passion that was unrequited?

In view of his son's rather dramatic good looks and tempestuous nature, that seemed unlikely, but perhaps Annie was just one of those girls who don't want to get involved in the customary steamy adventures of adolescence, and who could blame her? But if Annie, with her spectacular physical endowments, was Ebon's *belle dame sans merci*, Ben felt sorry for his son. Perhaps Annie and her reserve explained some of Ebon's moodier days. . . .

Ebon was coming up from the boat now. He wore only dungarees, and his muscular torso was mottled with grease.

"Hey, I got the engine started," he announced with a grin. "Want to take a spin with me tonight, Annie?"

"I'm sort of scared of boats."

"With Ebon I wouldn't say you had much to worry about," Rose said. "And congratulations, Eb! I hear you were an authentic hero today."

203

"Like my Tom," grammie said. "By god, he'd charge anything when he got his dander up!"

"My dad, too," Rose added. "He took on three state cops when he thought they were hassling a friend of his."

"Yeah, but my Tom always won," grammie retorted. "That was the English blood in him."

"I really didn't do anything," Ebon said. "Dad handled the situation with a ton of sweet talk."

"A fearsome weapon," Rose replied.

"Come *on*, Annie," Ebon said, putting his hand on her shoulder. "There's going to be a moon and everything. . . ."

Ben saw Annie's shoulders contract, and not with pleasure. "Please, Eb. Your hands are all over grease—"

"I'll *wash* them. Come on, just take a short spin with me."

"*Okay.*"

A short while later Ebon and Ann trotted down the steep trail to the boat. A half-moon rose from behind the purple outline of a distant mountain, casting a silver path on the still waters of the lake, with the planet Venus visible just above it. Grammie took her knitting from a bag and Rose fitfully napped on the chaise. After a while Ben saw the dark outline of the small cruiser emerge from the shadows by the shore and head slowly toward the center of the lake. Perhaps his father had stood on this terrace watching and worrying when Ben at Ebon's age had taken Heidi out for just a little spin. Heidi like Ann had also seemed aloof for a long time, and he had gone through all the tortures of longing to touch while knowing that his hand would not be welcome. Heidi, of course, had been quite right to try to avoid him. Almost all they'd had in common was an appreciation of a moonlit night and the fierce symmetry, as the poet said, of each other's youth— which, of course, had soon betrayed them.

Suddenly Ben found himself hoping that Annie's powers of resistance would be greater than Heidi's, and that his son was more responsible than he'd ever been. A few hours of enjoying too much moonlight aboard the *Indian Princess* and drinking too much wine had convinced Heidi she would be disgraced forever if she didn't marry Ben. Perhaps that quaint belief was more sinful . . . or at least more dangerous . . . than anything they had done, more deserving of the final punishment: twenty-four years of a too often loveless marriage.

Still, he reminded himself, young people were more sophisticated nowadays, or at least were supposed to be. Once when Ben had tried to alert Ebon to the dangers of too much too soon, he had detected a smile of something very like condescension on his son's face.

In the distance the *Indian Princess* crossed the bright path of the moon and disappeared into the shadows of a faraway mountain, her port running light glowing like a ruby on her bow.

"It certainly is a lovely night," Rose said, sitting up and stretching. "I'm sorry I dozed off."

"You're supposed to be resting," grammie said. "I always say, if your mother had rested enough—"

"I know."

"Nobody could ever get Amy to quit working," grammie said to Ben.

"If she had quit working, we all would have starved to death," Rose said, "so let's drop that one, okay?"

Still muttering, grammie increased the tempo of the clack of her knitting needles.

"I'm going to bed," Rose said. "If I'm going to sleep, I might as well be comfortable."

She kissed grammie on the forehead and moved toward the house, her walk as gracefully energetic as it had always been. Ben went with her, conscious of the fact that grammie was following them with her eyes, probably wondering if they were going to share the same room.

"I'll build you a fire, Rosie," he said loud enough for the

old woman to hear. "These rooms get a little damp in the evening."

The breeze from the lake had been blowing through the big open windows, and the master bedroom was indeed chilly, though fragrant with the last of the lilacs and the roses which had been sent as get-well presents. After closing the windows, Ben lit a fire that Ebon had laid in the big stone fireplace.

"Would you like some music?" he asked. "I think this old phonograph works. Some of the records date back to my father's time."

"What are they?"

" 'Rhapsody in Blue' . . ."

"Oh, play that!"

The music was a little scratchy, but still, for him, magical in the moonlight. Rose stood warming her hands at the fire. "Would you like some champagne?" she asked.

"I don't think we have any."

"The girls from my old office at the mill sent me a bottle. I put it in the refrigerator. I'll change while you're getting it."

When he came back with the champagne and two glasses, he found her sitting on a pillow in front of the fire. She was wearing a pair of her old white pajamas, which were now too big for her. The firelight flickered on her hair. He handed her an ordinary wine glass filled with champagne.

"I can just have a sip," she said. "You drink it."

"There's quite a lot to celebrate today," he said, and told her about the speed with which their papers were moving off the newsstands, as well as the business he had done with the Albany *Star*.

"God, you do make things happen."

"It's my line of work, Rosie."

"I know, but with most men I've known, including, I'm afraid, my father, the only thing you could count on was that they'd screw everything up."

"Patience. I may fit into that category yet," he said, lying

206

down on the hooked rug beside her. "One day does not a *New York Times* make."

"Don't worry, you'll be terribly, terribly successful and then you'll get a terribly, terribly beautiful secretary with boobs out to here and then you'll start taking some terribly, terribly long business trips. Isn't that what always happens?"

"Rosie, cut it out . . . are you really worried that I'd ever leave you?"

"Hell no! But if you must know, hell yes! I've seen it happen before."

"Sure. Your father left your mother, and no doubt when she was ill . . ."

"It wasn't his fault, really. He couldn't make any money here. He was no help so he went back to Ireland. He was going to send money home—"

"Did he?"

"Hell no. Dad can't even pay his own bar bill."

"That must have been rotten for all of you, but I'm not your father. History doesn't have to repeat itself."

"I understand that in my head, darling, but you know how it is. I was even getting the jitters when you were a little late getting back this afternoon."

He sat up and put his arm around her.

"Somebody told me once that love can last only between equals," she said. "If a woman can't give sex or money or do any work of any sort, what would you say her chances were?" Her diamond ring flashed in the firelight as she nervously stroked back her hair.

"I don't think theories apply to our situation—which, I remind you, is temporary."

The diamond flashed again as she repeated her nervous gesture and said nothing.

"Rosie, forget the words. Like they say, actions speak louder. I've changed my life, such as it was, to be with you. I'm *here*, and *I'm going to keep on being here*."

207

"I know, Ben," she said, taking hold of his hand. "I'm sorry to be such a drag. I just get the blues, you know? Thanks for letting me talk them out."

"Anytime."

"It's all such a . . . sort of vicious circle. The *least* I should be is good to be with, some jokes and good cheer—"

"You are."

The cockatiels, whose cage had been covered for the night, suddenly started chirping to each other.

"It's those damn birds that depressed me," she said. "They're worse than the hummingbirds."

"I thought you'd like them."

"Sure! Do you know what they do all day long? They make love! First they screw and then they celebrate, chirping up a real storm. . . . Let's go to bed, Ben. At least I can feel you next to me."

They got into the big spool bed. She lay with her head on his shoulder, her hair soft against the side of his face. The scratchy Gershwin record kept repeating itself.

"You make me feel so *warm*," she said. "I was cold all the time in that damn hospital, no matter how many blankets. . . ."

"I've been cold a long while too, Rosie."

She moved, pressing her lips to his cheek, and he put his arm around her.

The spool bed squeaked.

"This is a very old bed, isn't it?" she whispered.

"It's been in my family for a hundred years, I guess."

"Think of all the things that must have happened in it. . . ."

He knew his mother's father had died in it but he did not tell her that. He remembered many nights with Heidi in this bed, and he did not tell her that. What he said was, "I think I was probably conceived here. My mother and father spent their first summer in this cottage, and I was born the next April."

"Nine months from July!" she said, counting them on her fingers. "How wonderful! Good old bed!"

She sat up and patted the headboard with her fingers.

Returning to his arms, she kissed him hard. "I wish we could conceive a son," she said.

"When you're better, maybe we will."

She began to stroke his chest, then his belly.

"I think you'd better stop that."

"You promised I could be in charge of this department. Do you feel . . . You do . . . Lie still!"

"I can't lie still."

"Pretend you're at a wicked massage parlor," she said, getting up and pulling the blankets off the bed. "Have you ever been to one?"

"No."

"Why?"

"Loveless sex is not exactly my thing."

"Well, this isn't loveless."

From the drawer of a bedside table she took a bottle of baby oil and started rubbing it on his chest. As she worked downward, he involuntarily contracted his knees.

"Don't you like this?"

"Yes. I'm also, I guess, a little embarrassed."

"Well, it's our first time. To tell the truth, I'm embarrassed too, but if we learn together . . . try to relax and tell me anything you want me to do . . ."

She didn't need him to say a word. Her hands and lips were so loving that any once embarrassing aspects of the situation disappeared. The climax left him momentarily breathless. She snuggled beside him, throwing her arms around him.

"Was it all right?"

"It was marvelous."

"Oh thank you, Ben. You don't know what that does for me—"

"You don't know what it does for me, either," he replied wryly.

"I *can* give a little. And my heartbeat hardly increased at all. When I started enjoying it too much, why I just began reciting the Gettysburg Address to myself, and then Joyce Kilmer's 'Trees.' That brought my pulse right down."

They laughed together.

He'd been asleep for only three hours when Ben woke up with the distinct feeling that something was wrong. Rose slept beside him, a lovely smile on her face, her breathing soft and even, but from the glow on the terrace he knew that the living room lights had been left on. He put on pajamas and a bathrobe. The lights in the kitchen were also blazing. Checking Ebon's room, he found a tangle of clothes on the floor, but no Ebon. Tapping on the door of Ann's room, he received no answer. After knocking louder, he was answered by grammie in the next room.

"They ain't home yet. You figure they're all right?"

"Sure, grammie. Eb's good with boats."

Pouring himself a Scotch, he glanced at his watch. It was almost three-thirty in the morning. Hadn't Ebon promised Annie to take only a brief spin? Well, he wouldn't be the first young man to keep his girl out late on a summer night.

Moodily he walked out onto the terrace. The half-moon had sunk behind a mountain, but the stars were so bright that the lake still glowed. An early morning haze was gathering in the distance, turning the horizon milky, giving the dark tops of islands a look of floating in midair. The narrow, crooked lake was deep, but full of unmarked rocks and subject to storms which could come twisting through the mountain ravines with astonishing ferocity. Many an ocean sailor who had expected a small Adirondack lake to be calm had left the bones of his boat in the tangle of branches which covered the bottom of Lost Lake two hundred feet down in some places.

But now there was little wind and Ebon had been brought up on the lake. Since childhood he had taken to the water, as he had to the forests, with an easy mastery that had caused Heidi to boast about her ancestors, some of whom had been *couriers du bois*, early French explorers who had been as much at home as the Indians were in the wilderness and waterways of the frontier. He also recalled how, when Ebon had developed an uncanny ability to repair marine engines, he had infuriated Heidi by remarking, "It must be that old *couriers du bois* blood coming to the fore again."

Only in automobiles had Ebon caused his father worry, and that was not because of a lack of skill, but a not unusual teenage recklessness.... Now, suddenly, Ben found himself worrying about the possibility of this recklessness overcoming his son's natural caution on a boat.

The hands of his watch crept toward four. If Ebon wasn't paying attention in that mist, he could easily blunder out of the crooked channel, splitting the old boat like a rotten melon on some rock. Probably he and Annie could swim ashore, but the lake was still cold this early in the summer. Fire was always a hazard with a gasoline-powered boat. And most probable of all, a night with a pretty girl like Annie would be difficult to end. There had been many dawns when he and Heidi had come sneaking into the house, hoping to escape the wrath of his sleeping parents....

"What the hell have you been doing, Ben?" his father had once roared, a question he obviously could not answer truthfully.

"The engine conked out, dad," he had replied, or, "We ran out of gas," or, "The mist got so thick we had to anchor."

Afraid to press the matter, his father had glared at him, finished off the glass of whiskey which had helped him to keep his long vigil, and had walked unsteadily to bed....

Perhaps nature has its own system of punishments, Ben thought, and the wayward son becomes the worried father almost before he remembers to wind his watch. Sipping his whiskey, Ben paced up and down the terrace.

The silhouette of the mountains was beginning to show black against the sky when he heard voices on the steep path from the boathouse. Ebon was singing a Scottish song that

211

Ben had taught him long ago and that his father had learned from an old Harry Lauder record: "If you can say it a braw bricht moonlit nicht, well you're all right if you can!"

"Damn it, be *quiet*." Annie's whisper, sounding very cross.

Soon Ebon was climbing the stone steps from the path to the terrace with Ann steadying him. She was wearing her white bikini with a gray sweatshirt, he his dungarees and an old tweed sports coat with no shirt. Her sweatshirt was grease-stained, as was his tanned chest. He was carrying a bottle of red wine that spilled as he staggered to a chair.

"Hello, old dad!" he said with a foolish grin. "You just getting in? What do you mean, getting home so late?"

"I'm sorry," Ann cut in. "Honestly, I haven't been able to do a thing with him. . . ." She sounded, and looked, entirely sober.

"What happened?" Ben asked quietly, astonished at the anger he felt toward his son.

"Well, first the engine broke down. . . ." Ann said. "Well, I'm not sure whether it really did, or whether it was one of *his* jokes. So we just anchored and sat out there. Forever. He said the engine was flooded and had to drain—"

"You don't understand carburetors." Ebon was shaking his finger at her, and grinning.

"Go to bed, Eb," Ben said. "We'll talk about it in the morning."

"Hey, don't tell me what to do, old dad . . . I'm a sight taller than you are . . . come on, stand up, let's measure—"

"Go to bed, boy," Ben said, his voice rising along with his anger. "I want no nonsense—"

"I thought you weren't going to call me boy anymore."

"When you act like one, that's what you get called. Now, damn it, go to bed."

Ebon took a swig from his bottle, the red wine trickling down his chin and naked chest. Then, with awkward dignity, he started walking toward the house. Halfway there he stopped and turned to Ann. "Are you really mad at me, Annie?"

"I'm not mad at you," she replied wearily. "Go to bed."

"You sound mad at me and you look mad at me," Ebon observed mournfully. "Can I have a kiss?"

"For god's sake, Eb, what do you want from me? I'm sick of all this . . . Will you please, *please* get out of my life for a few hours? . . ."

Looking shocked, Ebon took a dramatic swig from his bottle and went off to his room. Ann sank into a chair on the terrace, buried her face in her hands and burst into tears, and before even attempting to talk to her Ben hurried to get a blanket from his bedroom and covered her with it.

"Lord, I hope we don't wake up Rosie," Ann said. "This is just what she needs, a giant row."

"Rosie is fast asleep. What can I do to help?"

"Oh, I don't know, Ben . . . I'm all confused. First Eb gets furious at me, then I get furious at him. Is that what they call love?"

"Sometimes."

"I hate it when he drinks like that. I hate pot. I hate just about everything he wants to do. I don't know why I even go with him—"

"Does he get like this often?"

"Quite a lot. At least, ever since his mother left him here— I guess he's got an awful lot on his mind—"

"Like what?"

"College, for one thing. Did he tell you that he heard?"

"No."

"I guess he's scared, and he's mad at his mother."

"Why?"

"Well, the word from the colleges went to her because her place in Florida is listed as his legal address. She was off in the Bahamas someplace and didn't even read her mail for about two weeks. Then she opened the letters, even though

213

they were addressed to Eb. When she called him she acted all broken up because he didn't get into Fair Harvard."

"Did he get in anywhere else?"

"Sure. Columbia and the state university."

"Well, Columbia isn't so bad. Why doesn't he want to talk to me?"

"He doesn't want to go to Columbia and take premed or predentistry, like his mother wants. He wants to go to the state college in Albany and study forestry. He's sure you'll say no."

Forestry for Ebon seemed almost inevitable to Ben, and yet he had not expected it. He shrugged. "If that's what he wants..."

"In two years, he says, he could be a forest ranger."

"It sounds like sort of a dead end to me," Ben said, "but we're different people, and I've no intention of giving him a hard time."

"There would be a lot more he could do if he finished a four-year course.... Ben, I feel awful about this."

"Why?"

"I shouldn't tell you this, but Eb is planning his whole *life* around me. I think he's taking the quickest route to a job so we can get married, and I'm not even sure I want to get married, to him or anybody else."

"Have you told him that?"

"Yes. He just says he'll convince me. And then he wants to ... well, mess around, and when I say no, he gets drunk. I'm sorry, I don't mean to sound like this but—"

"Why do you see him if you feel this way?"

"I *like* him, I guess maybe I even love him in a way, sometimes... I mean, anyone would when he's at his best. But one thing I *don't* want to do is to get married early and join that awful Twenty-three Club down at Joe's bar. Sis has really read the riot act to me about that. And I *don't* want to get pregnant, like nearly half my class at school." A shy, half-embarrassed look came over her face. "Ben, I know I'm young, but I've had my eyes open for a long time. It may sound corny, but I want to amount to something. People around here think that's crazy talk, but I really do."

"I'd bet you will, too."

"Sis and grammie have saved every dime they could to give me a chance. I think I'd be crazy if I booted the whole thing just because the damn moon is out."

"You got it," Ben said with a smile.

"But Eb . . . he can't see beyond the damn moon. When I say I want to live in New York and travel to Europe, he gets mad. All he wants to do is live in the damn woods. What am I, some kind of a squaw? I hate the damn woods. I'm sorry, but I do. They're creepy and wet." She smiled and Ben smiled back.

"Seriously, I don't know why Eb thinks I'm so just right for him. He talks about us sacking out in a sleeping bag on top of some damn mountain. He says he's going to teach me to cook trout on a campfire with just a bunch of sticks or something. If we get the right equipment he says that as a special treat we can camp on top of Mt. Marcy in the dead of winter. And when I don't just go *ape* over that idea, he says he'll teach me!"

"Do you know what kind of work you do want to do?"

The shy look came back again. "Well, it's embarrassing saying this to you, but I think I want to work hard enough at photography to find out if that's it. I've been dying to ask you if you think I have talent, but I know that's baloney. You can't tell what I'll do, or what I can do. You can only tell me what I've done."

"I can guess at ability, but not at drive, and even ability without a crazy kind of drive just makes an amateur."

She nodded. "Anyway, I want to take pictures like crazy. If I get good enough, would I still have to go to college?"

"Desirable, but not necessary."

"Rosie shouldn't have to think about saving money for me now. Especially if she has an operation."

215

"Can your father help?"

"We're lucky when we can go a year without sending money to him. Things are tough in Ireland, I guess."

"We'll work it out. The paper's off to a good start. Maybe you won't have to worry about money."

Stretching wearily, Ann got up. "I guess I better turn in. Lord, the sun is coming up."

"Get a good sleep. Annie, I think you're sounding very sensible. And ... don't worry too much about Eb. What you're both going through is probably a kind of standard operating procedure for people your age. Believe me, I've been there. ..." And in ways he didn't like to face, maybe was still there. ...

"You know what Rosie said?" Ann was smiling now. "When I visited her in the hospital, she said she thinks you were sent to us. And grammie said maybe, but she's not quite sure yet."

Ben laughed. "Maybe we were all sent to each other."

"But some of us don't seem exactly sure for what," she added with a mischievous grin, and disappeared into the house.

16

THAT morning Ben had trouble getting back to sleep.
He honestly worried that Ebon might be going the route of
alcoholism, like Ben's father and, at times of stress, Ben himself. Although he had been angered by his son's behavior, he
could easily sympathize with the acute loneliness and the sexual hunger that he knew must be driving him. In a way girls
like Annie were a kind of trap set by nature. In appearance
they were so sensual and seemed to offer such promise of
delight that few young men could penetrate the disguise
enough to see an ambitious young person who just was not
that much interested in the complicated emotion of love at
the moment. If the world were more sensible, only women
who wanted to go promptly to bed would look like Annie,
and ambitious would-be photographers and world travelers
would be lean and boyish, a lure to the mind but not the body.

This, however, was clearly not a day for editing the world.
It was a day for accepting, accepting the constant fear that
Rose would have another heart attack, accepting the worry
that his son was undergoing more than the temporary upsets
of adolescence.

Fear seemed to breed itself as Ben lay rigid in the bed, trying not to disturb Rose by tossing and turning. With hospital
costs as they were, an open-heart operation could cost $20,000
or more. If he was going to send both Ann and Ebon to

college, as he wanted, that could shoot maybe $40,000 more. Although the paper had started well, it could be expected to stay in the red for at least a year, and despite the profit he had made from his house in Santa Barbara, he would soon be in financial trouble.

Threats as a news photographer weren't new, but the thought of the Radeaus bothered him all the same. The pictures which would appear in the *Star* would be cruel, as many good pictures were, and in a sense had been taken under a pretense of nominal friendship. Although there was a ferocity about this strange family of hill dwellers, he had also discerned a kind of courage even in the worst of circumstances. They wanted to be let alone in their agonies, and would fight for that right.

"You ought to be ashamed of yourself," the man accused of raping his daughter and killing his son had said, and his wife, sitting surrounded by a *Tobacco Road* crew in that litter-strewn, falling-down farmhouse, had said she would like to have him photograph her family and her home.

Out of all this the *Star* was sure to make a lurid story. The thing, though, that bothered Ben most was the thought that he wouldn't really blame the Radeaus for feeling that they were being victimized in their hour of distress, and he wouldn't be surprised if their outrage turned to old-fashioned mountain vengeance of some sort.

In the end a man has to trust in God whether he believes in Him or not, Ben thought. No one is ever really safe, but if danger occupies the mind too much, it corrodes everything. Glancing at Rose in the bright light of morning, he felt an urge to put his arm around her, but didn't want to wake her up. Her breathing continued to be soft and regular, a blessing in itself.

Ben was having Sunday breakfast alone at ten the next morning when Ebon came in, his sharp, tanned face bleary-eyed, an Alka-Seltzer in hand.

"Well, dad, I guess I have another lecture coming. Let's get it over with now."

"No lecture," Ben replied, and took a sip of his tea.

"No lecture, no advice?"

"No advice."

"And no punishment?"

"Not from me."

"Why?"

"I can't think of anything to say that you don't already know. And whatever you've done will have its own consequences, I expect."

"I see," Ebon said, sitting down.

"I wish I *could* help you," Ben said, "but I honestly don't know how. If you can figure out a way, let me know."

"Why the hell are you carrying on like this? ... Was Annie talking to you last night?"

"A little."

"You know, she's really a marvelous girl, but sometimes she can also be a bitch."

"Do you mind if I cut this conversation short?" Ben asked, getting up. "Let's all try to steady down with as few recriminations all around as possible."

"Sure, fine with me ... anyway, I got to go feed her damn horse. While *she's* out with her camera committing great art, that mare has still got to eat. Not to mention the other animals over there. So you see, I'm not entirely useless."

All her life, Rose had looked forward to the Fourth of July in Livingston, by far the biggest celebration of the year. Ticonderoga, twenty miles to the east, boasted on bumper stickers that it offered "The Best Fourth in the North," a slogan that the Livingston chamber of commerce liked so much that they blithely claimed it for their own.

The celebration in Livingston always started at nine in the morning, when a parade began from the village square down Main Street. After a day of contests and exhibitions there was a giant display of fireworks on the shores of Lost Lake and a street dance with a local rock band that lasted most of the night in the center of the village. These organized events contributed only a small part to the Mardi Gras spirit which took over the town. Every bar was so crowded that, in defiance of the law, trays of drinks were passed to the mob surrounding their doors on the street. According to long-established custom, the owners of the stately homes on and near the green held open house for their friends and leaders of the parade. When strangers wandered in, they were rarely evicted.

People who had moved away from Livingston long ago often returned for the Fourth, giving the holiday the flavor of a homecoming. The old and the middle-aged wore their Sunday best, while more freedom than usual was given to young people who liked to dress outrageously. Young women wore braless T-shirts, muscular men wore red satin shirts open to the navel, and long after the fad of "streaking" passed in the rest of the country, youngsters occasionally tried it again in Livingston on the Glorious Fourth, causing delighted boos and cheers before they were packed off for a few hours in the jail.

Summer people swelled the crowd and nearly doubled the prices in most restaurants. Families from nearby towns, where the Fourth was celebrated less gloriously, sometimes brought the total number of spectators to more than ten thousand, twice the normal population of the village.

"Last year we had eleven thousand people here," the police chief once observed with a straight face, "and almost a hundred of them were cold sober."

Fondly remembering all this excitement, Rose longed to accompany Ben as he covered the Fourth for their paper, but the thought of getting caught in a crowd scared her and she finally decided to stay in the van, where she could nap if she got tired.

The morning of this Fourth dawned cold and rainy. At

about eight-thirty Ben and the others got into the van, all except grammie, who said that if thousands of people went out on such a day to see a bunch of damn fools march, they could do it without her. Ebon drove as close to the action as the police would permit a press car to go while Ben and Ann prepared to take pictures. Rose sat in an armchair which Ebon had put in the van for her, feeling quite regal in a dress with a red, white and blue pattern. In her black leather bag she had her digitalis and a bottle of water, which increased her sense of security.

As they parked near the war monuments at the green, where the parade was making up, she slid open the side door of the van to get a better view. A troop of Girl Scouts that she had once headed saw her and gathered around to say they were glad that she was out of the hospital. Some of the old legionnaires joined them, and a tall man in a dripping Indian costume waved from the green, shouting, "Welcome home, Rosie!"

A man with a bullhorn announced the imminent start of the parade, and Rosie's well-wishers hurried to their places.

"Damn," Rose said, blowing her nose on a tissue. "There's nothing those people wouldn't say behind my back, but I do believe they're glad I'm alive."

"Don't you know that you're loved all over this town?" Ben asked with a smile.

"They love my old man more. Dad *really* gives them something to talk about."

A bugle blared and the parade started to move, headed by three octogenarians in the blue uniform of the American Legion, the last veterans of World War I in Livingston who could march in a parade. The shortest of the three, Ben knew, was a survivor of the Battle of the Marne, perhaps the worst butchery the world had ever seen, and also a survivor of some thirty years as a sweeper in the paper mill, which he often said he hated worse than the army. The tallest of the three had been in the Marines only about four months and had

221

never left Washington, but during a long career as a state senator he had become a professional veteran, and now stepped along very smartly for an old man. The stout veteran in the center of this trio Ben had never seen before, but he obviously had rather too well fortified himself for this march in the rain, and had a terrible time holding his flag erect.

Ben could not understand why the beat of drums and the blare of bugles made him so emotional . . . in all the wars he had seen, no one ever played any music, nor had flags been much in evidence. Still, the three old World War I veterans walking in the rain with their teetering flagpole moved him, and the solemn beat of the drums sounded like the echo of footsteps from the past. Getting out of the van with his camera, Ben studied the three leaders of the procession. They had the sunken faces of old men, but even the one with the wavering flag was holding his head high, and there was pride in their eyes as they led the whole Fourth of July parade. Ben tried to catch that glint in his camera. As the men came abreast of him, on impulse he snapped to attention and gave them a full military salute. It was promptly returned by the man nearest him, the professional veteran. The others kept staring straight ahead but they were smiling as they marched into the driving rain.

Into this rain the veterans of four wars marched, the drums sounding duller as they became soaked, the bugles often ragged. Only about twenty young men represented the hundreds who had gone to Vietnam from that region, and they walked with a certain defiance which made them, alone amongst the veterans, look like fighting men.

Perhaps for the sake of contrast, a girls' marching band followed, a dozen nymphs with trumpets and drums followed by more who carried fake rifles of white wood. The rain had molded their uniforms of red satin to the forms of their nubile bodies, and there was something wonderfully incongruous about their military accouterments.

"They're the ones I want to fight," Ebon said.

222

"You would," Ann said. He didn't answer back.

The girls' marching band was followed by a solemn phalanx of businessmen in raincoats, the members of the chamber of commerce. One of these was a tall, handsome man about forty years old who strode along with military bearing.

"Do you know who that tall fellow is?" Rose asked.

"Not exactly," Ben replied.

"That's Harry Richardson. He owns the Birdseye Motel. About five years ago, everybody thought he was finished in this town."

"Why?" Ebon asked.

"A maid went in to clean one of the rooms in his place and found him there with a young man. She started to scream and all hell broke loose."

"What did they do to him?" Ann asked.

"The state took his liquor license away for a while and there was talk of running him out of town, but it finally blew over. Still it must take guts for him to march like that in the parade. This is the first year he's done it since then."

Next came a new ambulance belonging to the emergency squad and another with EDWARD CASE FUNERAL HOME in large plastic letters on the sides. These were followed by a luxurious new pickup truck with a sign LIV. MED. ASSOC. Three armchairs had been placed under a well-rigged tarpaulin in the back. In these sat the town's three physicians, all in their seventies but still imposing men as they waved at the crowd.

"I bet they have their emergency equipment with them," Rose said. "A jar full of leeches, a lance for bleeding people, and a hundred forms for collecting medicare and the mill health insurance."

"Now, now, sis," Ann said. "You know that grammie swears by Dr. Bill."

"That's just because he doesn't use any newfangled modern methods like sterilizing his instruments. I'm sorry, Ben, but just maybe I wouldn't have had rheumatic fever if that bastard had learned how to control a child's fever."

223

"Could you sue him for malpractice after all this time?" Ebon asked.

"Probably not. I'm not just talking about myself. Those three old vultures draw down at least a hundred grand apiece in this little burg, maybe two hundred, with all the health insurance people have. And for all that money we get medical care about as primitive as anything this side of the African bush. Would you let me write a column for the paper about that, Ben?"

"You're the publisher, but you better damn well document it."

"Everybody has horror stories about the hospital around here. We've got no obstetrician, we've got no pediatrician—we got nothing except three senile GP's who chase out every young doctor who wants to come in."

"Document it."

"That'll be easy, but you'll have to make me one big promise: if I get sick again, don't put me in that place, no matter what the emergency. If I wake up to see old Dr. Bill come fumbling at me, I'll die of fright right there."

Not much caring for this turn of the conversation, Ben said, "Anything you want, Rosie. Let's go up to see the firemen work out. There's always a picture there."

Just before he started, Ben saw a carrot-haired young man approaching with a hot-dog wagon under an umbrella.

"Anybody want a hot dog?"

Both Ebon and Ann did. As the vendor grew near, he said, "Hi, Mr. Winslow. That was some show you had on television this morning—"

"What show?"

"That stuff about the Radeaus with all them pictures. They gave you credit."

"Oh, yeah," Ben said. "The *Star* has its own TV station that gets its news from the paper."

"Will they pay you for it?" Ebon asked.

"I guess. I keep thinking about the Radeaus. They probably don't read newspapers, but they have one damn big television set, I noticed."

"Are you really worried about them?" Ann asked.

"I guess I'm just in no mood for a lot of trouble."

"I don't think that that bunch kills people," Rose said, putting a hand on his arm, "except their own kin. They destroy property, but I've never heard of any of them being up for murder until now."

"Well, that's a real comfort," Ben said. "Let's go see those hook and ladders work out."

Ebon skirted the village to avoid traffic and started up a long hill. Coming in the other direction Ben saw a truck loaded with logs going unusually fast down a steep grade. As it came near, it suddenly swerved toward them. Ebon expertly gave way, scrambling on the soft shoulder of the road before regaining the pavement. "Wow! That was *close.*"

As the truck had thundered past, Ben had caught a glimpse of a large bearded man. It was, of course, ridiculous to think that only Radeaus had beards, and there was no evidence that the near-accident had been deliberate. Still, Ben's heart was pounding, and he hoped that Rose hadn't been similarly affected.

"Are you okay?" he asked her.

"It's a funny thing about being worried about my insides," she said. "I don't worry so much about anything coming at me from the outside. I feel damn near magically invulnerable."

On a broad level field at the top of the hill, fire engines from Livingston and five surrounding towns were drawn up in the rain. The crews of the hook and ladders were competing to see which tall rig could be raised first while the men from other red trucks raced to a nearby pond, rolling great reels of heavy hose, or dragging it like an endless snake. As

225

the engines supplied pressure, the hoses stiffened and a nozzle writhed until captured. Three of the big hoses gushed at almost the same time as their crews pulled them toward empty oil drums, which had been set afire with gasoline. The Whitehall volunteers put their barrel out first, with the Defiance Hose Company of Ticonderoga placing second. When the Livingston Hose Company won third place, its members turned their hoses on their burly chief, making him dance and claw the air for a moment, as though he were trying to climb right up into the sky.

Ann caught this bit of action with her camera while Ben was changing his film.

"You have a good eye, Annie," he said as she clicked away. "You know a good picture when you see one."

She flushed, and smiled. "If you do a book on a small town, is this the kind of stuff you want?"

"I want whatever interests or moves you and me. I'll give you credit for everything of yours I use."

That, Ben soon realized, was the best thing he had ever done for the manufacturers of film, for Annie on this day began a nonstop program of photographing Livingston as though it were the scene of every crime and human triumph in the world, which, come to think of it, in some microcosmic sense it was. Shortly before noon the rain stopped, but the heavy fire engines sank into the muddy field as they tried to get to the road. Two yellow farm tractors arrived to help and there was much floundering around with chains and cursing.

"What happens if there's a real fire now?" Ebon asked.

"That depends," Rose replied. "On one Fourth a few years ago, a poor little old drunk who lived in a trailer up on Sellick Hill Road dropped a cigarette behind the pillows of his couch. When he saw a few wisps of smoke, he panicked and called the fire department. A few minutes later fifteen engines roared up, every piece of equipment in the county, and about forty hoses almost washed his trailer right off the hill. A real

226

over-save ... but the boys got carried away in the spirit of the day...."

At Ben's request, Ebon drove toward the office of Livingston *Life,* parking on a side street a few blocks away when the traffic became impassable. Rose stretched out on the mattress to rest and Ann stayed with her while Ebon walked with his father to the office. The middle section of Main Street had been roped off and was crowded with people drinking beer, strolling with children on their shoulders, playing guitars and singing.

"Boy, am I glad to see you!" Lillian said. She was sitting at a typewriter while two secretaries they had hired were answering telephones.

"What's up?" Ben asked.

"The place is going crazy! First, you've had two more threatening phone calls. One in the same kind of raspy voice that had called before. The second spoke in not much more than a growl."

"What did they say?"

"Don't ask me to repeat it! I wrote it down. And I gave copies to the police."

The first caller had said, "Don't think you can keep crapping on us and get away with it, you lying two-faced bastard—"

The second: "Men can die and houses burn. Soon, you cocksucker, you will learn."

"The guy's a poet," Ben said, handing the paper to Ebon.

"Good God, dad, do we have to take this kind of crap? What are the cops doing?"

"They say they're looking into it," Lillian told him. "They're trying to get the phone company to help, but they say short calls like that are almost impossible to trace."

"It *must* be the Radeaus," Ebon said. "Why can't *we* call *them* up? Threats can be a two-way street."

"What do you suggest we say?" Ben asked sardonically.

" 'If my house burns, yours will too. I can bleed but so can you.'?"

"Why not? Let me make the call." Ebon's earlier compassion for them had vanished.

"Come on, Eb, we're supposed to be pros. We just report crap like this to the police. We don't break the law ourselves."

"It's no laughing matter," Lillian said. "Both those calls came in about ten minutes after the hour. Do you know WXYZ has those pictures you took on every news program? I think that every time they're shown, those people just keep getting madder and madder."

Ben shrugged. "Like I said, occupational hazard."

"The *Star* just came in," Lillian added. "It's carrying the same pictures."

She handed him the Albany newspaper, which was folded to show the half page he had supplied. They had used his headline: CHARGES OF INCEST AND MURDER MAKE STRANGE HOME BREW. With captions giving further explanations, there was his picture of Roger Radeau in jail, with his infuriated face and his fist raised. Beside it was a shot of the Radeaus' dog, looking like the Hound of the Baskervilles, a picture of Mrs. Radeau looking sunken-faced and grim, and her two glowering sons, whom Ben had caught with his camera before they put down the ax and the baseball bat. The picture he had taken of the house and the yard was captioned A GRIM SCENE FOR A GRIM DRAMA TO BE UNFOLDED IN LIVINGSTON COURTS.

Ben felt a curious mixture of emotions when he looked at his handiwork. The photographs were dramatic but they also were a fine example of conviction by newspaper, because no one could possibly look at them without assuming guilt. To a degree Ben still felt he had capitalized on the misery of some poor degenerates who probably should go to jail but who should not be put on exhibition in a sideshow which now, apparently, was being televised coast to coast.

I'm going soft, Ben thought, soft and sentimental. A guy

rapes his daughter, kills his son and I weep great tears for him and his darling family, who apparently turned him in but now are trying to defend him. I photographed their gory tale and if they don't like it... well, when Roger Radeau leads a Boy Scout troop, I'll make him look all-American good-guy.

"God, you really can do things with a camera," Ann said, studying the newspaper. "How come when I take pictures the people always look bored?"

"There also have been a million calls congratulating you for the TV stuff," Lillian added.

"That figures," Ben said. "I could start the *New York Times* around here and nobody would much care, but one crappy news program on TV makes me a celebrity."

"Don't knock it. About a dozen people wanted to buy space. I referred them to Herb Mahoney. Is that right?"

"Yeah, Herb is going to handle the advertising for us from now on."

"I hope you know what you're doing," Lillian said, pursing her lips.

"Look, he sells space better when he's drunk than anyone around here does sober. So let me worry about it—"

"Yes, sir. Do you want to see our next edition? I've got the feature page ready."

"Later. I've got to cover Howie's speech."

"He sent us an advance copy. He comes out four-square for America, hates the Park Agency and wants to be a state senator. Some scoop."

When he got back to the van, Rose complained that the car was hot, even with the windows open, and she asked to go back to Cliff House. She looked a little feverish and Ben was worried about her as Ann helped her across the terrace to the bedroom. The thought that this secluded summer cottage with only grammie, Rose and Ann in it now might be the target for the men who made the threatening phone calls scared him more than he could afford to let on.

"Can I take the car while you listen to the speech?" Ebon asked when he returned to the van. "It's kind of a pain, but I promised Annie that I'd take care of her horse again today."

"I've got some stuff I have to get out at the farm," Ben said. "Those speeches never start on time."

They circled the village to avoid traffic and soon arrived at the dirt road leading to the farm. Recently the sun had dried it to the consistency of concrete, but the rain had turned it to mud again. The fields on both sides of them were still oceans of waving green grass, in which the grove of maples, the farmhouse, and the outlying barn with its leaning silo rose like an island ahead. The quiet was broken only by the bouncing of the van.

"I love this place," Ebon said suddenly. "I've been happier here than I've ever been in my life."

"Will you think I'm horning into your territory if I say that I have been too?" Ben asked.

"No. It's those women, Annie, Rosie and even grammie. They're just not like anyone I ever met before."

"How? I'd really like your explanation."

"You tell me," Ebon replied with a grin. "I can't put it into words."

"Neither can I," Ben said. "But I sure as hell feel it."

"Too much, maybe—me, anyway," Ebon said. "Want to help me with Jill? That's what the fair Annie calls her mare."

Shoving a sticky sliding door, Ebon entered a big, dimly lit barn with a box stall at one end and a hayloft overhead. From a shadowed corner the mare came slowly toward them, her ears pricked forward, sunlight from chinks in the wall casting bars on her chestnut coat. She snorted. Ebon stroked her neck and her nose.

"I can't put her out in the pasture because she can go right over those brokendown fences," Ebon said, "so I've given her the run of the barn as the next best thing."

"She's a beautiful mare," Ben said, looking at her delicate fetlocks and legs.

"She's part thoroughbred, part Morgan, a damn good combination. Annie raised her from a colt. She's all broken up about getting rid of her."

"Then why is she doing it?"

"She doesn't want Rosie to know, so don't say anything. With things going as they are, she figures she just doesn't have any right to spend the money or time it takes to keep a horse right."

"I'll talk to her."

"I wouldn't, dad. I tried. Annie looks as though she's made of butter, but when she makes up her mind she's granite, believe me."

"When is she going to sell her?"

"She's already been advertising. Several people have looked at her, and one guy from Vermont, I think, is just about ready to buy. He offered eight hundred and said he'd think about the thousand Annie wants."

Ben was stroking the soft nose of the horse. "Annie must feel as though she's giving up a child."

"I guess that's why she likes me to feed it, she gets to grieving when she comes down here herself."

"Why does she think she needs a thousand dollars right now?"

"She wants to help with Rosie's hospital expenses and the operation. She doesn't want to put any more off on you than she can help."

"God, the two of them! Everybody says their father is a hell of a bum. What do you suppose he did to get two daughters like that?"

"He went back to Ireland and left everything to his wife. He didn't stick around to contaminate them."

Ben filled a galvanized washbasin in a corner of the barn with water while Ebon cleaned up the earth floor of the barn with a shovel before pitching a mound of fresh hay from the loft. He also gave the mare a measure of oats from a sack in

231

the box stall. With a rusty scythe he stepped out into the neighboring field and cut fresh grass, which Ben raked up and carried to the mare.

"Well, I guess she's okay now, except for exercise," Ebon said. "Tomorrow I hope I get a chance to work out with her. You want to go into the house before we go back?"

The key was hidden in an old tin can, which was in the woodpile on the porch. The interior of the farmhouse was hot and airless. Without the people in it, there was nothing to distract attention from the worn linoleum floors, the frayed rag rugs, the absence of drapes or any luxurious ornamentation. This was a house which for over two hundred years had been devoted to essentials: warmth in mountain winters; the economy of small rooms, low ceilings and small windows which made a wood stove suffice in most conditions. No delicate antiques were there to boast of the house's centuries. Instead there were sturdy overstuffed chairs, couches and beds to offer comfort after a hard day's work. There were also books, old and new, lying on almost every table and in shelves which covered most of one wall in the living room. Pausing to look at them, Ben found rows of Dickens, Mark Twain, Robert Louis Stevenson and Conrad surrounded by thinner volumes distributed by the book clubs. A variety of magazines ranging from *The New Yorker* to the *Farm Journal* were piled in the small room usually occupied by Rose.

"There are more books around here than I ever found in Santa Barbara," Ben said.

"Rosie's mother was an English teacher," Ebon told him. "Didn't she tell you that?"

"No."

"She's very proud of it. Her mother even had some stuff published. She was trying to write a book when she died."

Death—somehow it seemed to meet Ben every time he turned a corner. He continued to the unused wing of the house, where he had stored everything that had been taken out of the house that he had considered his own. As he was filling a suitcase with clothes he could use that summer, he saw in a closet the cases containing his father's guns.

"You remember when I taught you how to use this?" he asked Ebon, picking up the shotgun.

"I was too young," Ebon said, accepting the 12-gauge when Ben took it from its case. "I was scared to death." He broke the double-barreled gun and inspected it to make sure it was not loaded.

"That's a good attitude to have about guns," Ben said, taking a Marlin carbine from its case. Levering it open, he held it up to the window to make sure it was empty. Rummaging around in the closet, he found a box containing both shotgun shells and .30-.30 cartridges, along with cleaning kits. "I don't think this ammo is more than three or four years old," he said. "It would shoot . . ."

"You up to some target practice?" Ebon asked with a grin.

"Not now. Call me crazy if you want, but when I get threatening phone calls, I begin to like the smell of a gun. No harm in keeping the shotgun in my bedroom and the carbine in the van."

"Would you actually use 'em?" Ebon asked. "Or *when* would you use 'em? That's kind of a ticklish question, isn't it?"

"All I know right now is that when I hear a door slam at night after those phone calls, I'll feel better if I know that somewhere I can draw the line if I have to. . . ."

Howie Hewat had just begun his speech when Ben and Ebon entered the crowded, bunting-draped gymnasium of the high school where the Legion picnic had been moved to escape the rain and muddy fields. His bulky figure draped in a dark blue business suit with a star-spangled tie in the colors of the flag, Howie was a surprisingly effective speaker. His evocation of the glories of the past and his celebration of the spirit of independence down through the years in this mountain valley did not, however, last long.

"All this history is glorious indeed," he continued after taking a deep breath, "but let us be frank: we can't eat it. In the midst of national plenty and state plenty, Livingston County is starving! Even with the mill going full blast, we have an unemployment rate of twenty-eight percent, higher even than Essex County, which is chronically the capital of depression in New York State. Our children are leaving as soon as they finish school because there's no work for them here. Good men are on relief year after year. Business of almost every kind shrinks every year and nearly everybody but Eddie Pace is going broke!"

Old Ed Pace, the undertaker, was sitting at the speakers' table near Howie. Accustomed to being the butt of jokes, he grinned tolerantly. The crowd laughed.

"Don't think I'm not serious," Howie continued. "We must ask ourselves, why are we broke? And we all know the reason, the Adirondack Park Agency, the most vicious kind of dictatorship ever to be spawned by our fair democracy—"

This accusation was greeted by loud cheers. A man beside Ben jumped on a chair and yelled, "You tell 'em, Howie! Tell it like it is!"

"I will," Howie said, holding up his hand for quiet. "Now you all know what the Adirondack Park Agency is. It was created by the Rockefellers and other great nature lovers who want the Adirondacks, including our valley, to be 'forever wild.' They love the beauty of the forest. They love chipmunks and deer, raccoons and even skunks! The one living thing they don't love is people, the people who live in these mountains. You see, the trouble with people is, they're not scenic. If we could learn to be cute and kind of sit up on our hind legs and beg for peanuts, why, hell, the Rockefellers might love us!"

The hall exploded with laughter, and many in the audience beat plastic plates on the tables to show their approval.

"Because people ain't as cute as bears, the Adirondack Park Agency is trying to keep them out of this whole region, including our valley," Howie went on. "Now, they don't drive us out with guns or poison, like rats. They just do the next best thing: they confiscate our land. And I say *confiscate!* They like to call it zoning, but when you tell a man he can't sell less than forty-three acres of land, you have reduced the value of his land enormously and you probably have made it impossible for him to sell it at all. Telling him he can't sell a lot less than eight acres is better, like having an arm cut off is better than being killed. This whole crazy patchwork of zoning they've imposed on us drains our life blood. It's hated by everyone but the city people, who like to have a park up here they can use without paying for it—"

After more cheers and table-pounding, Howie continued, "Now let me tell you a little story. Not so long ago my wife and I were sitting on the porch of a little camp we have up at Lost Lake. We have an outdoor fireplace down near the water, but it don't draw too good and we hardly ever use it. Anyway, on this morning I smell meat cooking. I walked to the end of the house and saw smoke pouring out of that chimney. Some people in bathing suits which left very little to the imagination had set up a picnic table in my backyard, and believe it or not, they were prying boards from the bottom of my old garage for firewood. When I told them to get the hell off my property, they were very indignant.

" 'What the hell!' one of them said. 'We're in the Adirondack Park, ain't we? This is as much our land as yours!' "

The crowd roared.

"These people really do think they own the Adirondacks," Howie said. "And with this forty-three-acre zoning, they're not far wrong. A lot of folks can't afford to pay taxes on land they can't sell. A lot of those forty-three-acre tracts are reverting to wilderness. We're going to be 'forever wild,' all right, if we don't do something about it."

"What, Howie?" a bald man shouted. "What should we do?"

"First of all, we have to bust that zoning like a rotten egg. With that, we can bring some industry in here, businesses of many kinds. So there will be jobs for people and money enough to live like other Americans."

"But how are you going to bust the zoning?" the bald man shouted.

"I won't pretend I know all the answers to that one," Howie replied, wiping his forehead with a handkerchief. "The Adirondack Park Agency is nothing but an appointive bureaucratic committee. It's backed by the Rockefellers and their successors. In fact, it's backed by just about everybody in the world who loves nature without having to pay for it. The only people who hate it are the people who live here, the people whose land is being zoned, not bought by the State to make a park. We suffer great losses without compensation. Still, I think the Agency can be licked. The only place to do it is in Albany, where all the strings are being pulled. You have to be one of the power boys to have any chance in this kind of battle."

Howie paused and took a deep breath.

"Which is why, ladies and gentlemen, I am running for the State Senate, starting right now! I am running as an independent candidate because I do not want any political party to impose its views about the Park Agency on me. If you will send me to Albany, I will break the chains that Agency has wrapped around us or damn well die trying! Guarantee it . . ."

While the audience stood to applaud, Ben and Ebon made their way through the crowd to the fresh air outside.

"I always thought he was such a bastard," Ebon said. "Is he really all that sincere, or does he just want to get elected?"

"The truth is, I don't know for sure," Ben said. "In a lot

236

of ways, Howie for sure is an SOB and a thief, but I suppose that that doesn't mean he can't help this town, even if it is for his private reasons. I haven't even made my own mind up about the whole Park Agency issue. Is it better for us all to starve here among scenic wonders, or to put up a huge smoky factory that will enable everyone to buy new cars and trailers?"

"Is that the only choice?"

"No. Like most towns everywhere, we can contrive to get the huge smoky factory and starve to death anyhow."

Ebon laughed. "You don't believe in happy endings?"

"I never knew a government that made one. Individuals, sometimes, if you can stop the story with the wedding."

As they approached Cliff House, Ben found himself increasingly worried about Rose. He wished the doctor had told him more about what symptoms might warn him of an approaching heart attack. When he thought of the gasps that had started her last one, the rigid way she had sat up in bed, desperately struggling for air, he was terrified all over again. This noon when she asked to be taken back to Cliff House, she had been breathing a little hard. Perhaps he shouldn't have left her. . . .

He found, to his relief, Rose sitting at a table on the terrace looking very well. She had put on a festive red sundress to greet the improvement in the weather, and was eating corn on the cob.

"For the first time in a long while, I feel famished," she said. "Annie's been waiting on me hand and foot. I feel quite spoiled."

"Have you eaten, Ben?" Ann asked, coming from the kitchen.

"Eb and I have been busy—"

"Sit down then. I've corn, salad, hot dogs, and watermelon."

As Ann brought in a tray of food, Ben reflected that she

had changed markedly in just the few weeks he had known her. When he had first met her, she had seemed to be a very pretty girl, but shy, often awkward and inclined to leave all work about the house to her sister. Yet as soon as Rose had gone to the hospital, Annie had taken over, blossoming into an efficient, admirably mature young woman. Her secret plan to sell her beloved horse to help with the bills filled Ben with real respect, as well as sympathy for her. Ben's own daughter wasn't old enough yet to show such qualities, but she had always been surrounded by so much money that sacrifice would be a new word for her. Ann smiled as she handed him his plate of food and without thinking he gave her a pat on the arm. "Thanks," he said. "I wish Rosie would hurry up and marry me so you can be my sister-in-law."

"We'll have a double ceremony," Rose suggested. "Ben, do you take these two women—"

"I do, I do," he said quickly, and Ann giggled, blushing a little.

"When they get to the part where they ask if anyone objects, speak up or forever hold your peace, you'll hear from me," Ebon said from his seat on the wall. "I'll fight to the death for my woman, even against my old man...." He tried to say it in the light, bantering spirit of the rest of them, but it didn't come out that way.

"Well, I guess the Radeau family has nothing on us," Rose said, and then rather quickly, "Annie, I'm still hungry. Is there anything left to eat?"

"Grammie baked an apple pie for dinner. Would you like to dip into that?"

"I'd love it!"

"How about a topper of ice cream?"

"Lovely. The doctor told me to get my weight back up as soon as I could. This is like sinning on doctor's orders. Lead on."

17

LATER that afternoon Ben saw the television program which featured his photographs. The tone of the announcer's voice made them appear more lurid than ever and when the picture of the Radeau house appeared, altogether dark and sinister on the small screen, the voice-over theatrically intoned, "Is this a house of horrors?" before going on to say softly that the answer awaited the trial.

Imagining that bleak woman who with such odd naivete had given him permission to photograph her family and her home, sitting before a television set with her fierce-appearing sons, Ben found his fists tightening. Up on Chasson Hill, where all the cousins and uncles of the Radeau family lived, this news program no doubt had a high rating. Feeling melodramatic himself, Ben got the shotgun from the car, and to avoid alarming Rose hid it on a top shelf of his closet with a box of shells.

While the others were taking a nap, Ben and Ebon returned to the village to continue their coverage of the Glorious Fourth. Outside Joe's bar a fight had broken out between a burly logger who was bleeding at the nose and a young athlete with a bloody T-shirt emblazoned with the number thirteen. Too drunk to land solid punches, the two flailed

239

away at each other until Big Duke, the cop, pushed his way through the cheering crowd.

"All right, now, folks, move it!" Big Duke said, twirling his club. "Move it on out."

The crowd thinned and the fighters ran off together, laughing like happy conspirators.

"Did you ever get in a fistfight, dad?" Ebon asked.

"Nope."

"Never?"

"Not since I was fifteen."

"What do you do when somebody challenges you?"

"They don't very often. I'm always polite to people bigger than me."

"Hasn't anybody ever taken a poke at you or insulted you?"

"Plenty of times."

"What do you do then?"

"Run. My old man told me that if I lost a fight, I'd wind up in the hospital, and if I won, I'd wind up in court."

"And you don't feel ashamed?"

"I'd be more ashamed if I bashed somebody's skull or got my own head knocked in. In Korea they had me teaching hand-to-hand combat for a while. I've seen enough to keep my hands in my pockets."

"I'll remember you're a pacifist if I ever decide to tell you to go to hell," Ebon said with a determined grin. "If I started shoving at you, what would you do?"

"Try my damndest to beat the bejesus out of you," Ben replied cheerfully. "Fathers and sons, you know, are beyond rules."

Tables for a pie-eating contest had been set up on the village green. To Ben's astonishment, Howie Hewat was one of the contestants. Across the table from Hetty Marcel, a fat lady who had served as town clerk for years, Howie put on a barber's apron and sat waiting expectantly as big blueberry pies were placed in front of him and his opponent. Forbidden to use their hands, the contestants dived in when the starter shot off his pistol. The crowd cheered as they gobbled. The fat lady finished first, but when Howie climbed on the table, his face a dripping purple mask, he got a standing ovation. The pie-eating contest probably got him more votes than his speech, Ben guessed, as he took Howie's picture. The town tended to tolerate immorality and even thievery in a "good sport."

A tug of war followed with the teams on opposite sides of a mud pit, into which they tried to pull each other. Howie, who had changed into white coveralls, joined this event, too. The occasion was billed as "The lawyers versus the firemen," and Howie's team included four of his legal assistants in addition to Pete, who looked very unhappy in his white coveralls as he picked up the rope at the spot nearest the mud pit.

On the other side the firemen in black slickers and boots took their positions. The starter fired his pistol again and the men set to struggling, slipping and sliding on the damp grass. As the cheering crowd pressed in around them, the young firemen began to have their way. Pete was the first to be pulled into the mud pit, where waist-deep in the mire he continued to struggle so gallantly that the crowd loudly applauded. Perhaps unwilling to stop the fun too soon, the firemen relented a little, allowing Pete to scramble out and help pull them to the brink. Then, with a final heave, the firemen pulled all the lawyers into the mud in a tangle of white coveralls. The first to recover his footing, Howie stood up, wiped the mud from his face and shouted, "We're going to sue!"

Laughter, and a man appeared with a hose to wash off the losers. Lifted to the shoulders of the winning team, Howie was taken on a triumphal tour of the crowd. All this Ben recorded in more detail than his paper could use. He was beginning to think more and more about a book.

When he got home Ben found Rose asleep. He lay down beside her, and apparently without waking she took his hand, holding it softly but with the barely perceptible caress of her fingertips. There was a smile on her face, which had lost some of its hospital pallor in the sunlight on the terrace. Her wrists still looked so thin, though . . . he brushed his lips over the nearest one, then went to sleep.

Two hours later Ann called them. It was dark, almost time for the fireworks to begin. Sitting out on the terrace, they saw the first skyrocket fly up from the park just a mile away on the lake. It was followed by many more until the sky was crisscrossed by multicolored showers of sparks, all reflected in the still waters.

"Who pays for all this?" Ebon suddenly asked.

"The firemen take up a collection," grammie said. "Half for fireworks, half for beer—"

A rocket that ended its arc with a tremendous explosion interrupted her, echoing off the mountains. And then came the grand finale, rockets of different colors fired from both sides of the lake and meeting overhead in a fiery network. From the park they could hear the sound of clapping and horns honking in approval.

"Well, there goes one more Fourth," grammie said. "Maybe the firemen deserve their beer at that . . . they sure put on a good show."

"You want to go to the street dance, Annie?" Ebon asked.

"Oh, gosh, Eb, I'm so tired I could drop, and I want to get up early tomorrow to develop some pictures. Are you game for that, Ben?"

"Sure."

"Why don't you go to the street dance anyway, Eb?" Ann asked mischievously. "Maybe you can pick up one of those city girls who just come up here looking for one of our handsome country boys."

"Because, dear heart, I'm plumb wore out . . . they've been chasing me all day. I'll turn in, if nobody minds."

Ben looked away, trying to ignore the tension between the two.

At nine grammie turned on the television set, and to Ben's discomfort listened again to the story about the Radeaus. Saying she was tired in spite of her nap, Rose went to bed, too, and almost immediately fell into a deep sleep. Feeling tense, Ben went out on the terrace. Because the street dance in the village had become so crowded the previous year, a second band, this one featuring country music, was playing in the lakeside park. Its amplified music echoed off the hills and was magnified and distorted by the water, a cacophony in Ben's ears of twanging fiddles, booming basses and a chorus of nasal voices singing the season's hit, "I'll always keep you in my heart, although you've gone away. . . ."

Soon the music awoke Rose, who came out of her bedroom wearing a short cotton nightgown that made her look like a child in the darkness.

"From every damn mountainside let nonsense ring," she said, yawned and perched herself on an arm of Ben's chair. And it was at precisely that moment that the music stopped and they heard fire sirens in the distance, on the other side of the village.

"Those firemen must be worn out," Rose said.

The telephone rang. Ben did not believe in presentiments but something made him run to pick up the receiver. The operator said, "Ben, the Kelly barn is on fire, maybe the house too. The firemen are on their way. . . ."

Ebon and Ann came running from their rooms as he hung up, and Rose had hurried to stand beside him.

"The barn's on fire," Ben said, his voice curiously flat.

"*Jill* . . . oh, my god . . ." Ann said.

"We'll get her," Ebon was saying as he was already headed toward the car.

"We'll all go," Ben called, "but Rosie, you stay here?"

"If the barn goes the house probably will too," Rose told him. "I'll stay in the car, but I *have* to be there."

243

Throwing on a coat, Rose walked quickly to the van, refusing to let herself run. Ben got into the back seat beside her. Ann was sitting in front and Ebon drove, tires screeching as they came out of the driveway at top speed.

"Easy, son," Ben said. "There're people here, not at the house—"

"My *horse* is there," Ann said, close to tears.

As they drew clear of the village, they could see a red glow in the sky over the old farm. They passed two lumbering fire engines before they turned onto the dirt road. The sound of sirens filled the air, and blue lights flashed on the battered cars of the volunteers while red lights revolved on newer official vehicles. A police car went ahead of them, its siren adding to the din.

Ben couldn't avoid a mental image of Ann's beautiful mare being burned up alive.

Annie, he guessed, was having similar visions. While the van jolted over the dirt road, she kept urging Ebon to hurry. Smoke obscured the farmhouse like a fog and the barn was exploding like a Vesuvius, sparks from the hayloft erupting into the air.

"It's too late—" Ebon said.

But Ann had slipped from the van and was already running toward the barn, disappearing, engulfed by a cloud of smoke. Ebon followed after her, catching her as she headed toward the door of the barn, which was now wreathed in flames.

"I've got to see—"

"You'll get killed." Coughing, he pulled her back to the place where Ben and Rose were standing, near the spot where Ebon had cut grass for the horse that morning. Weakly they sank down on the grass, still coughing.

Ann said nothing. But she was thinking of the beautiful chestnut foal she had raised, now on a funeral pyre set by some degenerate person who made threatening phone calls.

Two fire engines arrived, ran hoses to the river and began

spraying the barn, which made the flames burn with a ruddier glow, and mixed the dark gray smoke with white steam. Otherwise, nothing changed. Spectators came running from all directions, standing in concentric circles around the fire. The crowd swelled until Big Duke and his men had to set up police lines. A third fire engine now arrived and put a search-light on the back of the farm, where the weathered boards were beginning to smoke in the heat from the barn and where Ben saw seven words painted in outsize letters with out-rageous red paint: NEXT TIME THE HOUSE, AND MAYBE YOU.

"*Damn* them," Rose said. "Do we just sit and take this, Ben?"

Before he could answer, there was a roar as a hose was brought to bear on the smoldering side of the farmhouse, wetting it down and causing the wet red paint of the warning to run.

"Evening, Ben," a nasal voice said.

Turning, Ben saw old Ephram, who was wearing a fire-man's raincoat and boots.

"Hi, Eph."

"This is what I call a real old-fashioned Fourth of July," Ephram said. "When I was working for your grandfather, stuff like this was commonplace—"

"Barn-burnings?"

"Barn-burnings, house-burnings, threats—the works. If you think you got trouble now, you should see this town when there's a strike or a long layoff at the mill—"

"I've enough trouble now."

"Want me to handle it, like I did for your grandpappy?"

"How?"

"Well, when people started messing around with your grandpappy's property, their own tended to get messed up too. Wasn't long before people got the word, nobody ever threatened or bothered him. . . ."

"I'm listening."

245

"You got plenty of friends around town, Bens. A few of us might take a run up to the Radeau place. The time to act is now, so they get the point."

"I'll go with you," Ebon said. He had come up unnoticed from behind with Ann.

"Well, Ben?" Rose said.

"I'm going too," Ann said bitterly.

"Wait a damn minute," Ben said. "I want to think—"

There was a crash and a torrent of sparks as the roof of the barn collapsed and the crowd pulled back.

Winking in the grass a few yards from the barn Ben saw an empty pint whiskey bottle, and wondered if it had been dropped by one of the crowd, *or* by the man who'd touched off the barn. He imagined one of the bearded Radeau men arriving with a bottle of booze in one hand and a can of gasoline in the other. Maybe he'd swigged the whiskey for courage, or used it to help him savor the result of his damned handiwork. . . .

Taking a handkerchief from his pocket, Ben moved quickly through the heat to retrieve the bottle and showed it to Big Duke. "Can you test this thing for fingerprints?"

"What the hell do you think this is, Ben, a TV show? We got no equipment for that kind of stuff—"

"How about the state cops?"

"I guess they could if they wanted to, but short of murder one, I never seen them mess around with it. It's not such hot evidence anyway when you get to court."

Taking the bottle in the handkerchief from Ben, Big Duke sniffed it. "Home-brewed corn," he said. "Some clue. At least half the farmers around here drink it. Well, I'll take it back to the station anyway. We'll put our electronic computer gadget on it. Every self-respecting police department has to have one these days."

Disgusted, Ben stood staring into the huge bed of embers which marked the end of the fire. Barn-burners were almost never caught, he knew very well. Someone at least should have looked for footprints in the mud before the firemen and the spectators had obliterated them.

Rose, Ann and Ebon looked as dejected as he felt. Ann glanced fearfully at the embers, then turned to the crowd standing there impassively, their faces white in the floodlights from the fire engines. Some had brought six-packs of beer, which they sipped, discarding the cans in the grass. Others had brought sandwiches. . . . All of them just sort of *stood* there, watching the embers turn the water from the hoses to clouds of steam. "Do you think the house will go too?" a stocky woman asked no one in particular.

Ann turned to her, her hands doubled by her sides. "Get *out* of here, the show's over, you . . ."

The woman stared at her, laughed and took her companion's arm. Nobody made a move to leave.

"Didn't you hear her?" Rose called out, going to Ann's side. "This is private property—"

Ben went to Big Duke and repeated Rose's statement. "This *is* private property, Duke. Can't you get these people out of here?"

Moving people was what Big Duke did best. He strolled toward the crowd twirling his nightstick, his tall, bull-shouldered frame impressive. "All right, folks, let's move it. Time to move it on out . . ."

Muttering, the crowd retreated into the night, but strangely didn't disperse. As the smoke subsided, the moon could be seen overhead, riding on a thin white cloud in a clear sky. The surrounding fields of grass looked light gray, unrippled by any wind.

Ann turned to Ben. "It was like they were waiting to see what was left of poor Jill in there. God, it's so awful—"

"You did right, baby," Rose said. "They were just hoping that the house would go too."

Putting her arms around Rose, Ann suddenly began to cry. "Rosie . . . why . . . *why* did it have to happen to a beautiful—"

A small boy from the neighborhood ran from the crowd up to Ann. "Don't you own a horse?"

"I *did* . . ."

"Well, there's one grazing in the field out by the river. It ain't fenced in or anything—"

Ann ran toward the river, with Ebon following.

"Do you suppose? . . ." Ben started.

"Usually there're no other horses near here," Rose said, "but don't let's get our hopes up."

As he waited Ben imagined a Radeau, his bearded face slack. The man carried the can of gasoline in one hand, the bottle of corn whiskey in his pocket. He opened the barn door a crack, saw the mare, and hesitated. The mare probably retreated to a dark corner of the barn. The Radeaus, like most farm families, had always owned horses. Perhaps the moonlight in the barn had been strong enough to give the intruder some idea of the beauty of the young mare. Shoving the barn door all the way open, he may have walked quietly up to the horse, trying to quiet the fast beat of his own frightened heart. Taking her halter, he had perhaps led the mare to the door, slapped her hard on the flank. As the horse bounded into the moonlit field, the intruder might have watched her for just a moment before sloshing gasoline around the barn, wetting a narrow path to the outside that would act as a fuse. Tossing a match onto this, he would have watched the sudden *woosh* of flame before running across the fields to the place where he'd left his car. He'd felt some satisfaction because at least he couldn't bring himself to leave a young mare in a burning barn. . . .

. . . Except this might well be no more than a romantically hopeful notion, Ben realized. The boy had probably seen nothing but someone's plough horse put out to graze. . . . And then there was no more need to speculate—the beat of hooves and the chestnut mare loomed out of the darkness, carrying both Ann and Ebon on her bare back. Ann was hugging her neck, and both were shouting with joy. Without saddle or bridle, the young mare still seemed under perfect control as she stopped short of the smoldering ruin of the barn and tossed her head.

"I bet she got out by herself," Ann said when they were talking over the affair later that night. "I bet they were trying to steal her and she got away—"

"I don't know," Rose said. "The Radeaus may be pretty rotten, but they know horses. I doubt if even your Jill could get away from them if they didn't want her to."

Privately Ben was pleased by the thought that even the Radeaus were not entirely monstrous. It helped him to make the decision to ask Ephram and Ebon not to make retaliatory raids on the Radeau barns. All of which gave him a good, warm, almost righteous feeling until he reminded himself that Rose's barn had still been burned and whether the horse had been released or not, a grim warning had still been painted on the farmhouse. Worse, there was no way he could see how to avoid stirring up the Radeaus again. The wire services were already demanding more news about the "house of horrors on Chasson Hill." There would soon be a murder trial, which Ben would have to cover.

Ben was too experienced to worry about his courage. He knew that he didn't have any. No sane man had courage if that meant an absence of fear, however much one might respond to a dangerous professional challenge. What Ben figured he did have was an ability to do what he had to do, often hating it, with his stomach griping, his bowels quite literally in an uproar, often with a head cold, a malady that seemed to affect him especially in stressful moments. It had been that way in Korea and he'd covered four more such wars as a combat photographer. He'd quit when one of his best friends was killed, and he'd realized with a shock that he wasn't at all sure anymore why he kept getting involved in all the mayhem anyway. When he was young it had seemed

249

important to document warfare. In his middle age he realized that battles had been documented one way or another for thousands of years without changing anything at all.

But now he was in the middle of another battle of sorts in his own hometown. He sat on the terrace of Cliff House after bringing Rose home from the fire. She was in her bedroom taking pills and trying to get to sleep after the kind of emotional excitement her doctor had warned her to avoid whenever possible. And, damn it, there would be more nights of tension as the Radeau story continued to unfold and more acts of revenge were threatened, or committed.

It was time to establish some priorities. For his own sake and for Rose's his first job was to try to help her get well, to prepare herself physically and emotionally for the operation she feared so much. This was no damn time to be a Don Quixote crusading journalist. Besides, just how would the publication of the details of the Radeau debacle help anyone anyhow? . . .

Officially the court would have to decide what had happened in the "house of horrors," but after reading the police reports and talking to several members of the Radeau family while he photographed them, Ben was pretty sure that he already knew. On the night in question, the Radeau clan had gathered at the home of the father and mother for the innocent purpose of celebrating their twenty-fifth wedding anniversary. This event the mother, in her determined attempt to do things in the conventional way, had arranged. All the men got drunk on the corn liquor, which they manufactured themselves in quantity. The brothers began fighting over their fifteen-year-old sister, who was overdeveloped physically and underdeveloped mentally—an explosive and tragic combination. It was common knowledge in Livingston that incest was a frequent practice among many of the mountain people who lived in the hills and ravines on the fringes of the village. Ben had seen the reports of social workers— and not wide-eyed do-gooders but factual social reporters—

and so was not really surprised by the spectacle of a sadly retarded girl who had had intercourse with the male members of her family. At a drunken family get-together, the father could have hit his son either through jealousy or indignation. The other sons could well have taken sides. Whether the girl had been willingly taken or raped by her relatives would probably never be known since she'd changed her story from day to day.

The main point probably was that everyone drank so much that the next morning no one had a clear idea of what had actually happened. Half the men woke up in jail, half in the hospital, one with a fractured skull that had killed him. Now, not surprisingly, they were all saying whatever they thought would help themselves and each other. A kind of family loyalty was making the women retract the charges they had first made in anger when the whole mess had exploded.

All right then, Ben ... back to the original questions ... what would the public learn from detailed accounts of all this? Incest is not an activity recommended for peaceful family celebrations. Massive intake of alcohol is bad and does not lead to quiet anniversaries. Poverty is also bad, inbreeding, too, and hitting people, including members of your own family, can be dangerous. The great lessons he was supposed to risk Rose's health, and maybe his life, to provide?

The outraged citizens of Livingston could mount practically a small revolution against the Adirondack Park Agency, which was impoverishing them, in their own opinion at least, without attracting more than a paragraph of print in the Albany newspapers or more than a few minutes of time on some local TV talk show. But when a family of down-and-out hill people took to screwing each other, the whole nation apparently came to attention and faced toward Livingston, breathlessly eager for every detail.

Ben asked himself how his father would have handled the Radeau story, and decided he'd probably have given it three paragraphs on a back page. And not because of threats to a

251

barn or the pressure of local businessmen who wanted a clear image for the chamber of commerce.... "I just don't like to exploit people," Stephen had once said, a comment made almost casually but which had endured in his son's mind.

And still did, as he sat staring out over the mists of Lost Lake. Whatever their sins, the Radeaus *had* been exploited, which was why Ben's anger at their threats had been compounded by guilt. In all their actions there had at least been a crazy sort of spunkiness, a refusal to allow themselves to be exploited, a reaching, however wrongheaded, for some respect. Whatever else they might be, they were still men, they seemed to be trying to say.

Discovering that in a sense he admired the Radeaus almost as much as he was horrified by them, Ben decided not to milk their story. A few paragraphs on a back page when the case went to trial should tell the world all it needed to know....

Still too tense to sleep, Ben got himself a drink and sat watching two people in a canoe out on the lake who were continuing to celebrate the Glorious Fourth with sparklers. ...The word "priorities" kept going through his mind. It was strange, but Rose's doctor had told him some simple things that had scared him so much that he'd never really allowed himself to accept them. Or even face them.

"She will seem to recover her health," Dr. Knight had said, "but her heart has sustained injuries which cannot be healed without major surgery. If she doesn't get that, I don't know how long she might go without another attack. Maybe a few weeks, maybe a few months, maybe a year, but I do know one thing... the next attack will probably be fatal."

"How long before she can have the operation?" Ben had asked, feeling paralyzed.

"As soon as she gets her strength and weight back. Frankly I'm worried. I mean, her worry has me worried. Perhaps because of her mother's history, she's pretty terrified of the surgery, out of all proportion to the actual danger. And this panic of hers in itself can be an extra hazard. I hope we

252

can get her calmed down before we start surgery. Some delay might be justified if we can accomplish that. . . . She has to establish priorities. She can't seem to accept the fact that I want her to do no work at all, not until we get that heart fixed. I know she has an exciting new job but that would increase the stress. I also frown on sexual intercourse for her. It's hard to tell that to a woman who's just fallen in love, but she's so high-keyed that sex can impose real strain on her heart. Like I said, it's a matter of priorities. Prolonging her life comes first, second and third. Everything else should come afterward."

The doctor had picked up a yellow pencil from his desk and had started to doodle on a pad. "I'll say one more thing, which of course you know, but you might like my observation. Miss Kelly is, well, I don't quite know how to put it. I don't often indulge in personal comments. But here in the hospital, she's struck many of us as an unusual person. She has enormous vitality even when she's ill—a fact which no doubt has helped to keep her alive. And she has a wonderful awareness of the feelings of others. Not to mention a refreshing kind of honesty and a sense of humor that often kept the whole floor in an uproar. I guess what I'm saying is that I'm going to give you hell, Ben Winslow, if you don't help us save her life. . . ."

But tonight Rose had crowded close to the fire, helping Ebon restrain Annie. Ben now realized he should have insisted that she stay home to avoid the possibility of that kind of excitement. Except a damn sight easier said than . . . And although Rose had promised not to work, she was already writing columns on her own . . . And though they hadn't indulged in full intercourse, she had, with her urgent desire to please, seduced him into some fairly steamy sessions that despite her claims to the contrary had to involve some quickening of the pulse, even if she did recite the Gettysburg Address and "Trees" to herself.

The couple in the canoe began shooting off Roman candles

instead of sparklers ... What he had to do now was do like the doctor said and get her to calm down. And the way to do that was not to carry on and yell at her for not following doctor's orders. ... I've got to set an example, stay cool, work like hell to get her to accept the necessity of that operation, and soon. ...

Suddenly it seemed that maybe he should also repeat his request that she marry him. "Ask me in six months," she'd said, and they'd both understood why, but he suspected that even before her last attack she hadn't really considered herself fit for marriage, and now ... Still, the way she almost always wore her ring on her left hand, in spite of her refusal even to get formally engaged, made him believe that the idea of being his wife pleased her very much ... a better title even than Publisher ... Well, at least a near-tie ... And when people at the hospital had mistaken them for man and wife, she'd looked pleased and had hardly ever corrected them. ...

As for himself ... well, having barely survived one long, too long, loveless marriage, Ben wasn't so sure that he preferred matrimony to the kind of loving attachment he and Rose already had, but if it could help give her some kind of security, reassurance, he was *all* for it ... the fact that he would now insist on marriage before she received some miraculous cure from an operation might prove something to her—might give her a more realistic respect for her own worth, sick or well. And when she was married to him she might be able to accept money from him for her medical bills with less worry, and this was important, because he sensed that she was delaying her operation in the hope that she could somehow raise the money for it herself ... maybe by finding a way to sell part of her farmland, despite the zoning. And although she had talked little about it, he knew her well enough to sense that she was deeply concerned about what would happen to Ann and grammie if she never could work again, or died. ... She'd been forced to leave college after one year because of her mother's similar illness, and was now determined to give her sister a better chance. The desire to get security money for them was, he was sure, behind her frantic attempts to battle the park commission. So far she had got nowhere in this war, but if he were officially a member of the family, she might accept his help in solving these long-range financial problems, too.

So at least Rose would find marriage a *relief*, plus there was the fact that fundamentally she was a considerable respecter of the conventions, for all her verve in playing the role of self-styled mistress. She wasn't really very happy, he knew, conducting a love affair with Annie, Ebon and grammie as household spectators.... Okay, then why would she refuse him? Pride, not wanting to "saddle him with an invalid." Not to mention that she'd stayed clear of marriage before he met her, all during her twenties, odd for an unusually vital and attractive young woman in a town where most girls got married before they were out of their teens. From what he had heard of her father, he guessed that he had not led her to trust men much, or to look forward to matrimony as any great guarantee of happiness. Whatever the reason, he guessed that many men had failed to persuade Rosie to say yes.

So why should he be so sure that only pride kept her from marrying him? Maybe her well-developed common sense did, too. Forty-five years old, overweight, divorced after almost a quarter-century of marriage, no longer wealthy and with his reputation as a photographer gradually being forgotten, was he really a prize that a lovely, vital thirty-year-old woman should jump for? During her illness, the thought of security must tempt her, but she was too much of an individualist to marry just to get her bills paid and he would be gross if he tried to persuade her by dangling that prospect....

Feeling worn out and faintly irritated, Ben went to his room and changed into his pajamas before joining Rose in the big spool bed. She moved from the middle to make room for him.

255

"Hi, dear," she murmured drowsily. "Where you been?"

"Out on the terrace."

"Umm . . . what were you doing out there?"

"Thinking, believe it or not."

"I believe . . . what about?"

"The truth?"

"Not if it's too awful."

"I've been wondering how I can get you to marry me."

"Really?" She turned on her side, taking his left hand in both of hers, caressing his big knuckles.

"Really."

"Well, what's the problem?"

"You always tell me to wait six months."

The sound of her low laugh. "I always did like playing hard to get."

"I want to get married now."

"Why?"

"I want to grab you before you get smart enough to see you could do better."

"Sure," she said, pressing the back of his hand to her lips and biting his knuckles a little. "Any other reasons?"

"I'm sick of grammie glaring at me whenever I come in here."

"That's a reason?"

"When I go out to take pictures with Annie, I want people to know I'm helping my sister-in-law, not indulging a yen for nubile high school girls."

"In other words, you're coming down with a dangerous lust for respectability."

"Something like that. Hell, Rosie, you're just not the mistress type. You were born to be a wife."

"I think you may be insulting me."

"Please . . . no joke. There are also practical reasons—"

"Sure. With all my medical bills I guess I'd be a great tax exemption."

"All right, forget the practical stuff, let's just say I have this terrible, irrational desire to slice a cake with you, drink wine from a loving cup and carry you over a threshold. I know I'm a real old-fashioned male chauvinist pig, but to be truthful, I think I want to own you as much as possible and I want you to do the same to me. Freedom is great, but I think I'm too old for it."

"Oh my," she said, shaking her head and rubbing her eyes. "I'm still half asleep. Are we playing games, Ben, or have you really picked three o'clock in the morning for a serious proposal?"

"I'm sorry. It just happened."

"It's a lovely time, silly. Quiet and private."

"Do you want to get married at all?"

She closed her eyes and pressed her lips firmly together. There was a long moment of silence. "I bet you know everything I'm thinking," she said abruptly.

"Maybe."

"And I bet I know everything you're thinking. So we really don't have to talk anymore, do we?"

"Except for one word."

"*Yes*. Oh *yes*, Ben . . . I have no right to say that, but oh, it feels so good to give in . . ."

They embraced, and after a moment she said, "I would give anything in the world really to make love with you now."

"Priorities," he whispered, stroking her forehead. "The top priority is you."

She kissed him with such intensity that he began to feel his control slipping.

"Priorities," he whispered again.

"Oh, Ben, it's all so frustrating—"

"Not if we think of all the years we'll have if we give up a little now."

"I guess," she said, snuggling against him. "Anyway, I'm

257

going to be Mrs. Benjamin L. Winslow, the wife of the great photographer and scion of Livingston County. Mrs. Scion, they'll call me."

"And I'll point you out to all my friends whenever we go to a party. 'That's my wife,' I'll say, 'the one with that incredible smile and the waist like the stem of a flower.'"

"The one with no tits is more like it, until I gain my weight back ... oh, Ben, I want to be good for you—"

"I'll give you a fact and a question. Fact: Right now I'm happier than I ever have been in my life. Question: Does this mean you're good for me or not?"

"I'm happier than ever too. How can we be so happy when we can't even screw?"

"Perverts, I guess."

"Ben, hug me. I want my husband to hug me. You know, I already feel like your wife."

"Is it different?"

"Well, I'm turning sort of bitchy. Can I have charge accounts at all the stores?"

"In this town that won't pose much of a danger."

"Can I join the country club, the bridge club and the League of Women Voters? That's what all the married ladies do."

"You have my permission."

"And the Garden Club? Can I get a big hat and white gloves ... oh, damn it, Ben, I'm sorry ... here I am making dumb cracks when you're offering me a whole new life."

"Just a slight attack of tension."

"You mean, if I could screw I wouldn't joke?"

"Could be."

"Touch me, Ben. I love your hands. I was always embarrassed to tell you that, but I can tell my husband anything, can't I?"

"Absolutely."

"You have the most enormous hands, strong and yet so gentle ... what size glove do you wear?"

258

"Extra large, or size twelve."

"These big hands make me feel well-defended. And to think I'll never have to open an olive jar again . . . damn it, there I go again."

"Right, just stick to the good stuff."

"Okay. I love your hands and I love those thick shoulders . . . and, damn it, don't you love anything about *me?*"

"Well, I've been known to admire your ankles and legs. They're very delicate—"

"Before my boobs became the dear departed, did you like them?"

"Yes."

"I've always had an inferiority complex about my breasts. Who wouldn't with a sister like Annie? Before she was fourteen, my bras were too small for her."

"There's beauty and beauty . . . you'd make the better model."

"Will you take some pictures of me? After I get my figure back?"

"Sure."

"I'd like to have some really good pictures, a sort of record, if anything happened to me—I'm sorry, I know that's morbid. . . . Tell me some more you like about me."

"I like you for loving me. I was dying of loneliness when I met you."

"I can't imagine that."

"I like your warmth, which keeps so many people going—Ebon along with the rest of us."

"To be honest, that's been a little bit of a problem. There've been times when Eb didn't seem sure whether he was calling on Annie or me. He's getting over it, though."

"I guessed that."

"If you're not careful, you'll have a similar problem."

"What?" But he, of course, knew. And it startled him to feel as uncomfortable as he did.

"Annie is clearly all starry-eyed about you."

259

"She's all starry-eyed about learning to take pictures."

"For her the two go together. I realize it's just a schoolgirl crush, but I also think it may be upsetting Ebon, and you should be aware of it too—"

"Good god. Are there any more wheels within wheels?"

"Yes. Grammie has gone ape over you."

"Good. I've gone ape over grammie."

"But *I've* got *you*. Hold me, Ben."

He did, and after a moment she said, "Do you know that married love is safer for cardiac patients than hanky-panky?"

"I'm learning."

"I read an article on it in the hospital. The theory is that connubial love is less exciting. Isn't that awful?"

"Maybe we better not get married."

"But we have to, if only for my health. . . . Are you trying to back out of it already?"

"If you don't stop lousing up our married sex life, I just might."

"Shut up, Ben. Hold me, hold me very tight, tighter. Don't you ever dare let me go, Ben. Not *ever*."

Feeling too excited to go back to sleep, they got up at five to cook a celebratory breakfast. Setting a table on the terrace, Ben cooked waffles and sausage patties while Rose sliced a honeydew melon and prepared hot spiced apple cider, which she drank instead of coffee or tea, both proscribed by her diet. They had hoped to breakfast in the light of a glorious dawn, but the bad weather of the Fourth was returning and the breaking of the new day was marked only by leaden clouds in a strange formation, like the misty ruins of an ancient city in the sky on which the red ball of the sun bestowed a ruby glare. This apparition lasted only about a minute before it dissolved onto a solid pewter-colored cloud bank, and it began to rain.

Too happy to brood about bad omens, Ben moved the breakfast table into the living room and lit a cheerful fire there.

"What's our schedule?" Rose asked.

"It's up to you, but I think we should keep in mind that your operation shouldn't be put off too long—"

"I remember, I remember . . . how about August first for the wedding?"

"Why so long?"

"I want dad to come. He hates to fly. By the time he finds a boat, he'll need at least three weeks."

From what he'd heard of her father, Ben had not expected this show of family solidarity.

"We'll take a week for our honeymoon, if that's what you can call love without sex," Rose said. "I'll get good and rested. About the tenth of August you can take me to the hospital in Boston for my date with Mack the Knife."

Ben flinched but smiled. "Two things you have to promise me," he said. "We'll ask Dr. Knight if he gives his permission as well as his blessing. And we'll have a small wedding, just for the family. No exhausting shopping for a trousseau, no receptions, no guests. We just want a quiet wedding, followed by a week in Montreal or wherever you want it. Okay? Do you promise?"

"Cross my heart and hope . . ."

At a little after seven, grammie came in. "What are you two doing up so early?" she asked.

"Celebrating," Rose said. "Grammie, we have good news for you. We're going to get married, even though I gave this fool plenty of time to back out. . . ."

The old woman's blue eyes danced. And sparkled with tears. "Bless you," she said. "I was afraid you two would just fool around for the rest of your lives."

"We'll try that too," Rose said.

"Have you set a date?" grammie asked.

"August first. I want to give dad a chance to get here—"

"Rose Kelly," grammie said, pulling a straight chair up to

261

the table, "if you ask Dan Kelly over here you must be sick in the head."

"Come on, grammie, he *is* my father, and I promised him long ago I wouldn't get married until he'd met the man."

"Rose, I'm sorry to talk this way in front of Ben, but if he's going to be a member of this family he's got to know us warts and all. Your father, Dan Kelly, has never once come over here without damn near wrecking himself, you and all the rest of us. If you're as sick as I hear tell, you sure don't need *that*."

"I'm sure he's quieted down a lot. After all, he's almost sixty, grammie! And he'd be so hurt if—"

"Until they put that man in his grave, he'll be drinking, grabbing women, fighting and stealing money off of people. I don't want ever to see him again. And why do you want to put Ben through that? Remember what happened to that engineer feller at the mill who was sweet on you?"

"You talking about Bill Gardener?"

"Yes—your father was giving you a hard time, remember? He'd already lost his license but he insisted you give him the key to the truck. When he grabbed your arm, Bill Gardener stepped in, and you know what happened. Poor Bill was in the hospital for a week and I don't blame him for never wanting to see any of us again—"

"Bill deserved what he got, he called dad a crazy, drunken Irishman!"

"How could he be more right than that?" grammie demanded. "Why do you always defend him, Rosie? Defending him makes you just as bad as he is . . . how many times did I tell your mother that?"

Rose was breathing hard enough to alarm Ben. Her face was a bright pink. "Grammie, I hope I *always* will defend my father . . . if I ever have kids, I hope they will defend me. Now, if you don't want to see dad, stay away from my wedding. I love you, but he's closer kin."

White-faced, grammie wheeled her chair to her room. Rose

262

took a bottle from a pocket of her bathrobe and washed a pill down with cider. Then she stood up, holding her trembling hands out to the fire. Ben hurried over to her, put his arm around her shoulders.

"Why did she have to pull that in front of you?"

"She was afraid, I guess."

"Of what? A man almost sixty years old? Now I suppose you'll be afraid to meet him."

"I've met some fairly ... individual types in my time."

"You know, that may just be one reason I love you ... I think you can handle dad! You're the only man I ever met who makes me feel he could."

"You figure I should go into training?"

"I don't mean just physical force. Dad is a powerhouse in lots of ways. He can't help trying to steamroller people. I don't think he'll even try it on you."

"Sure, we'll probably get on fine together," Ben said without much conviction.

"He's charming in lots of ways ... mom used to call him Ireland's answer to Maurice Chevalier."

"I look forward."

"There's so much I could tell you about him, Ben. He wasn't around much when I was a kid, but when he was ... well, he was great to me—"

She was interrupted by Ann, who came in looking scared. "What's all the shouting about?" she asked, keeping her pink bathrobe closed at the throat with her hand.

"Oh, it's really nothing, Annie," Rose said. "The shouting part, that is. It's a shame that grammie managed to mess up a great occasion ... Ben and I are going to be married about August first—"

"That's *great*. Doesn't grammie like it?"

"She doesn't want us to invite dad to the wedding."

"Oh?" There was a moment of silence before Ann hugged Rose, then over to Ben, she stood on her toes. "I guess I can kiss you now," she said before giving him a peck on the cheek.

263

"Congratulations, I'm really happy about this...Ben, is it okay...I mean, can you still help me develop some pictures this morning?"

"Sure, I guess so..."—he looked at Rose—"give me an hour or so..."

A few minutes later Ebon, wearing blue jeans and nothing else, came in.

"I heard the news," he said. "Congratulations, dad. Am I supposed to call you mother now, Rosie?" After shaking hands a little stiffly with his father, he bent down from his majestic height to kiss Rose on the forehead.

"Looks like it would be more natural for you to call me daughter," Rose said. "I owe you a debt of gratitude, Eb. For bringing this here big Ben to me. And that's for sure."

"And Rosie to me."

"Anytime, anytime," Ebon said. "I'll take the gratitude as long as I don't have to take the blame if you two—"

"Don't worry about it," Ben snapped.

"Sorry," Ebon said. "I wish I believed in happy marriages, but I haven't seen many. Anyway, Rosie, I sure as hell hope you'll be happy. And if you can't make it with Rosie, dad, well..."

"Well, thanks for your good wishes," Ben cut him off, wondering what the hell had brought that on.

While Rose napped, Ben hurried through a session in the developing room in his office with Ann. Then went to his desk to telephone Dr. Knight at the Burlington hospital.

"Well, I like the idea of her getting married," Dr. Knight said when Ben had explained their plans. "Anything that gives her some sense of security should help, and we'd much rather operate on a happy person than a panicky one. I just wish you didn't have to wait so long."

Ben told him about Rose's father.

"I suppose it's a question of whether she'd be more upset by being told to rush her plans than the risk of waiting could justify. Hell, if she's agreed voluntarily to go to Boston, that's more than I'd frankly hoped for this summer. This is a time when she needs support, not carping. If my wife wasn't going to drag me off to Europe, I'd ask you for an invitation to the wedding."

The thing to do now was to get Rosie away from everyone for a little while at least, Ben decided as he returned to Cliff House. Since she was still napping, he went to the boathouse and inspected the *Indian Princess*. Ebon had not completed his work on her, but the old cruiser still looked ready for a tour of the lake.

"Do you think the doctor would mind my going out on the boat?" Rose asked an hour later when he asked if she wanted to take a trial spin aboard the *Princess*.

"Honey, from what I've seen of the lay of the land around here lately, the water is just what you need."

He helped her aboard the old cruiser and she looked around, surprised by the comfort of the galley, the two berths in the cabin and the pillowed benches in the cockpit.

"How did such a big boat get in such a small lake?" she asked.

"A lot of people used to have big boats on the lake, just as they had big hotels, big houses and big cars. This is a survivor, you might say."

Picking up a floorboard, he sniffed to make sure no gasoline had leaked into the bilge, a precaution his father had insisted on so strongly that he could no more start a boat without it than he could take a photograph without noting the nature of the light. The murky bilge smelled only musty but there was enough water in it to mirror the sky. Flicking a switch by the small brass ship's wheel, he started the whir of a bilge pump and leaned over the side to see if it was working. Rose sat on a seat in the stern, looking, by god, like a high school girl in her blue jeans and white sweater. She was watching him intently. While the pump splashed water from the bilge

into the lake, he unscrewed a heavy brass cap on the mahogany taffrail, took a yardstick from beneath the pillow on
the biggest seat and discovered that the gas tank was two-
thirds full. Next he opened a hatch in the deck, stepped down
to the venerable Gray engine and measured the oil.

"I love you," she said suddenly. "I love you for knowing
what you're doing. . . ."

"Actually, it's just an act," he said uncertainly and feeling
a bit uneasy. "If this old engine quits on us, we'll just have to
drift around until somebody brings Eb out to fix it."

When the bilge pump whined to announce its job was done,
he pressed the starting button. The old engine turned over
sluggishly, but when he pulled out the choke it came to life,
rumbling as though it possessed ten times the power it actually
had.

"Do you want me to help you take in the lines?" she asked.

"You just sit there while I display my mastery of the sea."

Stepping to the dock, he took the eye-splice at the end of
the bow line from a post and coiled the nylon rope on the
foredeck. Hopping back aboard, he slacked off the stern line,
gave it a sharp snap and flipped its eye-splice off the top of
its post. Then he went to the wheel, pushed the heavy gear-
shift lever, causing the *Indian Princess* to glide smoothly into
the lake.

"Where did you learn how to handle a boat?" she asked
admiringly, coming to sit on the high helmsman seat next to
the place where he stood at the wheel.

"My father. He spent most of his last years on this boat.
He'd fish every day, right up to the day the lake froze."

"Did your mother go with him?"

"She hated fishing. Dad would go alone or take me. Pete
hated fishing too.

"Could you and your old man talk?"

"About some things. He gave me a rather curious sex education. He said that sex was vastly overrated and 'mostly the
preoccupation of damn fools.' "

She laughed, perhaps a little ruefully. "I hope you can believe that, at least until I'm back in action again."

"Rosie, did you ever stop to think that there are worse things than just *loving* each other the way we do? What, for example, if you wanted thunder and lightning, more action than I could supply? For me that would be worse than temporary celibacy, I guarantee you...This way I can think of myself as a chained giant of virility, eagerly awaiting his moment of release. Such anticipation is quite a luxury at my age."

She laughed again. "Thanks for not complaining. I know that most men would. At any age."

"Well for us, for a while anyway, it will have to be love conquers all, including the lovers..."

"Yes," she replied, her voice catching slightly, and she put her hand on his arm.

The lake was shaped like a series of hourglasses, with the narrow parts full of islands of all sizes, from natural granite castles a mile long and a hundred feet high to tiny clumps of rock which supported only a single white birch or a lone pine tree. Although it was only sixteen miles long, it offered so many hidden bays and nearly landlocked harbors that Ben never felt he had fully explored it, in spite of the fact he'd virtually lived on it during the long summers of his youth. After crossing the wide part of the lake on which Cliff House had been built they entered a narrow channel with mountains rising steeply on the left and a flotilla of small islands on their right.

"It's funny," Rose said, "I've lived around here all my life but I've hardly ever been out on the lake. I've swum in it a lot, of course, but I've always been afraid of boats."

"Do you know why?"

"Maybe. Once when I was about eight or ten, I guess, dad came over from Ireland. One of the reasons I love him, despite *everything*, is that he always had great ideas, wonderful dreams...never mind that they most always came crashing

267

down, but at least no one can ever say he didn't *mean* well. This time he had this great plan for taking mom and me fishing and picnicking on an island in the lake." She paused.

"What happened?" Ben asked.

"He rented a rowboat with an outboard. Mom wasn't feeling well even then, but she loved being with him. She had a new green umbrella he'd given her to keep off the sun. It was calm at first. He sort of toured the bay, waving at people and cutting figure eights—he had never run a boat before and he'd *always* been a great showoff. At about noon he headed toward a big island for our picnic. All of a sudden it started to blow like hell."

"It does that on this lake."

"There was so much spray, I thought it was raining buckets, and the sky clouded over. Mom's umbrella blew away— I can still see it sailing over the waves, like a big kite. Dad tried to chase it. The waves got so big they were slopping into the boat." She paused again.

"You must have been terrified," he said, thinking of her as a big-eyed child in the wildly rocking boat.

"I figured dad could handle it, but then the motor quit. He kept telling us he knew all about motors and there was nothing to worry about. There was a wrench in a tackle box, and he started taking the whole motor apart, cursing as he hurt his fingers. It was his swearing, and the way his face got red and the panicky way he kept hammering at sticking parts that got to me. Every once in a while he'd put the whole thing together again and begin pulling the starting cord, yelling louder than ever when nothing happened. Once he almost fell overboard. Mother screamed. I knew she had a bad heart and I was terrified. Finally the starting cord broke. There was only one oar in the boat and he tried to paddle, but the wind was too strong. We could see the waves smashing on rocks ahead. Just when I thought we'd soon be swimming, a kid in a big Chris-Craft showed up and towed us back to the place where we'd rented the boat. That's where the worst of it started."

"How's that?" Ben asked.

"Well, dad was furious, of course. He had a bad sunburn—he can burn in no time flat. His knuckles were bleeding. He'd been scared and, of course, humiliated. His dream of a great day with his family on the lake had been shot down, like most of his other great plans. He had ... has ... a terrible temper, anyway, and he really let loose on the man who'd rented him the boat. He was going to knock him off the dock and he was going to sue him and he was going to see how far he could throw that motor into the lake.

"The guy who had rented him the boat had dark skin and black hair, a big, good-looking Italian about thirty years old. He was wearing bathing trunks and had a terrific tan. As dad ranted at him, he just sat in a tall lifeguard's chair at the end of the wharf and listened, shaking his head every once in a while as though he didn't believe what he was hearing. Finally he called a boy about twelve years old who was bailing out some of the other boats.

" 'Vito,' he said, 'take a look at the motor we rented to this man and see what's the matter with it.'

" 'The carburetor is shot,' dad shouted at him. 'The points are gone. The spark plug is giving no ignition. I *know* engines, I've built engines, I'm an engineer.' " Rose paused again. "Could I get a glass of water?"

"There's a cold jar of it in the refrigerator, also Coke and beer if you want it."

She disappeared and came back with a can of Coca-Cola. "Do you want me to go on with this tale of woe?"

"I can hardly wait."

"Well, dad's shouting gathered quite a crowd on the wharf. The boy, Vito, went to inspect the motor. In just about one minute he came back. 'Your trouble, mister,' he said to dad, 'is you ran out of gas. There's not a drop in the tank.'

269

"The whole crowd burst out laughing, most of all the man he had been yelling at. Poor dad just stood there, his face red from the sun and more so from embarrassment.

" 'There must have been a leak in the tank,' he shouted.

" 'I just filled it again,' Vito replied, 'and nothing's coming out. You really screwed up that engine, mister. Why did you have to strip the lug nuts?'

" 'You don't know what you're talking about,' dad yelled. 'You're nothing but a kid—'

" 'Now don't take it out on the boy,' the big man said, and he climbed down from the tower. 'I think maybe I ought to charge you for them stripped nuts.'

"The man was younger than dad, and taller, but mom and I knew what was going to happen. She moved forward and tried to hold his arm but she was too late.

" 'You bloody guinea,' dad yelled, and let go one of his rights. The guy ducked but dad charged him, butting him with his head and pushing him off the wharf. Then the boy tackled him around the ankles, and about five men from nearby boats jumped on dad. He threw a lot of them overboard, but then he went too, and like a lot of Irishmen, we found out, he couldn't swim. That surprised us, because he'd always said he could. Anyway, poor dad had to be rescued by the same man he'd attacked. Which, of course, was his final humiliation."

"I'm sorry," Ben said, "I guess I shouldn't laugh but I can't help it—"

"Dad's always good for a laugh," Rose said, but she wasn't laughing, or even smiling. "My whole family and all our good friends hardly need TV because we've got so many Dan Kelly stories. We all laugh."

Ben didn't miss the tinge of hurt bitterness.... "Well, whatever, that whole scene must have been pretty awful for you. And your mother . . ."

"*And* for dad," Rose said. "When they finally rolled him

270

up on the beach, he sat there coughing, his suit dripping. When he got the water out of his lungs, he just got up and walked to the car. He never again mentioned our great day of boating on the lake."

For a few minutes they didn't talk as he steered through a narrow passage between two islands, one of which had high cliffs, in the crevices of which stunted birch trees tenaciously clung to life.

"I feel guilty," she said suddenly.

"Why?"

"That story I told you makes dad out to be such a fool. He wasn't always that—"

"I'm sure."

"Can you stand it if I tell you one more story about him?"

"Sure, but please wait a few minutes until I anchor and can concentrate on your story. This channel is pretty tricky."

Fast outboard motorboats, many towing water-skiers, surrounded the *Indian Princess* as Ben emerged from the islands into a wide bay. Bouncing over the wake of the heavy old cruiser, the skiers waved gaily, but the snarl of their engines made conversation impossible. Ben steered toward a part of the shore that looked mountainous, with steep slopes of granite offering little shelter for a boat. Just when it looked as though he were going to crash the bow of the *Princess* into a great gray cliff, he turned to parallel the shore, keeping only about twenty yards off the rocks. Birches and hickory trees leaned toward the boat, almost touching her decks with their branches.

"The water is about a hundred feet deep here," Ben said. "See that land that looks like a point ahead?"

"It's beautiful."

"Watch it."

As he approached the "point," keeping close to the shore, the long finger of land appeared to detach itself from the adjoining hills and became an island, one of many islands it

271

turned out as they came closer, a crescent of rocks, shoals and tree-covered mounds that protected a narrow bay that ran into a mountain ravine.

"I never even knew this place existed," Rose said with near-awe. "Hey, it's shallow here. I can see bottom."

"This whole bay is shallow. My father and I used to love to fish here. See that reddish cliff ahead?"

"Yes."

"That's the bearing he taught me. If I head for that after having kept close to the shore we just passed, we go right between two patches of rock that are just under the surface of the water."

She could see the shoals on each side of them. "He knew what he was talking about."

"In navigational matters, anyway."

Coming on a new set of bearings, Ben turned toward the narrow end of the bay, which extended between two mountains as far as the eye could reach.

"Remember the Lost Lake Inn?" he asked.

"It burned a long time ago, didn't it?"

"The owner was jailed for arson. Anyway, they used to have a sandy beach right around this bend, the remains of it are still there. It's a fine place to swim."

Thick underbrush had now encroached upon the beach, but a crescent of yellow sand still offered soft footing for a few people. The bay here was only about a hundred yards wide. Slowing the engine, Ben turned off the ignition and glided to a spot only about a hundred feet from the beach. Going to the foredeck, he dropped a big old-fashioned Navy anchor, made the rope fast and went back to the cockpit.

"It's so *quiet* here," Rose said. "What happened to all the outboards and water-skiers?"

"Not many people know the way into this bay," he said. "Also, Green River empties into the lake just at the head of that ravine. It brings down all kinds of logs and branches from the mountains, sheer death for outboards."

"But our *Indian Princess* doesn't mind?"

"The *Princess* is made of sterner stuff . . . how about something to eat before we get to talking?"

"I'm famished, as usual these days. What have we got?"

"Nothing very glamorous. I bought an assortment of sandwiches in the village and some cherry turnovers."

"Yum! Can I get them?"

"When are you going to remember that you are supposed to be temporarily retired?"

She didn't answer him as he went below for the food, but stood looking with wonder around the secluded bay. The ruins of an old chimney and stone wall were still visible through the trees, but no house was in sight. Here there was no wind and the yellow stones on the bottom were as visible in the clear water as though the *Princess* were floating in air. The sun beat warmly on her head. Pulling off her sweater, she adjusted the top of the yellow bikini she wore under it. Birds sang in the bushes by the beach, not sweetly, but as though they were having an argument.

"Here we are," he said, appearing with a platter of sandwiches. "Hey, you look *good*, lady."

"Skimpy is what I look, but thanks anyway . . . tongue on rye, did I tell you that's my favorite?"

"You once told me you couldn't get tongue anywhere in town, and I asked the country store to get some in."

"Why didn't I think of that? I guess you have to be brought up rich to just tell a store to order something you want."

"You have to be rich enough to buy tongue. It's about two-eighty a pound."

She laughed and attacked the sandwich. "Why don't you take your shirt off? You could use a tan."

"I guess not."

273

"Why?"

"Just no."

"I bet I know why," she said with a smile. "You're afraid you're too fat to look good."

"That's not true. I *know* I'm too fat to look good."

"Well, I'm too thin and I risk it."

"Thin is prettier than fat."

"Ben, I'm your wife. Not legally yet, but in every other way. Don't be self-conscious with me—"

"I can't help it," he replied with as much dignity as he could muster.

"That's a terrible old shirt anyway. The cuffs are frayed, and do you know there's a hole in back?"

"I just use it for the boat."

"And I'm never going to see that beautiful chest of yours?"

"Heaven can wait."

Putting down her sandwich on the seat beside her, she stood up, walked slowly toward him and put her arms around his neck. He thought there was an odd gleam in her eye, but he was astonished when she put her finger through the hole in the back of his shirt, tickled him for a second, then suddenly ripped the whole shirt off his back, clawing with both hands like a woman possessed.

"*There*," she said when he stood with only a few shreds of cloth wafting from his belt. "Don't be shy with me, damn it . . ."

"I'm *trying* to be careful with you. I'm not all this modest, as you know. And right now I feel like ripping off that bikini top."

"You wouldn't," she retorted with mock terror, crossing her arms over her breasts. Then, her large eyes getting larger, she added, "Want to try?"

"Rosie, what would Dr. Knight say to this?"

"He didn't tell me not to rip off your shirt, and he said absolutely nothing about your ripping off the top of my bikini in good clean old married folk type fun."

274

"Rosie, please, let's take it easy—"

"Okay, okay, no more rough stuff, but do you mind if I take this thing off by myself?"

"Rosie, you know I've got nothing to say about it, so I'll surrender gracefully," and, kissing her on the neck, helped her to unbutton the top of her bathing suit. Her shoulder blades looked almost birdlike in the bright sun. Suddenly she turned around, her newly adolescent body tense. "It's nice not to hide," she said.

"Darling, you have nothing to hide—"

"You can say that again. Even if it wasn't very gallant."

"Oh, shut up." He kissed her. "But this is still a stupid thing to do—"

"Then I'll get dressed again . . . no, being together like this is good, Ben . . . I love the sunlight on your skin."

"Then lie down and soak it up with me. We'll recite the Gettysburg Address together, and if things get real bad, I know three lines of 'Trees.' "

He arranged the pillows from the seats on the deck of the cockpit. They lay on their backs holding hands, keeping their eyes closed against the sun.

"What do we do if even three lines of 'Trees' don't work?" he asked suddenly.

"Try 'O God Our Help in Ages Past.' I can teach you dozens of verses."

He laughed. "Rosie, celibacy with you is sexier than sex with anyone I've ever known—"

"Well, I bet you don't say *that* to all the girls."

At about four in the afternoon she said that she would like to take the kind of brief dip the doctor had permitted her and explore the ruins of the old inn. After getting in the anchor, he moored the *Princess* alongside the crumbling remains of a concrete wharf.

"Are we likely to run into any people?"

"Possible but unlikely."

275

"Do you mind if I stay topless? I guess I just want to be as free as I can."

"Bring a sweater with you. I'll take the towels."

The dirt road from the wharf to the inn was already overgrown with maple saplings. For Ben, who had visited the inn often in his youth, there was something eerie about the sight of the blackened foundation with its brick fireplace intact beneath a crumbling chimney. The spacious lawns which had surrounded the old inn had been returned to the forest, but some of the planting had survived. Snowberries, hydrangeas and lilacs now gone to seed grew in a big rectangle around what once had been spacious porches for the rocking-chair brigade.

"I can't get over how small the foundation is," Ben said, putting a blade of grass between his lips. "I remember it as such a big place, a regular Victorian wedding cake of an inn."

"I do too. I was always overawed when mom brought me here."

"I guess you're too young to remember the dances. Back in the thirties and forties they had dances here every Saturday night, with Japanese lanterns on the porches and a band on the terrace overlooking the lake."

"Mom told me about it."

"I have the strangest sensation," Ben said, jumping into the stone-lined rectangle of the foundation. "I can see exactly where everything was, as though it were still there. Here was the desk, with a big register held open by a piece of old cannonball, or grenade—that always used to fascinate me. Over there a string trio used to play before lunch and dinner. The dining room was over to the right, but on fine days most people ate on the terrace overlooking the lake. We can't even see the outline of that now because it had a board floor."

"With green and white awnings over it! I'm remembering too . . . they served lake trout on long silver platters with silver covers, or they looked like silver. Sweetbreads, too, which

I'd never even heard of before, and peach ice cream with real peaches and real cream—"

"With real ice cut in the lake and stored under sawdust . . ."

"And sometimes the string trio would play in a corner of the terrace while people dined," Rose went on. "It was always Mozart or Chopin with an occasional Strauss waltz, mother said. I was only here two or three times, but I can darn near hear them playing the 'Blue Danube' now."

"Heidi got mad at me and slapped my face in the cloakroom, right about here," Ben said. "I wish I had taken the hint."

"Why did she slap you?"

"I tried to kiss her cheek when I helped her on with her coat. In those days that was reason enough."

Rose smiled and shook her head.

"At one of those dances, I fell in love with a beautiful girl with hair like black silk and a red evening dress."

"What happened?"

"I took her out on the *Princess* and we lay down on the foredeck looking at the stars all night and vowing eternal love. Unfortunately, that was the Labor Day weekend. The next day she went home to New Jersey and she never came back."

"Did you try to get in touch with her?"

"The fact is I couldn't remember her last name, never mind her address. Her first name was Rita. Rita, Rita, where are you now?"

"In New Jersey," Rose suggested reasonably. "People who come from New Jersey always return, like boomerangs."

"I guess . . . You know, there used to be a formal garden over here," he said, walking to a level spot beside the foundation. "There were snapdragons and petunias, hollyhocks and morning glories on a trellis that surrounded a little nook with a stone bench . . . hey, look, the bench is still here."

277

Half-obscured by vines and tall grass the bench stood with only a slight tilt. Ben sat on it and crossed his legs.

"I'll be damned, what a souvenir. This was my glowering bench—"

"Your what?"

"When Heidi used to flirt and dance with other guys and otherwise behave like a normal seventeen-year-old, I'd come out here and glower. The idea was that she would be absolutely panic-stricken by my absence, but she hardly ever noticed it."

"Poor Ben...why couldn't we have met when I was seventeen? No, I take that back. I probably would have given you an even worse time."

She sat beside him on the glowering bench. For a moment they both stared at the ruin. A blue jay gave its raucous call and was answered by another. The air smelled heavy and sweet.

"Dad brought me here once," she said suddenly. "Can I tell you about it now? I want you to understand why I must invite him to the wedding..."

Her father, she said, had usually been away in Ireland during her childhood. One reason was that he could make a living in Ireland, where he had served an apprenticeship as an engineer for textile machinery, but he had no degrees and in America was considered uneducated. There might also have been other reasons: Rose was still unsure about the nature of her father's relationship to her ailing mother. At any rate, he was an absentee father. Amy, Rose's mother, never talked against him, but grammie was always muttering darkly about him. All Rose at the age of ten had of him were photographs, which showed a very handsome young Irishman and an occasional shilling wrapped in tissue or a pound note he sent her in the mail, usually with the briefest of letters. At her school there had been many fatherless children, some the result of divorce or desertion, but many who were illegitimate. During Parents' Day and other occasions when

278

fathers visited the school, Rose was mortified to find herself relegated to the library, where efforts were made to keep the fatherless pupils occupied. Anxious to prove, at least to herself, that she was not really one of these unfortunates, she had a bracelet made of Irish coins he had sent her, and wore a locket containing a picture of his head snipped from a snapshot. Unaware of its likely effect, she had showed these trophies to several other children. One tall fat girl had resented this. "You don't have no father, no more than the rest of us," she had said, "you just make all this stuff up..."

At the age of ten, Rose had been crushed. Perhaps, she thought, the charge was true. Perhaps her mother had just made up her father, the way the mothers of many illegitimate children did, she already guessed. Profoundly depressed, she put her locket and bracelet of coins in her school desk, from which they were quickly stolen, removing all trace of the handsome Irishman. Because her mother was already ill, Rose didn't feel she could mention her problems to her, and at the age of ten tried to be independent enough to survive on her own if necessary.

During this dark period her father, Dan Kelly, suddenly sent a cable announcing his imminent arrival aboard the *Britannia*. Looking flustered but happy, Amy arranged to take a train to New York to meet the boat. And feeling frightened but eager, Rose at the age of ten waited with her mother in the crowd on the wharf as the tugs pushed in the big Cunard liner. Finally the gangway had banged down, and the first passenger ashore had been this wonderful-looking man with a straw boater, a striped blazer, elegant white flannel pants, spotless white shoes and a cane!

"That's your father!" Amy had said, beaming. "Wave!"

Instead of returning the wave, Dan had come bounding up some concrete stairs, pushing impatiently through the crowd. While he enveloped his wife in an enthusiastic embrace, Rose had felt suddenly shy, wondering what she would do if he kissed and hugged her so hard. Instead he had stepped suddenly back from his wife, and standing very straight had tipped his hat to his daughter. "How are you, young lady?" he had asked. "You are a beautiful young lady indeed, but I guess I should get to know you a little better before I give you better proof of my esteem."

This was her father? This was Galahad. This was God. At that moment, Rose had fallen in love with him, abjectly, completely. While he waited to clear customs, Dan told his family that he'd had a stroke of great good luck. He had a new job that made him a salesman of textiles, not an engineer. He was, he was sure, a natural-born salesman, and had already brought in some big orders. He was in the chips. He was going to make up for all the hard times, and the way to begin was to buy a new car.

The next day they drove to Livingston in a shiny green Ford phaeton. With the top down they toured the village, waving at all their friends. After Amy went to bed to rest, Dan took his daughter on a stroll down Main Street, tipping his hat and twirling his cane. The next morning he even drove her to school in the open car, showing everyone that she had the most handsome father of them all.

"If you can stand it, there's more," Rose said.

Ben assured her he could.

"Dad knew that a lot of people in town didn't think much of him," she continued. "Some thought he'd just abandoned mom and me, and he'd been in a little trouble in the bars. Then, not long after he got home, there was that fiasco with the outboard motorboat I told you about. So a few days later dad decided to give a big dinner for all mom's friends at the Lost Lake Inn, the classiest place in town. You can't imagine what this meant to him. A man without much formal education, he was really proud to have a teacher as his wife. When he was unemployed, she seemed rich to him and he was very jealous of what he referred to as 'all her rich friends.' He was particularly jealous of the principal of the school. Somehow he had got the idea that mother was having an affair with this guy . . . yes, in spite of her illness. Dad's long suit has never been logic. Anyway, the principal was a rather elegant English type, and dad was *sure* that he saw him as nothing but an ignorant Irishman who couldn't even support his own wife."

"The dinner was here?" Ben asked.

"Yes, I'd forgotten just where it was until you mentioned the terrace by the lake. Dad got a long table right next to the rail by the water. He told mother to invite everyone she knew. The idea, of course, was to celebrate, and most of all to demonstrate his new affluence, but he called it a dinner in mother's honor. When practically the whole faculty of the school accepted his invitation, he was scared as hell, but cabled Ireland for more funds. This dinner had to be just right. He was always confused by menus, so he told mother to order the best of everything and got mad when she tried to economize. . . . Well, finally the great day arrived, and a fine sunny day it was. About thirty people sat around the long table, with dad at the head, me on his left and mom to his right. The principal, whom dad hated, was on the other end, looking just as impressed as dad wanted him to be. A special corsage of roses and gardenias arrived, and dad grandly presented it to mom. The guests were given a choice of cocktails or champagne, and there were wines for every course. I remember that we started with fresh brook trout, and then had duck l'orange, which I'd never had. The string trio played Strauss waltzes, and dad asked mom to dance. They were both terrific dancers, and I'll never forget them twirling around that terrace . . ."

"That's a lovely picture." Ben said. "And it's a very nice story—"

"I wish that were the end of it. Do you want the crash finish?"

"I can take it."

"Well, all went well till the waiter, a tall, thin, dark-haired guy, brought dad the bill. Even in those days it must have been staggering, for all those people, and dad wasn't used to American prices. Still, mom had warned him and he was prepared. Taking out his wallet, he counted out a fat stack of bills.

" 'Keep the change,' he said to the waiter.

"The trouble was, we learned later, the change amounted to about twenty-six cents. The waiter counted the money, looked at the check, and said, 'Perhaps there's a misunderstanding, sir. In this country we are accustomed to getting at least ten percent as a service charge.'

"It happened that there was a lull in the conversation and *everyone* at the table heard the waiter. To be made to appear cheap and ignorant after such a grand show ... do you see how he felt?"

"I sure do."

"What made it worse is that the principal said, 'Say, I'll leave the tip. How much was the check?'

" 'That will not be necessary,' old dad thundered. 'This waiter is going to apologize for his bad manners and be on his way.'

"The waiter said he didn't think he'd done anything to apologize for, that he'd served thirty people a large dinner and he ... well, he never got any further. Dad threw him in the lake."

"In the *lake?*"

"Yep. He just sort of sailed him right over the rail and then he threw his tray after him."

"He may not always have been the father of your dreams, but he sure had a sense of timing. . . ."

"He makes for good stories, but life doesn't stop with someone throwing a waiter in the lake. In this case the principal became the hero of the occasion by jumping in to save the guy. And the manager called the cops. By that time dad was plastered and he took a swing at one of them. Mother wanted to die—who knows, maybe that's partly why she soon did.

"... I tried to defend dad right up to the point of trying to bite a cop. And all the time this madhouse was going on, the string trio kept on playing, just like the band on the *Titanic*. I've never really liked the 'Blue Danube' since."

"I'll break my record of it."

"See? The story is still funny. But the cops messed up dad pretty bad and when he got home he lay on his bed, crying like a baby for an hour."

"End of the joke."

"But this is the real end of the story ... the next day dad got up early, I heard him singing in the shower. He put on his white flannel trousers and his striped blazer. All put together again. On the outside, anyway.

" 'Well, I guess we showed these country boys a thing or two,' he said to mom when he came down for breakfast. Then he told me to go out in the garden and get him a rosebud for his buttonhole. Finally he told us that he had urgent business in Ireland, got in his car and disappeared for another five years. . . ." Rose paused. "Damn it—"

"What's the matter?"

"I said I was trying to explain why I want him at our wedding, but all I do is keep telling you stuff that will make you believe everything grammie says."

"No, I do see why you want him. You love him, Rosie, and you're proud of him, no matter what. He's your father, it's not a crime."

"Is it crazy?"

"I loved my father, whose problems were different but probably just as bad. I certainly would invite him to my wedding, even if he was too drunk to stand up at my last one."

"Then you won't get sore if dad does something perfectly abominable?"

"Only if he upsets you ... maybe you ought to tell him that."

"A pronouncement in advance like that would *not* be conducive to peace, I assure you. . . . Hey, how about a swim, the sun's about to go down."

Although the doctor had told her to "swim like an old lady," Rose shed her bikini bottom on the beach and scampered into the water, where she was darting about like a trout until she heeded Ben's plea for caution. Leaving his clothes beside hers, he floated on his back beside her.

"This is marvelous," she said. "I feel like a dinghy beside the *Queen Mary*."

"Thanks . . . you said I was magnificent. Now I'm the *Queen Mary*."

"Sorry, tiger . . . say, do you hear mosquitoes?"

"They often come here at dusk."

"Why should I worry? If they bite me in the right places, they might even improve my shape."

"*Hey there!*" A loud, unpleasant voice.

Turning, they saw a tall man on the beach. He was wearing a wide-brimmed hat and a green uniform. He was standing with folded arms, a stance of stern disapproval.

"Oh, lord," Rose groaned, and Ben saw that she was genuinely frightened, not to mention embarrassed.

"Don't be scared," he said, "it's just our friendly forest ranger." Turning toward shore he called, " 'Hey there,' yourself."

"You come in, this is state land but it's not part of the park yet. You're trespassing. Didn't you see the signs?"

"No," Ben said. "You stay here," he told Rose, and began swimming toward shore. When he reached shallow water he stood up, looking terribly vulnerable, Rose thought, but he strode valiantly to the beach.

"This is a no-swimming area," the man said. "There's a fine. It's also against the law to tie up a boat where yours is—"

"All *right*, now please get out of here so the lady and I can get dressed. Go on to the wharf, where my boat is. We'll meet you there. Then we'll give you our names and you can do whatever you have to do."

284

The ranger looked at him. "Nude swimming is also against the law around here."

"No doubt. And no doubt it's also against the law for a ranger to stand on a beach while a nude lady is trying to get out and get dressed. Shall we get into that one?"

"I'll meet you by your boat, wise guy."

After waiting a few moments, Rose came out, and Ben handed her a towel. She still looked scared.

"Nothing can happen, maybe a small fine—"

"I know, but I hate this. I feel as though I'd been caught naked on Main Street—"

"Worse things could happen to Main Street. Leave the copper to me.... Why don't you go aboard the boat and take yourself a nap?"

When they were dressed, she followed him toward the wharf, where the ranger was standing, staring at the *Princess*.

"Can you prove you own this boat?"

"No," Ben said. "Now please be patient another moment and we'll get this whole thing straightened out."

He helped Rose aboard the boat and went to a drawer in the cabin, where he found a pad and a pencil. He sat in the stern and began writing quickly.

"What are you doing?" the ranger asked from the wharf.

"I'm writing our names to save you trouble. What's yours?"

"Lloyd Harris."

Ben wrote that on an inner sheet and handed the paper with his own name and Rosie's to the ranger. He was a little ashamed of having written his own name as "Benjamin Livingston Winslow," but in dealing with local officials, that rarely did any harm. He had also listed himself and Rose as "editor and publisher of Livingston *Life*."

Studying the paper, the ranger looked impressed. "Say, are you Ebon's old man?"

"Yes, I guess you could put it that way."

"Good boy you got there, a real woodsman...Say, I'm sorry I got uptight with you and your lady. I've had a hell

285

of a time with this place all summer. You know, city people walk in from the road and spread trash over everything. The reason you don't see it is we just raked up five tons of it and trucked it out. Before we did the bears were hanging out here as though it was a town dump. Some crazy kid shot one of the bears with a .22 and the bear tore his arm off. We got blamed, of course. Why didn't we tell 'em that dangerous bears were loose in the woods?"

"I guess you do have a beef . . ."

"Last year some drunk got himself drowned on this beach. That's why we're supposed to chase everybody off."

"I understand."

"Well, give my best to Eb. And tell your lady that I hope she'll forgive me. I'm no prude."

He left then, walking rapidly off the wharf.

Picking up the floorboard and quickly sniffing the bilge, Ben started the engine, cast off the lines, and steered the *Princess* away from the wharf.

"Safe at last," Rose said, emerging from the cabin. "Sorry I was such a coward. Did he give us a birchbark ticket or something?"

"Not a thing. I used influence.'"

"The Livingston name or the paper?"

"My *son's* name. Now I'm reduced to trading on the influence of my own kid. Generation gap, indeed . . ."

She laughed as he told her about the encounter. "Do you know why I got so scared?" she asked suddenly. "When dad starts arguing with cops, it always ends up in a fight. I could just see it coming—"

"Relax, I'm a complete coward. When you're with me there will be no fights. We may have to run fast sometimes, but no fights, I guarantee you."

He was quiet as he lined the boat up with the bearings to get through the shoals in the bay.

"It's been a wonderful cruise," she said. "How many miles have we been?"

286

"About eight."

"I feel as though I'd been around the world. Thank you, darling. By the way, I love you, Ben. How come you're able to make my life seem so safe and exciting at the same time?"

18

WHEN Ben got home the next afternoon he found a note asking him to call Bill Crawford at the Albany *Star*.

"Where the hell have you been, Ben? I've been trying to get you all day."

"Gosh, boss, I apologize. Please don't fire me, think of my wife and twelve kids—"

"To hell with your wife and your twelve kids, I have deadlines. I need a follow-up on the Radeau story."

"The old man hasn't killed anybody new yet, as far as I know."

"But they burned your barn down, didn't they? After making a lot of anonymous threats?"

"How did you hear about that?"

"When I couldn't get you I talked to your girl Lillian, in your office. She sounds pretty savvy."

"Well I hope she was savvy enough to tell you that we can't prove who made the calls or who burned the barn. There's absolutely no proof of any kind."

"Was it witchfire? Hey, that's not a bad caption for a picture of a burning barn with a story about no one knows who started it. . . . I assume you have pictures."

"A few, but they're not developed yet. Look, Bill, don't tie this thing to the Radeaus."

288

"I'll just give the facts and let people use their imagination."

"That's what I thought. Look, I'm kind of tired of this whole big-deal exploitation of some local hillbillies. Maybe I'm just a local yokel myself, but I'm going to play the thing way down in my paper—"

"You do what you want, but I got a circulation manager on my neck. We pay good money for your stuff, Ben. Are you so rich these days that you don't need it?"

"No," Ben said, thinking of Rose's medical bills and the college bills in his future. "I'll send you the film and a story to go with it. If there has to be a story about our barn, I guess I ought to be the one to write it," and control it, he added to himself.

Nonetheless, he felt in conflict as he drove down to his office to write the article and develop the film. He had, after all, made up his mind to play down the Radeau case as much as possible, but there was no way to avoid the intimation that the barn fire was a continuation of it. When he developed his film, he found one print which showed the lurid message that had been painted on the side of the building: NEXT TIME THE HOUSE, MAYBE YOU. In his article he quoted that, but also emphasized that the barn-burner had obviously spared the horse. As he handed his work to the driver of an Albany-bound bus, Ben still wondered whether he should have thrown it away. Sure, he needed money, and maybe he had more need for reestablishing himself as a professional *news* photographer, but the Radeau story, he felt certain, could lead only to bigger trouble.

He felt even more certain of it next afternoon when the *Star* appeared. Crawford had used his question, all right, as a caption for a three-column picture and story, a ridiculous amount of space for a barn fire. Still, his picture with the blazing old shed and the side of the house with its sinister warning was effective. And the caption WAS IT WITCHFIRE? lent a sardonic note to his own story, which made the point that it was not demonstrated that there was any connection between this relatively small disaster and the Radeau tale of alleged incest and murder.

Now his telephone would probably bring more threats, Ben thought wearily. Maybe more buildings would be burned. If he wasn't careful, he would find himself turning his own town of Livingston into a sort of Peyton Place . . . well, face it, it did have some similarities anyway, but the Radeaus were probably the least of it. . . . He turned to more cheerful thoughts, in particular the immediate prospect of exploring Lost Lake again with Rose aboard the *Indian Princess*.

The job for the Albany paper had delayed him, and it was almost four before he arrived at the boathouse. Rose was already aboard the boat, tidying up the cockpit. To his surprise, Ben saw Ann sitting on the helmsman's seat, examining the controls. He explained why he was late.

"I love just fussing around here," Rose said. "Do you mind if Annie comes? She's never seen the lake."

"Except at night with Eb," Ann said, "which isn't exactly the best way to appreciate the scenery."

"Glad to have you aboard," Ben said as he jumped down into the cockpit.

"I'm drawing the battle lines," Rose said. "Annie sides with grammie about dad. I told them you side with me, right?"

"Right."

"So, it's two against two, except it's our wedding. I wrote him airmail today."

"That's like lighting a long fuse, if you ask me," Ann said.

"Well, the decision is made, and it's mine. . . . And now I want to take Annie out on the boat so she'll stop hating me."

This time he headed for the largest of the islands at the other end of the lake.

"I really feel terrific," Rose said, stretching out on the seat in the stern. "Never thought I'd be in love with an Indian princess."

She had a new one-piece red bathing suit and was already

beautifully tanned . . . and still looking like a teenager to him. . . .

"Do you mind if I sit here?" Annie asked, indicating the helmsman's seat.

"Not at all."

She was wearing a green two-piece bathing suit, which was designed to be modest, but her proportions defeated it. Like her sister, she had that fair Irish complexion, which blossomed into all sorts of soft shadings of pink and white when touched by the sun, or embarrassment. As she sat on the tall seat, she often glanced at Ben, a quiet smile on her face, and he could almost feel her . . . well, her approval of him, almost like a warmth. . . . Those pictures of mine in the paper and on TV did it, he figured . . . the young lady had never really seen a picture escape the narrow confines of the camera and go public. If she could learn this magic trick, a glamorous life of world travel awaited her, didn't it? Instead of working as a secretary in the mill, or taking any of the other dull jobs Livingston had to offer, she could be off to romance and high adventure and god knew what else in New York, London, Paris . . . the camera was the key to the outside world, and he, she figured, the magic person who could teach her the secret of how to use it. Well, magician, watch it. . . .

Still, maybe it wasn't all that simple as he'd like to think . . . she was and she wasn't just a teenage schoolgirl . . . after all, she worked day and night, both to keep house for Rose and to develop her skills with that camera. She'd sold her horse without a tear to help with expenses and was becoming nearly as responsible in worldly matters as Rose was.

Beyond that, though, there was a dimension of Ann that remained a mystery to him. He'd sensed it, but until now hadn't been really aware of it. As far back as he could remember, the telephone in the house of most pretty seventeen-year-old girls rang without letup. In the old days he'd almost always got a busy signal when he tried, for example, to call Heidi, but ever since he'd known Ann she'd received *no* calls . . . and no boys on bicycles, or in jalopies, pursued her. At first he'd thought she'd just willingly and sort of naturally been monopolized by Ebon, but her relationship with his son appeared to be more than a touch less steamy than he had imagined. Was it possible for a seventeen-year-old girl who looked like Annie to be so consumed by family responsibilities and adult ambition that she was near-immune to the ordinary temptations of her age? . . .

He considered but couldn't really take seriously the notion that Ann had a teenage crush on him, but on the other hand perhaps he had encouraged something like it by spending so much time with her. And how did he feel? . . . Well, face it, would he have so easily given so many hours to a very *plain* young lady? Wasn't there something a little too pleasing, maybe even titillating about basking in the admiration of a statuesque—yes, she *was* that—seventeen-year-old girl? And wasn't there also something unbearably cheap and foolish about allowing even the most subtle, one-sided flirtation when he felt as he did about Rosie? . . . Damn right, there was. Whatever Annie was doing, he figured she was doing what came naturally, it was essentially innocent, but at his age he had no right to absolve himself if . . . unintentionally as it might be . . . he was somehow encouraging her. Perhaps his built-in guilty conscience was making him exaggerate the dangers, but there was something wrong with the present tableau: Rose lying on the stern seat, perhaps asleep, fifteen feet away, Annie sitting inches from his right shoulder, directing all those confidential looks, smiles, at him. It had been going on for an hour, and it was enough. He suspected Rose might think so too, even though she was the one who had invited Annie along.

"It's such a nice day," he said suddenly. "Let's just drift and sun for a while."

"Fine," Rose said, not sounding at all as though she'd been

sleeping. "The captain must get tired of running the boat all the time."

After turning off the engine he got himself a cold beer with cans of Coca-Cola for Rose and Ann. When Rose sat up to make room for him, he sat with her, she leaning against his shoulder.

Ann remained on the helmsman's seat. . . . "Say, do you guys mind if I talk shop?"

"No, honey," Rose said, a quiet smile on her face.

"Well, Ben, if you *really* are going to let me help you with this book *Small Town*, I wish you'd make up a sort of shooting schedule, a list of all the subjects you want me to take pictures of. Then I could just work on it whenever I get time—"

"Maybe we could do something like that, but I'm afraid I work mostly with targets of opportunity," Ben told her. "When I see something good, I shoot it. I don't think we should arrange too much of this."

"But can't some of it be set up? You once told me we should get shots of the Odd Fellows and those other outfits that dress up in fancy costumes, even with beards, swords and all that. Well, that can be arranged, can't it?"

"It might not be so easy. Some of those groups are more secret than the Pentagon."

"Well, I bet you I can do it. One thing I've found out is that almost everybody in this town likes to have his picture taken. At least give me a list and let me work on it?"

"Okay, you might as well try the Twenty-three Club at Joe's Bar," Ben said. "There's plenty of drama there . . . Rosie, I'm sorry, this is boring you to death . . . we should be talking about our wedding. I want to talk about it . . ."

"Wrong . . . you don't know how I love shop talk now," she said. "All my life I've had jobs I hated, now I *crave* work . . . God, I wish I could play more of a part in this thing . . ."

"You will, don't worry, and you may get pretty sick of it."

293

"Well, I'm no photographer, but I do have a few ideas. You want some?"

"Shoot."

"Stuff like the Odd Fellows sitting with their hemp beards and spears will be sort of funny, and the girls at the Twenty-three Club will be sort of sad, but if you're really going to do a small town, you ought to have something with some bite—"

"Like what?"

"Well, what about sex education? The photo would show a class of earnest kids and teacher. The text beneath would say something like 'For years the people of Livingston did not want their children to have sex education in their school. In 1978, however, twenty-eight high school and six junior high school girls became pregnant. Parents began to ask for sex education, but some maintained that schools are no place for that sort of thing. The debate split the town along religious lines. Finally a compromise was worked out. Livingston now has a class in sex education, but it is called 'The Life Adjustment Program.' There are four things which cannot be discussed in the Life Adjustment Program: masturbation, abortion, birth control and sexual intercourse. These are deemed too controversial for young people.' "

"*I* took that course," Annie said. "We spent a lot of time on Fallopian tubes. Mr. Ostrand said that they, at least, wouldn't get many people upset."

"Rosie," Ben said, "you're a Catholic and can say such things . . . how about doing the writing?"

"I wish I could, but I'm afraid that would come under the heading of work, and you know what Dr. Knight said—"

"I mean after your operation, we don't have to rush."

"Sure, I'd love it, but somehow it's hard for me to think about what happens after the operation."

"Well, right now we don't need a written text, but we could sure use your ideas," Ann said.

There was a moment of silence, during which Ann brought

a fresh beer to Ben without being asked and a fresh Coca-Cola for Rose.

"Damn," Rose said, "I just remembered that even Coke is on my verboten list and I've been guzzling it like there's no tomorrow."

"My fault too," Ben said. "We should carry that list with us."

"It would be like carrying the New York telephone book," Rose said, handing the Coke back to Ann. "Can you bring me a ginger ale, honey?"

The *Indian Princess* slept on the water, stirring only when a motorboat passed. The still surface of the lake gleamed like dark glass all around them. Adjusting her sunglasses, Rose took a bottle of ginger ale from Ann. "I've got a few more ideas, Ben. Forgive me, but I'm hung up on the schools. They spend god knows how many hundreds of thousands of dollars a year but they've forgotten how to teach *English*. They don't even get the kids to read novels or plays any-more—just the stalest textbooks."

"You can say that again," Annie said. "From the sixth grade right through high school, English is mostly memorizing the craziest rules of grammar you ever saw, which is funny because the teacher speaks the most garbled grammar you ever heard. I never would have heard of Dickens or *Treasure Island* or *Catcher in the Rye* if sis hadn't given me the books at home."

"That's interesting, but how do we photograph it?" Ben asked.

"Fortunately, both the principal of the school and the head of the English department look like what they are—idiots. I'd use their pictures to illustrate a brief text piece. And maybe I'd print a theme by a senior, a few paragraphs of it anyway, as a horrible example."

"We don't want to look unfair," Ben said.

"I know that's a danger, but damn it, Ben, it's true . . . and

295

let me give you one more crazy story before we get onto something better. Did you know that Howie has resigned as president of the hospital?"

"I heard he wanted time for his campaign."

"That's right. But Eddie Case has replaced him. Howie, god knows, is no bargain, but now we have an undertaker in charge of our hospital! Even the doctors have to report to him."

"Couldn't we get him for conflict of interest?" Ben asked with a straight face. "Does he want the patients to live or die?"

"Eddie's not a bad guy," Rose said, "but still the situation is crazy. We've got to decide how to handle the hospital. It's a public menace. What we should have here is just an emergency clinic and ambulances to Burlington, where people can get real care. You'll have no trouble finding pictures to prove it."

"I'm not too comfortable in the role of reformer," Ben said. "I'm not so pure myself, you know . . ."

"Okay, change gears. First, put the past into your book. Get into your own files and the archives of the library, have one section that shows the small town the way it used to be."

"Good idea," Ben said, and Ann nodded.

"Here's a better one, though it may sound sappy. Put some love in your book, all different kinds. Inevitably you're going to show a lot of hate—the Radeaus, street fights and all that, but there's also a lot of love in this town. And don't forget sex . . . sex, for heaven's sake, is the main preoccupation of practically everybody in this town from the age of six to sixty, and beyond. I bet we're much hornier than people in a big city. We have no big careers, often no jobs to occupy us, no theaters, no fancy restaurants, no big-deal distractions of any kind. Even the TV reception is lousy, and that John Wayne movie at the Empire never seems to change. If it weren't for sex, people would die of boredom. One more thing . . . when all's said and done, I hope the book shows that you love the town. Didn't Samuel Johnson say, 'If you hate

London, you hate life.'? Well, I feel the same way about Livingston. I can get mad at its schools and the hospital and all the damn fools who live here, but it's *me*, too. I love the place."

"In my fashion, I guess I do too," Ben said. "Otherwise, why do I keep coming back? . . ."

The air had turned very hot and muggy, and he began looking for thunderclouds, which soon began pouring over the mountains, forming themselves into the shape of a great anvil over the lake. "I guess we better go in," he said.

"Would it be dangerous to stay here?" Rose asked.

"Actually, the *Princess* is probably safer than the house. Lightning is always striking the trees around the house, but the *Princess* has never been touched."

"Then let's stay here," Ann said. "I bet I can get some great shots of the storm—"

"If you stay in the cockpit you're going to get mighty wet."

"I don't mind," Rose said. "I'd like to have a front-row seat for this thing."

Ben perched on the helmsman seat while Rose and Ann sat on the stern. Soon there was the intermittent glow of lightning on the other side of the mountain and the ominous roll of distant thunder. Gray clouds with white fringes raced across the sky, obscuring the last patch of blue, building up the anvil to monstrous size. Although it was not yet five-thirty, it grew surprisingly dark. A brisk wind sprang up, building into gusts that looked almost black on the water. The temperature suddenly fell, causing the women to put on sweaters.

"Rosie," Ben said, "this show may be more dramatic than you think. You sure you don't want to go in?"

"You still say it won't be dangerous?"

"The *Princess* and I must have been through a hundred storms like this. I used to love them when I was a kid—"

"Then sail on, damn it. The Kellys may have a better knowledge of firewater than fresh water, but we can learn . . ."

297

As the gusts increased, Ben started the engine. The old boat trembled a little as he headed her into the wind, like a good horse headed for a jump, he thought.

"Annie, there are some slickers in the locker below," he said. "If you two are going to stay out there, you'd better get them."

Annie hardly had time to get the foul-weather gear before the storm really broke. A white squall, stretching the whole width of the lake, roared toward them. The rain hit first like a brigade of fire hoses, driving the two women to the shelter which projected over the wheel. Then came the wind, heeling the heavy old cruiser a little, whipping the hair of the women around their faces and blowing an empty cardboard beer carton that had been left in the cockpit overboard. It lashed spray across the cockpit, although near the wheel they were dry. The windshield wipers had difficulty keeping up with the rhythm of the old boat's dance. Suddenly lightning struck a nearby mountain, followed by a crack of thunder loud enough to burst the eardrums.

Glancing at Rose, Ben saw her standing as though transfixed, her hand on the combing. Ann, less impressed or maybe more practical, went to the cabin below.

Putting the boat in gear, Ben steered across a small sea of whitecaps toward a mountain with a bald side of smooth granite which faced the lake. In this torrential rain, it was gushing like a waterfall, a regular Niagara two hundred feet high.

"Oh," Rose shouted above the roar, "thank you for showing me that!"

They were on their way back to the boathouse with the rain still pelting down when Rose saw an aluminum outboard motorboat drifting. A woman, a man and a child were waving frantically. Ben saw them at just about the same moment and turned to head toward them. Slowing a few yards from the boat, Ben called, "Where do you want to be towed?"

"Scotty's landing," the man replied.

Ben tossed him the end of a line, and they were soon steaming slowly toward the midsection of the lake.

It was almost eight o'clock when they got home. Ann, who had been sleeping below most of the time, hurried to get dinner, but Rose looked tired and felt a little chilled. She took Ben's arm as they walked to her room. While she took a hot bath, he changed his clothes. Soon he heard her calling from her bathroom, and hurried there. She was lying in her tub looking beautiful, he thought, but also very delicate . . . frail.

"Could you get me my shampoo? It's on my dresser."

He retrieved the bottle for her, noting its name, Wild Flower.

"That's not really why I called for you," she said, "but I guess you knew that. I was feeling lonely . . . how about keeping a lady company for a while?"

He closed the toilet seat and sat down.

"For your information you're the first gentleman I ever called into my bathroom to chase the blues, or anything else, for that matter . . . I think I'm going to like marriage."

"I hope so. It's not all wild flowers, though, I can tell you."

"What?" And then seeing him nod toward the shampoo bottle, laughed. "And by the way, I was very impressed by you as intrepid rescuer—"

"You've rescued a fair lot yourself, lady."

"Such as?"

"Annie, grammie, me for three. Ebon . . ."

"Maybe. Anyway, it's nice to hear. . . . Hey, you know I've gained six pounds? And my figure is starting to come back a little. It's like growing up all over again. I think I'm about to graduate to a training bra. Have you noticed?

"I've been sitting here noticing like all get out."

She was quiet a moment, then, not looking at him, she said, "Ben . . . when I go back into the hospital, do you know where they're going to cut?"

"No," he replied, closing his eyes for a fraction of a second. "I'm sure, though, that Dr. Knight could tell you if you really want—"

"I mean, when they say 'open heart surgery,' that sounds pretty scary, doesn't it? They must leave the whole heart open, or something."

"We'll ask Dr. Knight."

"The doctor told me the scars wouldn't be bad, but he didn't say where they'd be."

"We can ask him that too."

"No, I guess not . . . maybe I don't really want to know . . . Ben, thanks for putting up with me. I guess I'm just plain scared. And, Ben, I love you."

He got up, leaned over her, and kissed her. It was the best answer he had.

19

Rose's letter to her father had invited him to her wedding on August 1. On July 15, almost as soon as he had received her letter, she received a cablegram from him that said, ARRIVING KENNEDY WEDNESDAY MORNING SEVEN MEET ME DAD.

"Isn't it great he's coming so early?"

"It's very nice," Ben replied, trying to keep a dubious note out of his voice. His main comfort when hearing stories of Dan had been the thought that he would only be around a very short time.

"Wednesday! That's the day after tomorrow! I think I'll go down and get my hair done right away."

She left the cablegram on the kitchen table, where grammie soon caught sight of it. "Did Rosie want me to see this?" she asked Ben.

"I'm sure she wouldn't mind."

She scanned the message quickly. "Well, he ain't changed none. Nobody else would send a thing like this."

"How's that?"

"Would you come to your daughter's wedding two weeks in advance without even asking if it was convenient?"

"I guess not."

"Dan never in his life has cabled that he was coming if

convenient. He always just names a date and says he's coming, ready or not."

Ben shrugged.

"He almost always takes a boat, but this time he's flying. Why? Rosie told him you have a newspaper together and he suspects she's got a good thing, something he might be able to get in on. He can't wait to see."

"Are you sure he's that cynical?"

"Wait and see. Now look at the rest of this cable. He's getting into Kennedy at seven in the morning, and he says, 'Meet me.' Not 'Please meet me,' and he doesn't even have ten words here. And who the hell asks to be met at seven in the morning at that godforsaken airport anyway? Why doesn't he do like everybody else and fly on to Albany? And why doesn't he give a flight number and the name of his airline? It's easier just to let Rosie figure that out. I tell you, that man makes me mad just by cabling he's going to come here!"

"The thing to remember, I guess, is that Rosie loves him," Ben said.

"Well, if you love Rosie, you'll protect her from him. Whether you tell him about her heart or not, he'll run her ragged, just like he ran her mother ragged. You can't believe that man. Lordy, the last time he was here, I was already in this wheelchair, but he thought nothing of asking me to do his damn laundry for him. And all he did was lie around the house drinking."

"What do you suggest?"

"You should make Dan stay over at the farm. If he's in the same house with Rosie, she'll not get a minute's peace."

"I doubt if she'll permit that."

"You might talk her into it."

"I'll try."

"Now let me give you a few other pieces of advice." She hunched forward in her chair. "Don't you ever let that man drive a car. He'll tell you an Irish license is good here for six

302

months, or that he's got an international license, but that don't make no nevermind. He's been picked up for drunk driving so many times in so many countries, the only license he'll ever get now is for driving people crazy."

"I'll remember that," Ben said, fighting back a smile.

"Don't lend him money. The more he gets, the more he'll ask. I lent him a hundred bucks once a long time ago when that was big money. When I finally asked for it back, he said he could get it for me if he had another hundred to invest in his business."

"What is his business these days?" Ben asked, deciding he should learn all he could about the man.

"Funny business, mostly. He did pretty well as a textile salesman for a while, but that petered out pretty quick, the way everything does for him. Then he said he was in importing and exporting. What he does is import money from Rose and export bullshit, if you'll pardon my French."

Ben laughed.

"The other thing is, don't let him load any crap on you because the minute you do, he'll add ten more shovelfuls."

"For instance?"

"Well, Dan prides himself on being a real Dublin gentleman of the old school. Real Dublin gentlemen of the old school never carried suitcases or bags of groceries—they had servants to do those things for them. Dan doesn't have any servants, so he uses women, any woman he can find, including his relatives. Now, I've met Dan at boats and airports more times than I want to remember and he's like a child—he always has to be met. Why they don't just pin a note to his lapel, I don't know, but Amy always rushed off to meet him, and so does Rose."

"In a way I admire them for that," Ben said.

"Admire it if you want, but don't let Rose take his suitcase when he hands it to her."

"She wrote him about her illness."

"He knew Amy was sick too. Lordy, he'd probably load

his suitcase right on my lap in this wheelchair. God forbid he should carry it himself or pay a porter."

"I won't let Rose tote for him, I swear it," he said, wondering how much grammie was embroidering this description of what apparently was a long-time antagonist.

"Don't *you* carry his damn suitcase neither," she went on. "If that's the way you start, you're going to end by being his fetch-and-carry boy for good."

"I'll watch out for myself."

"Maybe, but you wait and see how clever he is when he wants something done. He'll start by saying, 'I've got an awfully bad back. Would you mind carrying my bag for me?' What you've got to say is, 'Sorry, I have a sore back too.' That's what my husband did, and it worked."

Ben laughed.

"I'm telling you what's going to happen when you meet him because it happens every time. As soon as he gets to your car, he's going to hold his hand out for the key and say, 'I guess I'll drive if you don't mind.' If you ask about his license, he'll swear he has one. If you still don't give in, he'll say he gets terribly nervous when anybody else drives. You just got to tell him that you get nervous too. You have to fight fire with fire."

"Well, thanks for the briefing," Ben said.

"One thing more. He's usually pretty well oiled when he comes from a boat or a plane. That means he'll have a chip on his shoulder. I figure you're young enough to take him without much trouble, but don't be surprised if he swings on you for what looks like no reason at all."

"Anything else?" Ben asked dryly.

"Well, I gave you the tip of the iceberg, anyway."

Rose returned with her hair all fixed up and a new dress of old-fashioned design that she'd bought to please her father.

"Rose," Ben said after complimenting her, "what if we fixed up the farm as a sort of guesthouse for the wedding? We could have a housekeeper of some sort look after the guests."

"Who would stay there?" she asked in surprise.

"Your father for one. I'm sure he'd be more comfortable there and you wouldn't have another body around here to take care of and wear yourself out over—"

"But he came all the way from Ireland to see *me*. He'd be terribly hurt—"

"Isn't your health number-one priority?"

"He's not going to bother me. Have you been listening to grammie?"

"Some."

"Do you know why grammie is really mad at dad? She blames him for mom's death, and that isn't fair at all. Mom had rheumatic fever, just the way I did, years before she met dad. How can you blame him for that?"

"Okay, okay," he said, "but don't you think you should stay home and at least let me meet your father?"

"The doctor said I could take drives. I wouldn't miss meeting dad for the world. Ben, that's that." It was one of the very few times she had spoken this way to him since they'd met.

"So I see, but I make no apologies for trying to save you some wear and tear."

He did manage to talk her into driving to New York the next day so they could have a restful night in a motel near the airport and be on hand for the seven o'clock flight. Although concerned about the expense, she agreed. She bought a fine shirt and had it elaborately gift-wrapped, with two expensive ties, as a homecoming present, and she made Annie thoroughly clean the room in Cliff House that their father was going to occupy, a job which Annie undertook with something of the look of a martyr. The curtains had to be washed, Rose decided at the last moment, commandeering Ebon to take them down and put them into the washing machine. Since vases of flowers would wither before Dan arrived, Rose gathered all available potted plants for her father's pleasure.

305

Ben wondered whether his daughter, to whom he sent a great deal of money despite the separation caused by divorce, would ever greet him so eagerly. For that matter, would Ebon? Whatever might be wrong with Dan Kelly, he certainly had the ability to cause his eldest daughter, at least, to look forward to his visit as though it were the Second Coming.

They left Livingston at about nine in the morning, with Ebon driving the van. Since Rose had been forbidden by the doctor to drive, Ben needed someone to take a turn at the wheel during the round trip of some five hundred miles. Beyond that, he had not seen much of his son for several days, and welcomed a chance to be with him.

Ebon was limping a little, he'd strained a ligament in his right leg while water-skiing, but he was fairly cheerful, even when he heard that Ann had insisted on staying home to take care of grammie.

For the first hundred miles Rose slept on the mattress that had been made up in the back of the van. When she woke up she asked Ben to come back and sit with her. As he slouched comfortably in the armchair Ebon had put there, Rose said to him, "Ben, I have a guilty conscience."

"Why?"

"I've been doing some work."

"Strenuous?"

"No, but exciting. Maybe I better let you finish it. I think I have Howie Hewat nailed but good."

"Explain, please."

A secretary in Howie's office, Debra Jones, somebody Rose had known when she worked at the mill, had telephoned her three days before. Howie had just tried to play his "hotel room game" with Debra during a convention in New York City, and now was having her transferred to the secretarial pool, in spite of her ten-years experience. The girl was so angry she offered to tell Rose and the new paper everything she knew about Howie's operations.

"What does she know?"

306

"Plenty. Howie is buying up options to purchase land everywhere he can in the valley. He works through dummy corporations, but Debra gave me their names. She figures he has options to buy more than five hundred acres."

"The SOB—buy land in an area where zoning keeps the price way down, then change the zoning and get rich."

"I think it's a little more complicated than that," Rose said. "He's corresponding with a plastics factory and a manufacturer of mobile homes. If he brings one of those in here, he'll make a mint selling them land and be a hero for providing jobs. Howie plans to have it made both ways."

"Can we make a map like your rattlesnake map, showing all the land he owns or has optioned?"

"That's what I've had in mind, for publication maybe two weeks before the election."

"Why'd you keep this to yourself so long, Rosie?"

"Because you wouldn't let me do any work. And Debbie won't talk to anyone but me. Neither will most of the farm people around here. I know them, but you try calling to ask if anyone has offered them money for their land lately! But lying here I got to thinking what it will be like when dad blows into town and I figured I was biting off more than I could chew. I got the Hewat story all done in outline, anyway, with plenty of notes. I'll need to make a few more phone calls, but the rest I'll leave to you."

"And I accept. Howic Hewat's head on a platter looks good to me!"

"Anyway, he won't sound so damn noble when he talks about changing the zoning if people know he's talking about his own land," Rose said. "Damn it, I hate the zoning too, but Howie's making a good fight into a cheap grab."

"Eb, have you heard all this?" Ben asked.

"Yeah . . ."

"Well, please be careful not to talk about any of it. I want to break this as news on our own schedule, not have it leak out."

307

"My lips are sealed. . . . You know, when I hear you guys talk about Howie and all, I'm damn glad I'm going to make trees my business. You take the people."

They got into the Skyways Motel a little after five in the afternoon. Although Rose had slept much of the way in the van she still felt rather tired and was beginning to get a sore throat. Although she'd been eating well lately, she ordered only a cup of soup and went to bed before it was dark.

"Ben," she said, "this bed has something called electric fingers. You put a quarter in."

"Do you want me to?"

"No. I hate electric fingers, the whole idea. I'd love your fingers, though. I'm just as tense as can be. Is it awful to ask you for a back rub?"

"I never refuse to give back rubs to beautiful women. Did you bring the oil?"

"It's in my suitcase."

She lay on her stomach, looking surprisingly small in the big bed, her body smoothly tanned from head to foot because of her sunbathing on the boat. Pouring some oil into the palm of his right hand, he rubbed his two hands together, warming them before gently kneading her neck.

"Harder . . . oh, that's good. How can such big hands be so gentle?"

He rubbed her shoulders. "Your shoulder blades make you look as though you were about to sprout wings," he said.

"If I fly, I'm afraid it will have to be with a broomstick. Do the small of my back."

He did, kneading it with both hands. She groaned with pleasure.

"Does this make you feel horny?" she asked suddenly. "Damn it, I'll kill you if you say, 'No, why should it?' "

"No comment."

"Ben, lie beside me a minute. At least we can have some pillow talk. *Hold* me, Ben . . ."

Stretching out beside her, he did. They kissed, and she

308

seemed to pour herself into it.

"Oh, Ben, why don't we just say the hell with it and love up a storm."

"You know why."

"The doctor told me to stop taking the pill. I suppose if we made love I might get knocked up and knocked out at the same time—"

In answer he kissed her again, this time more softly.

"We *could* fool around a little," she said, "the way kids used to do when they were afraid of getting pregnant—"

"We're not kids, Rosie."

"How can you have so much damn control?"

"Easy, when I think about the alternative."

"Yes. Ben, I'm scared."

"Of what?"

"Every boyfriend, every man I ever had ran as soon as dad arrived on the scene. I think he chased them away on purpose. He wants me to be the Virgin Mary or something."

"He has the father disease."

"I don't know why I asked him over . . . he does things to me inside."

"Maybe all fathers do."

"Maybe I wanted to see if you could stand up to him . . . hey, please don't hit him . . . I had a nightmare about your killing him, pounding his head off with your fists."

"Paging Dr. Freud!"

"And I have dreams of his hitting you too, but that's silly. When dad's sober he can be the most charming man in the world. When he gets drunk, he takes swings at people, but he hardly ever connects. I think that God disconnects his coordination at just about the time he disconnects his brain."

"That sounds like a pretty good arrangement."

"But thanks for having him at Cliff House. And thanks for putting up with him if he's awful. And thanks for putting up with me."

He pulled her close to him, moved as always by the clean

fragrance of her hair and the warm softness of her skin. She kissed his chest, biting it a little, and he felt her tremble like the *Princess* in a high wind.

"Rosie, we better stop this."

"Chicken."

"All I can hear is that doctor saying priorities, priorities, priorities."

"Maybe I have my own priorities," she said, gently rubbing his thigh.

He clenched his teeth. Suddenly he pushed her hand away and got to his feet.

"Puritan. Why don't you wear a funny hat?"

"Rosie, be careful. For the first time I am getting angry at you."

"For just wanting to fool around a little?"

"Once I held you in my arms while you almost died. That wasn't your fault, but if you refuse to take care of yourself and get yourself all worked up, you can bring this thing down on us again. I'm not settling for one night. I want a lifetime with you, so will you please get that straight and cut the con job until after the operation? Okay?"

"Okay, I'm sorry. God, you must get tired of me."

"I don't get tired, I get scared."

"Don't you get sick of it, though. You know what I mean . . . Why don't you find sort of a temporary replacement, or have you already? I'd have no right to object—"

"Rosie . . ."

"I have no right to ask you to be a saint just because I'm in this fix. In a really sane world, maybe I'd ask a friend to help you out. I know all kinds of nice women who'd be glad to take you over on loan."

"Rosie, please stop this."

"Why can't we talk about it? Why should I want you to live like a monk? Is that the way for me to hold you? Maybe I should ask Annie to help me out with this the way she does with the cooking—"

"Rosie, *cut it out . . .*"

"Come on, Ben, 'fess up, that idea doesn't turn you off so much, does it? I've seen you trying not to peek at those glorious boobs of hers, and I've seen the way she looks at you. Wouldn't that be a really civilized arrangement? At least we'd be keeping you in the family—" She was smiling, but it was to hide the tears.

"Rosie, I want *you* . . . and if I ever even tried to touch Annie, you'd chop off my hand, at the least."

"You're damn right I would," she said, and collapsed into a mixture of laughter and tears. "God, Ben, I don't know what's the matter with me, I'm really acting like a child and a bitch." He was lying beside her again, holding her in his arms. "I've been having nightmares too . . . I mean, about Annie . . . maybe that's what this is all about."

"I'm afraid to ask . . ."

"I have her seducing you, and it's not so farfetched . . . Annie's great but she's not the little angel you think she is, Ben."

"I know she's just a seventeen-year-old girl, without wings or halo."

"But she's different. She had a tough time when she was growing up, really tough. It's made her . . . well, sort of hard, and ambitious too. All she ever thinks about is getting out of Livingston and making it in some big city."

"I know she's ambitious, but I can't see that she's really very hard—"

"Look at the way she treats Ebon. She just keeps him nicely on a string, perfectly under control, like a well-trained dog."

"He doesn't seem to complain too much."

"Well, look at the way she treats dad. I know he's been awful plenty of times, but does she ever forgive him? Does she ever behave like she realizes that dad is trembling inside when he comes to this country because he feels he's just a big, dumb Irishman without any education or money that everybody laughs at? He knows we remember all the bad times he's

311

given us. When he smiles, he breaks my heart. He might as well wear a neon sign that says, 'Please, please forgive . . .' "

"Rosie, Annie may be too young for that kind of compassion. When you were seventeen, how did you feel?"

"Just like now. I loved dad and hated him and most of all saw a big, bewildered man who kept trying to do great things but always landed flat on his face. You don't have to be a genius to see that."

"How could a girl with so much heart have heart trouble?" he said, and smiled apologetically. "Sorry to be corny."

"God, history repeats . . . he kept saying that to my mother. . . ." She caught his hand, holding it in both of hers. "I've had to be in bed so much lately," she said after a few moments, "there's been nothing to do but think, and when you've got what I've got, well, you can't help wondering what would happen if . . . I don't mean the hereafter or anything big-deal like that . . . for some reason I never wonder about that . . . but I do wonder what would happen to you and Annie if I died—"

"We'd go into a state of shock, so please don't try it."

"What about after the shock? She'd be alone in the world. Dad can't even take care of himself, and grammie's too old. Would you be her guardian?"

"If that's what she wanted. . . . Look, Rosie, I hate this conversation, and it's beside the point. You're going to get better, no question, so—"

"But what if . . . ? Would you have an affair with Annie and marry her sooner or later?"

"Rosie! *You're* too young for me. Annie's almost thirty years too young. Do you think I'm altogether crazy?"

"Lots of talented, attractive men marry young girls, or at least live with them. Look at Steichen, Chaplin, Picasso—"

"You've really been chewing on this, haven't you?"

"Is it a forbidden topic?"

"Yes . . . no . . . hell, I don't know, Rosie. It's just so damn—"

"Hear me out. I happen to think it's not at all unlikely that you and Annie might get together . . . you could give her entree to the world she wants, and I guess you've already noticed that she's got more than a little to give you—"

"Rosie, can we cut this out pretty soon? It's making me damn uncomfortable."

"Why? Because it's crossed your mind too?"

"*No.*"

"You've never had the slightest passing little fantasy about Annie?"

"Rosie, you got me . . . I confess I have fantasies about screwing practically every female who crosses my path, from ladies of a certain age to nubile young things I could get arrested for. But they *are* fantasies, and I'm too old to start feeling guilty about them."

"Well, then you won't feel guilty about a couple of nights ago, when you called out Annie's name in your sleep—"

"Oh, god . . ."

"Don't apologize, you don't feel guilty, remember? Besides, I wasn't all that much bothered by it, but it did set me to thinking."

"Well, can we set these thoughts to rest now?"

"Not yet . . . you know, Ben, if you hooked up with Annie you might have a lot of good years, the way Chaplin did. And I promise you, Rosie's ghost wouldn't blame you a bit if you had the good taste to take up with our Annie—"

"Annie, I mean, Rosie—" He looked stricken.

"See, you can't even keep our names straight. Do you know that you mix us up quite often?"

"I've always done that with names. *Men's* too."

"Sure, okay . . . but without being too unfair to my sister I'm trying to give you a warning. You've gone through considerable hell for me and my family. Much as I love my little sister . . . well, I just don't want you to be hurt. Annie treats dad without pity, and Eb without passion, so far as I can see. She can work around in the kitchen for hours without knowing that grammie is even there. You'll have to figure out for yourself how she'd treat you if she ever stopped needing you—"

"Rosie, what in the name of god are we talking about all this for? The doctor said the odds are all in your favor if you have the operation."

"Even the favorite loses sometimes. I'm sorry, Ben—all this has been going round and round in my head and I had to unload it. Sorry you're the one to get it."

"Look," he said, hugging her tight, "why don't we fantasize about what we can do after your operation? Like flying to Paris. I know the most sinfully luxurious hotel we can hole up in for a week and live like the sheiks, who stay there all the time."

"What's the name of it?"

"Le Bristol. We'll have a real king-sized bed and a king-sized bathtub of black marble and huge towels that come out of slots in the wall where they're kept warm. Our suite will have a refrigerator stocked with the finest wines. The carpets on the floors are so thick you can use them for beds, and what goes on in bed . . ."

She laughed. "Did you ever stay in a place like that?"

"Why, my name is well known at Le Bristol—or was for about two days ten years ago. I was in Paris to cover the automobile show for one of the old picture magazines, I forget which. It was a last-minute assignment and all the hotels were jammed, except Le Bristol, which damn few can afford, including yours truly. Two other photographers and myself rented the royal suite and put it on our expense account. That's the kind of thing we got away with in those days."

"I wish I'd been your loyal assistant."

"So do I. That whole suite was made for making love, and all I had with me were two fat, hairy old photographers. I swore that when I met the girl of my dreams I'd bring her there, and I will as soon as you're better. Bet on it."

"What color are all these thick carpets?"

"Lemon-yellow and white, I think."

"What are the walls?"

"Covered with lime-colored silk. There're crystal chandeliers on the ceiling."

"I hope I spend hours looking at them," she said, and sighed wickedly. "Oh, Ben, I love you. Thank you for taking me to such a splendid hotel."

THEY got up at dawn the next morning and met in the dining room of the motel at six. Ebon acted subdued. His eyes were bloodshot.

"Sorry, folks," he said. "Late night at the bar. They must have put something funny in the ginger ale."

"Tell my father about it," Rose replied with a smile. "One thing he's a real expert on is hangovers. He knows a thousand cures."

As they drove to the airport they found it was already hot and muggy despite the fact that the sun hadn't yet risen above the buildings.

"How do you know which airline to go to?" Ben asked.

"Aer Lingus, of course. He wouldn't take anything but an Irish airline."

Ebon let Ben and Rose out near the place where passengers arrived and went to park the van. Almost an hour went by before he returned, hot and exasperated.

"All this time I've been circling around looking for a parking space," he said. "I finally found one clear on the other side of the farthest lot. There's a maze of one-way roads around it. We better walk to it because I'll never figure out how to drive it back here."

"No need to hurry," Ben said. "The plane seems to be getting in at nine, not seven."

"The cablegram was wrong or dad got it mixed up," Rose said. "He doesn't like being too predictable."

They had a second breakfast, which none of them really wanted, in an air-conditioned restaurant that made them shiver. Ben and Rose read the *New York Times* while Ebon toured the airport. When he returned he was carrying handfuls of pamphlets published by the various airlines extolling the beauties of Hawaii, Alaska and Europe.

"I thought I'd bring these back to Annie," he said. "This way she can put her big dreams on a regular flight schedule."

"It's funny," Rose said, "except for Le Bristol, Europe doesn't tempt me much."

"Do you want to stay in Livingston forever?" Ben asked.

"I guess my ideal would be to live the way our doctors and lawyers do. They make Livingston their headquarters and spend a lot of weekends in New York or Boston. In the winter they take cruises to the Caribbean, then back to Livingston, where they can be big frogs again. They really have the best of all worlds."

"None of that for me," Ebon said. "I want a log cabin by a pond so far back in the mountains that we'll have to bring in supplies by chopper."

"And do you expect a certain restless young lady to share this charming retreat with you?" Rose asked.

"Maybe . . . sooner or later people get sick of travel." But there was a question in his voice when he said it.

His father, almost pointedly, he thought, said nothing.

At eight-thirty they learned that the plane would be two hours late. Rose seemed to become increasingly tense as they sat in a waiting room leafing through magazines. As Ben got her a cup of water for her pills, he wished even more that he'd been able to convince her to stay home.

At twenty minutes to eleven Rose led the way to a window

317

through which they could see passengers going through customs. Soon others crowded around them, pushing for a place at the glass. They stood there being jostled for what seemed like an eternity before Rose suddenly shouted, "There he is!"

Even Ben recognized him from his advanced billing. Approaching a customs counter, the big Irishman was indeed an imposing figure. Silvery white hair, well cut and well groomed, a fresh, rosy complexion, much darker in hue than that of his daughters but striking, a glint of blue eyes, thick white eyebrows, the nose of an old battler who had lost a few, and a strong chin—all of which made him very senatorial-looking. He was wearing a seersucker jacket with a rose in the buttonhole, gray whipcord pants and shiny black shoes with the narrow toes common in Europe. He had enormous shoulders and his belly was still flat enough not to call attention to itself. His distinguishing feature was intangible . . . like Rose, he had enormous vitality, a quality evident in the intensity of his mobile face and all his body motions. He was handsome in a rough, virile kind of way that seemed out of context with his somewhat dandified manner of dress. It was easy to see why Rose and her mother before her could be proud of him, even when he misbehaved.

Tapping with a coin at the window, Rose finally attracted his attention. Suddenly he grinned, waved enthusiastically, gestured toward the line he was waiting in, shrugged and grinned again, the ingenuous grin of a small boy. The line to the customs inspector was very slow. To entertain his daughter while they waited he suddenly did a little soft-shoe dance while he whistled a tune that the dividing window made silent. The people around him smiled and laughed—Dan could be a good comic. Encouraged, the old Irishman took a few rubber-legged steps, staggering in a circle while the people behind him backed up to let him keep his place in line. When a few people clapped, Dan gave them a deep formal bow, complete with winning grin.

318

More charming than expected, Ben thought, and he could see why Rose's mother had called him Ireland's answer to Maurice Chevalier. Glancing at Rose, he saw that her eyes were tearing as she laughed.

Before long Dan emerged from customs carrying two large battered suitcases of imitation leather which he dropped as Rose threw herself on him. They embraced like lovers, with Dan lifting his daughter six inches from the floor at one point. They told each other how wonderful they looked, and then Rose suddenly said, "This is Ben, dad, my wonderful husband soon to be."

Dan directed a sharp glance at his future son-in-law. For just a split second Ben thought he caught a shrewd, calculating look on his face, like that of a salesman sizing up a customer. The ice-blue eyes hardened, with disapproval? Seeing himself as the old Irishman must see him, Ben wondered whether he appeared much too old for Rose, and to put it bluntly, too damn Protestant, too *English*, for god's sake, in background for the daughter of a man named Kelly. Well, something must have caused that flash of hostility that froze the old man's face before he smiled again and said, "Glad to meet you, what's your last name?"

"Winslow."

"His middle name is Livingston," Rose added. "His mother's people founded the place."

"Some of Rose's people were Irish kings, Mr. Winslow. Did you know that?"

"No, but it doesn't surprise me at all."

"It's a bunch of bullshit too," Rose added. "Come on, dad, let's not do the royalty bit. I want you to meet Ebon. Can you imagine that this enormous man is going to be my stepson? I think they call it that because I'm going to need a stepladder to kiss him."

"Nice to see you, lad," Dan said, making up for the fact that Ebon was three inches taller by nearly crushing his hand.

Ben was aware that Dan had not shaken hands with him.

Whether deliberately or not, he could only guess.

"I'm afraid we've quite a long walk to the car," Ebon said, "but it will be easier than trying to bring it up here."

"No matter, lad," Dan replied in his musical Dublin accent. "I will ask you and your father to give me a hand with my bags, though. My shoulder has been giving me a terrible time."

Remembering grammie's forecast, Ben smiled, but he did not want to ruin Rose's happiness by fighting over luggage. He picked up one suitcase while Ebon picked up the other. Both were startled by the great weight of the luggage.

"I think we should get a porter with a handcart," Ben said. "We have quite a ways to go."

"Now, none of that."

"We'll pay for it, dad," Rose added soothingly.

"None of that. I have valuable articles that I don't want to give to them people."

"Come on, dad," Rose said, taking his arm affectionately. "Ebon has a sore leg and a hangover. No reason for Ben to carry heavy weights for long distances in the sun. So you have a choice of calling a porter at our expense or carrying the stuff yourself. Which is it?"

"Will you give me a hand?" he asked.

"Me? Didn't I write you that—"

"Well, call a porter, then. I'll pay for it myself." This last with profound feeling.

Pushing a big handcart with the suitcases, a tall young porter followed Ebon, Ben and Rose to the car. Making sure that the fellow did not make away with his luggage, Dan marched beside him like an armed guard. When they finally reached the car, which was parked in the middle of a shimmering island of asphalt going soft in the noonday sun, the porter put the suitcases in the back of the van.

"Thank you, my man," grand Dan said, and gave him a handful of coins, mostly coppers. The porter stared at them.

"These are foreign coins," he said. "The banks won't exchange foreign coins—only bills."

"It's good money and you better be grateful for it," Dan said, squaring his big shoulders and doubling up his fists at his sides.

Rose quickly took three dollars from her purse and handed them to the porter, who touched his cap and pushed his cart away, shaking his head.

"Now, why in hell did you give that bastard all that money?" Dan bellowed. "Why didn't you let me handle it in my own way?"

"Because I don't want you fighting the first hour you're in the States. Now let's get started home."

When they approached the front of the van Dan said, "Say, this is a fine-looking vehicle. What do you call it?"

"It's just a delivery van."

"Does it drive good?"

"We have no complaints."

"I think I'd like to try it, if you don't mind. Could I have the key?"

Looking at the big hand extended toward him, Ben again thought of grammie. How could anyone be so predictable?

"I'm afraid that Ebon or I will have to do the driving," he said. "As you can see, it belongs to the newspaper, and only employees can drive it. Company rule."

"But who's to know?" He gave a huge wink. "It's been a long while since I drove an American car on an American road." He continued to hold out his massive hand.

"Dad, don't make me fight with you so soon," Rose said. "You're here ten minutes, and you pull this nonsense again—"

"What's so bad about asking to drive a car?" All innocently.

"Because you have no license, as you well know, and we would have no insurance if you got into an accident."

"Why, of course I have a license. My Irish license is good here for six months, and I have an international license."

"Show them to me, dad," Rose said wearily.

"Why, they're in my suitcase there. I don't want to bother unpacking them now. I don't see why you're all so unreasonable but I suppose I'll just have to make the best of it. What can a man do when even his own flesh doesn't believe him?"

"Dad, if I'd swallowed your line of bull, I'd have been dead before the age of three. Now get in the car and behave yourself, or go back into that airport and fly yourself back to Ireland."

With a great show of injured dignity, Dan got into the van, automatically appropriating the seat next to the driver. Fortunately, Ebon had put the air-conditioning on the moment they arrived with the baggage, and it already was taking effect.

"Why, it's cool," Dan marveled. "Air-conditioning in a lorry. I tell you, when a fellow comes to America, he never knows what to expect next. . . ."

Soon after they were under way Rose gave her welcome-home present to her father, who ripped open the gold paper as eagerly as a child. After admiring the shirts and ties he said, "All I can give you back, my love, is this." Taking the rather wilted rose from his buttonhole with a flourish, he held it out to her. "I wish this were a million bucks," he said.

"Well, dad, so do I," she said, and taking the travel-weary flower, started to put it in her hair with just the right mixture of respect for his gesture and humor at its proportions. "Ben, if I were in the South Sea islands, where would I put this to show I'm betrothed?"

"It depends what island you're on. On Mooka Tonga, where I had an assignment once, you'd eat it."

"Eat it?"

"What the hell is he talking about?" Dan said.

"On Mooka Tonga a girl eats her flowers when she's betrothed. You see, they don't have any mouthwash or stuff like that to sweeten the breath."

"Very sensible," Rose said. "What do the men do when they get betrothed?"

"They go to the witch doctor to get their head examined," Ebon said.

322

"Were you in this crazy place too?" Dan asked.

"Ebon was born on Mooka Tonga," Ben said. "The witch doctor proved to be quite a capable obstetrician, even if he did rely pretty heavily on shaking spears and beating drums."

Dan's big, blunt face looked resentful. "This is all a joke, isn't it? Are you one of those wise-guy Americans who like to poke fun at so-called foreigners?"

"It's just a *game*, dad," Rose said.

"Well, how the hell am I supposed to know what Mooka Tonga is? It's no sillier a name than Chattanooga or Ticonderoga . . . I don't like people who take advantage of people."

Nobody said a word, but as Ben drove, tight-lipped, the two weeks stretching ahead from now to the wedding suddenly seemed very, very long.

Dan napped, waking every hour or so to reach into his pocket for one of the miniature bottles of Irish whiskey he'd brought from the plane. About twenty miles from Livingston, he roused himself. "Are you going to keep on living in Livingston when you get married?" he asked Rose, as though Ben somehow wasn't there.

"Sure."

"I never could see how you can stand that burg. There's not a proper restaurant nor pub in the whole town, and the people all talk as though they were holding their noses. Why don't you come back to Dublin with me? Now that's a real place to live and pretty soon you'd find a real man."

Which, of course, was not lost on Ben, who forced himself to keep quiet.

"Dad, if Ben isn't a real man, the pope isn't Catholic."

"Don't blaspheme, girl."

Dan kept up a running commentary of uncomplimentary remarks about Livingston as they drove through some of the poorer sections of town, most indirect insults aimed at him, Ben suspected, though also from bad memories Dan had of the village.

323

"The animals in the Dublin zoo live better than most people here do . . . and to think that Irishmen used to believe that the streets of America were paved with gold!"

When Ben approached Cliff House, however, and Dan caught a glimpse of the big Victorian "cottage" on the hill overlooking the lake, he fell silent until he felt constrained to caution Ben and Ebon to carry his bags carefully, as he followed them to the flagstone terrace which ran to the edge of the cliffs a hundred feet above the softly lapping waves.

"Do you own this place?" he asked Ben.

"My family does."

Dan looked around, his sharp blue eyes appearing to take in every detail. Ben felt he could almost hear the wheels in his head print out the word MONEY. . . . The old Irishman even looked at Ben in a somewhat different way, a sort of mixture of deference and resentment.

"I'll show you to your room, dad," Rose said.

"Not now. Have them put the bags in my room and bring me a whiskey here."

Did he always stand uttering commands in another person's house, or did his air of authority grow as his inner confidence waned, Ben wondered, but Rose had just finished a tiring trip and damn well wasn't going to be *anybody's* waitress. This kind of nonsense should be nipped in the bud. "Rosie," Ben said, "remember the doctor's orders. Please lie down for a while. I'll show your father where the whiskey is so he can mix his own drinks."

"Thanks, Ben," she said, with relief, he thought, and left the terrace.

Dan glared at Ben.

"Now, the whiskey is in the kitchen in the locker to the right of the refrigerator. Feel free anytime you want."

"Is Annie in there?" Dan asked.

"I believe she's in the kitchen getting dinner."

"Tell her to come out here."

The harsh tone startled Ben, and in spite of his desire to

avoid upsetting Rose he felt an undeniable anger rising. He looked out over the lake, where a fleet of small sailboats with brightly colored sails was racing. The silence seemed to hum.

"I said, tell her to come out here," Dan repeated.

Turning to look at him, Ben saw that he was standing up, his body bent forward, his fists doubled up at his sides. His face was a livid red. Let me try to understand just what the hell is going on, Ben told himself. Was Dan upset because instead of rushing to meet him Annie and grammie had withdrawn to the kitchen, as though to postpone the moment as long as possible, or did he actually think that when he met another man he had to establish his top spot in the macho pecking order immediately? Well, none of it meant a damn beside the importance of handling the situation in a way not to reduce Rose to tears.

"Excuse me," Ben said suddenly, "I have things to do, so if you'll pardon me . . ." He started to walk off the terrace.

"Where's Rose?"

"She's resting. She's really not to be disturbed when she goes to her room. It might help, Dan, if you talked to her doctor about that—"

"I *know* about heart trouble. My wife had it."

"So I understand."

"The doctors mostly talk bullshit."

"If that means you think Rose doesn't need rest, you're wrong."

"It means that Rose is my daughter."

Ben felt his blood coming to a boil. He bowed his head, fighting to get control.

"You can't think I mean her any harm," Dan suddenly added.

"No, of course not, but I think you could harm her if you wear her out—"

"Have you been talking to grammie?"

Fortunately Ann appeared just then in her bathing suit. She appeared reserved, self-consciously correct as she said,

"Hi, daddy. Nice to have you here," pecked him on the cheek and withdrew to perch on the arm of a chair with her arms folded in front of her.

"You're looking good, Annie, but why are you running around without any clothes on?"

"I've been sunning and swimming."

"Well, go put some clothes on. And before you start, bring me a whiskey with just a little water on ice."

"Yes, daddy." She replied so primly he didn't catch the echo of mockery. She walked toward the kitchen, exaggerating the swing of her hips just a trifle.

"That girl will be in trouble all her life if she don't watch out," Dan said. He was looking directly at Ben when he said it.

Dan tried, but a lifetime pattern was difficult to break. Not only did he find it convenient to have Rose bring him whiskey, tea, cigarettes, matches and snacks at all hours of the day and night, he needed proof of love, like a small child. It seemed each time Rose did his bidding, Dan felt a bit more secure, or perhaps less insecure . . . playing amateur psychiatrist had never appealed to Ben, but he needed some explanation, other than his own private suspicion that Dan was simply the biggest bastard since Attila the Hun.

And sometimes Ben got angry at Rose for appeasing Dan, but he also admired and understood, grudgingly, her love for her father, and agreed she was right when she said that it cost her less to get him a cup of tea than to fight over it.

Most days Ben worked in the newspaper office and had to trust Annie to protect Rose as much as possible—which Annie did with a kind of sardonic good humor he'd never before seen from her. With Ben, Annie was still all soft, a seventeen-year-old country girl, but her father brought out a kind of toughness, in both the good sense and the bad, which Ben had never suspected in her . . . though he recalled what Rose had said. Annie liked to chew gum, strut around in her bikini because Dan detested it, and once when Dan caught her arm while he was calling her down, a look came into her eyes that made him pull back his hand as quickly as if he'd grabbed a wildcat. Maybe, Ben thought at the time, he had . . . Ann, at a young age, was already clearly a woman of parts.

Ben found the evenings at Cliff House almost unbearable now, with Dan spouting orders about adjusting the air-conditioner or the heating system, or something. He could tolerate no television program for more than five minutes, and since he could not or would not learn how to operate the set himself, kept ordering Annie, Rose or grammie to change channels or adjust the volume. He grew near-violent when Annie played rock records in her room and was constantly threatening to break every one. He preempted the telephone, and without keeping track of the costs made endless calls to Boston, New York and Dublin. During these long-distance conversations, he became furious if anyone in the living room talked, or if the washing machines in the kitchen were used. "Turn that damn thing off" was his slogan.

During the first week of this Ben tried to remind himself that there weren't many days to go until the wedding and that peace at any price was what Rose wanted and needed. Still, the endless hours of being ordered about put more than a little strain on his own concept of himself. When Dan would walk menacingly toward him in high dudgeon, with his big fists doubled up at his side, Ben felt tempted to demonstrate some of what he'd taught as a hand-to-hand combat instructor in Korea. Dan as a barroom fighter had apparently learned nothing about self-defense. When he talked about his exploits, it became clear that the roundhouse right was his only weapon . . . a crooked nose and mouthful of false teeth testified that he had left himself wide open.

Of course it would be easy to jump all over the old man, but what kind of triumph would that be, clobbering a sixty-year-old man?

Still, it was hard not to be tempted when Dan got drunk, as

he often did, and started pushing people around. When Ebon refused to drive him to the village one night, Dan tried to pull the keys of the van from his pocket, wrestling him to the floor before Ebon pulled clear and ran off, laughing. Once when they had a few people in for cocktails, Lillian Fletcher, his assistant editor, complained to Ben that she couldn't get Dan to stop patting and pinching. When Ben took Dan into the kitchen to ask him to cut it out, Dan declared, "No man can talk to me like that," and shoved Ben aside so violently that he almost lost his balance. And the old man stood there, waiting to fight, his fists outstretched, his groin, belly and face open for a shot. It was awfully tempting . . .

The next day, though, something happened that gave Ben some hope. He'd just come home from the office. Dan met him at the back door. "Ben, I have something important to discuss. Can we talk private-like?"

"The terrace."

"There are always people around."

"How about the car?"

They sat in the front seats of the van, parked behind the cottage, and Dan proceeded to make his pitch with practiced charm. He wanted to borrow two thousand dollars right away to buy linens in Ireland for export to Boston. If that deal worked, as he was sure it would, he wanted Ben to invest another five thousand dollars they'd use to make an even bigger killing. He had a friend on a freighter who would bring the stuff in, by implication without having to pay duty. He had another friend in a big department store who was waiting for the shipment. The deal was sure-fire . . .

"I don't know much about this sort of thing—"

"I need the money," Dan said urgently, "things have been bad for me, real bad lately. I haven't wanted to bother Rose with my problems, and I don't like coming to you but—"

"I don't know. I just might go for it, but there are some strings."

"What does that mean?"

328

"Well, for starters it means you'll shout no more orders at people, especially Rose, and understand that no one in this house is your servant. You'll get your own tea, your own food and booze. You'll adjust the TV yourself or take what's there. You'll carry your own suitcases—if you're strong enough to muscle people, you're strong enough to carry your bags. You'll be *quiet*, you'll stop yelling at Annie, and you'll never allow any unpleasantness to happen where Rose can hear it."

Dan's face grew redder by the minute.

"I didn't yell at no one."

"You don't even realize you're doing it. Now, if you can break that habit, just maybe we can work together, and if we can work together I'll get up the two thousand."

"When?"

"The day Rosie and I are married, if I see that the leopard can really change its spots. But if you're going to keep on playing household tyrant, you can stick all the money I'll give you up your nose and still breathe with your mouth closed."

"Jesus," Dan said, "I never took shit like this from anyone, not in my whole life—"

"Shit, Dan, is what you've been making us all take ever since you got here. Do you think you have a god-given right to walk around my house like some tinhorn dictator, yelling orders at everyone, sick or well?"

Dan's face turned fiery and Ben saw his fist come up.

"Now, if you hit me, some things will happen. For example, there'll be no money for you and I'll charge you with assault. With your record that won't sit too good."

The fist trembled but did not move.

"Let me tell you something about your damn fists," Ben went on. "Stop trying to scare me. I've lasted through five wars, including the one in your backyard. I know a little how to fight if I have to, but Rosie would be too upset if you got mussed up. So I don't fight, but I don't scare either, and I'll thank you to stop balling up your fists or raising your fists at me whenever you get mad and feel like it. All you're proving

329

is that no one could work with you on any deal—"

"I don't want your bloody money." He was clasping and unclasping his fists now, his face pouring sweat.

"Good, but if you can't go along with what I said, go back to Ireland right now. Rosie will be unhappy, but that will be better than all the trouble you make. And don't talk to her now and get her all upset. I mean it, Dan."

Getting out of the car, Ben slammed the door behind him and walked toward the house. Then, feeling sort of guilty, he paused and turned. The old man was sitting with his hands covering his face. Feeling worse, Ben walked into the house. His insides were churning when he poured himself a drink, and he felt like perfect hell.

21

THAT night Dan sat silently on the terrace and ate dinner without uttering a word. When he wanted the salt at the other end of the table he ostentatiously got up and retrieved it himself.

"What's the matter with you, dad?" Rose asked. "Are you feeling all right?"

"As well as can be expected," Dan replied with a slightly quavering voice, "for a man my age."

Dan's silence persisted until the next morning, when he announced that he was too sick with a cold to get out of bed.

"Rosie! I feel terrible. Do you have a thermometer?"

After finding that he had a slightly subnormal temperature, he executed a double order. "Rosie, tell Annie to get me a cup of tea and just a wee bit of toast." To grammie, who liked to watch the morning talk-shows on television in the living room, he bellowed, "Turn that damn noise box off. How can a sick man sleep?" And when Annie brought his tea and toast he said, "Have you got that damn cold-air machine on? If you don't turn it down, I'll freeze to death."

Ben came in to see him a few minutes later. He lay as though mortally ill with the covers up to his unshaven chin.

"Sorry to *hear* you're not feeling well."

"That I'm not. Now, you wouldn't be holding me to your

331

bargain while I'm like this, would you? Even in America a man can ask his daughters to take care of him when he's sick."

Ben left, shaking his head.

During these last few days before the wedding several new arrangements had to be made. At first they had planned a quiet family wedding with no reception. When Rose had felt that close friends would be hurt, Ben planned a modest, small reception at the country club, where Rose would not have to worry about serving drinks or cleaning up. The difficulty was that both of them had been born and brought up in Livingston, and it was hard to draw a line between close and not so close friends.

"Oh hell," Rose finally said as she studied a list. "Let's just have an open house, or an open country club for everyone. It won't cost much to make gallons of champagne punch, and maybe we owe it to the paper. How often do an editor and a publisher get married, anyway?"

"Rose, you shouldn't get in the middle of a mob scene."

"We'll just stop in for a few minutes, take our bow and scoot off to Montreal. Everybody will think we're too horny to stay."

Then there was Dan, still in his sickbed. "Rose, who's going to marry you? Have you asked a priest? Sometimes they can be very understanding."

I'm not really a Catholic anymore, dad, and Ben's an Episcopalian."

"So I suppose you'll have some damn Anglican fake priest."

"We're going to have a civil ceremony with a justice of the peace."

"Who?"

"Mike Murphy. Didn't you and he used to be drinking buddies a long time ago?"

"Mike Murphy? He's a plumber, isn't he?"

"He's a plumber and a justice of the peace."

"You mean my daughter's going to be married by a plumber?"

"Well, he's a pretty good plumber, anyway," Rose said.

"He's also a drunk and the worst skirt-chaser in town. Rosie, can't you find yourself a decent man at least for this? What kind of marriage can you have if you make your vows to a drunken skirt-chasing plumber?"

Ben was determined not to react to the pot-calling-the-kettle-black, or to the obviousness of the "decent man" crack. Not now, in front of Rose. Instead he said, "Mike Murphy performs a fairly dignified ceremony, from what I hear, but we can change if *you* want, Rose. How about Harry Alpert?"

"He's in bankruptcy court and he's always been an awful gyp as a used-car dealer."

"How about Elmer Peterson?"

"Ed Case's assistant? Come on, do you want to be married by an undertaker?"

"He's not an undertaker, he just runs the furniture end of the business."

"Which includes coffins." Rose shivered.

"It really doesn't, but I guess the echo is there. The trouble is, we know too much about everybody. And solid citizens don't seem to take the job of JP around here."

"How about old Judge Williams? He can marry people, can't he? He was a friend of your father, wasn't he? And when mom died, he was very nice to me about the probate stuff. At least we'd feel we were standing up in front of a friend, and he *looks* like a priest even if he isn't one."

Old Judge Williams was also known to Ben as a hanging judge, but Rosie didn't seem aware of it. "Judge Williams it is, then. To tell the truth, Rosie, you're the only part of the wedding party that remotely interests me. If I had to, I wouldn't mind standing up with you before the devil himself."

She crossed herself, one of the few times he had seen her do it. "Don't say things like that," she said. "I'm not exactly

333

religious anymore, but I still get the shivers. Besides, no point in asking for trouble, which we already get plenty of, right, darling?"

He nodded emphatically, and kissed her.

Two days before the wedding, the house reached such a feverish pitch of preparations that Ben's worries about Rose's health became acute.

"Rosie, let's play hooky," he said. "Annie, grammie and Ebon can handle everything here. This wedding isn't going to be much if the bride is flat-out exhausted."

"Where do you want to go?"

"How about a day of just sunning and lying around aboard the *Princess*?"

She agreed immediately. Putting on a new yellow bathing suit and a beach coat with a pattern of big, brightly colored butterflies, she eagerly led the way to the wharf, where the *Princess* lay bobbing restlessly in a strong but warm south wind.

"I can feel my whole body relax the moment I get aboard this boat," Rose said as she sat on the after seat in the cockpit while Ben made his preparations for getting under way. "What's so magic about her?"

"The *Princess* has been around long enough to learn the secrets of life."

"What are they?"

"Go slow. The modern boats go rushing around the lake at about thirty knots. Who could relax aboard them?"

"What are her other secrets?"

"Play it safe. Modern boats are always busting their wheels on rocks or getting swamped in a storm. The *Princess* is built to keep us alive."

"Any others?"

"Be comfortable in the cabin or out here. Be economical— a slow boat like this uses about a tenth the fuel fast boats take."

"And be proud," Rose said. "I think the *Princess* is a very

334

proud-looking lady. . . . And I think she has another message . . . make love. The whole cabin and cockpit is all over mattresses. Good lord, how many conquests have you had here?"

"This dial here on the instrument panel keeps track of that important statistic, along with the engine hours. It now reads 4,268."

"I bet you're like a used-car dealer and set it back."

"The *Princess* doesn't allow that."

"Tough lady. . . . Why was she named the *Indian Princess?*"

"Back in my grandfather's time some ambitious soul decided that Lost Lake ought to have a steamboat, like Lake George. They brought in people to build a small paddle-wheel excursion boat, and they named it the *Indian Queen.*"

"Sure, I remember hearing about it. She sank, didn't she?"

"Unfortunately the captain got drunk one night and ran right into a mountain. I was about six years old and had a great time picking up menus, life rings and other stuff in the water. To me it was just like the sinking of the *Titanic.*"

"Was anyone killed?"

"Nope. It was a quiet moonlit night. The people just walked off the bow into the woods. From what I heard, they lit a bonfire and continued their party until boats came for them."

"What happened to the captain?"

"I think he became a justice of the peace."

Rose laughed, and he started the engine, took in the lines and caused the *Princess* to glide in her quiet way toward the center of the lake. She lay on the after seat, her right arm shielding her eyes from the sun. "I have all kinds of things I want to talk about," she said. "Do you mind, or do you want to be quiet?"

"I want you. Carry on."

"Well, I feel sort of dazed, what with all that's coming up. First of all, have you made reservations in Montreal?"

"At the Royalton. It's not Le Bristol but it will be comfortable. I reserved a nice two-room suite."

335

"Well, I have this crazy worry," she said, sitting up. "What do people *do* on a honeymoon when they can't screw? Pardon my bluntness, but it's a good question, isn't it?"

"We'll be *together alone*, which is enough for me. And one point of all this, Rosie, is to get you away where you can really rest up for the operation. The doctor wants you to get some more weight back."

"God, you'd think Mack the Knife was the eager bridegroom. I even have to get my figure in shape for him."

"We're talking about strength."

"I'm sorry, when I think these things it helps to say them."

"I know."

"Anyway, Dr. Knight has no business complaining about my being too thin anymore. Men are starting to whistle at me again. . . . One of those big loggers whistled when I came out of the Fashion Corners yesterday. You should have seen his face when I ran up and kissed him."

Ben laughed. "Rosie, I never have been able to figure out how much you tell the truth and how much you make up to suit."

"Well, he did whistle, and I *felt* like kissing him. Now, isn't that a duller story than the one I told you?"

"It is."

"By the way, how many women *did* you really have aboard this boat?"

"Actually I think the grand total was more like three."

"See . . . you've no right to throw stones."

Ben opened the windshield a few inches, and the warm breeze felt good.

"I'm still worried about our honeymoon," she said suddenly. "I can just *see* us sitting in some fancy hotel room playing checkers for a whole week."

"What do you suggest?"

"Why don't we save our money for after the operation? Could we really go to Le Bristol?"

"Honey, I'm going to be in a mood for the biggest celebration in the world when I take you out of that hospital!"

"Have you already booked me in?"

"Dr. Knight has, at Mass. General for August tenth."

"Oh . . . I didn't realize he'd done it already. . . . Has he signed me in as Rose Kelly or Mrs. Benjamin Livingston Winslow?"

"I'll check on that."

"I think Mack the Knife might be sort of more careless with Rose Kelly than with Mrs. Benjamin Winslow, don't you think?"

"Rosie, I wish you didn't have to torture yourself so."

"And you too . . . Ben, I'm sorry—"

"Don't be, honey. You're afraid, and you wouldn't be human if you weren't. And believe me, I'm afraid too, even though I'm absolutely convinced that the danger is minimal with modern proven techniques. I'm being selfish now, because there were years when I was so damn miserable I didn't much care what happened to me . . . which is when it's easy to be brave. But now, ever since I met you, Rosie, I've wanted to *live* more than I ever have in my life. I'm what they call middle-aged, but most men like me aren't going to live to be ninety. It's at least early afternoon for me, not midday. Somehow, though, this doesn't scare me. From the first day, you've been able to give me the most outrageous ability to hope. Our getting married is a very important statement of that hope for me."

"Yes," she said, coming to kiss him, "and for me too."

He stood with his left hand on the wheel and his right hand around her delicate shoulders. There was a moment of silence, during which the old engine of the boat seemed to beat rhythmically, almost like a heart.

Rose brought them back. "Ben, instead of going to Montreal, could we just stay here, aboard the *Princess*? At least there'd be a lot more things to do than play checkers. We could see all the islands. I'd even like to shine the brass and do a little varnishing. I'd *love* to get the *Princess* all fixed up."

337

"We'd be a little cramped, wouldn't we? A week can be a long time on a small boat, especially if you're not used to it."

"Not if we found a great place to tie up, with a beach and plenty of room to wander around. Do you know a place anything like the Lost Lake Inn?"

"That's one of a kind, I'm afraid. The rest of the lake is all crowded with motorboats."

"I bet I know how to go back there without being hassled by the rangers."

"How?"

"Call ranger headquarters and tell them you want to do a feature story on the ruins of the inn and the good job the foresters are doing to protect them from vandals."

Ben laughed. "That probably would do it."

"Yup, and Ebon has a wonderful big tent. If he lent it to us, maybe we could set it up right in the old lobby, where the string trio used to play. We could bring steaks and fresh peaches and fresh cream and eat as well as anyone ever did there."

"I wish I could play the violin."

"Annie has a portable record player. You favor Chopin or waltzes?"

"You've got to come to dinner in an evening gown, and I'll need to get a striped blazer with white flannels."

"Let's do it, Ben! It will be so much more fun than some stuffy hotel with bellboys leering at us. I wouldn't mind if we were really going to be deserving some leers, but I'll be damned if I'll be leered at for playing checkers and staring at churches."

He said he'd make "a reservation" at Lost Lake Inn as soon as they got back to shore. Meanwhile Rose asked that he head toward the beginning of the channel that led to the rock-strewn narrow bay on whose shores the inn had been situated. Rose stood by the helmsman's seat, the wind rippling the light cloth of her beach coat so that the big butterflies appeared to flutter.

There was a long interval of silence before she said, "Ben, I've been thinking about those things I said to you about Annie the other night—"

"Please, honey, no apologies . . . besides, you probably weren't so far off the mark."

"No, thanks for the indulgence, but it's crazy . . . I've always been jealous of her. I was thirteen when she was born and thought mom was my personal property—"

"That's understandable."

"She was always prettier than I am, even before she got that fantastic figure."

"Rosie, you two are beautiful in your fashions, and it's too much for any one man."

"Well, I won't argue with flattery, but the point is, I practically made out Annie to be just a cold, calculating little bitch and of course she isn't . . . she's been marvelous with me ever since I got sick and, god knows, she has her reasons for staying away from dad as much as she can."

"Amen."

"And she has reasons for avoiding grammie too. . . . When she was growing up, first mom and then I was working. Grammie really raised her. It's maybe hard to see now that she's so old, but grammie was one tough taskmaster."

"I can imagine."

"When Annie was about fourteen she got in with a bad bunch of kids and we were all really worried about her. Grammie tried to lock her in her room like a small child and some things were said that were pretty hard to forget. Actually, Annie doesn't treat grammie badly now . . . I think she's still a little afraid of her. And Annie has just done something very generous. . . . Believe it or not, I'm ashamed to admit it, but I've been jealous enough to be afraid that Annie would outshine me at my own wedding. For a while I didn't even want to have her stand up with me. I could just see her in some great strapless low-cut number while I looked like a bandaged yardstick."

"Rosie, don't demean yourself."

"Well, I could just see you being a little slow about re-peating your vows to me because you were peeking down the neck of my kid sister's dress."

"Hey, now you're doing it to me."

"You couldn't help it. You'd be standing there wishing like hell you were connecting up with Annie instead of a rail you'd have to play checkers with on your honeymoon—"

"Rosie, can't you concentrate on the *fact* that in less than a month you're going to be all cured?"

"If Mack the Knife doesn't have a bad day."

"Nowadays, like I said, it's considered a fairly routine operation whose techniques have *worked*."

"I know . . . well, let me finish about Annie. . . . I never told her about my crazy fantasies, of course, but maybe she guessed. Whatever, all on her own she chose a very plain dress for the wedding, a beige thing that completely covers her. She's going out of her way to give Rosie the star role, which I think shows some pretty decent instincts in a girl her age, don't you?"

"I do, which is what I can't wait to say officially. Enough for a while about Annie, though. Okay?"

"Okay, skipper. Sail on."

Which he did, through the winding channel to the wharf at the Lost Lake Inn.

"Do you want to tie up here?" Ben asked. "The Mountie and his merry men may yell at us, but my influential son can always clear us."

"Sure . . . let's live dangerously."

After mooring the boat they walked toward the ruins of the inn as birds in surrounding trees warned each other.

They sat on one of the stone walls that marked the old foundation. "We could put up the tent right over there," she said, "and we could grill the steaks in the fireplace. We can put Annie's record player on that stump by the old terrace. The boards are gone but the ground is still level. Wouldn't moonlight dancing be better than checkers?"

They walked around the site of the old hotel, and following a rusty pipe that ran inland they discovered a spring of pure mountain water. The shed over it was crumbling, and they could see their faces reflected in the half-shadowed light as they looked in.

"Gosh, Ben, I bet we could live here forever."

"A little chilly, come December."

"Eb says they have gear now that lets people camp on top of Mt. Marcy in the middle of winter."

"Okay, we'll dance in the moonlight on the snow."

"Ben, let's do it!"

"I'm afraid the *Princess* wouldn't much like the ice—"

"We could come here with snowmobiles and buckets of champagne. We could string up Japanese lanterns all over the place. Think how they'd look on the snow . . . do you have a snowmobile?"

"I can get one."

"Ben, I'm leading into one of my oldest fantasies . . . maybe with you we can actually make it happen . . . come on back to the boat and I'll show you."

She hurried along in front of him. When they got into the cockpit, she looked up and pointed. "The trees are too thick here. I want to show you something about Big Iron Mountain. Let's go out in the lake."

When they were a few hundred yards from shore they could see the mountain she wanted, the highest in that part of the Adirondacks, an imposing peak topped by granite towers and giant blocks of gray stone, some of which were wet and smooth enough to reflect the yellow sunlight, like the lights of a distant city.

"See that?" She took hold of his arm. "Ever since I was about fourteen I've wanted to drive a snowmobile up there . . . first with Clark Gable, then it was with Jimmy Dean, and now you. The last and best."

"I'm in impressive company. What do we do up there?"

341

"We go right to the very top and we build a tremendous bonfire that can be seen for miles around. We cut branches up there and keep it going all night. . . . In my dream my lover and I build a lean-to up there to protect us from the wind. We spread out bearskin rugs in there and we watch the fire. . . ."

"Do I get to make love to you in the dream?"

"Like crazy . . . and the bonfire turns the whole top of the icy mountain a gorgeous orange. People will see the flames from miles away, they'll say it's a signal fire and ask what its message is . . . and all snug with the wind howling outside we'll know what the message is, won't we, Ben? . . .

He started to say he guessed so, to ask her what it was but she stopped him with her finger on his lips, her eyes glistening.

"Don't dare ask," she said, "just tell me we really can go up there in a good snowmobile, even if we can build just a little fire that would last only a few minutes."

"We'll try it if you want. I promise."

She kissed him enthusiastically. "How come you're so great at making all my dreams come true?"

It was nearly four in the afternoon when they got home to find Dan up and about, wearing pajamas and one of Ben's bathrobes. He seemed glad to see them, which made Ben wonder.

"Rose, come into the dining room. You too, Ben."

As Dan opened the dining room door, Rose saw a dozen goblets of Waterford glass lined up beside a neatly folded pile of Irish table linens. The heavily leaded glass sparkled as brilliantly as tinsel.

"Here's your wedding gift," Dan said gruffly. "I carried it all the way from Ireland."

"Oh, *dad*," Rose said, and hugged her father as though it were forever. Her eyes were wet as she proceeded to hold up each goblet to the light from the window and to inspect each piece of linen.

342

A half hour later, alone with Ben in her room, she talked about her father's gift, which he agreed was beautiful. "Oh, Ben, beautiful in more ways than one . . . he's never given me *anything* like that in his whole life. And he didn't really bring those things over to give me—he always crams his bags full of stuff to sell. That's the way he gets his spending money over here. But something made him change his mind and give us everything he had."

Ben thought of Dan's attempt to cover his real intent with the ploy about a linen business, and realized that the man was far more complicated than he'd thought . . . he hadn't been willing to admit he needed the money for his daughter's wedding present and so tried to save face. No crime in that. To the contrary, considerable honor. And in the end he'd given up his last chance to make some money in the States, just as Rose had said. No question, a man of parts . . .

That night Rose put one of the Waterford goblets on the table beside her bed. It gleamed in the moonlight from the window, like the reflection of a star.

"Sometimes," she said to Ben, "you have a day that makes up for all the bad years. This was one."

343

THE wedding day, as they say, dawned bright and clear. Rose had promised to sleep as late as she could. Ben was up at six. Hearing him in the kitchen, Ann put on her robe and came in to help him cook breakfast. The sound of her voice brought Ebon in his usual blue-jeans bottom and bare chest. Sun streamed through the kitchen window. Bacon sizzled, and the coffeemaker made low gurgling noises.

After breakfast Ann said she was dying to give Ben her wedding present, which she'd just finished the previous night. Wrapped in white tissue paper with a red ribbon, the gift consisted of two hinged silver frames containing photographs she'd taken of Rose and Ben. Both portraits' quality surprised Ben. So much of Rose's intensity and warmth had been caught in the beautiful triangle of her thin face, as well as a trace of her humor in a slightly lifted eyebrow.

"You take better portraits than I do," he told her, and meant it.

Ann showed her pleasure. "Guess who taught me?"

Ebon showed something this side of ecstasy, said nothing, and soon went out to wash the van for the wedding procession.

Ben went out to the boat to ready it for the honeymoon. As soon as the stores opened he bought ice and a variety of fancy foods, liquors and wines. When these were stowed in the roomy lockers of the cabin he picked every flower he could find in the neglected gardens around Cliff House. With roses, hollyhocks and tiger lilies blooming from a coffee pot and a chipped cocktail shaker, the cabin of the old cruiser could not exactly rival Le Bristol but it had a distinct charm of its own, and when Ebon brought down his tent, along with stacks of fresh towels and sheets, the *Princess* looked ready for the happiest voyage of her long life.

The wedding was scheduled to take place at eleven o'clock in the morning on the terrace. For the men, in the August heat, it was white suits. Dan wore one that Ben had outgrown, which didn't exactly please either of them.

Grammie wore a black dress, the only good one she had. Ann's beige was modest and unobtrusive, as Rose had said, but nothing could hide the way the girl held herself, or that beautifully modeled face with the perfect complexion, flashing eyes and almost luminous brown hair, now lightened by the summer sun. Ben did not see Rose or her dress that day in advance of the ceremony. She hid in her room, and all he heard from her were occasional yips of dismay when something needed quick alteration, and her delicious laughter when she was pleased.

Promptly at a quarter to eleven Judge Williams arrived to perform the service. He was a short, slender man about seventy years old with a sensitive face that was capable of easy mirth, easy tears. He was known among the courthouse gang as Weeping Willy because he had been heard to say to a young man who had been convicted of murder, "I know you have had a very hard childhood and I weep to think of the hardships a long prison term will work, not only on you, but your whole family. Nevertheless, you did kill a man. I hereby sentence you to life imprisonment. You're lucky you're not getting the chair."

Weeping Willy wore a dark blue suit that was too warm

for the day and made him sweat profusely, causing large drops to form like tears under the bags beneath his eyes. Unfortunately he felt called upon to say, "Marrying people is nothing new to me. I've handed out plenty of life sentences before, but in jail there's always the chance for a parole."

Ben forced himself to laugh. As soon as the judge walked in, Dan recognized him as the man who had fined him five hundred dollars for drunken driving (second offense), five years before, and five hundred dollars more for giving a state trooper just the smallest tap on the chin. Dan stood in fear of the judge making some reference to this, but Weeping Willy looked right over the old Irishman's head.

At precisely eleven o'clock, Weeping Willy stood on the terrace facing the house. Ben and Ebon waited in front of him while Dan went into the house to get Rose. Ben stared at the lake, now a cobalt blue flecked by whitecaps. He could hardly wait to get all this ceremony over with and get out on the *Princess*, where Rose and he could be alone.

Hearing steps, Ben glanced over his shoulder and saw Rose approaching on her father's arm. The broad-shouldered old man in white linen looked truly magnificent, and Rose, in a short dress of white silk with appropriate ribbons and bits of lace, Ben felt, was downright shocking in her beauty. Her delicate chin held at a proud angle, her big dark eyes flashing under a crown of glossy dark-brown hair, she could well have been the Irish princess of her father's fantasies. The silk clung closely enough to her slender body to show she was no longer childlike in her delicacy. She looked as strong as a young dancer and as graceful as she came toward him. The judge took some mimeographed papers from his coat pocket and shuffled through them.

"You look *fantastic*," Ben whispered to Rose.

"No falsies, either," she whispered back.

The judge cleared his throat. "Ladies and gentlemen, we are gathered here together . . ."

Came then the familiar words, the vows, the same words

346

that had joined Ben to Heidi long ago, and that had joined Heidi to the dentist who was her husband now. Still, they seemed new as he repeated them with Rose, or at least newly meant. When it was time to kiss the bride he brushed his lips against hers, surprised when he found them open, waiting for the kiss. The little gathering laughed as he clasped her in a full embrace.

Ebon and Ann then wheeled out a tea table with an ice-bucket of champagne and glasses. A few minutes later Ben got the judge aside and asked him how much his fee was.

"Nothing," Weeping Willy replied.

"Why?"

"I like Rose, always did. I seen her hold her whole family together when her mother died and come down in the middle of the night to get her old man out of jail. That girl's got spunk. I hope you can give her a run of good luck. She sure deserves it. . . . Now remember, I done you a favor, so don't ask me no favors in court. . . ."

Ben wondered if he meant for himself or for Dan.

At noon Ben and Rose got into the van, which Ebon had not only washed but decorated with a spray can of removable red paint. JUST MARRIED! was emblazoned in huge letters all over it. Paper streamers were tied to the door handles, and when they started the car they discovered they were towing a long tail of tin cans and an old frying pan. They headed toward the country club for the reception, with Ann and grammie following in Rose's pickup truck while Ebon and Dan brought up the rear of the procession in the jeep. It took about fifteen minutes to reach the country club. Toward the end Rose sat with her fingers in her ears to drown out the din, but her face was flushed and she looked delighted.

The parking lot at the club was already almost full when they got there.

"Gosh, we're popular," Rose said with a grin. "Or do they all think we're going to serve real champagne instead of punch?"

347

Feeling like a privileged character, Ben left the van on the edge of the lawn near the entrance, just behind Howie Hewat's white Lincoln Continental. Howie had not been personally invited to this reception, but he was too much of a politician to miss a gathering of this size, and how, he asked himself, could the *president* of the country club be kept out?

The main room of the club was jammed with people of all ages, and there was a cheer as Ben and Rose entered. Someone handed them glass cups of punch, and they stood in front of an empty fireplace, shaking hands and chatting with old friends.

It was, Ben reflected, quite a sensation to be in a room at the age of forty-five with maybe half your high school class, including the girl you took to the senior prom (now a stout real estate saleswoman), a tall, dark accountant who had kept trying to take Heidi to a motel and who probably had succeeded, an old teacher who had from the start encouraged Ben to be a photographer ("You got talent on you plain as your nose"), and even a woman who had been his mother's maid in his early youth, a lady whom he remembered as huge and stern but who now looked tiny and frail.

As if all these currents from the past weren't enough, Pete suddenly appeared with Ephram, carrying their mother in her wheelchair through the door, though Virginia was so lost in the clouds of her own senility that Ben had not expected her to accept his invitation to either the wedding or the reception.

"She heard about it on the radio and asked to come," Pete said as Ben came up to them. Leaning forward, he added, "She thinks you're marrying Heidi again. She was telling me how much she always liked her."

Ben kissed his mother's damp cheek and felt his fingers gripped in her trembling hand as she stared at Rose through thick, gold-rimmed glasses.

"Such a lovely girl," she said. "I know you two are going to be very happy together. . . ."

The strange thing was, Ben realized suddenly, that Heidi

and Rose *did* look a lot alike . . . both petite brunettes, though Rose's coloring was more striking and no one could match the vitality in her face. And come to think of it, his mother had also been a petite brunette . . . was it possible he'd gotten fixated on one remembered image of love?

Hurrying back to Rose's side, he wondered whether any of the fragments of her past in this room might be upsetting to her. She had been far too tasteful, and considerate, to talk about any past love affairs, even though she liked to kid him about his, but he could not believe that a woman as vital as Rose could reach age thirty without having left at least a few lovers behind. Now as she stood beside him, a handsome young engineer from the mill shook her hand and kissed her on the cheek with some obvious emotion. Suppressing a twinge of jealousy, Ben did not allow himself any questions. Rose's color was flaming a little higher than usual as she gave her husband a quick kiss on the lips before turning to the next person who wanted to congratulate her, a woman of about fifty who had been a close friend of her mother's.

"Aunt Harriet," Rose said, and throwing both arms around the portly lady in a dark blue dress, danced her around. "Did you come all the way from Boston?"

"I would have come from China, and I can't stop thinking how happy Amy would have been today! She always said she hoped you'd marry an *interesting* man, and your Ben certainly seems to be that. . . ."

After proudly introducing Ben to Aunt Harriet, Rose asked her if she liked living in Boston.

"Sam likes his job, but we both want to get back to Livingston. Boston is a fine city, but, you know, it doesn't have the *cultural opportunities* a small town has. Why, I don't even know where the juiciest scandals are cooking. . . . That's *barbaric*." They laughed and hugged each other.

Next to congratulate Rose was Debra Jones, the girl who had called to give information from Howie Hewat's files. A rather hard-looking woman of about twenty-five years with a good figure aggressively displayed in a tight blue dress, she held Rose's hand for what seemed a long time, asking where she and Ben were going to live . . . she seemed disappointed when Rose said they were going to move back to her farm in the fall. Ben, overhearing, suspected she wanted Rose to live out her own Cinderella-like dreams. Rose might have a prince, albeit stout and middle-aged, but where was the castle in the likes of Livingston?

Standing near the punch bowl, where Ann was filling the glass cups, Howie Hewat spotted Debra ("that bitch the Jones girl") in deep conversation with Rose. After their go-around at the last convention, Debra had unreasonably, he felt, told him that he better be damn careful with her, because any secretary can hang her boss higher than a kite if she wants to. A politician who puts a girl in charge of his files leaves himself wide open, he thought, rather pleased with his pun, if not the inspiration for it.

"It would just take one telephone call, baby. *You* figure out who to . . ."

Howie had thought she was threatening to call his superiors in the paper company and knew they would pay little attention to her. But as he watched Debra talk to Rose, it occurred to him that she very probably had called Ben's newspaper. Something like panic took hold of his guts. . . . Calm down, he told himself, that bitch wouldn't know enough to dig out his real estate deals. Still, if she just Xeroxed everything, Ben would soon figure it all out . . . Ben . . . the sight of him standing there so calm and smug beside Rose infuriated Howie. He damn well remembered how Ben had gone after him about kickbacks and about his little deals with some women. And here was the great Ben Winslow, who'd discarded Heidi, whom Howie had had the hots for, walking off now with Rosie, smartass bitch, in his opinion, but who also had enough fire in her to touch off any man . . . including himself, even after all these years. And now the two of them were getting out a paper that should have been dead before

350

it was born but was already running the *Recorder* ragged and threatening to have an important say about anybody who wanted to run for office in the town, and maybe beyond. . . . Howie wondered what Ben was really after. His grandfather, after all, had been the unquestioned boss of the county for half a century. Had Ben come home to claim that position, as though by some ancestral right? Well, he bloody well would have a fight on his hands. . . . He was sick of this sweet punch and went to the bar in the next room for a real drink.

At the bar he found Dan, sipping a double Scotch on the rocks. Dan had resolutely stayed away from the punch bowl, just as he'd promised Ann and Rose. But while Rose felt herself in a room full of friends, Dan felt himself surrounded by people who thoroughly disapproved of him . . . that old friend of Amy's, Harriet, for example, had constantly disobeyed the biblical injunction never to come between a man and his wife—he remembered how she had openly tried to persuade Amy to leave him, something he would never forget. In fact, Harriet had even given Amy information about the cost of a divorce and had talked her into seeing some crazy head doctor in Burlington who seemed to specialize in ending marriages not healing them. When she died Amy had been in the process of negotiating a divorce, something not even Rose knew. . . . And as if the sight of Harriet playing up to Rose now weren't enough to set a man's teeth on edge, he saw that Judge Williams, who'd given him such an unfair fine for having a little car accident, sipping punch and chatting it up with old Mrs. Winslow, a for-real rich old bitch if there ever was one, and now, God help him, Rosie's new mother-in-law . . . grammie, sitting in *her* wheelchair near the door, was keeping an eye on him, he was sure, and no doubt couldn't wait to tell Rosie he'd gone to the bar. . . . And to top it all off, here came that big fat bastard with the plummy face, Mr. Howard Hewat, who'd defended him . . . some joke . . . in court after a barroom misunderstanding about six years ago,

351

which had resulted in another big and unfair fine. . . .

Howie gave Dan a quick, penetrating glance as he ordered a martini. Rose's father, he remembered, a crazy Irishman if there ever was one. Ben must really have the hots to be willing to marry into a family like that . . . they'll give him nothing but trouble, and you won't find Howie Hewat weeping for *that.* . . .

With a curt nod at Dan, Howie carried his martini back to the reception room, now more packed than ever. A four-piece combo from the high school orchestra was setting up its instruments on a low bandstand in a corner. Howie half-emptied his martini and carried the glass in his left hand. He couldn't stand the *look* on Ben's face, but he told himself it was clear that the man had a lot of friends in town and he'd better keep his feelings to himself until the November elections at least.

Walking to the bandstand now, he tapped the brass cymbals over the bass drum with his Cornell signet ring. As the crowd quieted and turned his way, he announced, "Ladies and gentlemen, I hope you don't mind an interruption for a toast to the happy couple!"

Cheers.

"I've known lovely Rose and Ben here all their lives and am honored to count them among my dearest friends. Oh, sure, we've had our differences, the way close friends do, but no one is more welcome to these tired old eyes than Rose and there is no man I respect more than Ben Winslow. This town is lucky to have such a talented, devoted couple in its midst. Their fine new paper may sometimes be at odds with me and the *Recorder*, but a free press is the American way, just like competition is. One reason why I want to win the election for state Senator in November is that I want to keep Livingston just the way it is, except I'd like to see a little more money added to the mixture!"

After a ragged cheer and a few catcalls, Howie said, "Well,

this isn't the time or place for politics. Let's drink to Rose and Ben! Here's to you, dear friends . . . may life and love both be long for you."

Everyone drank. Rose stood up with her arm around Ben.

"Oh, hell, I know he doesn't mean a word he says," she whispered, "but just for today, I *want* to believe even him. . . ." She leaned against Ben a little, and he noticed that her breathing was just a bit labored.

"Are you feeling all right?"

"All right? Wonderful, is more like it. . . ." But Ben wasn't persuaded.

"How long do we have to stay?"

"Oh, let's dance a little and drink a little punch and hear all our enemies say how much they love us a little more. Ben, don't worry about me. I forbid it. The doctor said that happiness is the best medicine. . . ."

Back in the bar one Cory McLaughlin, who worked at the mill, recognized Dan as Rose's father and a man from the old country.

"I'm a janitor and I cleaned out Miss Kelly's office," he said. "She had a picture of you on her desk and she told me you lived in Dublin. Your daughter is certainly a fine lady, sir."

Which restored Dan's spirits considerably. Cory bought him a drink and Dan returned the gesture.

"There was never any luck in a sober wedding," Cory said, and they promptly had a round of doubles.

When a plump, pleasing woman of about forty sat beside Dan at the bar, she asked if he was the father of the bride.

"It is my proud privilege to say yes," he replied in his most melodic Dublin accent.

"I heard her father was a real Irishman. Now I see where Rose gets her good looks. She has your coloring."

Dan had not heard kind words from a woman in a long

353

while. He asked her name. It was Helen DeRosia and she worked in Fashion Corners, where she had often waited on Rose.

"It's a pleasure to sell her clothes," she said. "Anything looks good on her. She's a regular model. Anything I take off one of the mannequins fits her, and she's always so friendly and nice."

"She is that, but how about you? Surely a beautiful young lady like you doesn't need a model!"

It had been an equally long time since anyone had called Helen DeRosia "a beautiful young lady," and though she knew the compliment was outrageous, she blushed, and said happily, "I never heard real blarney before."

Seeing that Dan was now otherwise occupied, Cory McLaughlin departed, and Dan, moving his bar stool closer to Helen's, took her hand. "Now let me tell you how to tell the difference between blarney and a sincere compliment, dear lady . . . do you mind?"

"Not at all."

"A man who's giving you blarney can't look you in the eye, hold your hand and put his left arm around your shoulders at the same time. Only a sincere man can manage it. . . ."

Helen DeRosia's husband, who worked in the mill, now came to the bar, looking for his wife, who had argued with him that morning because he wanted to go fishing instead of to the wedding reception. When he found her holding hands with Dan Kelly, he was understandably angry. Helen would start up with anyone once she got a few drinks under her belt, he reflected darkly, and the fatter she got, the more she was interested in strangers. Still, this white-haired fellow seemed too old to worry about. Pat DeRosia ordered a double shot of rye with ginger ale at the other end of the bar and walked out without even disturbing Helen and Dan, who were too engrossed to notice him. For a long while, Pat figured, he really would be able to get Helen's goat by asking her if she had heard anything from her senior-citizen lover. Lover . . . some joke. The old bird was obviously years beyond that sort of thing. . . .

The punch was running out, and Ann sent Ebon to get some bottles from the bar and mix a new batch. The original mixture had seemed much too weak and too sweet for him, so now he substituted ginger ale for champagne, mixed in orange juice for coloring, and added enough vodka to make a man know he had had a drink. After two cups of this concoction, Cory McLaughlin, who had done well at the bar, went to sleep on a couch in the men's locker room. He was the first casualty of the reception.

Old Doctor Bill and his equally aged assistant, Dr. Thorndike, came to the country club to play golf. They had not heard of the wedding reception, and were taken aback by the crowd, which made it impossible for them to get a bite to eat before embarking in their electric carts. While they tried to make their getaway, however, grammie spotted the two physicians, whom she admired, and began thanking them effusively for coming. Left with little choice, they went to congratulate Rose and Ben.

"Rose, I delivered you," Dr. Bill said.

"I bet you say that to all the girls, Dr. Bill," she said.

"I delivered Ben too," Dr. Bill said. "I could say that to almost every person here."

"That he could," Dr. Thorndike put in.

"Anyway, we wish you every happiness," Dr. Bill said. The two old doctors, spiffy in leisure suits they had bought in New York, then strolled toward the golf course.

"Damn it, he makes me so mad," Rose said. "He didn't deliver me, mom had the sense to go to Burlington. And I bet he didn't deliver you, either. What right does he have to practice medicine when he's senile?"

355

"Mother had an obstetrician come from New York," Ben told her. "She didn't have much confidence in Dr. Bill even when he was young."

"But he *thinks* he delivered everybody in this town. I would have called him on it, but not today. Today I'm even ready to marvel at the medical skills of Dr. Bill. He's your basic, picturesque old country doctor and on my wedding day I love him. . . ."

As the crowd thinned a little, the band began to play a selection of old favorites Rose had chosen. More used to rock music and parade marches, the youngsters stumbled a little on some of the nostalgic chords, but the melody of "Stardust," their opening attempt, still sounded sweet and true.

"I think we're supposed to dance the first number," Rose said.

Ben uneasily led her to the dance floor, thinking how *young* she looked, her face as wonderfully open and eager as a young girl at her first ball. Her face, though, also felt hot as she pressed it against his, melted against him in a way he'd always hoped girls would when he was young. They danced effortlessly, even he, slowly circling the floor, so engrossed in each other they hardly heard the wedding guests clapping.

"I'm glad that you're such a good dancer," she murmured.

"I never was before."

After they had circled the floor several times the band began to play, "Our Love Is Here to Stay," and several other couples came out onto the floor.

"Let's take a break," Rose said. "Would you mind getting me a glass of punch?"

When he came back with the drink he found her sitting on the edge of the bandstand. She seemed to be breathing a little hard, perhaps from the exertion of dancing, and before taking the glass from him she pulled a tissue from a pocket of her dress, unfolded it, and picked out one of her pills. She put it under her tongue and took a swallow of the punch, almost spitting it out when she discovered how strong it was.

"Whew, how did the punch get to be a haymaker?"

"I don't know. . . . Rosie, let's go home. The *Princess* is waiting for us."

"Just a few more minutes. I'll only have one wedding reception, Ben, at least I hope—"

"I don't want you to get tired, honey. And don't forget, the whole staff of the Lost Lake Inn is waiting for us."

"I won't keep them waiting long. Don't *worry*, Ben. God won't let anything happen to me on my wedding day."

Soon Ann and Ebon began to dance, a striking couple indeed, Ebon tall and darkly handsome, Annie a sunny young princess in her own right. She might be somewhat aloof to Ebon most of the time, but they at least danced like people in love, Ben thought, each quick to catch the slightest response of the other, exchanging glances and smiles.

"They're lovely," Rose said. "I wish they could live their lives the way they dance. . . ."

Howie Hewat now appeared on the dance floor with Carol, his ailing wife. Howie's big broad face was fixed in a set smile as he glided about with his wife's face buried in his expansive chest, the band playing "Just One of Those Things." The irony was lost on them.

Suddenly there was a stir in the crowd around the dance floor as Dan pushed his way from the bar, followed by Helen DeRosia, whom he held by the hand. Taking his full-bosomed partner into his arms, Dan began to dance with surprising grace, especially considering that both of them were obviously more than a little drunk.

"Oh, no!" Rose groaned. "He *promised* he wouldn't drink today."

"Well, at least he seems to be having a good time—"

"God, there's going to be trouble, there *always* is trouble when he drinks."

Much of the color had drained out of Rose's face.

"Let's get out of here then," Ben said.

357

"We can't just leave him. Do you know what these people do to him when he gets out of line?"

"Eb and Ephram can take care of him."

"He won't listen to anybody but me. Just wait 'til this dance is over and I'll talk to him."

They watched as Dan and Helen continued to dance, holding each other as closely as Ebon and Annie did. When Dan turned, presenting Helen's back to them, they could clearly see that his big hand had slipped lower, until it was gently kneading her ample buttocks.

"Oh, no," Rose groaned. "Why does he always have to make a spectacle of himself?"

They weren't the only ones to notice. Howie Hewat, guardian of country-club morals, glared at Dan. And Pat DeRosia, who had been following the progress of his wife's flirtation with "the old geezer" so that he could punish her with it the next day, now decided that he'd had more than enough. It was one thing for Helen to have fun and games with a senior citizen at the bar, quite another for her to disgrace herself and her husband's name in front of all these people . . .

Pat strode toward the dance floor. The music stopped. Dan and Helen still kept their arms around each other while he whispered in her ear and patted her extensively.

"All *right*," Pat said as he walked toward them and put his hand on Dan's arm. "Enough, by damn, is enough . . ."

"Take your hand off me," Dan exploded, jerking his arm away.

"Dad," Rose cried out . . . "please, please—"

"Let go of my wife!" DeRosia shouted, putting his hand on Helen's arm and pulling.

"Let her alone," Dan said, and gave DeRosia a push on the chest that sent him reeling.

"Stop it. You can't behave like that in this club," Howie intoned, and came lumbering forward to grab hold of Dan's arm. He never had a chance. Dan let loose his roundhouse right, and Howie was perhaps one of the few men in the world who couldn't duck it. Dan's big fist caught him square on the jaw, causing him to collapse on his back, his eyes glassy.

At this moment Rose ran forward to restrain her father, with Ben following close after her, but before they could get to him, nearly every man at the reception, including members of the band, jumped on him, swinging their fists to teach a foreigner what happened when he tangled with one of Livingston's own.

Ben caught Rose in both arms as she tried to get in to defend her father.

"*Let me go*," she said between clenched teeth. "They'll kill him . . ." She was breathing with obvious difficulty now, and her face was chalk-white.

"Eb will take care of him," Ben said. "I'm going to take you home."

"I can't leave him." She was staring at the small hill of writhing bodies, which Ebon was shouting over.

"Forgive me," Ben said, picking her up. "I care about *you*."

"You . . ." Her breath caught and her eyes were staring. Holding her in his arms like a child, he ran for the van. Ann followed him, then rushed ahead to open doors.

He put Rose down on the mattress, she started to speak, gasped. Her struggle for breath became desperate, and to Ben's horror, the symptoms of the heart attack he had seen her suffer in Vermont were repeated. She sat bolt upright, her whole body rigid as she fought for air. Her fists were clenched at her sides, her eyes stared unseeingly and her mouth gaped open in a mask of tragedy. Then there came that nightmarish blood-flecked froth on her lips.

Ben scrambled for the driver's seat while Ann sat beside Rose, hugging her. Burlington was more than fifty miles away. The local hospital Rose hated, but maybe it had emergency treatment, oxygen or at least adrenalin. It was only two miles away.

Driving so fast that he almost had two accidents, Ben skidded to a stop in front of the local hospital's front door. Rose was utterly limp as he took her from Ann's arms. Her eyes were open. He made himself think that was a good sign.

"I'm scared," Ann said. Her face was white as her sister's, but she stayed ahead of him, opening doors as he ran with Rose in his arms. They entered a lobby with one young woman at a switchboard.

"Emergency," Ben rasped, his own breath coming hard. "Doctor . . . get a doctor—"

"The emergency room is downstairs, sir," the girl said. "You go down that corridor and take the first elevator on your left—"

"Get a doctor," Ben yelled. "She's had a heart attack."

"Well, if you will go to the emergency room, sir, they will take all the appropriate steps . . ."

He ran with Rose in his arms down the corridor, Ann ahead. After taking a wrong turn, they found the emergency room, which appeared empty.

"Doctor," Ben shouted at the top of his lungs. *"Emergency."*

An elderly nurse came from a dispensary.

"What happened?"

"Heart attack—"

"Put her here," the nurse said, indicating a high stretcher on wheels.

Ben put Rose gently down. Her eyes were staring in a way that terrified him, a stare too well remembered from Korea, Vietnam, Ireland . . . The nurse put her hand on Rose's wrist, examined her eyes. After taking a stethoscope from a hook on the wall, she loosened the front of Rose's dress. She listened for what seemed a long while before she spoke. "I'm very sorry, Mr. Winslow. She's gone. There's nothing we can do."

"Get a doctor! What the hell is this business of just having a nurse handle a thing like this?"

"It's Saturday afternoon, Mr. Winslow. We only have three doctors and one is on vacation—"

"And the other two are on the golf course. Call them."

"But she's gone. What's the use?"

"Adrenalin . . . it helps sometimes, doesn't it . . . what about oxygen, massaging her heart, using shock—"

"I'm afraid it's too late for any of that . . . When Dr. Bill comes in he'll examine her and write up a death certificate—"

"Get him *now*, you hear me? . . . Get that old bastard out of his golf cart or I'm going to nail him to this wall with my own hands—"

"I'll try," the nurse said. "I understand you're upset, but there's no need to go on like that."

No need. Jesus.

She pushed the stretcher with Rose on it into a small adjacent room, where it stood crowded against a hospital bed. She did not cover her with a sheet. Ben almost let himself think that was a hopeful sign.

"You can wait here if you want," the nurse said. "I'll do everything I can to get the doctor here as soon as possible."

"Thank you."

"I would like to say," the nurse continued, "that with only three doctors, we can't even pretend to have a doctor on duty here twenty-four hours a day, seven days a week. Dr. Bill works very hard . . ."

Ben did not answer, did not even hear. He and Ann stood by the stretcher, looking at Rose's face, which was still contorted by her struggle for breath, her eyes still staring without sight. The front of her dress, which the nurse had unbuttoned for the stethoscope, still was agape. Ann carefully buttoned it, pulling it straight. Ben smoothed back Rose's soft hair. Her forehead was warm, and the hair had that silky quality and the familiar fragrance of wild flowers.

He began to sob, an explosion of grief. He sank down on the hospital bed near the stretcher, crumpling up the covers to bury his face. He felt someone's arms around him . . .

361

Ann's. She was crying too. He turned to put his arms around her and they wept together, at last subsiding into a kind of mute exhaustion. All he could think of was that this sorrow was finally beyond his endurance, more than he had even the will to survive. Death was always the final answer, wasn't it? Why did so many people think it was wrong to embrace death when the pain of life got unbearable? . . .

Dr. Bill knocked quietly before opening the door. He had just come in from bright sunlight, and his old eyes took time to adjust to this dimly lit room. Ben and Ann stood by the stretcher. The physician perfunctorily ran through the steps the nurse had taken.

"She's gone," he said, then shook his head. "Didn't this young lady just get married today?"

"Yes," Ben said. "You congratulated her."

"Yes. I'm sorry, very sorry indeed."

"Thank you."

"Do you want an autopsy?"

"No," Ben replied. At least Rosie would be spared her date with Mack the Knife.

"Do you want me to call Ed Case for you?"

"I guess so." An old local joke went that when anyone asked one of the old-timers how he was, the standard reply was, "Well, I'm not ready for Eddie." Now Rosie was.

"Well, I think you might as well go along now," Dr. Bill said. "Ed will be sending his people over before long. Spare yourself. Go home and have a stiff drink. Do you want a sedative?"

They said no. Ben stood there looking at Rose, trying not to imagine what undertakers did. He focused on her hands. The nurse had folded them on her stomach, and in the dim light from the window, the diamond ring he had bought for her in Santa Barbara and her brand-new gold wedding band gleamed.

They walked to the van in a daze, and he drove toward Cliff House the same way until he approached it and saw the

362

cars, people already there to sympathize with grammie—someone must have brought her home. There were two police cars, probably about Dan. He knew he couldn't face all these people now, and found himself parking the van near the boathouse and walking toward the *Princess*, which lay rocking gently, prepared for a cruise. Ann followed him without a word. When he stepped into the cockpit, she said, "Can I go too?"

"I don't know whether you should. I have to get away for a while."

"So do I. Don't leave me alone, Ben. Please?" There was panic in her voice.

"Get aboard," he told her, and started the engine. Casting off the lines, he steered toward the Lost Lake Inn without thinking. He felt as if he wanted to hurry and shoved the throttle all the way down, making the old *Princess* strain through the water.

It was a beautiful afternoon, the kind he and Rose had hoped for. As he threaded the narrow channel toward the ruins of the old inn, he began a rush of what-ifs . . . what if he had had the wit to get more training and equipment for an emergency? What if he had not let her waste her strength on a big reception? What if he had asked Ephram or Ebon to stick with old Dan and make sure he didn't get into trouble? What if he had somehow forced Rose to have her operation much earlier?

He moored the *Princess* at the old wharf. From a locker in the cabin he took a quart of Scotch whiskey, a bottle of soda and two plastic mugs, which he put over the top of the whiskey bottle. He carried them to the old foundation, sitting down on a wall he and Rose had sat on. Ann followed him and sat a few feet away on an old nail keg.

"Annie," he said as he opened the whiskey bottle, "I'm afraid I am now going to get drunk. It's not right, but I am going to."

"Go ahead."

363

"If it bothers you to see me drunk, you can walk right up an old road over there about half a mile and find the highway. There's a gas station where you can call a taxi."

"It won't bother me."

He filled a plastic mug half full of whiskey and splashed in soda. He forced himself to drink it fast, and found his nerves were screaming at only a slightly lower pitch. He filled the mug again.

"Rosie would have more guts," he said abruptly.

"When mom died she got drunk. It's the only time she ever did. We had to put her to bed after the funeral."

"Thank you for telling me." He drank the second mug. "Annie, do you want some?"

"I would if I could, but it will make me sick."

He filled his mug a third time.

Ann moved to a more comfortable spot on some leaves where she could sit with her back against a tree. . . .

Later his memories of that night were never very clear. He did not eat. He just sat drinking the whiskey, finding that it at last diminished his feeling that he was going to explode. When darkness came, there were fireflies and he remembered how Rose had liked them. After a while Annie brought blankets and cushions from the boat. He drank a lot more before he lay down and let her cover him up. Sleep came, suddenly but brief. When he awoke a full moon was shining through the trees. It was chilly and some small logs blazed in the old fireplace under a coffee pot from the boat. Ann was attending to the fire. For a moment he thought she was Rose, and almost reminded her that she was not supposed to drink coffee.

"How do you feel?" Ann asked.

Sleep had made him forget for an hour that Rose was dead, but now the realization of it hit with fresh force. He filled his mug with more whiskey, noting that the bottle was already half empty.

364

"Annie, I loved her so much."

"That made her very happy."

"For four months. Do you realize that's as long as we knew each other? And we were married four hours."

"It was the best time she ever had."

"Me too. I was married twenty-three years the first time and four hours the second. My second marriage is the one that will stay with me. All my life."

"I believe that."

"Do you think she would have lived longer if she'd never met me? Please be honest."

"Of course not. Ben, she knew she had a bad heart for a long time."

"Because some stupid, incompetent doctor didn't know enough to keep a child's fever down."

She didn't tell him that her father would get mad when they called a doctor. They were all thieves, he said, and believed it. No . . . no point in telling Ben that now. . . .

Katydids were singing their dry, repetitive song in the surrounding woods. Ben filled his mug again with whiskey and now sipped it slowly. The moonlight was so bright that every detail of the ruin stood out. The grass looked silvery on the level ground where the old wooden terrace had stood. Rosie had wanted him to put on formal clothes so that she could dance with him there in an evening gown. Well, he had on a white suit, and in the distance he could hear music from some boat on the lake, but Rosie was missing. Had Eddie Case already taken her into his workroom? . . . The thought doubled Ben over and he was sick to his stomach in the dry leaves.

Ann helped him to move the blankets and the cushions away from there. His stomach cringed, but he had another mug of whiskey before lying down and trying to sleep again. But what he did was think of how Rosie had wanted to make love to him in spite of her sickness . . . to him . . .

365

for him . . . just as she had for so long exhausted herself trying to give to her father, Annie and grammie. Until in the end she gave more than she had.

Annie sat beside him now, rubbing his back. At one point the liquor and the grief turned him quite wild. He began shouting that God was crazy, that any poor son of a bitch with or without a high school education could run the universe better than the incumbent. Any fisherman or farmer, or even an advertising man, would know better than to kill a beautiful, generous young woman on her wedding day . . . "Don't worry, Ben, God won't let anything happen to me on my wedding day . . ."

After he got through lecturing God, with all kinds of threatening gestures, he decided that he wanted to go swimming, the way Rose and he had on the nearby beach. He wanted to swim all around the lake, he said, and began ripping off his clothes and heading for the beach.

Ann asked if he wouldn't like to try a little cold wine before his dip and persuaded him to go back to the boat with her to get it.

He would not touch the celebratory bottles of champagne in the ice chest but took a bottle of cold Chablis and drank at it before discovering a bottle of vodka. Clutching a mug of it, he returned to the ruins of the inn, rubber-legged, and collapsed onto the cushions, unconscious.

After covering him with blankets, Ann lay down beside him. She was not as calm as she had appeared to be, not by half, and lay close to Ben, needing his warmth, even if he was drunk. All her life, she had depended on Rose alone for what she really needed . . . love, food, shelter . . . Rose was gone. Ben was the strongest, most wonderful man she had ever met. The sound of his deep breathing was reassuring. Huddled close to him, Ann finally slept.

23

IT was nearly three in the morning when Ebon, who had been worried about the disappearance of Ben and Ann, found the *Princess* was not at her wharf. Borrowing a launch from his Uncle Pete, he set out to look for the cruiser, and knowing that his father liked the bay by the ruins of the old inn, he quickly located the boat. No one was aboard. Exploring the foundations with a flashlight, he soon came on Ben and Ann lying under blankets in a corner. Ann awoke as soon as he played the flashlight on them, and self-consciously began to try to explain the situation. Ebon looked stone-faced as he helped his father back to the cruiser and put him in a bunk, then arranged to tow the launch while he piloted the *Princess* home.

"It's been some day," he finally said after negotiating the narrow channel. "On top of everything else, I find you asleep with my grieving father—"

She slapped his face, hard.

"I'm not implying anything—"

"I don't see how you can even *think* such a thing at a time like this. Your father *had* to get drunk. Can't you understand that? He wanted to swim the damn lake."

"I guess I should be thanking you," Ebon said. "I'm sorry.

Maybe we all should be excused for what we do or say at a time like this."

It was ten the next morning when Ben woke up in his bed at Cliff House. He did not have a hangover in the usual sense—he had drunk too much for that. He felt that Ben Winslow had disappeared and had been replaced by a creature from outer space whose bodily functions dealt mostly in fire. He didn't much care. Rose was dead.

In the kitchen he found Ebon helping Ann wash the breakfast dishes. Blinking at them in the bright sunlight from the window, he felt he was, somehow, seeing them for the first time. Ebon, wearing only his dungarees, would have been a good study for Rodin. Tanned almost to the color of bronze, he was mysteriously muscular . . . he had no program for regular exercise, as far as Ben knew. Beside him Annie in a white one-piece bathing suit was all soft and feminine . . . was some basic contradiction involved here? Wasn't Ebon the one who was basically soft, at least when it came to planning his life and that sort of thing, while Annie's ambitions were supposed to be making her tougher than she looked? . . .

"Good morning," she said. "Tea, coffee, ice bag, Alka-Seltzer, aspirin?"

"Leave out the tea. Thanks for rescuing us, Eb."

"We were getting a little worried . . . Dad, there are a million calls for you . . ."

He nodded. "How's grammie?"

"She got drunk too, in her room. Now she's watching TV, with the only ice bag in the house on her head. She asked us not to talk about Rose. She said that right now she can't stand it."

Carrying a Bloody Mary that Ann made for him, Ben went to the living room. The old lady's face was etched with suffering as she sat in her wheelchair, her feet propped up on a hassock, a pink plastic ice bag on her wispy white hair. She was watching a famous morning talk-show host on television, and her eyes hardly moved from the screen as Ben entered. There was no reaction when he kissed her forehead.

"He's talking to child-abuse people," she said in a flat voice. "People who beat up their kids, sometimes kill them. He says it's a human problem."

Ben sat in an armchair, willing to exchange the problems of child abuse for his own.

"He's a nice looking boy, a lot like a man I used to know in County Cork, but you never know what he's going to talk about. He has queers up there and people who have been raped and even people who done the raping. And he says everything is a human problem."

"I guess he's right about that."

Silence. Then: "What are you going to do about the funeral?"

"We'll have a memorial service, I guess. We have a family plot in the cemetery."

"Seems funny to have her in Protestant soil. Rosie had her quarrels with the church but she was never a Protestant."

For a moment Ben found himself wondering whether a justice of the peace could bury people, a civil ceremony with a civil cemetery. He said, "Rose would want us to do whatever makes for the least trouble. I don't mind a Catholic cemetery."

"Thanks, Ben," grammie said, dabbing at her eyes with a Kleenex. "I got to admit, this was bothering me. Her mother was always a good Catholic and so were all her people, going clear back to kingdom come. I'll talk to Father O'Malley. He's coming to see me in a few minutes."

The talk-show host was now talking to an attractive housewife who had written a book about her "philosophy of joy." She said that one secret of happiness was clean living, that the pleasures of adultery and such weren't all they were

369

cracked up to be. While his head throbbed, Ben sipped his Bloody Mary and tried to concentrate on the philosophy of joy, nothing else.

"What are you going to do about Dan?" grammie suddenly asked.

Ben shook his head. "I haven't even begun to think about that."

"Rose would want you to get him out of jail. She always did, even when she had to take out a mortgage to raise bail."

"I'll do my best."

"He'll probably go right back to Ireland. He always does when he gets in a jam."

"Good," Ben said.

Still feeling as though he had become some odd creature he did not know very well, Ben called Judge Williams.

"God, I'm sorry for you," Weeping Willy said. "I haven't felt so bad since my own wife died. But I guess life has to go on. I suppose you want to know about Dan Kelly."

"What are the charges against him?"

"It's not my case, but I looked into it. They've got him on about a dozen charges of assault and resisting arrest. He took a swing at Dr. Bill when they got him to the hospital to have his face stitched up, and he butted Big Duke right in the belly on the way to the jail. I never knew a man who gets so crazy drunk."

"How long can they put him away for?"

"When you figure that, don't forget that Howie Hewat will make sure he gets the maximum. Have you heard about Howie?"

"No."

"Howie's lying up there in the hospital with his jaw broken in three places. It's going to have to be all wired shut for months. Can you imagine a politician with his jaw wired shut just before a big election?"

He knew that sounded funny, but wasn't laughing. As

370

Rose had said, all the stories generated by her father sounded funny. And weren't.

"I guess Howie has a right to be sore," Ben said.

"He's sputtering so much, they can hardly get him to shut his mouth long enough to get it wired. He says he's going to hang Dan by his balls over a slow fire, if you'll pardon the expression."

"What can he really do?"

"You got to remember that Dan's got a record of assault as long as your arm. Frankly, if I was the judge I'd give him ten to twenty at least. And he'll also be liable for Howie's medical costs. Dr. Bill is just giving him a temporary job, he's going to Boston to get the thing done right. God knows how many thousands the thing will cost."

There was a short silence while Ben's head throbbed.

"Then of course Dan will have a lawyer to pay," the judge said. "I don't know anybody around here who wants to go up against Howie on a thing like this. You'll have to bring somebody from out of town."

There was another pause, during which Ben saw most of the savings he needed for Ebon and Ann go down the drain.

"Of course, you could just let the old bastard stew in his own juice in the jailhouse. Or there is another solution . . ."

"What?"

"As a judge and a lawyer, I can't recommend it. But you *could* spring him on bail, then let him jump bail and fly back to Ireland, never to return, on pain of being locked up forever. They'd never bother to extradite him on any charge less than murder."

"How much is the bail?"

"A thousand dollars. Now, Ben, don't you help him jump bail. You shouldn't be caught helping a man to break the law. Remember, I advise against all of this. I'm just listing all the possibilities."

"Thanks," Ben said.

371

"Did I ever tell you what your father did for me?"

"No."

"He kept a story out of his paper that would have hurt me bad. No point in telling you what the story was—I still don't like to talk about it. I never asked him to bury the damn thing. He told me he threw it out just because he had more news than he could handle that week."

"I know what he meant," Ben said, and thanked the judge again before hanging up.

An hour later Ben appeared at the jail. Dan was sitting in a cell close to one occupied by Roger Radeau, who was to come to trial soon—for second-degree murder and other charges. The thin, now pale backwoodsman looked respectable compared to Dan, whose rumpled white suit was streaked with blood, who had one side of his face bandaged and the other badly bruised.

"Ben!" he said. "Where have you been? What took you so long?"

"I came soon as I could."

"Rose would have got me out of here in jig time—"

"Rose is dead, Dan."

"I know." The big man's legs sagged, along with his face, and he sank down on his cot. He did not cry, but the half of his face that was visible suddenly seemed to die.

"Are you going to write him up in your paper too?" Radeau asked. "Are you going to put his picture on television?"

Ben didn't answer. Dan stood up slowly. "When are they going to let me out of here?"

"When they finish their paperwork. I just paid the bail."

Dan did not ask how much that was. He hitched up his pants and smoothed back his hair. "Rose never let me stay in jail as long as this," he said again. He sat there looking as though he himself had died.

After he'd taken Dan back to Cliff House, Ben allowed

himself a shot of Scotch, but managed to resist the strong temptation to blot everything out again. At the newspaper office Lillian Fletcher was getting out the next edition, and he proceeded to force himself to search through his files for his best photographs of Rose. He also developed a roll of film Ann had just given him, steeling himself to look at the first image that appeared . . . Rosie was standing in her wedding dress on the terrace with the lake in the background, her slender figure arched in a motionless dance, her face showing vitality and joy. . . .

"Happiness is the best medicine," she had quoted her doctor as saying.

He decided to devote the bottom half of the front page to these pictures and wrote a simple text to accompany them:

> Rose Kelly Winslow, the publisher of this paper and the wife of the editor, died here Saturday afternoon of a heart attack, shortly after her wedding. The daughter of Dan. M. Kelly and his late wife, Amy, she had long lived with her grandmother, Ida M. Nolan, and her sister, Ann M. Kelly, on their farm on County Road. Mrs. Winslow graduated from the Livingston High School in 1964 at the age of 16, and attended Boston University. Speaking as the editor of this paper and her husband, I cannot find words to express the special qualities which made Rose such a joy to me and such a comfort to so many others. In her memory there is courage and inspiration as well as sadness. In the worst of the many difficult circumstances she endured in her short life, she never gave in to despair herself and would not want others to. These words of course fail to convey the strength and beauty of this free-spirited woman. I hope the accompanying photographs will do better.—B.L.W.

After making sure that Lillian understood the layout he wanted, Ben walked aimlessly down the street, returning hurriedly to the van when too many people tried to stop him to express their sympathies, most of them talking with heartfelt emotion which Ben found unendurable. Suddenly

373

the world seemed to be moving too slowly for him. He wanted to get the funeral and the interment over with before the strength he felt dissipating so fast deserted him entirely. Just before he left the house grammie had said something about arranging a wake, a prospect Ben regarded with sheer horror, but he also knew it was one more thing he could not allow himself to run away from.

Cliff House was surrounded by the cars of people who'd come to bring sympathy, hams, casseroles and cakes. Unable to face any more outpourings of emotion, he went off to the *Princess*. He forced himself to go through the elaborate safety precautions before starting the engine, reminding himself that he still had responsibilities if nothing much else to look forward to. In the widest portion of the lake he cut off the engine and drifted. Taking from its hooks beside a bunk a fine old pole of bamboo that his father had once used, he started casting with a small spoon. He recalled how as a boy he'd never been able to understand why his father spent almost every available hour in pursuit of small fish, or why he drank so much. Getting a mug and a bottle of brandy from the locker in the cabin, he let himself drink just enough to turn down the volume of his misery that still sounded like a scream inside his head. The lake was very still, reflecting both the *Princess* and the fluffy clouds overhead. He'd once read somewhere that Eskimos in kayaks suffered something called the mirror disease . . . when caught, surrounded by the reflected images of the ice floe on a windless sea, they occasionally lost all sense of direction and went mad. He felt now as though he had this same dizzying sense of disorientation. Ever since he had met her, Rose had in a real sense been his compass, giving him the impetus, the direction, to start the paper and to love and take on responsibility for several people. With her it had all been a joy and had meaning, without her the whole exercise —without being self-pitying—seemed pointless. Why, for god's sake, publish a weekly newspaper in a small town he'd

374

worked hard to escape from when he was younger? He rarely saw much of his own mother, was he really the sort to take care of another old woman in a wheelchair? A nursing home, face it, would be inevitable for grammie sooner or later. And as for Annie, did he really want to get involved with his son's girl professionally . . . or possibly, if he didn't watch it, any other way? The best thing for Annie now would be to go to a good boarding school until she was ready for college. If he helped her financially, she could hardly expect anything more. Nor could Ebon when he went to his school of forestry.

Then, with Dan back in Ireland he'd again be as solitary a character as he'd been when he appeared in Livingston the previous May—only four months . . . Now that his newspaper was doing well he was sure he could sell it, maybe at a good profit. Lillian Fletcher, who obviously enjoyed editing it without supervision now that Ben was away from the office so much, had hinted that her husband had left her enough to buy it, and if that didn't work out Pete had said outright that he and Howie would be glad to buy the paper and merge it with the *Recorder*. It seemed he could leave Livingston footloose, fancy-free with money in his pocket, if he wanted that.

And where would he go? Back to Santa Barbara? He tried to see himself joining some of the other aging beach boys and beach girls on the sand, middle-aged sun worshipers, bulging beach-blanket bunnies, or if not that crowd, then people who could get him invitations to cocktail parties in the great mansions on the hilltops overlooking the sea. And if he was lonely in all that splendor, surrounded by all those brilliant, glittering people, it would only be because he would again be locked into his own glass dome of loneliness, the way a turtle is locked into its shell.

Rosie had released him from that glass dome, but now that she was gone he felt it clamping down over him again. Maybe the ticket was some sort of violent action, the way it had been when his marriage fell apart and he'd taken on foreign assignments. Claudia Simpson, his agent, had told him she could get him back in that league again if he ever wanted, mentioning the possibility of an assignment in Russia or China. If a man traveled far enough, and fast enough, he could damn near outrun himself. For a while, anyway.

Finishing his mug of brandy he went below to the head, a tiny lavatory in the bow of the boat. He saw that Rosie had left her butterfly beach coat hanging on a hook on the door. It was swaying a little as the *Princess* rolled in the wake of a passing motorboat, as though it had a life of its own . . . This has got to stop, he told himself. It's one thing to love and another thing to drown in bathos. Rosie would have said, "Gee, Ben, I thought you were a *Protestant*. Why don't you leave all this teary sentimentality to us Irish Catholics? We at least know how to do it. . . ." With a half smile—his first in a century—he folded the coat into a drawer and returned to the cockpit.

The day of the funeral was cold, the first warning of fall. A stiff north wind rattled the windows of Cliff House. Ragged gray clouds raced across a blue sky, alternating sunshine with shadows. Ben was startled by the beauty and size of the Catholic church, which he had never before entered, and he was gratified to see that practically the whole town had turned out to honor Rosie.

In the pew beside Ben, Dan stood in one of Ben's dark suits, one side of his face still bandaged, a doleful yet somehow incurably comic sight as he kneeled and crossed himself, like an old pirate being converted. He was drunk enough to need Ebon's steadying hand when he tried to get back on the pew after kneeling, but there was no fight in him on this day, rather a look of tragedy in his one exposed eye, a vulnerability in his trembling lips. Ben was glad the old man would go back to Ireland the next day, instead of to jail.

Ann wore a black dress she had bought from Helen

DeRosia at the Fashion Corners the previous day. She looked composed as she helped grammie with a prayer book, but the composure fell from her and she began to cry halfway through the service. Ebon gave her his handkerchief and sat holding her hand, looking strong in his new role of protector and at least emergency head of the family.

Although the mass was sung in English, Ben could understand very little of it. He examined a stained glass window that showed Christ holding a lamb, and sentimentally thought of the lambs he'd seen in the field near Rosie's farm soon after they had met. It seemed necessary to think of Rose during her funeral mass, but oddly difficult. He did not want to think of her in her coffin in the hearse waiting outside the church door. The memory of her telling him how she wanted to build a bonfire in winter on the highest peak of Big Iron Mountain was better. People, she'd said, would think it was a signal fire and they would ask what its message was. And she'd stopped him questioning her about it, saying they both would know, wouldn't they? . . . Except he really didn't. . . . She had laughed about the actors she'd dreamed of taking there when she was a young girl, and had included him in her fantasy of watching the bonfire burn, covering the icy peak with an orange glow. She'd made something of a joke out of it all, but he still liked to think of her signal fire as big as a burning house on the icy summit of the great mountain, and her words about "what its message is . . . we'll know, won't we?" haunted him.

The mass was over. The family got into Virginia's old Cadillac, with Ephram, dressed faultlessly in a chauffeur's uniform, driving. They tailed the hearse to the Catholic cemetery on the edge of the village, while a long parade of cars followed them.

There was a brief ceremony in a ring of people surrounding the open grave, where the mat of fake grass had slipped enough to expose the red clay. Wind blew the burly priest's surplice. Again Ben tried not to think of Rosie in that gray metal coffin. He'd shocked Ed Case and grammie by refusing to look at her after leaving her in the hospital and had insisted on a sealed casket. Somehow he thought that Rose would like her privacy in death, as she had during her illness at the hospital.

The old phrase, "ashes to ashes, dust to dust" sounded to Ben as though he had never heard it. They're not putting ashes or dust into that grave, he thought—they are burying Rosie, my beautiful Rosie. The awfulness of that thought made him dizzy, then nauseated. Please don't let me be sick, not here, not now, he prayed. That prayer, at least, was answered.

24

AFTERWARD they went back to Cliff House. Some
of grammie's friends had spread out in the dining room the
many foods which had been donated, and Ebon had set up
a bar in the living room. The house quickly filled with people, many of whom Ben could not remember seeing. A lot
of old women thought it necessary to hold Ben's hand and
tell him in detail what a fine woman Rose had been. Dan
spilled a platter of potato salad he was trying to pass. Ann
cleaned it up.

After about an hour Peter arrived, again carrying his
mother in a wheelchair with Ephram's help. Old Virginia
had been much moved by the news that the bride she had
seen on Saturday had died that very afternoon.

"Such a beautiful girl," she kept repeating to Ben. "So
young. I don't understand it. I've known Heidi ever since
she was born, and she never once had heart trouble. . . ."

Howie Hewat, on his way from the local hospital to a
hospital in Boston, was definitely a surprise arrival. Howie
had his jaw and neck set in an uncomfortable-looking leather
device, and could only hiss out a few words between
clenched teeth. When Dan saw him, he promptly made for
the upstairs.

Appearing not to notice his assailant, Howie approached Ben. "Sorry, Ben," he said in a sibilant whisper. "Forget everything. Rose's death a shock, terrible shock. You might not think it, but I liked her, respected her . . ." Apparently this effort hurt his jaw, because he stopped with a grimace. Solemnly circling the big room, he shook hands with Ann and grammie, kissing both of them on the cheek. Then he walked out to the ambulance waiting for him.

"Howie may be just another politician," a woman said, "but at least he seems to care about people, and that's more than you can say for most of the breed."

Ben could almost agree . . . at least at a time like this when everything and everybody paled to nothingness compared to Rose's death. He took a Scotch on the rocks from his son and went upstairs. The party looked as though it would go on for hours. He had a craving for solitude.

When he came downstairs, it was mid-afternoon. Instead of thinning, the crowd had increased, filling every chair in the big house and on the terrace. Somewhat but not really to Ben's surprise, Dan was sitting at the upright piano in the living room, playing in his barroom style and singing in his Irish tenor, which was true in spite of his being drunk. Ben cringed, though, at the song he selected—"My Wild Irish Rose."

Getting another drink from Ebon, Ben went out onto the terrace. The wind was increasing, and waves dashing against the cliffs below sent up spray to the birch trees beneath the wall that surrounded the flagstones. Despite the wind he could still hear the tinkle of the piano and Dan's plaintive voice. Rose hated that song, she had told him once. "To me, it's just a sure sign that dad's drunk."

It still was, but the emotion that Dan was pumping into that refrain now came from more than alcohol. If there was anyone in the world who really had loved Rose, Ben realized, almost as much as he did, it was Dan Kelly, and in that there was a sense of kinship, no matter what had happened.

Feeling guilty about again ducking out on the wake, which was getting bigger than the wedding reception had been, Ben beat another retreat upstairs. Grief, like rank, has its privileges, or ought to, he decided as he lay down. This time he actually slept for about five hours.

It was dark when he awoke. The big house seemed oddly quiet. All the guests had gone home, no one was in the living room but Ann, Ebon and Dan, who was lying on his back in the middle of the rug. Holding a bottle of beer, Ebon was standing over him. As Ben entered, Dan began shaking his finger at Ebon, looking straight up at him.

"You have a lot to learn, lad," he said in professorial tones. "Just because your father is rich you can't go through life without the Bible and the moral principles which the church teaches . . ." And still flat on his back, he proceeded to give Ebon a mini-sermon, pausing from time to time to refresh himself from the glass of whiskey he held in his right hand.

Ebon's lean, narrow face looked saturnine as he asked questions, egging him on . . . "How about drink, Dan? Does the church have anything to say about booze?"

"Ah, drink is a curse, especially in excess," declared Dan in ministerial voice. "A man who can't hold his liquor can never be trusted. You must learn your capacity, lad, or take the pledge and be done with it."

"How about fighting? Do your moral principles have anything to say about that?"

"You should never raise your hand against your fellow man . . ."

Suddenly the concept of his son ridiculing the old man upset Ben. This, he was sure, would not be the way Rose would like to see her funeral end.

"Ebon," he said sharply, "get out of here. Let him alone—"

381

"What the hell did I do?" He was fairly drunk himself, Ben saw.

"Whether you realize it or not, you were taking advantage ... I can understand the temptation, but it's not right, not now ... Why don't you go off somewhere, collect yourself, and try to sober up—"

"*Me* sober up? Is this the night when all the drunks read lectures?"

"You do have a real mean streak, Ebon," Ben replied evenly. "And not the best sense of timing ..."

"Come on, Annie," Ebon said disgustedly. "Let's take a swim in the boathouse. There's no wind there."

"I'm going to stay here," Annie said. She had been sitting on the sofa, looking as though she were trying to pretend that none of this was happening.

"Come *on*," Ebon repeated. "It's early yet. There's a lot I want to talk to you about—"

"I have to help put dad to bed."

"Leave him there. With his moral principles, he'll get a great night's sleep right there on the floor."

"You know, you really can be a bastard sometimes, Eb. Why don't you just go on to the boathouse? I'll stay here ... at least the talk won't be about the mating habits of pine trees—"

She'd hardly gotten the words out when Ebon turned and left without a word, slamming the front door.

"Sorry," Ann said to Ben, "but sometimes he just ..."

"I know ... well, let's get Dan to bed."

With help Dan was able to stagger into the nearest bedroom. Ann helped to pull off his clothes with practiced skill, and after covering him up gave him a quick kiss on the forehead.

"Rosie? ..."

"Good night, dad ... God bless ..." The tears stopped her from saying more.

Amid the shambles of dirty dishes and glasses left by the wake, they sat on the living room couch, almost too exhausted to move.

"Well, it's all over, isn't it?" Ann said suddenly. "Now we have to try to sew our lives back together."

"We still have to get your father onto that bus tomorrow. We can't load him on there drunk," Ben said.

"He'll sober up. I think he wants to go home . . . You're not going to fly off somewhere too, are you?"

"I haven't really thought much about the future."

"I have a bad dream where you go off to Timbuktu and leave me here holding the bag all alone."

"You wouldn't be left holding any bag here. If I did go somewhere, you could go to a boarding school. It might be a good change for you, Annie."

"I don't want to go to some damn little rich girl's boarding school, Ben . . . I want to stay here and do a book on this town with you. Have you forgotten all about that?"

"No." He stood up.

"You used to be so high on it."

"I used to do a lot of things . . ."

"I know . . . me too, but I can't stop thinking . . . if you do go to Timbuktu, will you at least take me along as your assistant?"

"Maybe." He was beginning to feel uncomfortable.

"Well, photographers do travel with assistants sometimes, don't they? Like movie producers. And I have learned a lot about cameras . . ."

"That you have," he said, "and if I could take an assistant I can't imagine a better one—"

The words were barely out before she was throwing her arms around his neck and kissing him.

"*Thank* you, Ben . . . Now I can go to bed and dream about Timbuktu without being scared . . . And you know something, Ben . . . I don't think Rosie would want us to let every hope we ever had die with her. In fact, I think she'd be real sore if we did. . . ."

In the morning Dan tried to be businesslike about getting ready for his long flight, but although he had crossed the Atlantic dozens of times, briefing him for the trip was like preparing a child for travel. Ann wrote a timetable showing when and how he was to change from bus to plane in Albany, and from LaGuardia to Kennedy airports in New York. Ben had given her money to buy his tickets at the local travel agency. She handed them to him in a small manila envelope.

Dan looked through this dubiously. Ben had foreseen this and took two hundred dollars in twenty dollar bills from his wallet.

"Thanks," Dan said perfunctorily as he put this money in his own wallet. "Say, Ben, are you still interested in that little business deal we talked about? I don't know whether you think you can work with me now, but I sure did the best I could . . ."

A pause while Ben rubbed his chin and Ann glanced down in embarrassment. Finally he took out his checkbook and wrote a check to Dan for two thousand dollars. It was crazy in more ways than one, but he had a distinct feeling that Rose, or whatever part of herself she had left with him, was smiling even more broadly than the old man was.

They didn't take Dan directly to the eleven o'clock bus, he was *supposed* to be skipping bail on his own. They let him off by the bank with his suitcases, which were now much lighter than when they had held what became his wedding gifts. He walked briskly to the place where passengers waited for the bus, and was shrewd enough to tell several people that he was off to visit friends in Albany. After the bus arrived, he was the first one aboard, pushing himself through the crowd with apparent urgency. When the big Greyhound passed them a minute later, Ben and Ann saw him at a window near the front. He did not return their wave. He was sitting very straight, staring ahead stern and unseeing as the figurehead of an old ship heading into its last Arctic gale. . . .

When the bus had disappeared around a corner Ben drove Ann back to Cliff House. Some friends had taken grammie for a drive and Ebon had gone on a solitary camping trip in the upper Adirondacks, planning to be gone about a week. The big house seemed to buzz with silence.

"Whenever Rosie was blue she said hard work was the only cure," Ann said. "I've seen her start washing walls in the middle of the night."

What Ben decided was to take two weeks off and paint the *Indian Princess* after sanding her down to bare wood. He'd do it alongside the boathouse to have electricity for power tools, but he hoped everybody would ignore him, as though he were on vacation far away.

The harder he worked, the less he thought and felt, which was the desired effect. No slave under the lash ever labored with more intensity or for longer hours than Ben Winslow did during that August. When he'd removed the varnish, the beautifully shaped taff rail and all the other mahogany looked nakedly new. After three coats of varnish, the *Princess* appeared ready for display in a showroom. The rejuvenation process was good and pleasurable therapy. Lying in a narrow bunk at night, with aching shoulders and bruised knuckles, he had more of a sense of accomplishment than his camera had given him in years.

Every day or so Ann would come down to observe his progress, bring hot food. She looked tired, and when he asked whether taking care of Cliff House was too much she brushed her hair back and said, "That's nothing, I'm really working on something else."

385

"What?"

"It's a surprise . . . when you finish with the *Princess* it will be ready for you. . . ."

The hard physical labor had left him so exhausted that his curiosity and anticipation were dulled. That afternoon he rubbed the corroded brass fittings with steel wool and buffed them with an electric machine before polishing them. The ancient binnacle, the cleats and all the other hardware gleamed like new-minted gold. He thought how pleased Rosie would be to see how grand the *Princess* looked.

Laboring harder than ever, he painted out the cabin, changing the rather dark green to a rich cream color. Ebon had recently painted the topsides and the decks, so there wasn't much more to be done. Frightened by the threat of leisure, Ben spent the last days of his two weeks time-off painting the anchors silver and the old engine a bright red that somehow made it look as though its horsepower had just been tripled. . . .

Finally he was done. Every muscle still ached, but he felt a great deal saner than he had at any time since Rose's death.

He found Ann and Ebon sitting on the terrace.

"Are you all finished with the *Princess*?" she asked.

"I guess that affair has ended," Ben said ruefully.

"Well, are you in a mood now for me and **my** big surprise?"

"You better be," Ebon said. "She's been going ape."

"We have to take the van," she said. "Let's hurry while we have plenty of light. You coming, Eb?"

"No . . . it's your gig, I have a lot of stuff to do . . ."

Ann asked him to drive to grammie's old farmhouse, which now stood baking in the afternoon sun. When they went in the heat was stifling.

"We ought to open some windows here," Ben said. When she snapped on some lights, he saw that she had carefully laid photographs on the floor of the living room—more than a

386

hundred. To increase the light, she raised shades and pushed back curtains.

"Now, *here's* our book. I couldn't get a good enough idea of it while it was in the files so I took out everything we have and laid it down here. Are you mad at me?"

"No, it's fascinating."

"I shot a lot of new stuff that we talked about, too. See, here are your fraternal-order kings in full regalia. I had no trouble at all with the Odd Fellows but those old Masons gave me fits. I finally got a few to pose outside their hall or Temple, I think they call it."

He congratulated her. She really was extraordinarily good. . . . She managed to catch so-called typical people and yet rendered them as *people*, not just types. She had an eye, no question.

"Damn it, Annie, don't ever again ask me whether you have talent. You have it to burn. I mean it."

"What are we going to do about it?" she asked, her eyes a challenge.

"What do you want to do about it?"

"For starters, I want to get this book published. How do you go about that?"

"We can wrap up what we've got here and take it to my agent in New York. If she can find some publisher who'll buy this sample, we'll get a contract, then we'll have to work like hell to finish the job."

"*When?* When can we go to New York?"

"I think we need to add a few more pictures, but I guess we could do it in a week or so."

Ben found he was almost as excited as Annie at the prospect of taking the work to New York. These photographs were only a start, but a damn good one, and he felt sure he and Annie could build them into a good book, maybe even an exciting one. Excitement was what Annie gave off, and it was impossible to be with her without it catching.

387

"Where will we stay in New York?" she asked him.

"I always liked the Algonquin."

"Oh, I've heard about that. The artists and writers stay there. When the book's published will you go on the talk shows the way the authors do?"

"Maybe, if they want me."

"Will you take me, or do I wait in the wings?"

"You'll be co-author, and I'm sure the TV people would rather show you than me. You'd be a sight kinder to the camera."

"Can't you just see me standing up there giving everybody the secret of my success?" Ann said with a grin.

"Sure, and what is it, Miss Kelly?"

"Why, sir, hard work, faith in God, and being smart enough to have a terrific brother-in-law. Of course on the late shows I'll throw in that I was subjected to *unspeakable* indignities on the way up."

"Not by your terrific brother-in-law, I hope."

"Wouldn't that be a great rumor to get started? It might really get them interested."

"It sure would in Livingston."

"I was meant for the great world, not Livingston," Ann said, meaning to sound as if she was kidding but not quite succeeding.

On the fifth of September Ann and Ben started for New York with a van loaded with a collection of about 150 photographs stored in big leather portfolios. A middle-aged widow had been found to stay with grammie in Cliff House for the three days they'd be gone. Ebon did not go . . . he had to attend an orientation program for freshmen at the state college in Albany. Besides, he said, he'd only be a fifth wheel. He said it, but he sounded as if he hoped they'd talk him into it, and looked distinctly unhappy when they didn't.

On the drive to New York that September day Ann wore a tweed skirt and a cashmere sweater that was awfully like one Rose had frequently worn. She also carried a lemon-yellow suitcase with Rose's initials on it, which Ben remembered he'd brought to Rose in the Burlington hospital after grammie had filled it with clothes and books.

"I had to borrow Rosie's suitcase," Ann said. "I've never even had one. I hope you don't mind."

"Of course not," Ben said, and told himself he had to learn not to mind. Why was it bad to be reminded of her when he loved her so much? Why did any sign of her, from a few strands of her hair in a comb to the old farmhouse where she'd been living when they first met, remind him less of the happiness she'd given him but so much of the loss? Time . . . it would take time, he told himself.

They left Livingston a little after seven on a crisp, blustery morning, hoping to check into the Algonquin Hotel in New York before keeping an appointment with Ben's agent Claudia Simpson at 4:30 in her office only a few blocks away. He noted that the maple trees in Livingston and the surrounding forest were already beginning to blush in anticipation of their nakedness as their leaves were ripped from them by the first cold winds of the season, a conceit that would have made Rosie smile, but that he somehow would have felt ridiculous mentioning to Annie, who looked sternly practical as she sat beside him, studying a map of New York.

"You get to the Big Apple often?" he asked with a straight face.

"Don't kid with me," she said. "You know I haven't ever been there, but I've been dying to go as long as I can remember . . . Rosie was always going there on business or something but she couldn't take me and would never let me go alone. Anyway, New York was too expensive for us and too complicated, what with grammie and all."

Ben concentrated on passing a truck that was piled high with logs.

"Rosie did take me to Boston, though, and to Montreal twice. I'm lucky. Most of my class has never been out of the valley. Plenty of even *grammie's* friends have never been out of the valley. I feel sort of strange about never having seen New York, but then, I figure, what the hell, New York has never seen me. And plenty of New Yorkers have never seen Livingston."

"Right," Ben said, "they're the real losers. Well, New York, here she comes. Look out . . ."

Ann nodded happily and squeezed his arm.

As they drove south and came down from the relatively high altitudes of the Adirondacks, fall gave way to summer again, and there was no more color in the leaves of the trees. This apparent reversal of the seasons pleased Ben. If he only drove fast enough, he might come to apple blossoms and it would be May again, when he had first returned to the valley and had met Rosie.

Reversing time—another conceit which would have amused Rosie, but Annie clearly was not much interested in small talk.

"What's this agent like that we're going to see? I don't even know what agents *do*."

390

Claudia Simpson was difficult to describe, he discovered as he tried to do it. A fiery, energetic woman of about sixty, she ran one of the few small talent agencies that could compete with the relatively new Hollywood-based monsters. She actually respected writers, painters and photographers so much that she often nursed them through divorce, alcoholic bouts and bankruptcy, but if she concluded that their talent had finally run out, she was equally capable of showing them the door with a brief note that "I find I need to concentrate on a smaller list of clients."

One of Claudia's extra strengths was that she also genuinely admired good publishers and producers almost as much as she did the people whom she represented. She made it her business to know every important publisher and producer on both coasts and thought of herself as a marriage broker who brought all these difficult, talented people together. She was helped in this by her husband, David Simpson, a well-known theatrical and literary lawyer.

None of this, though, really described Claudia, Ben felt. Perhaps she could best be understood at the parties she gave almost every weekend either at her penthouse apartment overlooking the Hudson River or at her house in Connecticut. In making up her invitation list, she was an unabashed celebrity hound. She often stalked a famous writer or actor she had not met by cultivating his circle of friends, one of whom might finally bring him to one of her "little get-togethers." Despite that her agency didn't handle their kind of business, she invited the top models of the day to her parties on the rather sound theory that beautiful women often attracted interesting men. Political figures who were honorably in the news were included as another kind of bait, as were a few well-publicized professional athletes. It was, of course, possible that Claudia was nothing much more than a professional snob, but Ben found something admirable—at least gutsy—in her determination to be surrounded by nothing but the best, the brightest and the most beautiful. If you were the world's best, or just New York's best in just about any field, Claudia loved you, even if she saw no chance for direct profit.

Claudia's own New York had no slums and was a city of "winners," while Livingston was, in a not altogether bad sense, a village of "losers." Perhaps that was why he'd run back there after losing in New York and finding something considerably less than salvation in Santa Barbara, another city of "winners."

Yes, four years ago he had, in many ways, become a loser in New York. Upset . . . confused by his impending divorce and sick of carrying a camera from war to war, he'd gone from one fairly arid affair to another, and had taken pictures as empty as he felt. Claudia had been patient at first, but Ben had also been drinking enough to make him barely tolerable. She'd continued to have enough faith in him to keep him on as a client, but she'd also chopped him off her invitation lists. He told himself he'd been bored by her weekly parties anyway, but when the gracefully handwritten little notes stopped coming, it hurt more than he liked to admit. He was not wanted. Even by his own agent, someone he'd known for a decade. She and her world were closed to him. Now, of course, it no longer mattered, but at the time, though he bawled himself out for being a damn fool for caring, he'd tried to work harder than ever, and when the results had failed to produce anything of any interest even to himself, he'd run, first to Santa Barbara and then to Livingston.

Now, as he drove back to New York with Ann, Ben didn't know how much to tell her of this personal saga. All the poor girl had asked, after all, was what is Claudia Simpson like, and what does an agent do?

Unwilling to destroy her Olympian image of him, Ben left himself out of his description of Claudia Simpson. "Basically, she's a salesman, a middleman, she'll try to sell our stuff to a publisher for the best deal she can get."

So there, Claudia Simpson. He almost smiled.

Every depressed middle-aged man, Ben concluded a few hours later, should be given the opportunity to introduce a seventeen-year-old small-town girl to New York City for the first time. Driving toward Manhattan on the Saw Mill River Parkway, Ann got no breathtaking glimpse of the skyline, but she didn't need it. Even Yonkers astonished her with its endless brick apartment buildings, and when she first glimpsed the Hudson River and the George Washington Bridge, she gasped with delight. Ahead of them the Empire State and Chrysler buildings shone in the afternoon sun, while the twin World Trade towers reached all the way up to a bank of low-lying smog, a tan mist.

"Ben, how long did you live here?" she asked.

"Off and on for maybe five years altogether."

"How did you ever leave?"

"Walked up to a window and bought a ticket."

"Come off it . . . what could you ever find in Livingston that you couldn't find here?"

"You want a serious answer, okay . . . I couldn't start a newspaper of my own here. And I never met anyone like Rosie here, I never met anyone even remotely like her at all anywhere."

"That's nice," Ann said, patting his arm, "but I don't want to start a newspaper and there's no one like Rosie back in Livingston anymore either. Oh, God, I want to live here . . ."

Ben said nothing. He was driving in three lanes of speeding traffic which seemed crowded and dangerous after the streets of Livingston. Nervously he edged away from a taxicab that seemed intent on pushing the van into a concrete wall.

"If our book goes okay, do you think I could get a job as a photographer here?"

"You're seventeen, Annie. College should come first—"

393

"Why don't you move back here and give me a job as your assistant? I bet we'd make a terrific team . . ."

"Well, do you think you could at least finish high school before we team up?"

"Don't make fun of me, Ben. I'm serious."

He knew it, but he didn't. He dropped the subject as he edged into the proper lane, shot down a ramp and emerged at 57th Street. As he drove south and then turned east on 44th Street, Ann stared at the slums and crowds of blacks and Puerto Ricans, all entirely unfamiliar to her. When they stopped at a traffic light, a derelict in an old army overcoat staggered toward them, hand outstretched.

"A quarter, only a quarter, a quarter . . ."

The light changed and Ben started the car with a jerk, getting away before the man put his hand on the door.

"Why does he have to beg?" Ann asked. "At home they'd lock him up for the night or put him in the hospital to get better."

"You want New York . . . he's part of it."

"I still want it . . . I don't know, it's funny, but I already almost feel at home here. Is that crazy?"

"Annie, I don't know. If you feel it, I guess it isn't crazy. I'm no expert on what makes sense, that's for sure. . . . 'As they drove he remembered Rosie telling him she'd like to make Livingston her headquarters but visit New York the way the town's doctors and lawyers did. She'd said there was a two-way effect going on . . . that small-town people appreciated the wonders of Manhattan more than the people who lived there, and that nothing increased her love for Livingston as much as a stay in the City. Both seemed especially true to Ben as he drove across town. Jostling crowds, stalled traffic, frantic blowing of horns, crumbling slums that seemed much more desperate than the vine-covered shacks and trailers at home made him long for the mountains, but the shining tower of the Pan Am building ahead and the gleaming new skyscrapers on Sixth Avenue seemed to give silent testimony that this was also a place where aspirations could grow as high as the buildings without losing contact with the ground.

Knowing that the van was too tall to enter most garages, Ben left it in a parking lot and loaded their portfolios and suitcases into a taxi. When the handsome Irishman in derby hat who was the doorman at the Algonquin Hotel helped Ann out, she smiled and said, "Thank you, sir." He clearly loved it as he took the bags from the cab. Ann watched while Ben paid the bill, and helped him carry the portfolios. While they waited in a small line before the registration desk she whispered, "Why did you give the driver two dollars? We only rode about a block—"

"*That's* New York too, honey."

"Well, at least one thing I could do to live here is drive a taxi!"

A bellboy led them to the seventh floor and showed them two adjoining rooms with a connecting door. When he asked them if they wanted it unlocked it was Ann who nodded firmly. Ben gave him a dollar.

"A dollar?" Ann said. "For carrying those little suitcases? I could do that, too." She looked around the small but lavishly appointed rooms. "Why, staying here, I wouldn't call the queen me aunt!"

It was an Irish expression Rose had often used.

"What's the matter?" Ann asked him.

"Just tired, I guess . . . look, it's only about three. Would you like to have a late lunch before we see Claudia?"

They ate in the Rose Room, which at that hour was almost deserted. Deciding to avoid real alcohol before seeing his agent, Ben ordered a glass of cold Chablis and eggs Benedict.

"I'll have that too," Ann said, having no idea what they were until the waiter brought them.

At a little after four they found it difficult to get a taxi, so despite the awkward portfolios decided to walk the few blocks to Claudia's office on Sixth Avenue. As he neared their destination Ben began to feel butterflies in his stomach. Up until now he had not allowed himself to remember the cold objectivity with which Claudia could flip through a portfolio of his work.

The vast marble lobby of the office building had such a high ceiling that they felt their own stature reduced to midget size as they walked to the elevators. Ben punched a button for the forty-second floor. The doors silently closed and the machine shot up, accelerating with more speed than Ann had ever felt. Looking startled, she quickly grinned and said, "Well, I always knew you'd take me up in the world, but can't we wait for my stomach to catch up?"

"The ride down can be worse, Annie."

A pretty, stylishly dressed young receptionist took Ben's name and asked them to sit down. The walls of the waiting room displayed the efforts of some of the best photographers in the world, all pressed in glass without visible frames. During the Vietnam war two of Ben's studies of infantrymen immediately after a battle had been included in this select gallery, but obviously no one wanted to look at the faces of exhausted soldiers now. Feeling hopelessly out of date, Ben sat with the portfolios on his lap while Ann walked from picture to picture on the walls, studying each closely.

Finally the receptionist led them down a long hall to a corner office with big windows. Claudia was sitting behind an ornate antique desk, wearing a severe but attractive gray dress and a heavy gold necklace. Her face was much thinner and older than Ben remembered. Her short hair had gone from gray to white, but was still elaborately coiffed with small curls over her forehead. Her large dark eyes were still quick; no one could look more shrewd, more alert.

"Well, Ben," Claudia said, standing up. "You look marvelous! No wonder! I saw in the *Times* that you got married. What a glorious new bride you've got for yourself!"

Standing beside Ben, Ann blushed.

396

"I'm afraid there's a little misunderstanding," Ben said quickly. "This is Ann Kelly, my sister-in-law. She's collaborating with me on this project." He didn't want to go on about how Rose had died, not now, not here.

"I'm sorry," Claudia said, not in the least flustered. "I admit I did think you were robbing the cradle, Ben, but then, who am I to criticize? Anyway, you have a lovely sister-in-law and I bet your bride is just as beautiful—"

"Yes."

"Now, what's this project you've got? You've brought something I can see?"

"Let me tell you a little about it first," Ben said, and told her it was to be a book of photographs called *Small Town*. Then on a long narrow table that stretched from one end of the room to the other along the west wall, Ben opened the portfolios and chose the best of the photographs to place in a line with their typewritten captions. Claudia, holding in her beringed right hand an ivory cigarette holder without cigarette, bent over each photograph, studying it closely without change in her expression. First she examined the landscape of the village in the valley, taken from on top of the hill on the entering highway. She looked at Howie dipping his face into a blueberry pie, at a fireman leaping into the air as he was squirted by a high-pressure hose, at Roger Radeau snarling from his jail cell, at the dignitaries of the fraternal orders in their ceremonial robes. And at a picture of Rose running toward Ben, arms outstretched.

"That's a lovely-looking woman," she said.

"Yes, I know."

The rest included a meeting of the Poetry Society, the World War One veterans on parade, Ann's picture of the hungry-eyed young women in the Twenty-three Club at Joe's bar, the ancient pictures Ben had found of the old *Indian Queen* puffing up Lost Lake with smoke billowing from her high stack and all flags flying, and finally Lost Lake Inn as it had stood in all its Victorian glory, alongside a

picture Ben had recently taken showing Rose standing in the midst of the ruined foundations.

Claudia put her cigarette holder between her lips, sat down behind her desk, and broke the uneasy silence by telling them first the good news . . . the photographs were good, the idea was good, and then the bad news that with production costs the way they were publishers were wary about expensive picture books. . . .

There was another silence during which she put a cigarette into her holder, but did not light it. Then she strolled back to the table and examined the photographs again, taking longer this time.

"Look, you need more kids," she said suddenly, "and more pretty girls and more dramatized situations, like those firemen actually battling a fire. Some of this is pretty static."

"It's just a start. There's no end to the material," Ben told her.

"Damn it, I like the idea, Ben . . . believe it or not I come from a small town—West Harding, Ohio. This stuff rings a bell for me—"

"Every city is full of people from small towns."

"Then there ought to be a market . . . I'll push this, Ben. I'll get the ball rolling and we'll just see where it goes."

"That's all I wanted to hear," Ben said, and Ann, who had been looking distinctly glum by now, smiled.

"How much of an advance do you want?" she asked. "Money's tight."

"Just earnest money, I'm a big-time small-town newspaper publisher these days."

"Now, that's smart. I won't name names, but I have photographers who are doing company portraits these days, men who were stars on *Life* and *Look* and the old *Trib*. Everything's changed . . ."

"And nothing has."

She looked at him, didn't push for an explanation. "Are you two going to be in town for a while?"

398

"We're going home Sunday," Ann told her quietly. "I wish we weren't though."

"Well, we're having our usual little get-together tonight," Claudia said. "Why don't you come and bring your charming collaborator, Ben? Dave would love to see you."

More than anything else that Claudia had said, it made him hope that their book would be sold. Claudia might at times appear enigmatic, but one thing was certain: no failures were invited to her little get-togethers.

26

Ann was obviously excited when Ben told her about the gathering of celebrities she could expect. After they returned to their rooms in the hotel she put on a simple dress of green Irish linen, exactly like one Rose had often worn, because Dan often sent his daughters identical garments.

"I know I'm going to look pretty ridiculous in this," Ann said, "but there's no time to get anything fancy."

"I don't think anyone could call you ridiculous," Ben told her. Indeed, Annie with her exuberant breasts, narrow waist and fine legs—not as delicate as Rosie's, though—was hardly likely to go unadmired in any group, especially with her finespun hair, which had been bleached from chestnut to dark gold by the summer sun. Of course he'd been aware before that she was an attractive girl, but being wholly taken up with Rose as he had been, he'd not *really* noticed . . . and the fact that he was doing so now made him distinctly uneasy . . . guilty?

The penthouse apartment Claudia and her husband occupied was in a building on 45th Street near the Hudson River and did not look at all impressive; the surrounding structures were mostly commercial. Ann was disappointed until Ben led her out of the elevator onto the top floor and they entered a luxurious apartment with walls of glass surrounded by a broad tile terrace with views of the Hudson and panoramas of the City. It was dusk when they arrived, the lights of the George Washington Bridge resembling a giant's necklace of diamonds spanning the river. As daylight faded, electricity was turned on all over the City, transforming it into the biggest multicolored light show in the world.

Claudia and her guests were gathered in the living room to avoid the chilly wind that whistled around the corners of the building. Before joining them, Ben waited while Ann took in the view around the terrace.

"Oh, Ben," she said, kissing his cheek with considerable enthusiasm, "I never imagined anything like this. Thank you for bringing me."

Inside, in a living room so large that fifty people did not make it seem crowded, Claudia's guests at first glance seemed an odd mix. Some of the men were in conservative business suits. Others looked like tweedy professors, and still others wore blue jeans and open-necked shirts. A more sizable contingent sported coats in pastel or brilliant colors, ascot ties, and trousers which were fitted so tightly that one wondered how their occupants ever sat down.

The women, though, were in full flower . . . actresses, models, highly competitive wives of highly competitive men. Several of them wore "old-fashioned"—now new-fashioned— dresses with lots of wispy cloth, low circular necklines and no bras. Some had chiffon sleeves so voluminous that they had difficulty handling a knife and fork. A fine statuesque blonde had a high neckline, but her dress left wide gaps from beneath her arm to her waist, giving a startling view of the sides and, as she moved, the graceful undercurve of her breasts. When Ann saw her, she seemed almost as awed as she had been by the view from the terrace. Ben's reaction to the guests was essentially different. He was stunned to discover that not one of the celebrities who'd attended these get-togethers a few years ago remained. *Sic transit gloria* . . .

Claudia warmly greeted Ben and Ann, then introduced

401

them to the other guests, ticking off their acomplishments and affiliations with precision . . . "Ben, this is Harry Arnold. Harry has the most marvelous show opening at the Hartman Gallery next week, you *mustn't* miss it. And Harry, Ben Winslow has the most wonderful new project, a collection of photographs that are *top secret*. And Harry, this charming young lady is Ben's *collaborator*. Can you believe it?"

"I believe, I believe," said Harry, "and should you ever get tired of collaborating with him, come on down to my house, honey, and collaborate with me. Sorry, that's from an old song . . . also, though, from the heart . . ."

The names soon blurred as Claudia introduced them to more people. The blonde woman with the holes in her dress turned out to be a model Ann recognized from shampoo commercials on television.

"What do you say to someone who sells shampoo on the tube?" Ann whispered to Ben. "Do you congratulate her on a great performance?"

Before long Ann was surrounded by middle-aged men who felt compelled to offer her sausages on toothpicks, crackers with caviar and tiny meat pies. She attracted more attention than the model who displayed such interesting aspects of her breasts. As Ben watched and listened to Ann talk to these strangers it was not difficult to see why. A fresh-faced seventeen-year-old, full of unaffected excitement about the city, Ann provided a kind of stimulus which, he suspected, most of these men had forgotten. There were no holes in her dress, but when she laughed, there was such a delicious commotion that none were necessary, and her smiles of delight when people paid her compliments made them try their damnedest to think of more.

At the buffet supper Ann insisted on serving Ben and dutifully refilling his wine glass.

"What do you have to do to get a girl like your Annie to wait on you like that?" Harry Arnold asked as Ann appeared with coffee.

402

"I heard that," she said with a smile. "I'll tell you, Mr. Arnold, he just treats me *good*, that's all."

"Photographers," declared Harry, and went to get some coffee for himself.

Ann and Ben said their farewells to Claudia at about eleven.

"Good night," she said, kissing Ben. "Dave would have loved to see you, but he felt rotten tonight and stayed in his room. Come again."

Her husband often stayed in his room during the parties, Ben remembered, and had the curious impression that he could pass away there without Claudia missing a beat. Nonetheless Claudia was a good woman to have on your side.

"What did you think of the party?" he asked Ann when they were alone in the elevator.

"I loved it!" she said. "I've never felt so glamorous . . . all the people there thought I was your mistress—"

"Yes . . . well, I know it was a kick, Annie, but you did lay it on a bit thick . . . 'he just treats me so *good*' . . . Thank god you didn't bat your eyes."

She giggled delightedly, hooked her arm through his, and when they got out of the elevator asked if they couldn't take a walk to Fifth Avenue.

"At this hour, in this part of town? It could be dangerous."

"How?"

"Muggers."

"Is all New York like that?"

"Lots of it."

"I love it anyway. Can we take a taxi to Fifth Avenue? I've always wanted to see it."

In the taxi she asked, "How did that woman in the ventilated dress get to be a model? She's no more beautiful than lots of women—"

"Maybe she went to modeling school and got an agent."

"Is there a school for absolutely everything?" She was grinning.

403

"I guess so."

"Is there a school for mistresses? If so, everybody there tonight thought I'd graduated—"

"Annie, cut it out."

"Yes, sir."

The taxi stopped at the corner of 57th Street and Fifth Avenue. Few of the great stores were fully illuminated, but there was a glow in many of the windows. After staring at several displays of women's clothing and furniture, Annie started hopping up and down to keep warm, and from sheer enthusiasm. "Fifth Avenue, I love you," she chanted. "It doesn't make the old Fashion Corners look too good, does it?"

He told her he guessed not. When they returned to the Algonquin he found that the evening had left him surprisingly tense and decided to go to the Blue Room for a drink. She insisted on going with him.

"Nobody ever thinks I'm under eighteen," she said. "Even last year I could order anything."

The small, intimate bar was crowded, and they sat over a tiny corner table while he drank Scotch and she sipped ginger ale.

"Could *I* be a model?" she asked abruptly.

"Hey, I thought you wanted to be a photographer."

"Why not both?"

"Why not, indeed."

"Could you teach me how? You've worked with models, haven't you?"

"Yes, but I'm not much of a teacher in that line—"

"But you take wonderful pictures of me. If we put some in the book, couldn't that maybe get me started?"

"Modeling can be a pretty cruel business."

"How?"

"I'm afraid models are supposed to stay about twenty pounds underweight, for one thing."

"I'll diet. You watch. I can do that . . ."

After he had two more Scotches they went to their rooms. She thanked him, saying good night, and hugged him and kissed him on the cheek. After going to her room, she reappeared almost immediately. "Do muggers ever get into hotels?"

"Rarely."

"Do you mind if I leave my door open a crack?"

"Of course not."

Her bathroom was on the other side of a partition next to his. When he heard her shower start to run, there was no way for him to avoid an image of her beautifully molded young body standing under the shower, looking up while the water streamed over her face and breasts.

Hell, Annie was enough to inspire such fantasies in the mind of a bishop, there was no reason to feel guilty, he lectured himself. And with the lecture came the realization that this evening he'd gone far longer than he had before without constantly thinking of Rosie. My god, Rosie had been gone not quite a month, and here he was already having erotic fantasies about her sister.

It was a comfort to realize that Rosie would not be shocked at all. To the contrary . . . "Why do you always feel so guilty," she'd said to him.

He tried to hold that memory as he went to bed, but slept less than soundly.

In the morning Ben ordered breakfast sent to the rooms, partly because he was tired and partly because he wanted to demonstrate one more big-city luxury to Ann. She stayed in her room while the waiter set up the table near Ben's bed. When she came in she was wearing nylon pajamas. They were decent enough, except that when the light from the window hit them just right, or wrong, the outline of her fine figure was visible with startling clarity, and when she moved, the free play of her breasts was simply *there*. During breakfast Ben, to his annoyance, found himself not really looking at her, actually feeling embarrassed, for god's sake. He could hardly ask her to go put on something else, something more, as a 19th-century throwback father would . . . and besides, she'd definitely and properly be hurt. And, along with that brief flash of sanity, it occurred to him that if a forty-five-year-old man can't stand the sight of his seventeen-year-old sister-in-law in her pajamas, isn't it the man, not the girl, who has a problem?

After breakfast Ben took Ann to the Museum of Natural History where she was in awe of the skeletons of dinosaurs, and to the Metropolitan Museum of Art, where she was even more awed by a display of horses and warriors in full medieval armor. They went to Sardi's for supper before seeing *The King and I.* At the restaurant a truly earthshaking event happened in Ann's life: she saw Marlon Brando, in the flesh! Actually, she didn't see him for very long. The great man simply came in, chatted with a friend at the bar for five minutes, and left. Ann would not have recognized him at all if Ben hadn't pointed him out.

"Why, he's short!" Ann said. "And fat! I love him anyway, though, he's still Marlon Brando."

If such a climax could be topped, Yul Brynner of *The King and I* did it, bedazzling her with oriental splendor. Between acts she said, "All these girls the king has are his mistresses, right?"

"Concubines."

"Aren't they about the same thing?"

"About."

While the King ordered Anna and his concubines about, Ben indulged the notion that maybe his Ann was developing a fantasy of her own (teenage version) about being his mistress in wonderful, adventurous New York, which could have no more to do with reality than what was going on up there on the stage. If so, it would be his job to cure her of it. Of course, it would.

That night he had five Scotches in the Algonquin's Blue Room before going to bed and getting to sleep, without fantasies. At least any he could remember.

At eight the next morning they breakfasted in the hotel's Rose Room, Ann savoring her glass of freshly squeezed orange juice but eating only a soft-boiled egg . . . she'd embarked on her diet. She did, however, get a responsive waiter to give her the recipe for eggs Benedict.

"After all," she said to Ben, "there's no reason why you can't live like a king at home too, is there?"

She slept most of the way home to Livingston, giving Ben too much time to think. Mostly about the potentially explosive combination that Ann was revealing herself to be . . . fragile and vulnerable, ambitious and seductive. Thank god he couldn't tell the future.

Back at Cliff House they were surprised to see the jeep, which Ebon had driven to Albany for his orientation program.

Ebon met them at the front door, quickly told them that the state college administrators had showed him how forestry could be big business these days, not just a woodsy cop's job. And even though he had to be back for classes the next day he'd driven the hundred miles from Albany because he couldn't wait to tell this to Ann . . . that his prospects were a damn sight better than she'd seemed to think. . . .

Her reaction was something less than he'd hoped for as she launched into what a "marvelous time" she'd had, how "fantastic" New York was and that she was "in love—"

"Who with?" he said, startled.

"With New York, with Ben, with you . . . our book is going to be published—"

"Now, that's nowhere near certain yet," Ben told her. "Claudia has just agreed to try to find us a publisher."

"She'll do it! Don't you know I'm a witch, Ben? I can see into the future . . ."

"What do you see, witch," Ebon asked, his mood darkening.

Not catching it, or not wanting to, she went on about how she saw "our book being a bestseller" and "we're going to get rich and famous; Ben and I are going on TV to promote it . . . we're going all over the country, aren't we, Ben?"

"Great," Ebon said, "I'm sure you'll be a great big smash."

"Nothing is certain yet, Ann," Ben murmured, not failing to catch Ebon's tone.

"Not for you, maybe, but I tell you the future holds no secrets from *me* . . . I'm going to be a model *and* a photographer and probably an actress too . . . look, I've already started to lose weight . . ."

"Dad," Ebon said, trying to ignore her for the moment as though she were an overexuberant child, "do you think it's right for you to encourage all this? What's going to happen when she comes down to earth—"

"People who have talent and self-confidence can do anything," she broke in. "Look at Marlon Brando. Everybody thinks he's some kind of great stud but he's hardly taller than I am and he's fat."

"What the hell has Marlon Brando got to do with any of this?"

"We saw him at Sardi's, in the *flesh*. He got where he is on the strength of his talent. Why can't I?"

The question hung in the air, as they went into the living room to say hello to grammie and Mrs. Wilmot, the widow who'd been caring for her. Grammie expressed her customary opinion of New York as that filthy Sodom and Gomorrah not fit for decent Christians, and after a few moments of that the three of them escaped to the terrace. It was getting dark quite early now and there was just enough of a glow left in the sky to show the ripening colors of the trees on the mountains. The quiet waters were a deep blue. There was nothing to be heard but katydids.

"I bet you didn't see anything in New York to beat this," Ebon said, gesturing toward the view.

"Oh, Eb, you're wrong . . . New York is so . . . *alive.* . . ."

"With what?"

She answered with a look and shake of her head, and they just sat there in big wooden chairs that Ben's father had bought in Vermont long ago. The stout maple legs of the chairs teetered a little on the flagstones, comfortable as rockers.

"Ben, can I get you a drink?" Ann asked, breaking the uneasy silence. "Or how about something to eat?"

"Just like room service, right, dad?" Ebon said. "Fit for a king—"

"Well, maybe I'd treat you like a king if you treated me like a queen . . . Ben made me feel at least like a princess all weekend. May I bring you food and drink, kind sire?"

"A good healthy Scotch would be damned welcome," Ben said quickly, feeling a storm brewing. He was right.

"Do you really think it's right to encourage her in all this crap?" Ebon went at him when she'd gone to get the drink. "What's going to happen if she ever really tries to do what she said?"

"I don't know—"

"Well, I do . . . You talk to Bill Frango, the guidance guy at school. New York fucks our people over good. The older sister of a friend of mine went the route . . . she'd just won some beauty contest or other when she left and when she came back she was on booze, drugs and would screw anybody for twenty bucks . . . do you want Annie to go that route—"

"I'll take route twenty-two," Ann said, catching the last part of Ebon's speech as she returned with Ben's drink. "What's this about, Eb?"

"I'm just saying you ought to be a *little* realistic. Talk to Bill Frango. Ask him what happens when people around here go to New York to make the *big* time—"

409

"I did talk to Bill Frango. I think it's his job to discourage people, but at least he did tell me about Daniel Levinson."

"Who the hell is Daniel Levinson?"

"A ballet dancer, a really great one, in New York. He didn't come from here but he came from Ti, and Ticonderoga is even smaller than we are."

"You come up with one name out of all the thousands—"

"Eb's right, Annie, about the odds against," Ben said. "It's one thing to fly high, but it's also a good idea to rig, if you'll forgive me, some sort of safety net—"

"Which brings me, if you'll forgive me, to my mundane career," Ebon said. "That orientation thing taught me that foresters can be executives in charge of thousands of acres of timberland. Industry is using more wood than ever and they're farming trees like corn. Foresters can go into research or conservation. They can work damn near anywhere in the world—"

"How about New York, New York?" Ann asked.

"That's possible . . . of course it wouldn't come right away. Most foresters get ahead slow but steady. It's a job we could always count on. Does that sound like such a bad safety net for you, Annie?"

"No," she said, and sprang up to give him a swift kiss on the cheek. "Eb, I love your steadiness and all that, but please don't start rigging your safety nets before I even get off the ground. It's sort of demoralizing . . ."

"I'm just asking you to keep it in mind."

"I'll try, but it's hard . . . I think New York's bewitched me . . . like I said, I'm a witch who can see the future, which at this moment means taking a bath and going to bed early . . . But first let me freshen your drink, Ben."

Ebon pretended to throw up. Ignoring him, Ann took Ben's glass and skipped from the terrace.

"But first let me freshen your drink, Ben." Ebon mimicked her. "Jesus H. Sweet Christ."

Ben laughed, uneasily.

410

"Are you *teaching* her this crap?" Ebon asked.

"Eb, calm down. Ann is a delightful, high-spirited young girl . . . there's nothing for you to get sore about—"

Ann returned holding a round tray with a glass of Scotch and a ham sandwich high over her head, curtsied and bowed as the concubines had for the King of Siam on the stage. "I am at your service, sire."

Ebon couldn't take it and told her so.

"You're just prejudiced against concubines," she told him. "Don't be so narrow-minded, I'm just following the customs of Siam," and then before retiring for the night, gave Ben an enthusiastic hug with a kiss that landed on his ear. Ebon received something less exuberant on the cheek.

Both watched her as she ran, almost dancing, into the living room and upstairs. Finally . . . "I know you're not doing anything wrong, dad," Ebon said rather heavily, "but sometimes I just wish to hell that you didn't have to get so . . . well, so involved with her—"

This sentence was overheard by Mrs. Wilmot, the housekeeper who had been taking care of grammie, and who had come to the terrace to see if Ebon wanted something to eat. Unwilling to interrupt so interesting a conversation, she retreated into the shadows, though not far enough to be beyond hearing.

"Of course there's nothing *wrong*," Ben said. "I grant you it might be better if I were working with somebody else, but what can I do about that now?"

"I don't know," Ebon went on. "You take her to a hotel in New York, you take her to a Broadway show, you're off working with her somewhere most of the time. God, if anybody else but my own father did all that . . ."

"I understand."

"I wonder . . . Dad, do you mind if I'm really honest for a minute?"

"Shoot." He knew, of course, what was coming, and found himself vaguely irritated in advance.

411

"You've had an awful time. I understand that. God, Rosie's going almost killed me—I can imagine what it's doing to you. You're lonely, sure, lonely as hell. Annie comes along, crazy to work with you. She sounds like Rosie and she even looks a lot like Rosie. She's all full of some kind of hero-worship over you. Are you sure you can think of her as just some kind of little professional assistant?"

"Well, that's pretty honest, all right," Ben said, taking a sip of Scotch and feeling as though the son had reversed roles with the father. He didn't much care for that, though. Eb, of course, did have a point . . . a right?

"I don't mean to hurt you, but—"

"You're not hurting me, son, although I think you may be just a bit out of line. Look here, Annie's my sister-in-law and my pupil—the best one I ever had, and that's the truth. She's a very pretty girl who does remind me of Rosie sometimes. It's not wrong or unnatural for a man in the good sense to love someone like that—but that is *quite* different from a man my age imagining himself to be 'in love' with a seventeen-year-old girl. I'm not that foolish, Eb. After all these years I have too strong a sense of survival. I'm not going to do anything to mess up the rest of my own life, not to mention Annie's and yours."

"I hope I can count on that."

"Cross my heart and—" He cut off the phrase as Rosie once had.

"Well, I guess it's way too soon even to think about it, but sooner or later I hope you can find a wife or some woman . . . you know, closer to your own age . . . it might sort of clarify things for Annie—"

"You think she needs to have them clarified, do you?"

"Dad, she was absolutely ape over you even before Rosie died. And now all she ever talks to me about is you. She wants the full details of your divorce and what you were like when I was a kid and—"

"She's mostly in love with my camera, is my guess. Rosie

understood that for Annie a camera is a chance to get into the world, and I'm just the one who handed it to her."

"And she wants to thank you from the depths of her grateful little heart . . . look out, old dad, when our Annie comes on strong she's pretty hard to put off—"

"Eb, I'm not at total damn fool. After all, like you love to say, I'm your 'old dad' and while I've made some bad mistakes in my *old* life, I've learned a thing or two maybe as well. There's no good reason why I shouldn't help Annie and there's no reason why I shouldn't enjoy a bright, pretty young sister-in-law. Aside from memories, she's really all I have left from my marriage—" He regretted saying that last the moment it was out of his mouth.

"Dad, I hope you don't get to thinking that somehow you deserve Annie as a replacement for—"

"Don't say it, Eb." (The roles were getting reversed again, damn it.) "Of course I don't think that. Give me some credit, at least. I don't have many friends, Eb—hell, even most of my relatives aren't my friends. I have you and I have Annie —and I don't want to lose either of you. Do you think I'm enough of an old fool to do something that would make the two of you hate me?"

Ebon smiled, nodded, and gave his father one of his quick but strong hugs. "I'm glad we had this talk," he said. "I was the only guy in my class who spent orientation week worrying about whether his father was stealing his girl!"

Laughing, they walked into the living room. Still standing in the shadows at the edge of the terrace was Mrs. Wilmot. An inveterate gossiper, she had not chanced upon such a choice morsel since her preacher had thrown his wife and mistress down the same well some thirty years ago. She could hardly wait to get home to her own telephone.

413

27

Mrs. Wilmot's story fueled rumors that had already been started by those who'd taken note that Ben and Ann were so often together on the boat, in the office *after* hours, not to mention that trip out of town to New York. Ben, though, was not aware of the wildfire spread of gossip about him for another ten days . . . he was too busy preparing several articles for his paper, including the one Rose had started about the large tracts of land on which Howie Hewat and his associates had bought options prior to trying to have the zoning in the valley changed. The Radeau case was soon to come to trial, and Bill Crawford was already demanding more background information for the Albany *Star*. In addition to all this, Ben was helping Ann take some of the new pictures their plans for the book called for. He couldn't remember ever having worked harder in his life. He was grateful for it. Sometimes he even was unaware of the dull ache of his grief for hours at a time. . . .

It was seven o'clock on the evening of September 22 that Ephram telephoned Ben at Cliff House. "Can I come see you? I got something important."

"Of course," Ben said, and while he waited for Ephram he cradled a heavy glass of Scotch in his hand and sat on the terrace. It was warm for September, no wind ruffled the smooth surface of the lake. A few fireflies still floated like sparks in the darkness. He wondered what Ephram wanted, he never used the word "important" lightly. He was in fact, Ben reflected, a most curious man. Hired originally as a bodyguard by Ben's grandfather during a time of trouble at the mill, Ephram had remained all these years with the family, working as a chauffeur, instructor in the crafts of woods and lakes for the boys, gardener and general family all-purpose protector. When Ben's father had received threatening calls, as most small-town newspaper editors did, he had simply referred them to Ephram. When Ben's brother Pete had been accused of impregnating a classmate of his in high school (a charge that he indignantly denied), he ran in panic to Ephram, who somehow got the girl's father, a man who had been fired from the mill for drinking on the job, to drop it.

There always had been something intriguingly sinister and mysterious about Ephram. No one knew where he came from—he simply had walked out of the woods, Ben's grandfather had said. He was proud of his Mohawk heritage. Somehow he knew the inside story of every crime that had been committed in the valley in his time. Under his graying dark hair he kept records much more complete than the police files on every troublemaker or potential troublemaker in town. Ben did not doubt that he had burned down buildings owned by people who had threatened his grandfather. From his laconic innuendoes, Ben suspected he had also killed at least one man who had constituted a real threat to his grandfather, shooting him down during the hunting season in the woods, an unexplained and common accident. On the other hand he guessed that Ephram might like to make dark hints just to enhance his own image of himself as a surviving Mohawk capable of living up to his heritage. As a tutor for the boys, Ephram had been gentle and patient. Sitting by a

415

campfire, he had told Pete and Ben Indian legends and all sorts of folklore that was in no book. Even as a child, Ben had suspected that he made most of it up, but it was fascinating anyway.

Now Ephram came from the shadows at the edge of the terrace almost as silently as his forefathers might have done.

"Evening, Bens."

Sitting with his back to him, Ben jumped a little. "Evening, Eph. Can I get you a drink?"

"Not now." He sat on an old church pew. "You got trouble," he said without preamble.

"That's nothing new . . . what kind this time?"

"Howie Hewat."

"Well, *that's* nothing new. What's his beef this time?"

"Dan Kelly skipped bail and won't pay Howie's hospital bills."

"He's got a point there, but I'm not going to pay Dan's bills. If Howie can't learn to duck, he's got to take the consequences."

"He's also mad you've been digging up stuff on his land deals."

"I thought that might get to him."

"He's mad because his busted jaw might keep him from winning the election."

"Is he blaming that on me?"

"Maybe not, but it sure keeps him good and mad, though. He also says you're trying the Radeau case in the papers. Howie's a tough man, Ben. May not look it, but he is."

"How's he going to hurt me?"

"He's already started to stir up talk about you."

"What talk?" Ben demanded sharply.

"Ain't you heard? The whole town is saying you're taking Annie away from Ebon."

"Do *you* believe that junk?"

"No, but lots of folks do. They like to catch a guy like

416

you in a mess, Bens. You're too high and mighty for them. It was the same with your grandfather."

"Well, to hell with the talk. It's got to die down after a while anyway."

"Maybe, but you got a bad situation, Bens. Howie hates you. Now he's got some people who think you're as bad as he does. You don't know what they're saying."

"There's more?"

"Sorry, Bens, but some say, well, they let on you weren't good for Rose's health and now you can't wait to get to her sister."

Ben stood up suddenly and hurled the heavy glass of Scotch onto the flagstone terrace. It exploded into fragments of glass and ice cubes that gleamed in the light of a rising moon.

"Sorry, but I thought you should know about it," Ephram said imperturbably. There was a moment of silence, broken only by Ben's heavy breathing.

He sat down. "People always have to have a monster, a devil in the valley. Howie fitted the part for years but he's worked himself out of it. Now he's picked me as the ideal successor."

"That's about it," Ephram agreed.

"What do you suggest, Eph?"

"Take care of yourself. Keep out of the woods, for one thing."

"I have to photograph the foliage and mountains for my—"

"Forget it. There could be another hunting accident."

"Come on, Eph! That talk is just local folklore . . ."

"I *know* a dozen cases in the last thirty years. Why do you think more local people get killed in the woods than city people?"

"All right, all right, I'll stay out of the woods, even though I think it's crazy."

"Get as much fire insurance as you can on this place and

the Kelly farm. These folks are more likely to burn than shoot."

"Okay."

"Get a shotgun and a rifle."

"I have both."

"Get dogs. Guns won't do you much good if you're asleep."

"I don't want some huge damn dog jumping at every deliveryman."

"Big dogs are no good. They don't bark as quick as small dogs. You want dogs to wake you up, not to fight. Fight with a shotgun."

"What kind of small dogs?"

"Dachshunds. I got a friend who raises them. They ain't got papers but it don't take much pedigree to bark loud. I can get you four half-grown pups for two hundred dollars, all housebroke, injected and everything."

"Why do I need four?"

"Put 'em in different parts of the house. And a pack will bark quicker than one. Those hounds don't go just by sight or ear. They can smell farther than they can hear or see . . . One more thing. Don't drive on roads people expect. And Annie shouldn't go on the school bus."

"You think they might try to get to *her*?"

"Just mean talk, probably, but I'll drive her to school. Not a good idea for you to."

"Should I talk to the police?"

"Nothing to report to them yet. What I get comes direct from Pete, and his comes direct from Howie."

"God . . . my own dear brother mixed up in this?"

"Well, he works for Howie. All he did was tell me how Howie felt."

"You figure they're just trying to scare me? On account of my opposition to the land deal . . . plus old bad blood, of course . . ."

"Possible. Just don't take chances. You want me to bunk here for a while?"

"No. Jesus, I've got through wars all over the world . . . wouldn't you think I could survive in my own hometown?"

"You'd think . . . I'll be here eight in the morning to get Annie for school, and I'll bring the dogs."

After Ephram had left Ben reviewed the situation he'd described so darkly and decided it didn't seem as bad as Eph had said . . . So Howie was angry, no surprise there, but Howie had never showed any real inclination toward violence, except for the radio tower. And, sure, maybe inevitably considering the circumstances, people were spreading malicious gossip, but not everybody would stoop to that. Most of the people who'd known him all his life would be as disgusted as he was about the vicious tale Eph had mentioned. And even people who spread the nasty rumors weren't arsonists or murderers . . . Ephram was something of an alarmist, Ben concluded, however well-intentioned he might be. He was like an old war horse waiting hopefully for the trumpets to blow . . . Still, there was no point in refusing to take reasonable precautions, and since he agreed Ann might as well not take the school bus for a while, and could no doubt expect some taunts, he'd better talk to her.

He found her upstairs in her room, doing homework, her most hated chore of the day. She was wearing blue jeans and white T-shirt . . . which appeared to prove that anything Annie put on looked good. The walls of her room were lined by photographs she'd taken, including three big ones of Ben and one medium-sized one of Ebon—a distinction Ben's son had silently noted before going back to college.

"Hi!" she said, "who were you talking to out on the terrace? I was spying on you from my window, but I couldn't see or hear a damn thing."

"Ephram . . . Annie, he brought some unpleasant news that you need to be aware of . . ."

419

"What?"

"Well, I guess it's inevitable in a small town like this, but people are saying some pretty rotten things about us."

"Oh, *that*. They *always* talk."

"Did anything happen at school today?"

"Today, yesterday, tomorrow—they'll never stop. It's been going on since I was thirteen. I may not be famous in New York, but I sure am here."

"Was it worse today than usual?"

"I don't know!" Ann said, her face suddenly defiant to the point of toughness . . . and he remembered something of what Rose had said was one part of her sister's nature . . . "The word used to be that I was making out with the captain of the football team, then it was Sammy Sarto, then the English teacher, and now you've been elected . . ."

"Ephram is afraid it might get rougher than usual because *I* have so many people sore at me. He's volunteered to drive you to school for a while and I think it's a good idea—"

"You mean I'd arrive with a chauffeur in your mother's big Cadillac? No thanks! The kids give me a hard enough time as it is."

"Well, maybe you're right."

She looked at him, her face still defiant. "Don't worry about me, Ben. I've grown up in this town, pretty much on my own. From the time I was twelve, when the boys noticed I wasn't a little girl anymore, I've been fighting off their busy hands. Well, no matter what they do or how they talk, they just don't exist for me . . . and maybe now you can understand better why I just live to get the hell out!"

"I guess I can," he said, and kissed her on the forehead before returning downstairs.

In the morning Ephram gracefully accepted Ann's rejection of his services as a chauffeur, but opening the back of the old Cadillac he took out a large crate, which proved to contain four half-grown dachshund pups; at least there'd be protection at home. Ann, delighted, and having no idea of their real purpose, sat down and tried to hug all four of them at once.

It made, Ben thought wryly, quite a picture—an apparently happy study of innocence in an innocent small town.

Walking down Main Street to his office later that day, Ben was fully aware of the stony looks from Big Duke and several others he passed on the sidewalk. A pair of old ladies found it necessary to whisper pointedly to each other as he walked by, shooting glances. On the window of his office someone had soaped in large letters, BEWARE! GOD WON'T LET YOU GET AWAY WITH IT!

Still, as he had suspected, at least some stuck by him . . . Seth Peterson came all the way out of his hardware store to slap him on the back. "Don't let the SOB's get you down." And Joe would not let him pay for the beer he drank with lunch. "You got friends, Ben, you don't want never to forget that. . . ."

Least expected was the greeting from the Episcopal minister, a stern old man who had been his mother's pastor ever since Ben could remember. In dark clerical suit, Dr. Haltensberg was pushing a grocery cart in the Grand Union when Ben dropped in to pick up some meat for supper. "Ben, come over here." He led the way to a little-used corner, where the shelves were piled high with health foods. "I just want you to know I'm going to give a sermon on the evils of gossip and slander this Sunday . . . I may also include a reminder of 'let him who is without sin cast the first stone,' which isn't to say, of course, that I believe for one moment any of their nonsense . . . it's just for dramatic emphasis to make the point . . ."

Ben nodded, and kept back a beginning smile. He also reminded himself that he shouldn't let himself get carried away with relief . . . it wouldn't take more than one deranged, hostile person to take a shot at him or try some other drastic actions Ephram had warned him against . . . He was glad when, on approaching Cliff House, the four dachshunds set up a fearful row before he even touched the front door.

The target of hostility outside the house, Ben also found that he had an inside battle to referee. One sunny afternoon early in October Ann met him as soon as he'd come in the door of Cliff House. She was wearing a sundress with a low, scooped-out neckline she had recently made herself.

"Ben," she said with some urgency, "can I talk to you alone?"

"That sounds ominous. The terrace okay?"

"I don't want anyone to see us. How about the *Princess*?"

Feeling like a co-conspirator, he followed her down the path to the boathouse, where the *Princess* was moored. The afternoon sun shone on the recently polished brass and newly varnished rails. Ann leaped easily into the cockpit and Ben climbed into the helmsman's seat.

"Now what's the trouble?"

"Grammie! She's been on her way to driving me crazy for years and now she's succeeding."

"I didn't notice you two not getting along," but as he said it he remembered that Rosie had mentioned something about the two.

"She's always sweet as pie when you're around, but as soon as you go, she lights into me."

"How?"

"This afternoon she started in with this dress, which she said nobody but a comon you-know-what would wear. Then

423

she started asking me what college I'm going to . . . it turned out that what she was getting at was that I ought to go to a Catholic college or fry in hell."

"I'd just say I don't know what college I want yet," Ben said. "There's not much point in arguing with an old lady like that."

"She won't let go! And the worst thing she does is give me the business day and night about not doing the housework better. Ben, I have school, our book, and the damn housework. To me it's the least important but to grammie it comes first. Never mind finishing the book and getting into college, has the oven been cleaned yet?"

"I guess her generation was like that. Maybe we better hire Mrs. Wilmot full-time, then you can forget the housework. I agree, you have more important things to do."

"Ben! Would you do that for me?"

"It'll be good for all of us."

"I feel free, like I'd been let out of a cage!"

Swooping forward, she hugged and kissed him, full on the lips this time, her pink lipstick tasting faintly of raspberries, her hair still carrying the same haunting fragrance he remembered from Rosie and . . . for a moment he automatically put his arm around her, feeling the warm, smooth skin of her back where the sundress left it exposed. He withdrew his hand almost as quickly, as though he had been burned. (Have I? he thought.)

"You're *afraid* even to hug me!" she said, her eyes dancing. "Are you that chicken?" She sat on the after-seat, Rose's favorite spot.

"There are times when I crow like a rooster." (Bad joke.)

"I bet, and I bet I look too awful for you . . . do you think nobody but one of grammie's you-know-whats would wear this dress?"

"It's a pretty dress." He felt uneasy about where this seemed to be leading, and looked out across the sapphire waters of the lake to the brilliantly colored mountains.

424

She brought him back with, "Don't men sometimes want a girl so bad they don't even care who she is or what she is?"

"No doubt."

"Have you ever felt that way?"

(Careful.) "I don't think so."

"Why not?"

"I'm funny that way. I always seem to care who the girl is and what she is. Sometimes my standards are remarkably flexible, but I do care."

Ann laughed, tossing her head as she smoothed back a few strands of hair that had fallen over her face. "I love you, Ben," she said with a sudden smile . . . "oops, I know I shouldn't say that, but it's the truth."

"And you know, dear sister-in-law, what they say about the truth . . . it's in the eye of the beholder." And having delivered himself of that piece of purposeful if heavy-handed misquotation, he suggested they go back to the house.

"I don't want even to think of getting dinner yet, can't we take a little spin? And you could show me how to run the boat . . ."

After demonstrating his elaborate safety precautions, he let her start the engine and steer the *Princess* away from the wharf. She headed for the center of the lake, standing on her toes to see better through the windshield. The lake was ruffled to silver by a few gusts of a wind that was dying with the day. The fall foliage was nearing its full splendor now. Smoke from a distant forest fire hung like a gray mist over the other end of the lake and filled the air with a sharp autumn fragrance. The outboard motorboats of the summer people had disappeared, leaving the lake to twilight peace.

"I hate to see the lake like this," Ann said suddenly.

"I guess I'm supposed to ask why," Ben replied.

"Because it's times like this that make people love this place. They work a lifetime loading rolls of paper at the mill or cleaning motel rooms so they can live here. Well, you won't find me falling into that trap . . ."

425

In the center of the lake they turned off the engine and drifted. Lights were going on in the few waterfront cottages which were still occupied. The wind died completely and the night felt strangely warm.

"Let's go swimming!" she said suddenly.

"No."

"Why not?"

"We don't have bathing suits here, for one thing. I took them all up to the house when I painted out the cabin."

"It's getting dark," she said, her eyes challenging. "Who needs bathing suits?"

"An old man like me."

"Well, do you mind if I go in?"

"Please, Annie. Let's not build up a situation."

"Well, you've seen a naked girl before, haven't you? You wouldn't go *ape* or anything, would you?"

"Annie, take it easy. You have too much sense for that. Don't be a tease. It's not attractive, at any age."

"How do you know I'm just teasing? Maybe I'm one of those girls who deliver. I bet the king's concubines didn't just tease—"

"Annie, do you really want to go swimming?"

"Yes!"

"Okay," and to her astonishment he picked her up, still in her orange sundress, and threw her in the lake, carefully making sure that she fell clear of the boat. "So swim," he called when she came spluttering to the surface. "Cool off a little!"

Turning over on her back in the water, she called, "I never thought you'd do something like this." She began to laugh.

"I'm full of surprises."

"Help me up. It's cold!"

"I'll get the ladder." It took him a few minutes to rig the contrivance.

"My leg hurts," she said when he took her hand. "I think

I pulled a muscle when I fell. Could you step down and get your hands under my shoulders?"

He climbed awkwardly two steps down, twisting his body to try to help her. At the same moment she grabbed him firmly around the waist and kicked back with the full strength of her legs. Suddenly he was in the water.

"Tit for tat!" she yelled when he surfaced. "You can't say you didn't deserve it!"

"Little bitch," he roared, but exploded with laughter. Then, noticing that some almost invisible breeze was causing the *Princess* to drift away from them, he swam fast to the ladder.

If he had thrown Ann overboard to end her teasing, the maneuver had failed. When she came out of the water, the thin material of her orange sundress clung to her in a way that was more provocative than nudity, and there was nothing aboard for her to wear except Rose's butterfly beachcoat, which he had put away in a drawer. Nothing to do but get it for her. Before she put it on, he went below and changed into some old painting clothes he had left in a locker. When he came on deck Ann was standing near the wheel in the beachcoat, the butterfly pattern of which was just visible in the semidarkness.

"I always loved this coat," Ann said quietly. "Rosie said one day she'd give it to me . . ."

For no clear reason at the moment, Ben felt a rush of anger, which gradually subsided, to be followed by a not at all unclear, if disturbing, rush of desire, a temptation to take this girl here and now, to end this teasing game, to get down to the bottom line of whatever was adding here . . . And finally, with an effort, this too subsided, leaving him feeling exhausted and in a foul mood . . . "Let's go in," he said. "I have a lot of work at the office I should attend to tonight. And tomorrow will be a long day, for both of us."

427

29

Throughout the first part of October Ben and Ann kept almost frantically busy taking photographs for their book and the newspaper, including a week of following fire engines almost everywhere they went for Claudia Simpson's action shots, and since it was the dry season, they kept very busy.

The firemen, like most, had heard the rumors about Ben and Ann. Unlike most, they approved of what they heard, looked at Ben with new admiration, though their asides to him and frank appraisal of Ann were hard to take and offended Ben. On October 14 there was a party to celebrate the election of a new deputy chief. The volunteers were always holding elections of some sort that then had to be celebrated in their recreation room over the firehouse. This time the celebration was edgy because the election had been a hot one. Sal Paladrani, massively built owner of a garage and repair shop, was obviously the best qualified, but Brian Moran, his opponent, had gone around saying that with Tony Torillo as chief and Sal Paladrani as deputy they'd have a damn guinea fire department, so Moran was elected even though he was a terrible drunk and hadn't had a job in eight years.

At the celebration the two factions gathered at opposite sides of the big room, much beer was drunk, but when the alarm suddenly went off the volunteers sobered up as best they could, clambered aboard a big new hook and ladder and a smaller hose truck and went roaring off through the night, sirens screaming, red lights flashing.

Ben and Ann caught up with them just before they turned from the state highway up Garrow Hill Road, a country lane which led to an abandoned farm, now spectacularly ablaze. As Tony Torillo turned the big hook and ladder onto the dirt road, he ran into some deep potholes that caused him to brake suddenly. Brian Moran, who was driving the older fire engine, was following too closely and rammed the new hook and ladder, crumpling its shiny red rear. The shock was not great, and Tony was so eager to get to the fire that he didn't take time to inspect the damage. The two big fire engines went lumbering up the hill and parked just beyond the circle of fire which had enveloped both the abandoned farmhouse and its barns.

As he got out of his cab, Tony Torillo was shocked by the sight of the crumpled stern of the new fire engine, and Brian Moran, appearing at this very moment, added no little to his upset with "Why the hell did you have to jam on your brakes like that?"

"Because I didn't know a drunken Irishman was riding right on my ass."

"Why you . . . ain't they heard of rear-view mirrors where you come from?" said Brian, "or do guineas just use mirrors for oiling their hair—?"

Whereupon they swung on each other, and some fifty more volunteers soon joined in to defend their respective ancestral heritages. So while the old farm burned to the ground, shooting flames high in the air, the firemen fought a titanic battle against each other.

It was not true that *all* the firemen joined in. Sid Levi, owner of the Livingston Economy Store, said he didn't give a damn whether the guineas won or lost, and he was joined in this sentiment by a Greek who owned the Adirondack

Diner and by Willis White, whose mother headed up the local chapter of the Daughters of the American Revolution, as well as a dozen others. These brave souls did their best to get the hoses going and at least to wet down the surrounding fields to prevent the spread of the fire. The trouble was that these pacifists were not expert fire fighters; they hooked up the hoses improperly, quantities of water spilled, turning the ground where most of the firemen still battled into a sea of mud.

The pictures Ben and Ann took of the firemen hammering at each other in the mud while the old farm blazed in the background were memorable. The name of the farm, it turned out when Ben checked on it, was The Homestead, and he published a picture of the battle in his paper with the caption, WHILE THE HOMESTEAD BURNED . . .

Ben, of course, expected some reaction, but the anger of the villagers was far greater than anything he'd imagined. Showing up the firemen obviously made him more enemies than rumors about him and Ann had. Joe's bar fell silent when he entered, and instead of giving him a beer Joe sullenly mopped a counter, ignoring his order. When he got back to his office Lillian told him there was another threatening call, some man had said: "Ask that bastard this: if his house burns, who's he going to call?"

A few minutes later Ephram called. "What the hell's the matter with you, Bens? You can have your fun with the Republican party in this town and get away with it. You can say the Loyals don't know a pigskin from a pig's ass. You can even joke about the pope, but not the firemen, Bens. You know every famliy in town has at least one man in the Volunteers. It's the best fire department around—they're always winning those competitions. And now you come along and show them up . . ."

"I showed them showing themselves up—"

"Bens, words don't change the picture . . . First you get Howie fighting mad, then you get all the respectable folk upset over the rumors, now you got someone from every family in town ready to kill you. What's the matter with you, Bens?"

"What do you think I should do, Eph?"

"Sit down and hold your hands over your balls."

"That bad, huh?"

"Bens! That picture is going to be up in every firehouse. I bet it gets into Firefighters' magazine—someone from Ti or Whitehall is sure to send it in. People will make fun of our boys everywhere. You think they won't get back at you? My advice, Bens, is try Florida for a while. It won't get so hot down there."

Which, of course, he couldn't do. He couldn't leave his paper. He couldn't leave Ann behind with people sniping, or worse, at her, and he could imagine Ebon's reaction if he took her to Florida or somewhere else.

Ben soon began to feel about volunteer firemen the way 1950's politicians used to think about communists—they were everywhere. You never could be sure who was and who wasn't one . . . the pharmacist who glared at him and kept him waiting endlessly for a prescription, the man who almost ran him off the road with a balloon-tired pickup truck. He tried to keep a sense of proportion; it wasn't easy.

Neither was the persistent hostility he still felt when he and Ann were seen together on Main Street. And Cliff House didn't offer much relief, with grammie in her old age getting to be increasingly dictatorial to Ann and Mrs. Wilmot. The *Indian Princess* offered the only clear relief.

Nearly every afternoon now after they'd finished their work Ann and Ben went out to explore the islands or to drift on the broad bays of the lake. They'd sit polishing the brass or wiping the newly varnished brightwork with a chamois, helping the old *Princess* to retain her splendid new look. And usually Ann would wear a white bikini under a new red beach coat.

"Do you catch any flak from the firemen's kids at school?"

431

he asked her one Friday afternoon after the incident.

"Sure, but I don't even think about it. All I care about is the book. When will Claudia get us a publisher?"

"I'm not sure," he said uneasily, wondering what she would do if there was no book, no publisher. His thought was interrupted by the approach of a small aluminum outboard motor boat. An old man was steering and a woman of about the same age was sitting in the bow, surrounded by fishing tackle. They passed close to the *Princess*, peering at Ben in his dungarees and Ann in her beachcoat. They did *not* wave when Ben raised his hand in salute. Still staring, they circled the *Princess*.

"Maybe they think we've broken down," Ben said, mostly for Ann's benefit, and called out, "We're all right, we just like to drift, nothing's wrong."

The couple did not answer. Instead they circled the *Princess* once more before heading up the lake.

Suddenly Ann whipped off her red coat, and now in only her white bikini jumped up on the taff rail. Waving her red coat, she shouted, "Come back, folks . . . the show's just begun . . ."

The aluminum boat did not swerve as it retreated up the lake.

"Are you sore at me?" Annie suddenly asked Ben, still standing on the taff rail.

"I'm not sure that was too smart, Annie, but I surely know how you feel."

"The whole thing just bugs me. This whole town is full of *creeps*—"

"Now let's not exaggerate, Annie, there are some really great—"

"They're ugly and fat and old and drunk most of the time . . . they made fun of Rosie because she wouldn't be like them and they make fun of me and you too."

"Aren't we making fun of them?"

"They started it!"

432

"I'm not sure. But take it easy when you knock the old and fat. I'm not so young or svelte myself."

"You'll *never* be like them. And if you're afraid of getting fat, why don't you diet, the way I am? I've already lost sixteen pounds. You told me to lose weight and you haven't even noticed."

Ben had noticed, all right. He had been shocked by the fact that Ann grew to look like Rose more and more as she grew thinner. Already high cheekbones were emerging. Glimpsed from certain angles, the resemblance was enough to make him catch his breath. Ann's bosom was now much like Rose's when he had first met her, before her illness had worn her down. He remembered with startling clarity the glimpses he had had of Rose at the Elmsford Inn, a graceful nude who somehow managed to be both modest and delightfully flamboyant at the same time. He remembered Rosie laughingly trying to cover herself with a lobster bib. . . .

"I've noticed," he said with a careful smile. "If I kept complimenting you each time I noticed you we'd never find time to talk about anything else."

"That's *nice*," she said. "Keep it up."

"Enough, as they say, already."

"I know . . . I'm sorry"—she had an instinct for pulling up when she sensed she'd gone, or was going, too far . . . she switched to a less personal plane. "Tell me honestly, Ben, if the diet's working. Do you think I could make it as a model now?"

"You've got the looks, no question. But you still need the training."

"Do *all* models have to go to schools?"

"No. I guess some just start in somehow and pick up experience as they go along."

"Well, will you start me out?"—she tried to sound casual— "The book needs more girls, Claudia said. What am I, as they say, chopped meat?"

"We could try a few shots—"

"Somebody said we need a few nudes, can I do them?" Her face was carefully serious.

"Annie, I work with models I have no personal relationship with . . . you're my sister-in-law and friend, I—"

"I say that's bull! Every painter I've ever read about used his mistress for a model."

"I don't know where you pick up this kind of information," Ben said, "but regardless of how the great masters did it, I do not want to use my sister-in-law—*not*, by the way, my mistress—as a nude model, and an underage one at that."

"Who'd know? You wouldn't have to show my face clearly. You could do a great shot of me . . . standing under the waterfalls and sunning on a rock, shielding my eyes from the sun. We've talked about shots like that before—"

"No."

"Well, who are you going to use for those shots? Grammie?"

"No relatives."

"I bet you would have used Rosie!"

"Rosie was my wife . . ."

She turned from him, then back again. "I know, I understand, but I *still* don't see why you're so stuffy about this. My god, you're a professional, and I'm trying like the devil to be one. Why can't we just sort of relax and get some good pictures?"

He laughed. "The real reason is that I simply couldn't relax in a situation like that, Annie. I am human, after all . . ."

"Do you have the hots for me?" she asked abruptly.

"I guess I asked for that . . . Look, Annie, it's getting late . . . My god, it's Friday! Ebon's probably waiting for us right now."

He hadn't, of course, answered her question. Which each of them, in his fashion, was acutely aware of.

On the way in Ann sat on the helmsman's seat where Rose had once perched. He thought how he'd so often admired

434

the delicate curves of Rose's slender figure, her smoothly tanned legs, steeling himself to the necessity of celibacy, and finally loving her so much in the midst of her illness that he hardly cared. He surely had no such depth of feeling for Ann, but again the situation was he could look but not allow himself to touch. He enjoyed the excitement Ann created, the sense of intimacy that chased loneliness for a little while at least. She amused him and made him grateful, because how many men his age, after all, had the enviable if difficult job of dealing with a seventeen-year-old nymph who insisted on having a "crush"? Ann was a marvelous tonic for his ego, a delight to his eye, a welcome distraction to get his mind off the despair which still threatened to overcome him when he spent too much time alone. Often she behaved like an outrageous child, but in a way that was a relief, making her seem less a woman, less a temptation. . . .

Waiting for the *Princess* to return, Ebon angrily paced the wharf alongside the boathouse. Returning to Livingston from college a bit earlier than usual with some scuba equipment he had borrowed from his roommate, he'd looked forward to taking Ann on a brief diving expedition before the sun went down. Finding that his father and his girl had gone out on the lake aboard the *Princess*, he had gone to Joe's bar for a beer and hamburger. The hush that had fallen when he entered puzzled him. Big Duke smiled in an odd way. "How are you, Eb? How's your girl? How's your old man?" Much laughter.

A short, enormously fat man with a red face asked one of Howie Hewat's young assistants, "I wonder what young Eb plans to give his old man for Father's Day? Or did he sort of give at the office?"

More laughter. Ebon's face slowly reddened. He wanted to charge the whole crowd of giggling drunks but turned abruptly to go to his jeep, the raucous laughter still in his ears.

That people were gossiping, making bawdy jokes didn't surprise him. What bothered him was the thought that in Livingston gossip most of the time was solidly based on fact ... Would the whole town really be sniggering over his father and his girl if they hadn't done something to deserve it? ...

Parking his car by Cliff House, he hurried toward the boathouse, to find that although it was nearly dark there was still no sign of the *Princess*.

He paced the wharf now, fists doubled up at his side. Why did his wonderful big-shot father have to louse up every situation in his life ... some of his most painful memories as a young boy were of fights between his father and mother, building to her bitter accusations during the divorce. Their whole family had been smashed. Finding Ann and Rose was a terrific relief, and the months alone with them were the happiest he'd ever experienced, but then, of course old dad had to come back to louse that up, wearing out Rose, maybe, as grammie had hinted, even contributing to her fatal attack, and now horning in with Ann ... god*damn* him ...

Except, if he was honest, wasn't Ann almost as much to blame? Crazy-ambitious, she'd gotten. All she seemed to care about was money and being famous, for god's sake, and his father was spending double time encouraging her ...

And with the anger, and fear, came an image of Ann and Ben in bed together, maybe right now in the cabin of the boat, no doubt old dad teaching her all the tricks he'd picked up in Korea and Paris and all the other wonderful faraway romantic places he loved to sound off so much about. And Ann being a willing pupil, just so long, of course, as she got a chance to have her name on some damn photograph or other ... she'd actually called Ben "king" and herself a "concubine." Terrific ... disgusting. ... Closing his eyes he saw himself exacting fitting revenge ... breaking the gasoline line at the engine, waiting for the fuel to fill the bilges, wadding up newspapers and lighting them and throwing them into the bilge just before he jumped overboard ...

The copper gasline would melt and no trace of the act would be left . . . Who said it was impossible to commit a perfect murder? Perfect murders happened in Livingston all the time. No sweat, no sweat at all with cops like Big Duke . . .

He felt on fire himself as the running lights of the *Princess* glided into view now, Ann standing up forward in a white bikini that seemed to glow in the deepening twilight, getting ready to put out the bow line.

"Hi, Ebon," she called with a cheery wave. "Have you been waiting long?"

Leaning out from the wheel, Ben waved too. "Hi, son! Glad you're home."

When Ann jumped onto the wharf with her line, Ebon grabbed her by the arm and without a word marched her up the wharf toward his car.

"Ebon, you're *hurting* me—"

"What the hell is going on here?"

"Stay away from me, dad," Ebon told him. "For once in your goddamn life, just stay the hell *away* . . ."

Ben froze.

"Let me handle this," Ann called to him, her voice surprisingly firm.

The sight of Eb taking possession . . . yes, that was the word for it . . . of Ann so suddenly bothered him more than he liked to admit, more even than the cause of his son's explosion. And he realized—faced—that despite his intentions he'd somehow fallen into a bizarre sort of competition with his son for Ann, a game in which there couldn't possibly be any winners.

His stomach churning, Ben completed the job of tying up the boat and went to the cabin for a drink. Sitting at the small table there, he found himself remembering a grotesque experience of a friend of his at college, a sensitive young man named Timmy Blanchard. Timmy had been in love with a girl who worked in a bookstore because she couldn't afford college. After knowing her almost a year, he'd asked her

437

home to introduce her to his parents. Only a sophomore, he'd hoped to get permission and support to marry the girl. It didn't happen. What did happen was that his father, a distinguished lawyer of that era, had started dropping in at the bookstore, and it wasn't long before he'd made the girl his mistress and paid for her college tuition.

Ben could still remember Timmy's awful misery, hurt and anger as he recounted this seemingly improbable tale during a night of drinking . . . "I feel like killing my father," he'd said, "and you know, I just damn well might. I know where he keeps his guns . . ."

A month later he'd gone into the study of his father's elaborate house, forced open the gun cabinet and selected a double-barrel 12-gauge shotgun. Taking off his right shoe, he'd used his toe to trigger a blast that, literally, took his own head off. Less than a year later the father had driven his Cadillac convertible off a highway at great speed, and died in the crash. The girl? He'd lost track of her . . . One thing was certain, though, there were no winners. . . .

Hold that thought, he told himself, and then quickly realized he was being melodramatic. His and Ebon's situation with Annie was hardly comparable . . . after all, he had not made Annie his mistress and had no intention whatsoever of doing so. Eb had undoubtedly picked up on the ugly rumors, but the boy, while he might resent him at times, was certainly intelligent enough to separate mean gossip from fact and not cast his old man in a ridiculous villain's role.

Well, wasn't he? . . . Whatever, Eb's explosion made it clear he'd have to be more careful not to give substance to all the crazy talk. And suddenly he felt sorry for his son, putting himself in his place, asking himself how he would have felt if his father had started taking Heidi to New York and out on the boat. Except such a situation was literally beyond imagining, because Stephen had never shown any interest in any woman but his wife, and often, not much in her. Even so, just the fantasy of one's father bedding down

438

one's girl was somehow enraging, offensive . . . going against the natural order of things. A sort of variation on the old Oedipal thing.

Cut it out, he told himself. You've drifted too far with this thing. Back up, *cool* it, old man—what did Ebon call him that got him so angry? "Old dad"? Okay, "old dad," back off, play at most the role of a surrogate father with Ann, or get out of her life.

Which would mean leaving Livingston for some foreign assignment . . . lonely flights, meals in restaurants where no one knew him, hotel rooms and sex with women he'd never seen before and would never see again. Lonely drinking and lonely work he did not really give a damn about. Livingston wasn't exactly nirvana, but damn it, hadn't he had enough of that pointless, rootless existence for one life? . . .

He found Ebon and Ann on the terrace of Cliff House. Apparently—hard to believe after their display—they had made up. They sat on the old church pew now, leaning against each other, closely entwined. Ben's fine resolutions of only moments before, he discovered with a jolt, seemed to hold up poorly as he experienced a distinct feeling of—no other word for it—jealousy. Well, damn it, this was precisely the sort of nonsense he'd need to be aware of and make a special effort to control. He was a desperately lonely, grieving middle-aged man. And as such likely to be a particular damn fool . . . and having put even his least noble feelings in a proper box, he proceeded to go quietly to his room without bothering the loving young couple—god, so young—and might have made it except that the dachshunds began to demonstrate their ability as watchdogs.

"Dad?" Ebon called out.

"Yes."

"Want to talk a minute?"

Surprised that Eb was even talking to him, he went out onto the terrace. They were sitting a little farther apart now, but still holding hands.

"I'm sorry I gave you such a hard time," Ebon began. "I guess it was just that they all started some pretty rough needling down at Joe's bar, and being a hothead . . . like father, like son, I guess, I started believing all their garbage—"

"I told him," Ann said, "how you're so chicken you won't even take a picture of me in less than a Mother Hubbard dress. Some dirty old man, right, Eb?"

"I guess . . . but still, what with all the dumb talk and upset here, wouldn't it be best for you to go to a boarding school in Albany? My roommate has a girl who goes to a place called the Hudson River Academy. It needs students and would let you enter late in the academic year, according to her. And as a senior you'd have all the privileges and get a better education than Livingston High . . ."

"What do you think, Annie?" Ben asked.

"I think it's a swell idea, except for a few little items like the money, finishing the book, and of course there's grammie, who needs me . . . but sure, I'll think about it, I really will," and bestowed on both of them a smile that wouldn't stop.

Ebon appeared to be almost satisfied with what was in effect a careful turn down, and when Ben left them to go to bed, he noted that their two silhouettes had become one even before he'd moved off the terrace.

That night Ben had special difficulty in getting to sleep. At about two in the morning he had just dozed off when the dogs started to bark. At about the same time, handfuls of gravel rattled against the windows of his room. Almost immediately Ebon, wearing only his jockey shorts, came in, and Ann, in blue pajamas, soon followed.

"What the hell is going on?" Ebon said as more gravel rattled against the slate roof.

"They're giving us the treatment," Ann told him, her voice edged as it had been when she'd told Ben of the treatment she'd gotten at school.

440

Laughter, jeers came from the shadows surrounding the house. An open can half full of white paint landed on the roof outside Ben's window, leaving a swath as it rolled to the gutter.

Friendly folk . . . angry firemen, or keepers of the public morality, or part of Howie Hewat's revenge, or maybe the Radeaus'? . . . Ben had so many people against him, it could be any one or a combination thereof.

Whoever they were, they progressed to throwing ripe dead perch on the roof, accompanied by jeers and laughter, much of it sounding drunken, punctuated by the sound of beer cans rattling over the slate.

"We getting you out of the sack, Ben, or maybe you too *busy* to hear . . ."

"Why don't you get your shotgun?" Ebon said.

"To hell with them, let's have a drink and ignore the bastards."

"How about at least calling the cops?" Ebon asked.

Big Duke answered.

"People are throwing stuff at my house," Ben began.

"That's right? Terrible what people do, ain't it? Why do you suppose they'd do such a thing to such *nice* folks like you?"

Ben hung up, poured himself a shot of Scotch and put the phonograph on loud enough to drown out the jeers. It wasn't that there was any real damage being done, but the ugliness, the invasion of privacy was unnerving, and the inability to fight back was infuriating.

Gradually the catcalls and thud of objects thrown onto the roof diminished, the laughter in the night died away and the dogs went to sleep.

Ben, Ebon and Ann, targets, stayed awake for hours with their separate, uneasy thoughts.

At eight next morning Ebon woke his father and asked if he'd like to go scuba diving. Ben guessed that his son was trying to make up for some of the unpleasantness of the previous night by including him, and quickly accepted the invitation. After they'd hurriedly eaten breakfast, Ann prepared a picnic basket. Carrying that and the scuba gear, they walked down to the boathouse. As they approached, Ben stared at the empty wharf in disbelief. The *Indian Princess* was not there. She had entirely disappeared.

They ran out to the wharf, as though they could find the old cruiser hidden in a crack somewhere. In utter bewilderment, they looked into the boathouse, which was empty. Shielding their eyes from the sun with their hands, they peered in every direction. On this clear October day, there was no hint of summer mist. The boat was nowhere in this end of the lake.

"I'll call the ranger, he has a boat," Ebon said, and started running up the hill toward the house.

Waiting for his son to return, Ben told himself that it wasn't entirely reasonable for a grown man to be so upset by the loss of an ancient boat, but he felt grief-stricken nevertheless . . . the disappearance of the *Princess* was in a way like death: she was someone—all right, something—that he loved, she'd disappeared, and nothing but thin air remained. Beloved people and things suddenly seemed so insubstantial to him that he was tempted to throw both arms around Ann and Ebon just to *keep* them there.

Ebon's forest-ranger friend quickly arrived in a Boston whaler with a powerful outboard that took them down the lake at nearly forty miles an hour, and they hadn't gone far past the narrow part of the first hourglass when Ann gasped and pointed toward a point of land. The blue decks of the half-sunken *Princess* were so close to the blue of the water lapping over them they were difficult to see, but the freshly varnished sides of the cabin still reflected the sun. The *Princess* had been run on the rocks and sunk in about five feet of water. Her small mast was tilted at an unnatural angle and her cockpit flooded.

As the whaler drew close to the wreck, Ebon stripped to his shorts, his lithe, muscular body accented in the morning sunlight. Wearing one of the masks on top of his head, he dived cleanly over the side and swam to the *Princess*. Before climbing aboard the half-sunken hull he adjusted his mask and examined the bottom from stem to stern on both sides, then inspected the cockpit and water-filled cabin before returning to the whaler. Climbing aboard, he said, "I think she could be saved, dad. The keel and the garboards up forward are smashed, but there's no big hole. If we could get some help to lift her we could get a tarp under her. Then if we had some big pumps—"

"You better call the fire department," the ranger said. "Marine salvage isn't exactly their business but sometimes they'll do you a favor—"

"Forget it," Ben said, looking meaningfully at Ebon and Ann.

"It could have just been a bunch of drunks," Ebon said. "Why don't you try . . ."

"Wait a minute," Ann said, "every plumber has those gasoline-driven pumps, they'd be easy to get."

"Where do we get the manpower?" Ebon asked. "The lady we have to lift weighs about five tons."

"The Loyals," Ann said. "The Livingston Loyals . . . 'Now hear us, this song we sing, the Livingston Loyals can do anything.' Do you think I put in all those glorious years as a cheerleader for nothing? Get me ashore and I'll give them a call."

Ann made her call at the nearest ranger station and the resulting spectacle was enough to make Ben begin to forgive his town despite his various debacles. The captain of the football team responded to Ann by ordering his forces to Scotty's wharf, where a variety of small boats were rentable. When he learned of the emergency, Scotty said he'd hardly had any October business anyway and offered the free use of his whole fleet. Paul's Plumbing responded by bringing three pumps to Scotty's wharf and a variety of tools. The rescuers approached the wreck of the *Princess* in outboards, launches and speedboats towing canoes and rowboats. The young football players looked strong enough, Ben thought, to raise the sunken battleships at Pearl Harbor. Ebon directed the operation as they surrounded the *Princess*, floundering in shoulder-deep water while they tried to get a grip on the old boat's slippery sides. Three of them held a heavy tarpaulin the ranger had supplied near the bow, ready to slip it under the boat. Suddenly the captain shouted, "All right now, a one and a two and a three and *up* she goes . . ."

To Ben's amazement, the *Princess* lifted all of her five tons into the air as though she'd mastered the art of levitation. The tarpaulin was deftly pulled under the hull and lashed in place. An old Chris-Craft edged alongside to put the pumps aboard. Ebon cranked them up and great streams of water began to gush from the *Princess*'s cockpit. For fifteen minutes everyone watched the half-sunken hull closely while it gradually became evident that more water was coming out than was going in. Soon the *Princess* was afloat, rolling almost imperceptibly to the familiar rhythm of the waves.

The football team waited around another half hour in their flotilla to make sure that more efforts wouldn't be needed.

"Okay now?" the captain asked finally.

"Everything's fine," Ben called. "I don't know how to thank you, can I give you at least a few cases of beer?"

"That's okay . . . everything okay, Annie?"

Doing her cheerleader's strut on the stern, Ann chanted, "Now hear us, this song we sing; the Livingston Loyals can do anything," and the players laughed as they roared away in their boats, their outboards almost colliding as they played chicken.

The ranger towed the *Princess* to Clarence's Boatyard at the northern end of the lake, where she was immediately hauled out of the water. After examining her, Clarence's son

444

Jake, who ran the yard for his father, guessed that the damage could be fixed for about five thousand dollars. Which was certainly a lot of money, but for Ben held the good thought that at least one kind of resurrection was possible. And the sight of the young people doing a job for Ann, in spite of the rumors they must have heard about her in school, helped blot out the memory of the ugly jeers and snickering of those heroic souls who had thrown dead fish at his house in the middle of the night.

Ben also congratulated Ebon for his part in supervising the raising of the boat. Even Ann seemed impressed . . . "Hey, Eb, I knew you were pretty good, but I never knew you could do anything but stuff like rubbing sticks together to put out a fire."

"To build a fire, idiot," and gave her a playful shove. For a few moments they wrestled on the terrace at Cliff House like what they were—two very attractive young people physically complementing each other . . . How, Ben wondered, in his wildest imaginings, could he ever have even thought that Annie might prefer *him* to Ebon? . . .

No fool like an old . . .

Sᴜɴᴅᴀʏ afternoon Ebon went back to college, apparently pretty well convinced by Ann's good job that there was no truth in the rumors he'd heard. Ann seemed thoughtful after he had left and declined Ben's invitation to go down to the boatyard to see if they could hurry along the process of drying out the *Princess*. She did not bring him his supper and drinks as she had been doing, which Ben saw as one more sign that her crush on him had simply run its course, as, of course, it should. And if, instead of being relieved, he only felt more conscious of his acute loneliness than ever, well, that was a problem that a mature man his age ought to be able to handle by himself. Ought to . . .

He was in his office next morning when the telephone rang. Lillian answered. "Ben, it's for you."

"Another threatening call?" he asked wryly as he put his hand on the receiver.

"No, it's a Claudia Simpson in New York. You know her?"

Ben had been steeling himself against the possibility of disastrous news from Claudia for so many days that the imminence of a real decision from her was terrifying. His arm felt stiff with tension as he lifted the receiver.

446

"Good morning, Claudia, the weather in New York as good as it is here?"

"I'll put Mrs. Simpson on the wire in just a moment," a secretary replied, making him feel ridiculous.

"Hello, Ben!" Claudia finally was on the line.

"Hello, Claudia! Is the weather in New York as good as it is here?"

"Oh, it's a beautiful day. Dave and I just drove in from Connecticut and the fall foliage out there is fantastic. Well, I guess I don't have to tell you."

"The fall foliage is great up here too," Ben replied desperately.

There was a short pause, but to Ben it sounded altogether too pregnant.

"About that *Small Town* project you talked to me about, I think I have some fairly good news for you."

"Oh?" His voice was still determinedly casual if a little hoarse.

"I decided to send the presentation you gave me up to Unicorn Press in Boston. A guy named Bernard Gold is the unicorn. He started the house only about ten years ago, but he's been doing pretty well."

"Does he like it?" Ben finally got out.

"Very much," Claudia said calmly. "I just had a call from him a few minutes ago. We had to go back and forth on money a little, but he offers an advance of twenty thousand dollars. That's hardly a world's record these days, but it's certainly better than just earnest money."

Oh, thank you, Lord, Ben thought, and could almost see Ann's reaction to this news. And the sense of failure for the past five years was suddenly gone. Claudia misinterpreted his brief silence.

"Of course if you need more cash on the barrelhead I could try one of the bigger houses—"

"Oh, no! The twenty will do fine!"

447

"I'm glad because Bernie Gold seems to me to be just right for this book. He's a bear for perfection when it comes to reproduction quality of photographs. In this age of conglomerates he's one of the few fully independent publishers. You'll get decisions from a real publisher, not an office boy and not a committee."

"He sounds marvelous," Ben said, and indeed was ready to knight Bernard Gold and kiss him on both cheeks.

"To top it all, he's a small-town boy himself who really identifies with your project," Claudia said. "I didn't know that until this morning. Bernie looks about as small town as your basic mayor of New York, but he comes from Tatesville, Illinois. Apparently there's a huge underground of small-town people in every big city."

"We'll have allies," Ben said. "We country bumpkins stick together. Hick power."

"That thought was a factor in Bernie's decision. Now, Ben, he wants to see you. Can you get to Boston for a conference in his office at eleven Friday morning?"

"I'll make it."

"And bring your little collaborator. He was quite intrigued by the idea of having a pretty little seventeen-year-old girl involved in this. It could be a real publicity bonus and I will say that Bernie is something of a genius when it comes to pushing a book."

"Annie will be there if she doesn't have too much homework."

"What?"

"It's a joke. Annie is, to put it mildly, eager."

"Good." Claudia hesitated. "Do you want to include her in the contract or are you going to pay her a fee or—"

"Put her in the contract. She's done a third of the work, so give her a third of the profits."

There were more details, including the address of Bernard Gold's office. Finally Claudia said, "Well, I guess that wraps it up for now, Ben. I'm glad things are going well with you

448

for a change. Dave sends his best, and give our greetings to that new bride of yours. If she's as pretty as her little sister, I can't wait to meet her."

The wire seemed to hum very loudly before Ben brought himself to say, "Claudia, I should have told you this in New York, but it was just too rough. Rosie, my wife, died very soon after the wedding. She'd had a bad heart for some time . . ."

"Oh . . . I am so sorry, Ben."

"She changed me a lot, Claudia—all for the best, I think. It was wrong for her to die . . . I mean, she had such a marvelous capacity for life."

"Those are the ones . . ."

"Anyway, thanks for putting all this together for us," he said, his throat tightening.

He hung up, sat staring out the window, thinking of how delighted Rosie would have been with this news. Success. Rosie had known so little of it, but had made a triumph out of her life anyway.

He thought of calling Annie at school, but decided to hold the good news until she got home. Somehow this was a moment he needed to be alone with . . . or rather to be alone with Rosie, and almost automatically he found himself heading for her old farm. The bed of the long dirt driveway had been crushed by the heavy fire engines that had tried to put out the fire in the barn and rutted by the cars of the spectators. Before the ground froze it should be scraped and covered with gravel, Ben thought. Standing near the middle of the driveway, he looked at the old farmhouse that had given him so much pleasure that spring. The fields of green grass that had surrounded it, making the grove of maples around the building look like an island, now had mellowed to a fine shade of harvest gold . . . hay that should be cut back from the house to get rid of a fire hazard. The green maple leaves which had made the ancient building beneath them look so cool in summer now were red, yellow and

449

orange, a pyramid of color as brilliant as smokeless flames. The house looked curiously smaller than his memories of it, and he realized that the disappearance of the barn with the silo that leaned like the Tower of Pisa had diminished the whole farm. After parking near the front porch with its familiar stacks of firewood, he walked to the place where the barn had stood. The fire, of course, had left a tangle of charred wood and a few crumbling stonewalls . . . These too should be cleaned up before snow fell. . . .

Taking the key from its can in the woodpile, Ben let himself in the front door. After a summer of disuse the kitchen was musty and damp, but there was also that well-remembered fragrance of rooms long heated by wood stoves. The only sound in the kitchen was the hum of a refrigerator he had forgotten to turn off. The big round table at which Rosie had first served him dinner looked ready for another meal, with salt and pepper shakers already in place. Slowly Ben walked through the rest of this house which he had loved so much. Somehow the cozy feeling had disappeared. The small rooms, which had once looked snug, appeared cramped, and the cracked linoleum on the floors looked more dingy than practical. The warmth and charm of this old farmhouse, Ben realized suddenly, had come from Rosie, and for the most part had died with her. While she had been there cheerfully feeding the glowing stoves and the people, the house had seemed a protection against all the coldness in the world. Now . . .

Sitting on a living room couch with a worn cover, Ben looked around . . . this was where Rosie had spent her life, taking care of a sick mother when she herself was hardly into her teens, rearing a younger sister, keeping an irascible grandmother out of a nursing home; her slender income at the mill had been able to support this place, and that had been more important to her than new rugs or curtains or any adornment for herself.

He went upstairs, saw the small bedroom where Rose had

slept, the narrow iron bed and the few clothes hanging forgotten in a makeshift closet in a corner. Looking over the slate tiles outside the window, he saw the dormer of the room she had assigned to him, telling him jokingly that he could climb over the roof to visit her. And he sank down on the cot and had the first crying jag he had allowed himself since Rosie's death. Finally he stood up, telling himself that Rosie would hardly want him to celebrate his success this way.

From the beginning he'd intended to return to this farm from Cliff House as soon as the weather turned cold. Cliff House had a furnace for chilly fall days, but lacked the insulation and storm windows necessary for economy and comfort in the harsh Adirondack winters. Now he wondered if living in this farmhouse again would be possible for him. Why not get storm windows for Cliff House and have the place insulated? Then grammie and Annie could sell this building for some much-needed money . . . except as he had the thought he felt disloyal. Grammie loved this old house and had talked all summer of getting back to it. Ann would be sure to be upset at the very thought of selling this farm where she had been brought up. And, face it, he still found in these cramped rooms, if not the charm and warmth and the joy that had died with Rose, at least still some echo of her voice and footsteps. He considered whether Rose would like him to have the place fixed up. Grammie would welcome any improvements . . . new paint, rugs, curtains, furniture . . . partitions could be removed to make big rooms out of small ones—but no, then the whole atmosphere of the old building would be changed, and Rose wouldn't recognize it anymore. Still, he knew Rose had hated things to be shabby. He'd keep everything just the way it was but renew anything that was broken or worn. Remembering how happy she had been when Ebon painted a room, he decided to find a contractor who would put everything in shape before they had to move out of Cliff House.

The contractor he chose was a mountain of a man named Cyrus Horn, inevitably called "Horny." Horny Horn had an old farm on the outskirts of the village, in the barns of which he kept his trucks, bulldozer, back hoe and other equipment. On the bulldozer he had painted in large letters his slogan WE CAN'T MOVE HEAVEN, BUT WE CAN MOVE EARTH.

Ben found Horny in the driveway of his farm, where he was repairing the clutch of a tractor. Although he'd known the contractor for years, he didn't really like calling him "Horny" and "Mr. Horn" would sound stiff. "Cyrus" or "Cy" also sounded odd, because no one called him that except his wife and ancient mother. Ben tried to avoid any name at all.

"Good morning," he began. "I have a few jobs to do out at Rose's old farm." After discussing the driveway, the overgrown hay field, the wreckage of the burned barn and the interior work, Ben asked if he'd have time to do all that work in the next month or so.

Horny took off his painter's cap and scratched his shaggy gray head. "I'll give it a try," he said. "I got time, all right. The trouble is getting help. They say almost a third of this town is on relief, but damned if I can find anybody who wants to work. Now with the hunting season coming up, even the cops and the firemen will be off in the woods most of the time taking potshots at each other."

"I guess most of the work can wait, but I would like to get that hay field cut back away from the house as soon as possible," Ben said. "I hate to think of what a grass fire could do . . ."

"We'll get to her. How's Annie, Ben?"

The big man's smile was bland, and perhaps, Ben thought, he only imagined that there was a sly glint in his eye. Maybe he was getting paranoid. The most ordinary civilities were beginning to sound like jeers.

"Annie's fine. I think she may make it as a photographer. She's starting to sell her work already."

"Well, you never can tell, can you?" Horny scratched his head again. "I always knew she was a plum pretty little girl, but I wouldn't have guessed she was so smart. I bet you gave her a mite of help, though, didn't you, Ben? . . ."

"A man generally does try to help his family," Ben replied, feeling both angry and foolish as he returned to his car.

The taunts he and Ebon had received at Joe's bar made Ben decide to go to a place called Harry's Hideaway for lunch, a dark and gloomy saloon frequented by the unemployed of all ages, the retired, and a coterie of loggers and hunters much more interested in their own affairs than in gossip about others. As he drank his beer and ate a sandwich of Polish sausage, he kept looking at the flyspecked walls and cigarette-littered floor and suddenly wondered what on earth he was doing there . . . What the hell, he was a success again, wasn't he? Well, sort of . . . a twenty-thousand-dollar advance wasn't all that much, but he'd been around the course enough times to recognize the faintest aroma of approaching success even at considerable distance. Claudia's tone of voice told him a lot. When his work was going well there was almost a caressing sound in the agent's words and she asked about his family a lot. When it wasn't, her sentences were short, clipped and her interest in his relatives became minimal. This morning she'd talked to him in a businesslike manner, but there had been sufficient undertones in her husky contralto to make a man who didn't know her suspect that she was trying to start an affair. Ben, however, knew her. Her love was for a project that worked, a passion they both shared . . . And after *Small Town* why not *Big Town* (Manhattan) and *Village* (Greenwich) and *Rich Town* (Palm Springs or Palm Beach) . . . and how about coming off it, he told himself. Right now the immediate goal was a good meeting come Friday with Bernard Gold, and meanwhile it was back to the old drawing board, or rather the old typewriter ... he still had a newspaper and some unfinished business.

He had been sitting on his article about Howie Hewat's landholdings in the valley, excusing the delay by telling himself that the piece would hit harder if it were published closer to the November election, but he suspected his real reason was a disinclination to escalate the level of hostility. He had had to telephone so many people to nail down the facts that Howie inevitably must have learned what was in store for him. Perhaps he thought that the raining of junk on Ben's house in the middle of the night had been enough to make him shelve the article.

Now Ben took the folder containing the piece from the bottom drawer of his desk and examined the map that he had commissioned a high school art teacher to draw for him. In black areas the sketch showed the 134 acres in the valley which Howie owned and the 721 more on which he and his associates had bought options under various names. Ben's headline read HEWAT CONTROLS 855 ACRES IN AREA HE SEEKS TO REZONE!

He put the folder on Lillian's desk. "Run this, please, on the first page of the next edition," he told her.

"Do you mind if I come to work in a suit of armor afterward?"

It was possible, Ben realized as he went back to his desk, that his whiff of success was giving him too much courage. Determined to clear his desk of matters he'd been unwilling to decide on for weeks, he picked up the file on the Radeau case. After endless delays it was finally to go to trial on Wednesday. Should he avoid the whole distasteful mess the way the *Recorder* did, minimize it, or play it up, the way Bill Crawford at the Albany *Star* wanted?

"Lillian, do we have a file with the names of people who came in here looking for work?"

"Of course."

"Didn't you tell me a long time ago about an old guy who

454

was managing editor of the *Herald Tribune* years ago?"

"Hank Deering. He bought an old farm up on Berry Hill. He does special articles for papers all around here."

"Well, hire him and put him on the Radeau story. Tell him to handle it the way the *Trib* would have. I have to go to Boston Thursday and I may have to be out of town quite a lot."

"I'll take care of it," Lillian replied, looking pleased. With mixed feelings Ben had discovered that she liked nothing better than to run the paper while he was away. This was convenient, but it was a little disconcerting to have an employee whose face fell every time he came through the door and who beamed when he departed.

He left his office and drove back to Cliff House. It was a little after two o'clock in the afternoon, and Ann could be expected to return from school at about three-thirty. While he waited he sat on the terrace, admired the multicolored mountains surrounding the blue lake and tried to imagine what effect the good news would have on Ann. She would be delighted, of course. Probably she would jump up and down and hug him and of course there would be nothing wrong with that. Probably she would find their trip to Boston even more exciting than their visit to New York, because now their progress was tangible. When she learned of her share of the money, she might go on a shopping spree, and why not? On the dark side, might she decide to hell with school, being a success of sorts at seventeen? And what about old personal ties . . . what about Ebon?

Which, of course, was *the* question that had been nagging at the back of his mind. When Ebon had gone back to college, it had seemed they were safely—"safely," what was that?—together, but now, stimulated with her success, preoccupied with conferences in New York or Boston, excited by the prospect of a publicity tour clean across the nation, would Ann again want to discard Ebon's simpler world, and would Ebon become disgusted with her? And if he were with Ann on all or even just some of those jaunts, wouldn't Ebon's understandable suspicions grow? And grow?

There could be a complete break between Ebon and himself . . . what son could feel good about a father who kept running around the country with his girl, and who kept using special advantage to excite her admiration? Even if he had enough control to resist Ann's girlish—and womanly at the same time—temptations in all those adjacent hotel rooms, wouldn't his innocence be only technical? In effect, wouldn't he be taking his son's girl, whether he actually bedded her or not? As soon as he told her the good news, Ann's attentions and time would be concentrated on him, he suspected . . . suspected with admittedly mixed emotions . . . and for a dark moment he wondered whether he had, perhaps, subconsciously arranged all this—it was almost a standard middle-aged man's mode of courtship, after all, to involve a young woman by helping her with her career. Had he singled Ann out, both for her delightful self and her increasing resemblance to Rose, and now was he proceeding to seduce her with an efficiency that he would not admit but which his son would be smart enough to recognize? . . . No, damn it. Come down to basics. Sure, Ann might be easy enough to seduce, but he was also certain that it would be impossible for him to hold her for long. Rare men of genius like Chaplin and Picasso might have lived happily with women much younger than themselves for decades, but he was no Picasso or Chaplin, and for all his admiration of her, he couldn't quite see Ann in the role of faithful keeper of the dying flame of Ben Winslow's modest talents. When he began to slip, to bore her, she'd be off to Ebon or some other potent young man.

Let this thing run its course and he'd end up a lonely, disillusioned man without a wife *and* without a son. And that son's whole life could be scarred by the bitterness of losing his girl to, of all people, his father. Remembering Timmy, the college friend who'd committed suicide to escape just

456

such a situation, Ben felt a chill that his Scotch could not warm.

But, he decided, it was being melodramatic to let himself believe that their lives necessarily had to turn out disastrously. All three of them were good people. They weren't stupid. They loved each other in good as well as, admit it, dangerous ways. Above all, she was seventeen and he was forty-five. He was the one who was supposed to give the control and the direction. He was, after all, the adult here. Hold that thought, he instructed himself.

At a little after three-thirty Ben heard the school bus stop to discharge passengers near the end of the driveway leading to Cliff House. The escaping students laughed and shouted as they ran toward their homes. A few moments more and he heard Ann's footsteps on the stone stairs leading to the terrace from the driveway. She stepped now through the saplings which had grown around the entrance to the terrace, a slender girl in a brown sweater and tweed skirt carrying a heavy armful of books.

"Hi," she said, looking worried. "Why're you home so early? Everything okay?"

"Claudia Simpson called."

"What did she say?" Ann sounded and looked scared.

"We have a publisher!"

The books dropping in a jumble at her feet, she leaped over them, threw her arms around his neck and covered him with lipstick-smeared kisses before finally stepping back (he did not discourage her). "What did she say, tell me *everything*. What time did she phone?"

"About ten-thirty this morning."

"*What?* Why didn't you call me at school?"

"I guess I was trying not to exaggerate things. It's good news, but we should play it a little cool—"

"Oh, don't be cool *now*. When do we go back to New York?"

"It will be Boston this time."

457

"I love Boston too. *When?*"

"We'll drive down Thursday for a meeting Friday morning."

"Oh, wow!" And she broke into a wild Irish jig on the flagstones, ending in three cartwheels, face flushed and hair flying. "When do we get some money—is it awful to ask that?"

"It's not exactly an uncommon question in artistic circles. We get an advance of twenty thousand dollars."

"Twenty thousand dollars? You *mean* it?"

"I do, and since you've done a third of the work you get a third of the loot . . . which means that after Claudia's commission you'll get about six thousand dollars—"

"For *me?* For taking a few pictures?"

"I told you that you had talent."

She kissed him again, this time on the mouth. Holding her hands locked behind his neck, she kicked up her heels and swung. Catching her mood, in spite of himself, he twirled her around the way he had his daughter when she was a little girl.

"Six thousand dollars," she said as her feet touched the flagstones. "Ben . . . do you think God means this, or has He made a mistake?"

Before he could answer the sliding glass door to the living room opened and grammie was wheeling herself out. "What's all the commotion out here?"

"We sold the book, we have a publisher," Ann chanted.

"Well, I guess that's good . . . when you get done gallivanting around out here we've got some cobwebs in the bedrooms that ought to come down, Mrs. Wilmot's no good at getting into the corners and under the radiators."

When grammie had retreated into the house, Ann said, "What are we going to do tonight? We ought to do something absolutely terrific to celebrate."

"What would you like to do?"

"Drive to Burlington, maybe? They have all kinds of absolutely terrific restaurants there . . . hey, what do you know, I can afford to buy *you* dinner."

Ben had what he decided was an inspiration. "How about Albany? Then Eb can join us. I'm sure he'd like to help us celebrate. If we leave now we can get there around seven and be home by midnight."

"*Super!*" She hugged him again, then ran off to put on some festive clothes.

While she was changing, Ben telephoned Ebon at his college dormitory. "Hi, Eb, how'd you like a couple of visitors tonight? Annie and I have some good news, we'd like you to help us celebrate—"

"What kind of good news?" He sounded wary.

Briefly Ben told him, not mentioning the money.

"Well, that's great," Ebon said in a noticeably flat voice. "You want me to make reservations at some restaurant?"

The place Ebon chose turned out to be a students' nightclub with a deafening rock band and nothing to drink but beer or wine. During intermissions Ebon listened quietly to Ann's happy talk about the great sums of money she had coming, the trip to Boston and the chance for a nationwide publicity tour, which especially fascinated her, depressed him . . . his depression deepening with her talk about the possibility of assignments that could mean world travel. The more she talked, the more he drank—quantities of dark beer from a thick stein that a stout waitress in a red dirndl kept refilling. Each time the clamorous music started, he jumped up, grabbed Ann's arm in the middle of one of her sentences and led her to the dance floor. When the music wasn't playing it was as though they were strangers, but when she moved with him to the rock beat of the bull fiddle and drums they appeared to Ben to be almost one person.

Chewing on a thick ham sandwich, Ben reflected that his first mistake had been in letting Eb choose the restaurant. Was this his son's none too subtle way of showing his *old*

459

man that he didn't belong with the younger generation? Ann and Eb danced together with such sensual grace that he found the spectacle almost as painful as it was beautiful. Never in his life, at any age, had he been uninhibited and skillful enough to dance like that . . . in his youth he'd found the box step and the waltz difficult enough to master, and he couldn't help envy as he admired Eb's easy mastery as he danced a kind of duet with Ann, who was graceful and stylish enough to make even the most provocative movements amusing rather than vulgar. Strutting, twirling, she combined bits of the Hustle with the Twist and who knew how many other dances. In her shimmering, clinging green silk dress, she couldn't help turning every dance into a kind of fertility rite . . . there was no other, or better, name for it . . . The beat was rock, hard rock, and the din made his coffee cup chatter on its saucer. To Ben the crowd of some twenty dancers seemed to be clawing at the air, jerking like spastics in obedience to the orgiastic beat of the band. In the midst of it all Ebon and Ann somehow managed to preserve a kind of discipline that appeared to make their intensity all the stronger. If sparks had flown when he touched her, Ben would not have been surprised. He'd never felt older, more clumsy, more inhibited in his life. And, to his chagrin, he found that he had never, however absurdly, wanted this young girl more. His hunger would have been funny if it hadn't caused so much pain. Right, as they say, where he lived.

When the band quit for an intermission and they rejoined him in the booth, Ann reverted with startling ease to her excitement about the book and publicity, almost as though she and Ebon hadn't been dancing at all. It was almost scary, her abrupt, seemingly impersonal switchover. Ben warned himself to take note of it. Along with Ann's change, the vitality drained from Ebon's face and his depression showed as a kind of sullenness. Ben, on the other hand, woke up when Ann returned to the table, and he felt himself caught

460

up in her enthusiasm as she asked and he answered her questions.

The trouble was, the intermissions lasted too long. Ann's preoccupation with the book was understandable even to Ebon, but it began to sound obsessive. Ebon, morosely sipping his beer, finally broke in when Ann went on to say she might use the money she was saving for college to open a small studio in New York. "Now wait a minute, Annie . . . I really think you're just getting carried away by all this—"

"What do you mean by that?" She looked hurt and angry.

"You're talking as though you were already a big-deal great photographer and you're not. That kind of self-delusion can dump you pretty hard—"

"Your father says I have talent—"

"And he'll also say talent is common . . . isn't that *right*, dad?"

"I've said that talent is common, but real drive is rare."

"Well, I *have* real drive. To spare. Wait and see—"

"Annie," Ebon said, "I'm not trying to put you down, but you have to face some facts. I mean, you're only seventeen. Do you think you would have done a book if dad hadn't put you into one of his?"

"That's note quite fair, Eb," Ben put in. "I wouldn't have used her work if it wasn't good."

"But the book was *your* idea, wasn't it? And your name and connections are getting it published."

"What are you trying to do to me?" Ann said, on the edge of tears.

"I'm *trying* to bring you down to earth, where us ordinary mortals have to live."

"Eb, take it easy," Ben said. "What's so bad about a young girl having some dreams? You have yours too—"

"Wrong," Ann broke in. "He makes fun of my dreams because he never had any, except camping in the woods.

Damn it, Eb, I don't tell you what to do with your life, where do you get off telling me? Why do you have to make a disaster out of every good thing that happens to me? I thought we'd settled all this when you went back to college, now here you are at it again."

Tight-lipped, Ebon looked down. "I'm sorry," he said. "Forget it."

"I will . . . Ben, can we please go home?"

"Wait," Ebon said, not being able to carry off his show of indifference. "Annie, I'm sorry, I apologize." Then, looking as much at his father as at her, "I love you . . . if you're still interested to hear it . . ."

She sighed. "Okay, Eb, I know, but I'm tired, I want to go home."

"When do you get back from Boston?"

"Friday night," Ben told him.

"Well, Annie . . . will you see me Saturday? About ten? I'll take you down to the Performing Arts Center in Saratoga, I'll show you we have more than trees around here—"

"*Okay*, Eb," she said tiredly. "I'll see you at the house Saturday . . . now please, I have an awful headache, *please* take me home, Ben . . ."

Ebon decided to stay for another beer. He watched Ann take hold of his father's arm as they walked out to the car.

"God," he thought, "god*damn* . . . did anyone in the world have a problem like *this?* . . .

ALTHOUGH Ben was made to feel distinctly uneasy during the argument between Ebon and Ann, he soon afterward told himself that he was not, after all, even though he was the senior, in full control of three lives, and there were times when all one could do was to ride things out as well as possible. When on the way home to Livingston Ann kept alternately spluttering about Ebon, vowing that she never wanted to see him again, and lapsing into dark silences, Ben allowed himself a tinge of pleasure, as well as sympathy for both the girl and his son. Introspection, after all, always has its perils as well as its presumptions. He decided to give it up for the duration.

Thursday dawned as a perfect day of Indian summer with golden sunlight adding to the splendor of the autumn foliage and the golden fields of hay surrounding the village. Ann wore bluejeans, a T-shirt and an Irish cable-knit sweater for the three hundred mile drive to Boston because she often liked to nap on the mattress in the back of the van. Apparently talked out, she sat lost in thought as they hummed south on the Northway.

When Ben finally drove up in front of the Ritz-Carlton, Ann asked if it were a real fancy hotel and Ben told her it had never been called a flophouse, as far as he knew.

"This time at least I won't call the doorman, 'sir,' like I did at the Algonquin." She was shifting to, or settling into, her little small-town girl in the big city role.

The formally dressed clerk at the registration desk did not seem in the least surprised by Ann's bluejeans. After consulting his list of reservations, he said, "I hope you enjoy your stay with us, Miss Kelly."

"What are you supposed to say when a guy like that says he hopes you enjoy your stay?" Ann whispered as they followed a bellboy toward the elevator. "I wanted to say I hoped *he'd* enjoy his stay with *us*."

The bellboy ushered them into adjoining rooms which were furnished in a quiet elegance unique to the Ritz. After asking, without giving Ben an option, to have the door between the two rooms left open, she began walking around on her toes. When the bellboy had left she said, "Pardon me, but I'm afraid to walk on this carpet, I'm afraid to sit in chairs like that, and I'd *never* lie on that bed. Well, hardly ever."

Soon she spotted one of the outsized Ritz menus on the desk, and after studying it asked Ben to explain all the items written in French. The hors d'oeuvres had a special fascination, she'd never had any. "Listen," she said finally, "could I just have a whole bunch of hors d'oeuvres instead of dinner?"

"I don't see why not."

Before going down to the dining room she put on a yellow dress, the best that Fashion Corners had to offer, and good enough for Boston to judge by the admiring glances she got from several men in the lobby (very un-Ritz-like behavior). A senatorial-appearing waiter did not, however, smile when she explained that she wanted nothing but a variety of hors d'oeuvres but soon delivered them to her. A string trio played Chopin in a corner, three men in tuxedos who looked as though they might have been the same ones who played at the Lost Lake Inn what seemed so long ago.

After dinner Ben took Ann to the Bolshoi ballet, the first professional dancers she had ever seen. As the exuberant Russians soared into the air and almost tore the stage apart with their folk dances, Ann kept saying, "I don't believe it, I *don't believe it* . . ." She clapped with such enthusiasm that she stood out from the crowd and during the curtain call one male dancer blew her a kiss. She made a gesture of catching it and holding it up to her cheek. The dancer laughed. Ben had often been bored at the ballet. Not this time.

Afterward she asked if it were safe to walk at night in Boston, and because it was a zesty October evening with a harvest moon riding high over the steeples and skyscrapers of the city he did not feel like saying no. Running ahead of him on the sidewalk, Ann leapt into the air, doing a surprisingly good imitation of a *grand jeté en tournant*, a phrase which she kept repeating with relish after he'd told it to her.

"How come you know everything?" she asked with her mischievous grin. "Where did you go to college?"

It was a direct question that he had often done his best to avoid.

"Near here," he replied.

"Boston College? B.U.? I bet it was Harvard!"

"Guilty."

"Why didn't you tell me? Are you *ashamed* of it, for god's sake?"

"I don't know. When I was in the army I learned to keep quiet about it. You could get in a lot of fights. And I was embarrassed by my dad. Toward the end, when he was drinking a lot and my mother's family was giving him a hard time, he got to be a kind of professional Harvard man. All his pipes had an *H* on them and he had the big coffee cups, the chair with the seal and all that nonsense. He even made me go to reunions with him, and there wasn't much for me to do while he staggered around with his buddies. I loved

465

my father, but I never wanted to be like that."

"Like I can't stand all that Irish jazz," Ann said, and squeezed his hand.

He was surprised by his confession because his antipathy toward Harvard was part of a private pain he'd never explained to anyone, not Heidi in all their years of marriage, not even Rose, who from the first had been self-conscious, he felt, about her background and his somehow clashing. Fortunately Ann quickly dropped the subject, as well as his hand as she darted about the sidewalk again, imitating the leaps of the ballet dancers. When passing Bostonians glanced at her with amused astonishment, she said, "What's the matter, folks? Ain't you never seen a *grand jeté en tournant?*"

When they reached their hotel he took her to the Ritz bar—a discreet oasis offering the best martinis in the world—where she proceeded to order three, count them, three Shirley Temples as rapidly as she could drink them. This fine watering hole had changed not at all in the past thirty years, he noted. His father had often sat in that corner under the window with his reunion hat still on the back of his head, and Heidi had sat at one or another of these small tables when she was hardly older than Ann was now, a nervous young Livingston girl carefully dressed for a Harvard weekend.

"This is sort of a creepy place," Ann said, "nice and all, but creepy all the same." A moment later, she said, "Are all those Russian dancers communists?"

"Well, I doubt if they're Republicans." Not too funny, Ben.

"Well, if they can dance like that, where do I sign up? Actually I wish I never saw those Bolshoi people. I'll never dance again."

"You're a beautiful dancer—"

"I'm great with the Funky Chicken. Period."

Perhaps in anticipation of the hours ahead, Ben drank enough brandy to get really sleepy. When they returned to their rooms, Ann gave him an enthusiastic hug and kiss "for tonight and everything, everything," then went to her room.

He'd almost dropped off to sleep when he heard her come in.

"Ben, am I waking you up?"

"Not quite."

"I'm way too keyed up to sleep," she said, perching on the bottom of his bed, her pajamas a white glow in the dim light from the window. "I have a million things I want to talk about."

He shut his eyes, as though to hide from her the intense fantasy he had of her joining him in the bed, feeling her warm firm body against him, smelling the fragrance of her hair . . .

"Ben? Are you awake?"

"Just barely, honey. We have a big day tomorrow. After we see Mr. Gold, we can . . . we can talk all you want . . ."

"Okay," she murmured, obviously disappointed, and then her fragrance became reality as she kissed him on the cheek. "I love you," she said. "In a sister-in-law way, of *course.*"

And she was gone, leaving him to the pain and pleasure of the fantasy where he'd left off.

In the morning they had a leisurely breakfast in his room before their eleven o'clock conference with Bernard Gold.

"Do you always live this way when you leave home?" she asked as she tasted her shirred eggs, a dish she'd never had before.

"When I can afford it. Some hotels became a habit. My parents and my grandparents stayed here. Their theory was that we small-town people should enjoy the best of the cities whenever we get a chance. After all, we economize like crazy the rest of the time."

There were exclamations of delight as Ann lifted the silver top of a dish and discovered hot popovers.

"My diet is going to hell, but I'll start again when I get home."

There was a brief silence while she ate. Suddenly, without preamble, she asked, "Is Mr. Gold a Jew?"

467

"I doubt if he's a Presbyterian, but you never can tell."

"You're laughing at me."

"Annie, I'll tell you what the Jews are like if you tell me what the Irish are like."

"Well, mostly we drink and fight and go to church and have big families we can't support. Anyway, that's what Rosie told dad one day when he was saying the Irish were better than everybody else."

"Rosie did have a way with words when she got riled. Don't ask me to sum up a whole religion, Annie. It's silly. We're going to see one Bernard Gold. He has the reputation of being a good publisher. He had the guts to start his own firm. He stands ready to gamble about a hundred thousand dollars or more to bring out our book. He's a reputable businessman or Claudia wouldn't recommend him. What else do you have to know?"

"Yeah, but is he *nice?*"

"I imagine that like most publishers, he's nice when your work is good and makes money and not so nice when it isn't and doesn't."

The Unicorn Press occupied a dozen or so rooms on the third floor of an old office building not far from the Boston Common. Except for book jackets on the walls, there were no decorations. The bare wooden floors, the green metal room partitions, the stacks of filing cabinets and the old wooden desks reminded Ben of newspapers and editorial rooms of magazines where he'd worked. This atmosphere and the clicking of typewriters, the bustle of secretaries and harried-appearing young men in shirtsleeves made him feel at home. A receptionist asked them to wait in a small room with hard wooden chairs and no window. Through an open door they could hear a man behind a green partition shouting into a telephone.

"Damn it, Harry, I can't help it. I can't take this, one delay after another. A contract is a contract. If you can't deliver, I'm going to find someone who can. Monday is your absolutely last deadline. Don't even bother to ask me for another..."

"I hope that isn't Mr. Gold," Ann said to Ben.

A few minutes later the receptionist led the way to the partition surrounding the source of the conversation they'd overheard, which was indeed Bernard Gold. He was a tall, very thin man of about fifty with an ascetic face and a ring of black hair around his bald head. On this chilly October morning he was wearing a red shirt and gray work pants, as though he were going hunting. Seeing Ben and Ann, he stood up and his strident voice became surprisingly warm as he said, "Sorry to keep you waiting. Publishing is like being a supply officer in the army sometimes—I have to spend about half my time yelling on the telephone."

Ben grinned. "In a small way, I'm in the publishing business myself."

"Of course—your newspaper up there. Sit down. Is this the collaborator who impressed Claudia so much?"

He was charming as he offered straight wooden chairs with a flourish. After shaking hands, he sat behind his cigarette-scarred desk. "Pardon me if I get right to the basics. This is a hell of a morning for me. My editor, Mrs. Roper, is stuck home with a sick child and my assistant is in New York. About half my girls are out for one reason or another, probably the good weather. So I don't really know where I'm at."

He paused and lit a cigarette with a fancy gold desk lighter, which did not seem to go with the room. "Now to the basics," he said. "One, we love your book, the whole idea and the work you've done."

Ann sighed, and her look of tension turned beatific. Ben too smiled. For Ann, Gold had definitely passed the niceness test.

"My second point is this: we have to face the economic realities of reproducing photographs. I hope this doesn't upset you but I feel that we should keep this book as short as the

469

idea permits. People will buy a book with one hundred pictures as willingly as they will buy one with two hundred. Fifty would be a bit skimpy, but if we padded it out with text, we might get away with even that. I'm trying to hold our price down to fifteen dollars. The more we go above that, the more sales will fall. I'm also hoping for a soft-cover sale, something that could be sold for maybe three dollars. Are you with me on this?"

"Only fifty pictures?" Ann asked with disappointment.

"I'm not setting a limit," Gold replied. "I'm saying, be as selective as you can. You may find that the discipline of that may even be effective in artistic terms. And try to give me a text of about fifty pages, in addition to the pictures. Are you with me on this, Ben?"

"I can see the need for brevity."

"Which brings me to deadlines. I'd like to bring this out in the fall, a year from now. I have a hole in my list. Let's aim for October. That means I'll need finished photographs and copy before the end of April. That gives you about six months. Can you meet a deadline like that?"

"Yes," Ben said, and Ann looked surprised.

"Good! Now about publicity. I have a girl here who gets out news releases, but Helen Roper is the genius who makes people notice our books. She's gone over your project and thinks there's a chance of getting a presentation of *Small Town* on TV, not only to help sales directly but soon enough to help move the books into the stores before publication. It's just rotten luck that she can't be here today. She can be in touch by phone and mail, of course, but for a matter this important, you really should meet. Do you have to head right back for the hills, or is there any chance you could come in here Monday morning?"

"Oh, we can stay," Ann said, "can't we, Ben?"

"I guess so."

"Fine. Now one more thing. Our contract gives me an option on your next two books. Claudia fought that, but I held on. I don't regard that option as simply routine. I have several ideas which might be just right for you two. If I can figure out a way to keep the price of picture books down, we may be able to open up a new market, or reopen one that people thought would never come back. Are you with me?"

"I'm with *you*," Ben said.

Gold's telephone rang. Picking it up, he shouted, "God damn it, Harry, is that you again? No, not one more day. I don't care how much you have to kick ass, I'm not going to hold up a book that's already been advertised just because you..."

Pausing, he gave a cheery wave to Ben and Ann. "Sorry about this. See you Monday at about ten. Thanks so much for coming in."

"He's nice," Ann said as they went down on the elevator, "but something tells me we better meet our deadline."

Feeling so high they didn't know what to do with themselves, they strolled across the Boston Common. A brisk wind sent tattered armies of leaves scurrying ahead of them as they made their way between couples lying on blankets to catch the last of the autumn sun. Unlike the fields around Livingston, the Common offered no privacy, but some of the young people solved that problem by simply ignoring passers-by.

"Boy, these Bostonians really make out, don't they?" Ann said. "I thought they were all supposed to be such great Puritans or something!"

Ben laughed. "Proper Bostonians are on the way out, I guess."

"Let's sit here," Ann said as they approached an empty bench.

"It's a little chilly, isn't it?"

"Those people on the grass don't seem to mind." She smiled her smile. "Do you want me to keep you warm?"

"I don't think that will be necessary," he said, and turned up the collar of his sportscoat as he sat down on the bench.

For her meeting with Gold, Ann had worn her oatmeal-colored short-sleeved cashmere sweater and gray flannel skirt. The chill breeze put goose bumps on her arms. She rubbed them as she sat down, and it seemed altogether natural to put his arm around her shoulders to shield her from the wind . . . a fairly gross piece of rationalization, he instantly realized, but didn't remove his arm.

"You feel good," she said.

"Likewise."

A moment of silence, followed by, "Mr. Gold said so much so fast I'm all confused."

Likewise again, he thought, but for different reasons. "We'll get a letter spelling it all out."

"He really wants us to do more books?"

"Sounds that way. We'll have to see how things go."

"But the signs are good, aren't they? Wouldn't you say we have a damn good chance if we work really hard?"

"Maybe."

"*Probably*, I bet . . . Ben, can I work with you on the next two books?"

"I think we ought to see how this one works first."

"Well, don't you *want* me to work with you? You don't have to give me a share of the profits, I'll just need enough to live on and that wouldn't be much if we stayed together, and I'd have my college money . . . except what's the *point* of going to college if I'm already working with a great photographer?"

"Annie," he said softly, caressing the soft cashmere over her shoulder, "someday you and I are going to have to face up to some hard realities."

"Like what?"

"Like Ebon Winslow, for one. How do you think he'd feel if you stayed with me as my permanent assistant wherever the work took me?"

"Oh, Eb wouldn't even notice. He'd be too busy counting pine needles."

"That's not very kind, Annie." (Ben, you hypocrite . . .) "Be honest, you really love Eb, don't you?" (Don't be too honest . . .)

"Sort of." She blushed prettily. "Maybe I do . . . I guess . . ."

"Well, then, shouldn't *he* be the center of your life? Shouldn't you be planning things around him?"

"How can I? He doesn't plan anything around *me*. He knows how I feel about Livingston . . . What does he do about it? . . ."

"What would you do if Eb left you for someone else?"

"He'd come back, he always does."

A pause. Two boys started throwing a football a few yards away. Somewhere nearby a fire engine screamed, almost causing Ben to run for his camera and his car the way he did in Livingston. The wind blew leaves around the bench. Ann snuggled closer.

"Face this hard reality, sir . . . your little sister-in-law loves you . . ." And when he started to withdraw his arm she quickly added, "I mean, you're so big and warm and know so much . . ."

"Annie, I think you've got some things to sort out, to put in perspective . . ."

She straightened up. "Do I have to? Why can't I just let it all sort itself out. It will, sooner or later . . ."

"Well, they say sailors who just drift instead of steering often hit the rocks."

"What do *you* think I should do?"

She'd put the ball back in his court . . . God, and she was only seventeen . . . He watched the boys throw the football back and forth for several moments, took a deep breath for conviction he didn't feel, and said, "What I think is that in the long run it would be best for you to go up there to that Hudson River Academy Eb talked about for you. You'll be able to be near him and still have plenty of freedom. Next fall you can go to college wherever you like and keep on with your photography in your spare time—"

473

"Why are you saying this to me? You don't mean it." Her face was pale.

"I do . . . and it's because I care about you, about all of us—"

"Well, how about finishing the book?"

"It's pretty much all finished. I can tie up the loose ends."

"How about the next books?"

"We maybe could work together on your summer vacations if it didn't foul up you and Eb—"

"And how about the publicity tour?"

"Annie, I've never been much for those things, but I think it would be great fun for you and I'm sure you'd be good at it. Maybe you could get Ebon to go with you. The two of you, I'm sure, could sell anything—"

"Ben, you know what? . . . I think you're plain chicken." Her voice was cold as she got up. "Come on, old dad, let's head on back to the hotel and get you a *nap*."

The walk back was in stony silence. As they entered the lobby he broke it to ask if she would like to have lunch. She said no. Following him into his room she went to stand at the window, staring at the cars inching through traffic below. Her face was still pale and she was breathing hard. Ben felt a sudden, irrational return of his fears about heart attacks, but of course Ann was not ill. Just angry. Hell hath no fury . . .

"Annie, I'm sorry I upset you—"

"Come on, Ben," she said, turning abruptly to face him. "You're always asking me to face reality. Can you really face a little?"

"I hope so."

"I said you were chicken. I meant it. The only reason you want me to go to that school and stop working with you is that you're afraid we'll wind up in the sack together. Isn't *that* true?"

"No . . . yes . . . I guess that's one reason, but—"

"Well, why are you so scared of me? Do you think I'm

474

some little plaster virgin? Do you think I'd fall all apart if you touched me?"

"Annie, this doesn't have anything to do with virginity."

"But it has to do with little orphan Annie needing to be protected, doesn't it? Ben, you don't even know me. How can you have the nerve to plan my whole life without even taking the trouble to *know* me?"

"I always thought I knew you fairly well."

"How can you? You think I'm so cute and full of girlish enthusiasm and god knows what all, except it's all bull . . . We don't talk, not really—we just circle around each other. I could never talk to you the way I used to talk to Rosie, and sometimes even strong, silent Ebon. They're the only two who ever really knew me at all, and they never tried to plan out my whole life—"

"I'm sorry, I—"

"Do you *want* to know me? Will you let me *talk*? Will you be shocked and angry and stamp around, or do you really want to know me?"

"Of course I do, but I can't help suggesting you don't tell me things you'll later regret, Annie."

"Oh *boy* . . . talk about stuffy talk . . . just be a *person* for a while, will you?"

She lay down on the bed with her shoulders on the pillows.

"Now please *listen*. I'm not trying to make you feel sorry for me, but here are some hard realities, as you like to say . . . my father's a drunk and my mother died when I was twelve. Rosie did her very best for me, but I was a wild kid."

"So I've heard."

"Did you hear I got pregnant when I was fourteen?"

"No."

"Without Rosie, I guess I would have died. She took me down to Albany to get it fixed, all nice and legal. She never told anybody, including even you, and she *never* made me feel bad about it."

475

"That's the way Rosie would be."

"I'm *talking* about *me*. Do you want me to tell you how I got pregnant?"

"If you want to."

"I was thirteen. A guy asked me to go steady with him. He was fifteen and it was a big deal for me. Do you know what going steady meant then?"

"Not exactly."

"It was almost like getting married. I had a guy I could count on. He was my old man—that's what we called them. If other kids bugged me, he chased them away. We ate lunch together in the cafeteria. He took me for rides in his boat. He was a big handsome guy, and boy, was I proud of him. The only trouble was, he said that fooling around was part of going steady. He told me not to worry about getting pregnant, because he'd take care of it, and he said that even if that did happen, we'd get married. Young kids often get married in Livingston when the girl gets knocked up."

She seemed to be forcing herself to use street language, perhaps, he thought, to find protection in toughness, and to shock him into thinking of her as an adult.

"Anyway, I did get pregnant when I was fourteen. Rosie had explained everything, and I knew the signs. I wasn't too worried because I thought I'd get married and I kind of liked the idea. The only trouble was, my steady date didn't turn out to be so steady when I told him the big news. He said he couldn't marry me on account of my religion and before long he was even saying he couldn't be sure the baby was his. Finally he told me to get lost, in just those words. I was in a state of shock, the doctor in Albany said. And when I got back to school I didn't feel much better because my steady date was going all around saying I screwed everybody—that was his idea of insurance in case I tried to get money out of him."

"What a little SOB. Where is he now?"

476

"He's still in school. God didn't smite him. Of course the stories he told made it open season on me for all the guys in town and a lot of them got mad as hell when I didn't come across with hardly an introduction. I cried a lot, I admit it. And I started to dream about doing something that would make all those creeps have to look *up* to me for a change. I needed anything that would wipe the dirty smirks off their faces. I just happened to luck into photography. They had a darkroom in the school, and your books were in the library. I thought that if one guy who came from Livingston could get to be a big-shot photographer, why not little me?"

"I'm glad those books did something—"

"They did a *lot*. Eb was in my gym class, and when I realized that he was your son, I got up my nerve enough to make friends with him. You know, that was when your divorce was in the works and Eb was almost as mixed up as I was. Anyway, I was grateful to him because he *knew* how scared I was of fooling around, and never asked for much. That's how we got together . . . and we've been pretty much together ever since. More or less . . ."

"I'm glad you told me that about my son."

"Do you want me to tell you what I know about you?" The twinkle was returning to her eye.

"Shoot."

"Rosie and I could always talk. She worried all the time about being so sick that she couldn't make out with you. God, how she hated that. And she loved you for being so nice about it. She never could get over that."

"With Rosie it wasn't that much of a hardship."

"I know, but I think I understand one reason why you get so kind of edgy every time I touch you . . . do you know what I'm trying to say?"

"I'm not sure."

"Well, this may sound funny coming from somebody you think of as a *kid*, but I think you make sex too important,

477

maybe just because you haven't had any in a long while. I've been scared to death of it ever since I took that awful trip to Albany, but I feel safe with you . . ."

"Annie, I'll give you my best try at honesty by saying that I *don't* feel safe with you."

"I know, you're worried about Eb . . . well, I've just about decided I never could live his way for long . . . I guess I sound awful, but I don't want his good simple life. I don't mean to put it down either, but, well . . ." She smiled her special smile . . . "How're you going to keep them down on the farm after they've seen the Ritz, not to mention the Bolshoi? . . ."

"You say you've just *about* decided—"

"I say, what would *you* say if I just broke up with Eb, just solved the whole thing with a clean break? I'd move in with you and we wouldn't have to have Eb on our conscience, he'd be off with some other girl—"

"And where would we be ten years later?"

"How about here at the Ritz? You'd be fifty-five and I'd be twenty-seven. Is that so bad?"

"How about ten years after that?"

"Come on, Ben. Who gives a damn about what's going to happen twenty years from now? Probably the whole world will blow up. Don't laugh. Ben, I'm serious. I want to be your collaborator, your assistant . . . and your girl."

"Annie, it's a damn flattering proposition. I'm *not* making fun of you or taking you lightly. I know you're serious, but did you ever consider if I am? Don't answer that. It's a perfect example of my proven ability to louse things up by talking too much . . . Let's please leave it for now that we both need time to think. We'll need some fancy food for thought, and *that* at least is easy to solve. It calls for some puttin' on the Ritz. Well, we're in the right place for it." Feeling like an idiot, he hurried her out of the room.

478

At the luncheon table, where she ordered her first lobster, Ann did a quick change from the startlingly experienced young woman to a carefree seventeen-year-old who acted exactly her age.

"I want to see all the sights in Boston," she announced. "Will you show me every one of them?"

The first stop on their agenda was Harvard. As he drove over to Cambridge she told him, "Rosie brought me here once a long time ago, when things were rough for me. We drove down just for a lark in the old pickup truck. The traffic was terrible and we really didn't know where to go. Finally we located the *Constitution* and everybody got furious at me for climbing the rigging. We were lucky the head cop was Irish. Rosie put on her best brogue. The guy let me go but got sore when Rosie wouldn't give him a date. He escorted us back to our motel. I've never had a police escort, before or since."

Harvard Yard, like the Ritz-Carlton, had changed little in the past thirty years. Students wore dungarees instead of flannels, but the tree-shaded lawns surrounded by the great brick buildings which exhibited such a startling variety of design, from Colonial through Victorian to modern, were just as Ben

479

remembered them. Some of the students still carried green bookbags, and a tall, pink-faced professor who was walking toward the steps of Widener Library seemed to Ben to stride along with that peculiar mixture of arrogance and humility which a tenured job at Harvard so often bestowed.

Ann stood looking at the great marble columns of the Widener Library across the quadrangle from the white steeple of Memorial Chapel. "How many books are in there?" she asked.

"I don't know. I think it's supposed to be the biggest college library in the world."

Ann grinned. "You Protestants really do get it together sometimes, don't you?"

"Sometimes."

As they walked toward the administration building, she asked, "Were you happy when you were here?"

"Not very."

"Why not?"

"I missed my girl in Livingston. I didn't have many friends here. In my day Harvard was sort of prejudiced against blacks, Jews and small-town boys."

That couldn't have been the only reason, Ben reflected, but he had been acutely lonely throughout his college years. It came as something of a shock to realize that he'd been equally lonely throughout most of his life, had never really felt in full communion with another person before meeting Rose. Maybe she had cured him of whatever disease had made him isolate himself from other people. And now with Ann he had opened himself further than he had with anyone but Rosie . . . not fully, probably not so wisely either. . . .

When he showed her the great bronze statue of John Harvard thinking in his chair, Ann called out, "Hello, John Harvard, we bring you greetings from Livingston, New York. What have you got on your mind up there? . . . He's a dummy. Put him in a special class. What else has this place got to offer?"

480

As Ben showed her the bronze rhinoceroses outside the zoology building, he found that his thoughts were getting increasingly muddled, or perhaps clarified, if the wrong way. Maybe Ann was right and his old-fashioned mind just kept making too big a thing of sexual encounters. Why *not* turn this weekend into something more than a boring sightseeing tour? Why not eventually even go ahead and marry Ann? So what if it was only for a few years? Half a loaf . . . Rosie had foreseen a possible involvement with Ann . . . she'd said there was no reason why he couldn't have a long, happy marriage with her but had warned that Ann was capable of a certain toughness, a comment she'd later withdrawn, saying it came mostly from her own jealousy. It seemed the natural, flattering thing for her to say at the time, but in retrospect it occurred to Ben that it might have been one more effort at a brave front like her "Mack the Knife" talk. He wished like hell he knew, because his feeling of recklessness was growing. Life *was* short, Rosie would testify to that . . . he was already forty-five and a lovely young woman was practically begging to go to bed with him. Why examine all sides of every question like an old man? What was the matter with him? "Old dad," indeed. . . .

Back at the hotel, both edgy and tired from their sightseeing, they found the Friday afternoon cocktail hour in full swing at the Ritz bar. If Ben had been alone he might have spent a glum evening, as he had so many times before in his life, but Ann had some of her father's ability to strike up new acquaintanceships at a bar. She had, according to her, so few friends, except for Ebon, in Livingston that her outgoing manner surprised Ben. Here, as a stranger, she joked with people at nearby tables and was so saucily charming that Ben soon found himself surrounded by men and women who were pulling up chairs to join them. (Of course, he thought, she might also be telling him in her fashion that if *he* didn't appreciate her . . .)

They ate dinner with a group of new "friends" who had

just come from a wedding, Ben soon finding himself involved in toasting a bride he had never seen. Some of the wedding guests were Harvard students, handsome in their formal clothes. One tall blond young man with gleaming hair to his shoulders asked Ann to dance. Nothing wrong with that, Ben instructed himself as they glided to the sedate rhythms of the Ritz quartet, and with it realized that this was almost certain to repeat itself if he traveled with a girl so much younger than himself. . . .

Still swept up with the wedding party, they went to a discotheque, where the music was even louder than it had been in Albany. Annie danced with several of the young men and even persuaded Ben to try the Hustle with her. Trying not to be embarrassed—or wholly left out—he learned from her as best he could but felt fat, awkward and ridiculous nonetheless. After he'd beaten a hasty retreat to the table she blew him a kiss and went gyrating into the arms of the tall blond student—who just happened to be there? Not likely. He clearly was on her trail.

It was late when they got back to their rooms at the hotel. Ben's head ached from too much noise and too much booze, and he felt thoroughly down . . . The brave what-the-hell, gather-ye-rosebuds-while-ye-may mood of the afternoon lost in the reality of the hustle and a blond Harvard boy.

"What's the matter?" Ann asked, glancing at him as they came in the door.

"Just a headache."

"How about an Alka-Seltzer?"

"Too late to get one."

"I'll try the night desk. You hit the sack." A bead of sweat was still visible on her upper lip from the exertions of the evening.

Soon after he'd put on his pajamas and gotten under the covers she appeared with the Alka-Seltzer and a glass of water. He sat up, mixed and swallowed. Age will be served, he thought. Small joke.

He lay back down and she smoothed out his covers as if he were a patient.

"How do you feel?"

"Lonely, to tell you the truth."

"Mister, I know how that is."

She lay down on the bed beside him, put her arms around him. They felt so good that his muscles stiffened, as though from shock.

"Now don't get all tense," she said. "I'm not trying to get you to lay me. I know I said a lot of stuff a while ago, but to tell the truth, I'd just like to stay here for a while. Okay? . . ."

"More than okay, Annie. Much more . . ."

It was three A.M. when Ben woke up to find Ann asleep in her pajamas on top of the covers beside him, with a silk counterpane to keep her warm. Except for an occasional car outside he heard nothing except the soft, even sound of her breathing. She'd used a different shampoo or perfume; it smelled like Chanel No. 5, a scent he had often bought for Heidi long, long ago in their good days . . . come to think of it, nearly every woman he had ever known had used it, giving the fragrance all sorts of confusing connotations, some pleasurable, some still tinged with regret.

Ben had trouble getting back to sleep. Dancing with the wedding guests, Ann had been very much the belle of the ball, but in the dim light from the window, with her hair tousled around her head on the pillow beside him, she looked more like a vulnerable child. Or was that perception another of his defenses against a not unnatural inclination? Was he that uptight that he couldn't even accept this comfort from Ann without feeling threatened?

Much too tense for sleep, tossing and turning, he couldn't avoid waking Ann.

"What's the matter?"

"I can't seem to get comfortable—"

483

"I can take a hint," she told him, kissed him on the forehead, and headed for her room, pausing only long enough to smile sleepily, shake her head, and say, "You keep this up, and I may give up . . ."

Awaking soon after dawn, Ben tried to put her last line out of his head. It should have been what he wanted to hear. Should have been . . . Well, he'd take Ann to see the glass flowers at Harvard, then a Chinese restaurant, which should be a novelty since there were none in Livingston. In the afternoon a trip to the aquarium . . . a nice, proper program that sounded like the holidays he had arranged for his children when they were ten or twelve years old. . . . He began pacing his room, wishing she'd wake up. At eight he looked in on her, finding her fast asleep with the covers tangled around her waist. She'd discarded her pajamas and was lying on her stomach, exposing her smoothly tanned back. In the big bed, she looked tiny—she actually weighed not much more than a hundred pounds—but as she stirred he got a hint of the fullness of her breasts, the untanned sides of which stood out in contrast to her bronzed shoulders.

"Ben?" she said, suddenly opening her eyes.

He was, of course, embarrassed. "I'm sorry, I didn't mean to be like some peeping Tom . . . I just came in to see if you were awake and you looked so damn lovely . . ."

"Me? Sleeping Beauty?"

"That's right . . ." He was relieved she was letting him off the hook with her light tone . . . "And now, Sleeping Beauty, how would you like to have breakfast and go see the fabled glass flowers?"

"*Glass* flowers?" She sat up, somewhat negligently holding the edge of the sheet over her breasts.

While he described the glass flowers and their German origin, her hand with the sheet kept slowly slipping downward, only to remember its duty at the last moment. Or was he again being dramatic? . . . Was this a game or was she just being unself-conscious as she yawned away the sleep?

"Well, the glass flowers sound lovely," she said and yawning again casually approved the rest of the day's agenda.

While she dressed he ordered breakfast, and soon after he heard her telephone ring. Although he could not make out her words through the door, he could hear her talking excitedly and wondered who could be calling her at the Ritz. Finally she burst into his room.

"Ben," she said, "Trevor wants to take me flying! I've never been up in a plane, can I go? *Please* . . .

" 'Trevor'? What in the hell is a *Trevor*? Sounds like a stage name to me . . ."

"Don't be mean. His name is Trevor Peabody. No kidding. He's the one I was dancing with last night, the tall guy with the terrific hair. He asked me if I wanted to see Boston from the air, but I didn't think he was serious—"

"Is this guy a pilot?"

"He has his license and he belongs to a flying club. He wasn't sure he could get a plane but he has one now and—"

"Do you know anything about this joker, Annie?"

"He's in his second year at Harvard. You can't knock him for that, can you? I mean, being an old Harvard man yourself, and all . . ."

He winced—unnoticeably, he hoped. "What kind of a plane is he going to use?"

"Oh, I don't know. A Piper Cub or something. He says the autumn foliage is just beautiful from the air and I've never, never been farther off the ground than I can jump, please let me go, Ben, *please* . . ."

"I won't stop you, honey. Of course, go, have a fine time . . ."

In a rush of thanks she began making up her face and fixing her hair. When the waiter arrived with breakfast, she accepted only a cup of coffee, which she gulped down.

"What's the big hurry?"

"He wants to start early. He says that if the weather stays

485

good we might have time to go all the way to Nantucket. Do you know anything about Nantucket?"

Nantucket, fuck it, he said to himself . . . or rather meant to, but some escaped as a mumble.

"What?"

"I'm sorry, nothing, just a dumb private joke."

"Oh. Well, don't *worry* about me. He says he can land that thing anywhere. He must be a good pilot, Ben. His father was a flyer in the war and taught him. They have oodles and oodles of money. I got the idea that I was supposed to drop dead when he told me that his name was Peabody. He pronounced it funny . . . '*Pee*buddy.' "

"Funny money *Pee*buddy."

"Ben, are you mad? Please don't be. I'm having such a good time. I hate leaving you all alone here but I'll be back way before dark. Tell you what . . . you go see the glass flowers and tell me all about them." And giving him a quick hug and kiss on the chin, she almost danced out the door. If she'd done a few cartwheels in the hall on the way to the elevator he'd hardly have been surprised.

When she was gone he sat down in his room, slowly drank his coffee. The elaborate breakfast under the covered dishes tasted flat and he soon gave up on it. The day stretching ahead seemed endless.

But this is ridiculous, he lectured himself. A man nearly forty-six years old who can't spend one whole day in Boston by himself must be in a bad way indeed. Really? Well, so be it, but he found he had a violent urge to get drunk enough to blot out the hours until she came back.

He continued his lecture. What did he expect in what he could only call his fit of adolescent jealousy . . . that he'd lost her forever to a Harvard undergraduate who would bed her down in his Piper Cub while circling over Nantucket? And what did this say for his confidence in her . . . his respect for her? . . . While she'd been telling him about that business of her early youth he'd felt wholly compassionate, but it

486

seemed now that he was still enough of the stern old upstate New Yorker to suspect deep down—however irrationally—that one who has strayed will do it again. Good lord, what leftover Puritan self-righteousness . . . and he shook his head in disgust.

End of lecture. Very logical. But it did nothing for his anger. Didn't *he* have some rights here too? Didn't he have *some* right to be angry? After all, when a man takes a young lady to spend a weekend at the Ritz in Boston, does he have to expect her to *fly* off with some stranger she meets in a bar? . . .

Scared. He was scared too. Sure, chances were that Ann would return safely, but everyone knew that light planes flown by amateurs had a high accident rate. Ever since his father had died, Ben had been strongly aware of the fact that death could happen anytime, anyplace. Rosie's awful passing, of course, only reinforced it. Before Annie had been gone an hour he began imagining the state police calling him with news of an accident. Noticing that she had left her purse on a desk, he realized that that call could not come, Ann had taken no identification. If she and her Trevor Peabody were killed, how long would it be before anyone could identify her body? . . . In his mind she was a still white form—shaking his head to rid it of that awful vision, he suddenly realized that what he was presently suffering was probably a fair sample of what a forty-five-year-old man could expect if he was foolish enough to allow himself to be involved with a seventeen-year-old girl. It would not be just Ebon who'd be competing for her attentions but practically every male of her own age wherever she went. No matter how much her ambitions involved her with him, she'd be full of desires—innocent or otherwise—to dance, to talk and to fly, one way or another, with her own generation. Now how could he ever expect to overcome that?

Many times he'd decided to cool it with Ann, as she'd say, but giving her up was as hard as renouncing booze. In some sense Ann, he was beginning to realize, had provided a relief similar to alcohol during the months of his despair after Rosie's death. When his whole future had appeared to be wiped out, she had shown him that some possibility, some warmth was left. She'd reawakened his interest in his profession and might have saved him from one long last journey into the oblivion of alcohol. He ought to be grateful to her for that, no matter what happened.

But someday his trip with Ann—like a drug trip?—would have to end, he'd have to face up to the fact that nothing constructive could be built with her even if she wasn't his son's girl . . . except in facing it all the despair she'd helped to hold back for him came down on his head. The sensations of Rose suffering her last heart attack came flooding back, and along with them the old questions about whether he'd really done everything possible to prevent it, had he been forceful enough in urging her to have her operation sooner in spite of her fear of it, had it really been a good idea for a woman in her condition to get married at all even though it seemed a reassurance to her at the time? . . .

There was no *point* in such questions. No more. Rose was in her grave. He tried to think of her the way she'd been those happy times aboard the *Princess* and at the ruins of Lost Lake Inn. Few would believe it, but looking back he realized they'd lived at such a pitch of exhilaration that the enforced absence of physical love just did not seem that important. Living with a woman who, out of her love, wanted to *give* herself but couldn't surely was infinitely better than living with a woman who could but wouldn't . . . love without sex was more sustaining than sex without love.

He had thought of Rose's dream about building a signal fire on the icy peak of Big Iron Mountain so much that sometimes he half believed they'd actually done it even though they had never known winter together. His picture of the leaping flames and the orange glow on the ice was more vivid than most of his real memories.

The pull of Rose was overwhelming, lasting . . . and, at least in part, what he had been trying to do was make another Rosie out of Ann, and when Ann at the age of seventeen didn't act like her sister he became, all unreasonably if perhaps understandably, angry and frustrated. Which was unfair to everyone. . . . Maybe this young flyer, Trevor Peabody, had arrived at just the right moment, like a captain of cavalry in an old-fashioned movie. At least his improbable name fitted that role. And instead of being pettishly angry, he ought to feel grateful for being rescued. Ought to . . .

He paced restlessly up and down his narrow room. Suddenly he very much wanted to go home. At least in Livingston he could work off steam by varnishing the *Princess* or any number of repair jobs on his house. What did he do when he was going crazy cooped up in a hotel room and didn't want to get drunk?

He took a walk and wanted to see Livingston even more. On the streets of Boston he recognized no one and no one recognized him. After the familiar combination of friendliness and hostility in Livingston, this business of walking among crowds without any emotion at all made him feel like an invisible ghost.

Even the lovers stretched on their blankets on the Common annoyed him. One young man had his hand firmly under the sweater of his girl, and god knew what she was doing to him. And doing it right out in the open with kids skipping rope and playing ball all around them. The Puritan within wasn't helping much either. . . .

When he returned to the Ritz the desk clerk told him that he had received a telephone call and handed him a slip of paper: "Call Ebon at Cliff House." Ebon would be aware that Ben usually stayed at the Ritz when in Boston, but he had almost never telephoned his father when he was out of town. Feeling apprehensive, Ben hurried to his room and placed the call. Ebon answered at first ring.

"Dad, what the hell is going on? I was supposed to meet

Ann here this morning. How come you're still in Boston?"

"Oh, god, Eb . . . I'm sorry . . . there's been so much going on here that I guess—"

"I was going to take her to Saratoga, she knew that. Where the hell is she, anyway? Let me talk to her."

"She's out . . ." At least he'd be spared Trevor Peabody.

"Goddamn it, I got tickets for the Performing Arts Center . . . I'm really fed to the teeth. Just what big business deal made you change your plan?"

"No *big deal*, Eb, but we do have another meeting with the publisher Monday—"

"So now you get to shack up at the Ritz for a nice long weekend. Very convenient. What's going on? . . . Does Annie feel too guilty to talk to me—"

"Eb, cut it out, it isn't like that at all"—okay, he asked for it—"she's not here, and if you must know why, she's out flying over Boston with one Trevor Peabody, whom she met in the bar last night."

A pause. Followed by a snicker? "So you got stood up too." Grim satisfaction.

"Something like that."

"You know, maybe she's incurable, maybe we both ought to say to hell with her."

"Eb, stop putting me in this. And try to remember"—you too, old dad—"that she's a seventeen-year-old girl . . . I'm doing what I can, by the way, to persuade her to go to that Hudson River school you mentioned—"

"Really?"

"Yes, really. And I've had another idea. How would you like to go on the publicity tour with her, if it comes off?"

"What the hell do I know about that kind of thing?"

"You know enough to escort her. And if you want to go on some of the talk shows with her, that might be arranged."

"What would *I* say?"

"They'll be talking about small towns. You live in one."

"Well, I don't know . . . let's see what her highness says.

490

And if she ever comes down to earth tell her to call me soon as possible. And tell her I'm still mad as hell."

He hung up with a bang.

Ben was just about to go down to lunch when his telephone again rang. It was the doorman. "There's a Miss Kelly here with a fifteen-dollar taxi bill she can't pay," he began.

"Tell her I'll be right down," he said, and, puzzled, he hurried to the elevator.

Looking embarrassed, Ann stood beside the yellow cab, her pretty blue dress looking stained and rumpled. "Oh, I'm *sorry*, everything awful happened and I didn't even have my purse—"

"Let's talk about it upstairs," he said, and paid the taxi. She clung to his arm as they walked through the lobby. In the elevator she began to sniffle and he gave her his handkerchief.

"Now what happened that was so awful?" he asked as they entered his room.

"Everything."

"Could you be a little more specific?"

"Well, first of all, I got sick in the damn plane. I didn't know that planes are like boats. I ruined my dress."

"That, at least, can be fixed. What else?"

"All that character wanted was to make out, even after I'd been sick. Can you believe that? He was awful, worse than the guys at home. And I always thought there was just something specially awful about Livingston guys."

"Do you want to tell me what happened?"

"Well, first he put the plane on this thing called automatic pilot, which meant that his hands were free and I mean, free. Then when we finally came down, he said that this friend had lent him an apartment and he wanted to show it to me. When I said no, he tried to talk me into it and to fool around a little right in his damned sports car with people all over the place in this parking lot by the airport. I finally climbed right

491

over the door because I couldn't find the damn latch. He yelled at me and away he went. So I had to take a taxi home from the airport . . ." She stopped, wiped her eyes, and half smiled as she shook her head and said, "You know, the truth is that in a way it's really all my fault . . ."

"How's that?"

"Do you remember that party we went to at Claudia's apartment in New York? When you said I was your collaborator, a lot of people thought I was your mistress. I got a big kick out of that. It made me sound all worldly and kind of mysterious. I loved playing that role. So when this Trevor character asked me if you were my father, I just smiled and said, 'Not exactly,' and I said the same thing when he asked if you were my boss. So the idea of meeting this really hot young mistress type really gave him ideas, as grammie would say, and he used up his whole month's allowance to rent a plane."

Ben laughed.

"It's not funny, Ben . . . believe me, I'm never going to play *that* game again . . ."

He nodded, and when she'd had a chance to calm down, told her that Ebon had called.

"Ebon! Oh, god, I was supposed to go to Saratoga with him today. I completely forgot—"

"Me too, I'm afraid."

"He'll kill me! He's been mad at me anyway for weeks and now he'll really cut my head off!"

"Well, he wants you to return his call."

"I'm scared to. He'll tell me he never wants to see me again . . . and I miss Eb, Ben. I don't know what I'd do without him."

"I suspect he'll be very glad to hear that. I guess you ought to just say that to him, and let him take it from there." He didn't add that it indeed seemed a rather abrupt switch from her previous show of disaffection with Eb. Her agreement to the date to go to Saratoga had certainly appeared to be a grudging one, which would account for her forgetting it. Wouldn't it? . . . The young lady had at least seemed to be of two minds. Maybe it was a combination of his own paternal act and her getting more than she'd bargained for with Harvard's wild-blue-yonder Trevor Peabody that had swung her back to Eb. Hell, Eb should be thanking him for taking her off to Boston, not sore at him. Clearly, the stage was set for passionate, tearful reconciliation.

"I think I'll go downstairs for a drink," he told her.

In Livingston a dry martini was a most rare gem, and this one in the Ritz bar now tasted especially good. While he sipped it, he acknowledged that his abrupt departure had only been partly for the sake of discreetness. He also didn't especially relish being in on the details of their loving exchange when she called him. Not too fatherly of him, but there it was. He ordered a second martini.

When he went back upstairs, Ann was still on the telephone in her room, with the door shut. From the muffled sounds, it seemed that she was crying, and then there were exclamations of obvious pleasure. Ben paced for what seemed like a long while before the door opened.

"Everything's great . . . I think, sort of," she said, wiping her face with his handkerchief.

"What does that mean?"

"Eb was terribly mad at first, just like I thought. Not just because I forgot our date. He's sore because you and I spend so much time together, Ben, and then the Trevor thing had him all uptight."

"So I gathered."

Ann sat on the edge of his bed. "He doesn't exactly forgive me, not all the way . . . he says we've got to have a chance to spend some time together without anybody . . . you know, bothering us . . ."

"That sounds very sensible," Ben replied heartily, trying to buoy his sinking heart.

"The thing is, he wants to take me camping," Ann said.

493

"He says to hell with school and college and everything. He wants to take me out there in the woods for about a week—"

"That sounds pretty exciting."

"Ben, I *hate* camping. I used to have to do that when I was a Girl Scout, and it's *awful*. You sleep in wet blankets on top of rocks and roots. You eat raw bacon and burned beans. Besides that, I'm scared of the damn woods. They have bears in there and some people say there are still wolves around. I know they have wild coy-dogs and rattlesnakes and moccasins! Why does Eb want to take me to a place like *that*?"

"Don't forget that he's an expert out there, Annie. He'll no doubt have you almost as comfortable as you'd be right here at the Ritz—"

"Baloney. But I guess it doesn't matter. I'm going . . ."

"Anything else bothering you?"

"He still wants me to go to that school in Albany."

"I hear it's a good place—"

"All he's trying to do is get me away from *you!*"

"I'm flattered, but maybe he's trying to force a decision, Annie. I don't blame him" (but I don't like it).

"You're just trying to hand me over to him. Nobody seems to really want me anymore. Eb says we have to talk a whole *week* before he even can be sure anymore whether he loves me. I assume if I can't put on a good enough act about how much I love the woods, he'll trade me in for a raccoon or something."

Ben laughed, feeling altogether too cheerful in the face of her gloom. After all, if the week in the woods didn't work out . . .

Ann appeared considerably down all afternoon, and a Chinese restaurant and the glass flowers didn't much help. As she peered into the cases of crystal blossoms, she seemed to Ben a fragile girl with those large, vulnerable eyes in her delicate face, almost a kind of glass flower herself, perhaps in need of a mature man's protection—and promptly if reluctantly dismissed the notion as a fine bit of middle-aged self-delusion.

494

That night, saying she was "really tired," Ann went to bed early. After a few drinks at the bar, Ben turned in and lay for a long while, wondering if she would perhaps come in and perch on the bottom of his bed for one of her talks.

She never did.

33

Next morning it was raining heavily, a cold, bitter foretaste of winter. Before Ann woke up, Ben bought the Sunday papers and was reading them over the wheeled-in breakfast table when she came into his room wearing her white pajamas and a sweater. She still looked subdued. After giving her a cup of coffee he said, "What do you want to do today? Boston doesn't close up like Livingston does on Sunday."

He handed her the entertainment pages of the *Herald*, which she studied for a moment before saying, "Hey, look at the movies! I never knew any town had so many movies!"

"Can you find any you want to see?"

"Oh, *all* of them. I've never seen an X-rated movie. Can we see one of them?"

"I'd rather not."

"Why?" And with a straight, mock-serious face, "Afraid it would make you too horny?"

"The couple I've seen made me feel sick."

"But you've taken all kinds of nudes. You did a whole book of them."

"My pictures celebrate, not desecrate, or at least they're supposed to. What else?"

"How about an R-rated?"

They finally settled on *The Turning Point,* which so entranced her that she demanded to sit through it all over again.

"Now I'm *sure* I want to be a dancer," she told Ben as they left the theater, "except, of course, I keep forgetting that I've got to be a woodchuck."

Her appetite whetted, they went on to *The Goodbye Girl* later that afternoon and, in the evening, *Annie Hall,* both of which she also loved.

With eyes burning, they walked back to the hotel. "You see, it can be just *nice* for people to go to bed with each other," Ann observed as they walked along, "nice and easy ... Too bad it isn't that way in real life ..." She had the grace not to look at him when she said it and he, for once, handled it with silence.

That night Ben went to sleep without any trouble. He dreamed of Rosie and her signal fire on the icy mountain again. When he awoke the next morning, he had no clear recollection of the details of the dream, but some of its warmth stayed with him and he was in a better mood than he had been in for a long time. Was he finally coming out of it? ...

Promptly at ten Ben and Ann presented themselves at the headquarters of the Unicorn Press. Bernard Gold was still busy shouting into his telephone, but the receptionist led them into a corner office which, alone on that floor, was well furnished—comfortable leather chairs on a pale green rug, a kidney-shaped desk, heavy gold-colored curtains, and an impressive assortment of paintings and photographs. No one was there when they entered, but almost immediately a middle-aged woman of striking appearance stepped from an inner door. She was small, not much bigger than Ann, and her face clearly showed that she was no youngster, but she was dressed with such flair and her dark eyes mirrored such vitality that she hardly seemed to need the chronology of youth.

"I'm Helen Roper," she said with an upperclass Boston

accent that she softened with a self-deprecating smile. "Do sit down. I'm sorry I couldn't be here Friday. I've been wanting to meet you, Mr. Winslow. I've been following your work a long time. And I knew you'd turn out to be just as enchanting as your pictures, Miss Kelly."

She was so pleasant that Ben was taken aback when she said, "The book at hand is fine, of course, but I have a major change to recommend. Make it more personal. Think of the narrator in the play *Our Town*. In your small town, show us where you were born, where you went to school, where you got married, your family burial place. Make it more of a *personal* tour."

"I'd like to think about that," Ben replied.

"It would give the book a better point of view and would perhaps interest TV programs more. You could give, in effect, a kind of illustrated tour of your small town with some emotional value."

"What if Annie here did the TV stint instead of me?" Ben asked.

"That could be . . ."

"And what if her boyfriend accompanied her? He's a college freshman, very handsome, and he grew up in the same town. He could come in as a sort of counterpoint guide."

"Could be intriguing visually. Are you stepping out of this, Ben? If you don't mind my calling you that?"

"Well, who the hell wants to watch a fat old man who can't dance or sing?"

She laughed. "I wouldn't say that's an entirely accurate description of yourself, but you've got a point, I suspect. Frankly, if these young people have the poise and talent to do the job, they might indeed put together quite an act. We'll see."

For the next hour they discussed the proposed changes in the book. "I'm sort of confused by all that," Ann said as they left and rode down in the elevator.

"Don't worry about it."

498

"Do you understand what we're supposed to do?"

"We have to rearrange a few pictures, add a few, take out a lot and write a text."

"It *sounds* like an awful lot of work."

"Did I ever tell you that photography was easy? 'Infinite pains' is the operative phrase."

She nodded. "You know, I really would never get even one picture printed without you . . . Eb was right when he said that . . ."

Soon after they left Boston for the long trip home Ben felt unaccountably sleepy, so Ann drove while he napped on the mattress in the back of the van. Just as Rosie had, she drove with both skill and care. Recalling the old maxim to the effect that people drove the way they lived, Ben began to wonder whether Ann really had lived as recklessly as she sometimes appeared to do. To endure her tough childhood she'd had to be something of a survival expert . . . Seeing that Eb could give her the safety of his affection and loyalty and he could provide certain other kinds of security, wouldn't a real survival expert regardless of age use all wiles to hang on to both for as long as possible? And though it might at times seem calculating, wouldn't the action be mostly instinctive, beyond conscious control?

Eb now seemed alerted to the danger, for him, of this, and during their week in his woods wanted to force Ann to make her choice. Sooner than later he'd *have* to lose out, wouldn't he? And end up alone in Livingston . . . no, not quite alone, he thought, forcing a private smile. He would, after all, have grammie. Having entered a house with two beautiful young women and an irascible crone, he would be left with the irascible crone. Wonderful.

An hour after they passed Albany Ann got sleepy and Ben took her place at the wheel. Soon he turned off the Northway and drove along the state road which followed the river. When he'd come this way the previous May the stream had been a torrent, but now it was only a silver trickle in a rocky

499

ravine. As he passed the pine grove, which shielded the waterfall from the road, he heard no roar. Often he had thought of swimming in the pool at the bottom of those falls with Rose, but had also realized that the cold water from the mountains would not be good for her. Later he'd had fantasies of photographing Ann while she was wrapped only in veils of rainbow mist at the foot of the falls, and had demurred when she'd offered to try it. The only woman he had ever made love to on the ledges surrounding the pool under the falls was Heidi, and she had got such a bad case of poison oak that she had never forgiven him. He allowed a smile at that one.

When he got to the parking space on top of the hill which commanded the panoramic view of Livingston, he stopped the car as he so often did there. With the last of the fall foliage still giving its fiery colors to the trees, the village of Livingston looked more splendid than ever. The surrounding valley, which in spring had been a study in various shades of green, now had been turned by ripening hay to fields of gold, with glints of silver supplied by the river.

Without question a lot of people in that village hated him, Ben thought, but a fair number liked him as well and perhaps a few even loved him, or respected him. His son, at least, was no longer angry at him, or seemed to have lost much of his anger to judge by his latest telephone conversation with him. Probably Eb was impatiently waiting for his girl at Cliff House right now, his gear for the camping expedition already loaded into his jeep. Not to be dramatic, but why delay any longer . . . this trip was done. He forced himself to turn away and started driving down the hill.

34

BEN was right in his expectation that Ebon was waiting for him with all preparations for the camping expedition complete, but he was wrong in his assumption that his son was no longer angry at him.

After talking to his father on the telephone Ebon had packed his own camping gear into duffle bags, moving with the annoyed impatience he still felt over being stood up by Ann. Ben's reassuring words had helped some, but it had soon dawned on him that they did not change the fact that his father was almost constantly in the company of his girl, whether on trips or at home while he was at college. Nothing his father could say could obscure the basic fact that he had, in a way, moved in, monopolizing the time of a girl who'd been his constant companion for the past four years. Brooding about it, he found it hard to swallow that the two of them hadn't made love ... Ann, he knew, could be sexually vulnerable, and his father had gone storming around the world, living first with one woman then another for twenty years ... And even if he hadn't actually gone to bed with Ann, he'd damn well seduced her mind, turned her head, excited some pretty wild, unrealistic ideas that were fouling up his plans for life with her. Never mind the excuses, no question that his own intense if rocky romance with Ann—the only real one he'd ever had—had been made a lot rockier by old dad. . . .

His temperature definitely rising, Ebon finished stowing his own paraphernalia and went to Ann's room to see if he could find rain gear and suitable camping clothes of hers to pack. One thing he didn't want was to stand first on one foot, then the other, after his father returned. If he didn't leave practically the moment he could get Ann into the jeep, some kind of argument was sure to break out, and the way he felt now he'd better be careful not to let that get started . . . And then, rummaging about in a bottom drawer for dungarees, he came on four photographs of herself in the nude that Ann had taken. He was, especially in his mood, shocked. With him, Ann had always acted extremely reticent and downright scared when it came to actual sex, although she loved to tease. Now here she was in these four photographs, lying and smiling on her bed, flaunting her body like some cheap centerfold in a men's magazine. Remote-control mechanisms and self-timers on cameras were hardly in his mind, the thought never occurred to him that Ann could actually take her own picture like this. And since he did remember his father saying that he never used anything but professional models, he quickly, easily, jumped to the conclusion that old dad had lied in his teeth. He paced back and forth on the driveway leading to Cliff House. His mouth felt painfully dry.

And that was the way Ben found his son as he turned into the driveway, though still not close enough to see his face and be warned of his mood. Ann, who'd recently awakened, waved sleepily, and when Ben stopped the car got out and lazily stretched. She was astonished as Ben when Ebon ran up to her, grabbed her by the arm, saying, "Get in that jeep right away, we're getting *out* of here."

"*Wait* a minute," she said, pulling her arm free. "What in god's name is the matter with you, Eb?"

Grabbing her arm again, he said, "Don't talk, we'll do that

later, I want you to get in that car right now. Annie . . . now
. . . *please* . . ."

As he actually started to pull her toward the jeep, Ben
came up.

"Let go of her, have you gone crazy, Eb?"

"Maybe, but at least I'm not a damn liar and—"

"I don't know what's eating you, but we'll talk it out. First,
though, you better stop this manhandling . . ."

As Ebon continued to pull Ann toward the jeep, Ben put
his hand on his shoulder, and suddenly Ebon whirled toward
him.

In his rage, he was close to tears. "Dad, you get the hell
away from me . . . leave her alone, leave *us* alone . . ."

"Can you please try to calm down a little—"

"What's there to be calm about? You want me to stand
here whistling 'Dixie' while you screw up Annie the way
you did Rosie and mother and—"

"Eb, listen, for god's sake, listen—" And now he put his
hand on his son's arm.

"Dad, I'm telling you to get your goddamn hands off of
me, or . . . I'll flatten you, so help me God I will—" And saying it, raised his big right fist.

Ben stepped back. "If you're going to try to flatten me, Eb,
don't lead with your right, a real sucker punch . . . didn't I
teach you that? . . ."

And suddenly Ebon's tears of rage and frustration broke
out and Ann, who had been standing too petrified to speak,
instinctively hugged him. She was crying too, and suddenly
Ben himself wasn't doing too well. For a moment they stood
there, an odd, anguished huddle, until Ebon pulled back.

"Okay, so we all cry together, but that doesn't change a
a goddamn thing . . . everything's the same. Now, I want to
get *out* of here. Annie, you coming with me?"

Looking dazed, she nodded and followed him to the jeep.
He jumped behind the wheel and started the engine with a

roar. Avoiding so much as a glance at his father he sped out of the driveway and down the road toward the distant mountains.

So they were gone. Shaking his head with bewilderment, Ben went to the Cliff House kitchen for a drink, and, carrying it to the terrace, stood looking over the brilliant colors of the forest and the blues of the lake. The wind coming up off the water was cold. What specific thing had touched off his son's anger, he had no idea, but he had to acknowledge that the general situation merited it, had for a long time. His own technical innocence was not really much of a saving grace. What son wouldn't hate his father for doing what he'd done? ...

He resisted an impulse to get in the van and go after Eb in some dramatic attempt to straighten it all out, but as quickly realized the stupidity of that, given Eb's mood. If it were going to be straightened out, the next few days between Eb and Ann would have to do it. . . .

"That you, Ben?" grammie called from her room as he came back into the kitchen.

"Yes."

"Ebon going to take Annie somewhere?"

"Camping."

"She hates camping."

"Maybe she'll learn."

He returned to the terrace with a refreshed glass, felt the temptation to get blind drunk, resisted it . . . he needed *something* to feel virtuous about . . . finished off his drink, returned to the kitchen. "Grammie, we're got to pack everything up," he said. "It's getting cold. It's 'time to move back to the farm."

The farm did Ben good because there was so much work to do, to divert him from the final reckoning. Either because he could not find men to help him or because of an enmity, Horny Horner had not shown up. Looking at the surrounding

504

fields of hay which marched right up to the house, Ben again began imagining what a grass fire would do. How smart was it for a man with so many enemies to live in a tinderbox?

Buying himself an old-fashioned scythe, Ben felt like Father Time, for god's sake, as he started to cut the tall grass around the house. The job was made even more difficult by the four dachshunds who kept chasing the blade as it swished through the grass and soon escaped whenever he locked them in the house. Sweating in the cold fall wind, Ben felt some of the tension ease out of his arms, but the unfamiliar motion soon made his whole body ache long before the job was done.

The next morning Ben dropped in at his office to see how things were going. After assuring him that all was in order, Lillian gave him a copy of the paper with the article on Howie Hewat in it. Leafing through it, he tried not to think of Ben and Ann camping somewhere out there in the wilderness, but it was hard not to wonder . . . or to deny, even at this late date, that he honestly didn't know whether he wanted them to return the blissfully united young couple . . . or Ann coming back wanting only him. God . . .

To keep his mind off it all, he put in long days at his office and worked with shovel and rake until dark, cleaning up the debris left by the burned barn. During this waiting period Ben felt curiously as though he were only about half conscious. Nothing made much impact on him. Even when Howie Hewat came into his office to rant that the article on his land holdings was "inaccurate, unfair and unjust," and bound to ruin him, Ben didn't feel the satisfaction he should have as he said, "So write us a rebuttal, Howie," knowing Howie had none. And none arrived.

The continuing saga of the Radeau family, which unfolded in court, hardly excited in him the indignation that Bill Crawford wanted for the Albany *Star*. What it boiled down to, didn't it, was that a whole family of hopeless, miserable people had got roaring drunk. A young girl was pregnant, all kinds of accusations had been made and one man had been hit hard enough to die. The next morning no one was clear about what had happened or, understandably enough, wanted to remember. Soon, it was becoming clear, the old man would go to jail for a few years, and the family would continue pretty much as before . . . . Thinking about them, he decided recent events in his own family didn't quite put him in the Radeau class, but no denying his son *had* raised a fist to him and conceivably, if they all had been just a little more far gone or less sober, a violent fight could have resulted. Sure, contemplating a liaison with one's sister-in-law was not incest, but it was close enough to give more insight into it than as a vicarious bystander. At any rate, Ben for sure didn't feel like throwing stones at the Radeaus, and he was glad that the editor he had hired was restricting himself to brief summaries of the trial. Of course, the question was, would the Radeaus forgive him as easily as he did them . . . .

At night Ben slept in an old-fashioned double bed at the farm with the four dachshunds often snuggling against him for warmth. They howled if left alone in any room and seemed to be of negligible value as watch dogs in cold weather.

While he counted down the days of the week that he expected Ann and Eb to be gone, he was subject to various fantasies he could not control . . . Why not take Ann to Le Bristol in Paris? What a delight it would be to drive her around Ireland, her ancestral home. She claimed to loathe everything Irish but she'd change her mind fast enough when she saw that incredible countryside of emerald hills, some of them topped by crumbling castles that were old when America was born. Or Spain? . . . Travels with Ann became a game he played to get himself to sleep. How would Ann react to a bullfight? With initial fright and finally unabashed excitement, covering her eyes with her hands, but peeping through her fingers . . . how oddly detailed these fantasies were. His favorite of all involved chartering a ketch and taking her on a long cruise through the Bahamas . . . he'd once done a magazine piece on Bimini and could almost see Ann dancing down the only street of that island with the moonlight on the sand and the steel bands playing in nearly every little bar. And when they left Bimini he'd show her how to steer through the shoals on the Great Banks. In a bikini, or maybe without one, she would sit on the wheelbox, squinting in the sunlight as she glanced up at the sails while the wind tousled her hair.

Such was the stuff of dreams that often put Ben to sleep with a smile on his face. It was a shock to wake up the next morning and find that the pleasant warmth next to him came only from four shivering little dogs.

It was only six days since they'd gone off. It was just before dark and he was raking up the debris of the barn when he spotted the jeep coming up the dirt road toward him, jouncing over the rough spots. He walked carefully toward it, half waving. The jeep stopped a few yards away. They got out, both dressed in dungarees and T-shirts. As they walked toward him, they held hands and swung their arms. He didn't really need to be told anymore.

Ann rushed forward, kissed him on the cheek. "Everything's fine, Ben, really, just fine."

"I'm glad."

"I'm sorry I was so rough," Ebon said. "There were . . . you know . . . a lot of misunderstandings . . ." He gave his father a quick hug, then went on to explain about the pictures he had discovered in Ann's room. Except somehow that didn't seem very important to Ben. The gunpowder, after all, was always more the cause of the explosion than the spark.

"And . . ." Ann put in, "it looks like I'm going to that school both you guys think is so great . . . we've called in about it and I'll only be a little over a month late . . ."

"That's good."

More was said, which he didn't really hear, including her report on the joys of the great outdoors . . . smiles . . . jokes

... she kissed him on the cheek again, hugged him, and tried not to cry.

"Ben ... okay ...?"

"Of course, 'okay.' Are you kidding? ..."

"Well, so long, dad ... come on, Annie, we've really got to go, we've got a zillion things to do in Albany ..."

Hugging Ben, she whispered, "Thanks for living," and ran after Ebon. It was another phrase she had learned from Rosie, and he remembered when Rosie had said it to him....

"Was that them out there?" grammie called.

"Yes."

"Why didn't they come in?"

"They have a zillion things to do in Albany."

He escaped to the bathroom. In the mirror over the sink he got a glimpse of himself. He looked like he felt. No matter. Ann was gone and he must *not* let himself fall into the further trap of spinning fantasies about her coming back. Ann had gone *where she belonged*, and if she ever did leave Ebon, it would be for another young man ... at any rate, *not* for him....

Taking a six-pack of beer from the refrigerator, he got into the van and drove to the parking space on top of the hill which offered such a fine view of the town. It was good to watch the village as lights came twinkling on like necklaces, first down one street, then another. If he wasn't careful, he told himself, he'd dissolve into disgusting self-pity and drink himself right down the drain. Work, hard work, was an immediate solution, both on the newspaper and the book, but that wouldn't hold him together for long. Somewhere, somehow, he'd have to arrange a private life for himself better than, different from, existing on a farm with too many memories and an irascible old woman.

God, how he wanted Rosie back. There was never a hint of self-pity in her through all those years of self-denial and pain. Couldn't he be at least half as gutsy? ... He tried to

508

imagine what Rosie would say to him now, but no words came.

There was only the sound of a cold north wind whistling around the car.

Winter came early that year. Well before Thanksgiving, the persistent snows of the Adirondacks began to fall, covering the posters and pamphlets of the election which had been discarded on the streets of the village. Coming out of his office, Ben saw a picture of Howie Hewat smiling up at him, half obscured by the mounting flakes. Howie had, in no small measure thanks to Rosie and then Ben, lost the election and had gone off to Florida—some said never to return and good riddance. Except in a curious way Ben missed Howie. The loss of a good old enemy could be almost as painful as the loss of a good old friend.

Before the snow got too bad, Ben drove home to the farm-house and lit good wood fires in the stoves. Peering through the windows, he could see that the snow had already covered the hayfields, removing the threat of a grass fire. Now he could admit to himself his constant dread of seeing all those fields turn into a sea of flames in which the old farmhouse would explode. Of course, not all possible disasters happened, he told himself, and there should be some comfort in that.

The next morning he shoveled snow for an hour, finding solace as always in physical exhaustion. For several reasons he found himself wanting more snow, for winter to come in really hard and change the entire village. So much of the summer had been agonizing and during so much of the fall he had made a damn fool of himself, as he reconstructed the events, that he could hardly wait for a change of the entire landscape. Though the *Princess* would have to remain in drydock until spring, he could build a shack for ice-fishing that would give him another private place. . . .

That year heavy snows blanketed the region in early December, and before Christmas the temperatures plummeted to twenty below zero and the lake quickly froze. After the firemen had measured the thickness of the ice by boring holes in it, and after they'd tested its strength by having their fattest volunteers jump up and down on it, the children began skating and men pushed out their fishing shacks on runners.

Ben was helping Ephram push a shack to the west side of the lake one afternoon when he happened to look up at the ice-sheathed peak of Big Iron Mountain, turned to gold by the setting sun. Silhouetted like the mythic city of El Dorado against the azure sky, it was so beautiful that he caught his breath.

The next morning he rummaged through some of the gear that Ebon had left behind until he found a hatchet he could wear on his belt. Driving into the village he rented a snowmobile and one of the heavily padded suits made for people who ride those machines. On the rear seat he strapped a five-gallon can of gasoline. The owner of the contrivance towed it on a trailer to the beginning of the trails which led up the mountains. He stayed until Ben got the powerful little engine started and then with a wave drove away.

Ben had driven snowmobiles only a few times and he knew that there was real danger if one got off the trails, but on this day that didn't seem to matter. He felt almost exalted as he turned off the beaten track and sped upward, finding his direction by heading into the morning sun. Dodging through trees, he entered a glass forest that put man-made flowers to shame. Every branch and twig overhead was glistening crystal aglow with the sun, like the stems of goblets in candlelight.

Sometimes the runners of the motor sled thumped on hard-packed banks and sometimes they sent up cascades of soft snow like spray from the bow of a speedboat. He had to detour around steep granite cliffs and high hummocks of bald rock, ravines and brooks which ran too fast to be frozen, but he continued upward into the path of the sun.

Once he almost rolled into a deep gully, and while speeding across a mountain sheep pasture he narrowly avoided a wire fence, a kind of trap that had undone more than one unfortunate snowmobiler, he had read. His engine ran raggedly for a few minutes, making him wonder how he would get home without it, but the machine continued to hold together for about two hours while he made his ascent.

As he neared the top of Big Iron Mountain, the trees began to be shorter, as though reversing growth, and suddenly he was clattering over bare ice. Leaving his snowmobile, he unbuckled the can of gasoline and carried it, slipping on the ice as he walked upward. Soon the highest peak loomed ahead, glacial, forbidding, a defiant fist of rock raised toward the sky. It was not easy to mount it, but after falling several times, he succeeded. Fortunately the wind was not as high as he had expected, though the temperature was perhaps thirty degrees below zero here. Standing on the summit, he looked at the view of other white mountains and the white lake below, on which a whole village of fishing shacks painted in pastel colors nestled. Turning his attention to the ground around him, Ben saw that the vegetation here was not as sparse as it had appeared at first glance. In many crevices stunted fir trees grew with their branches spreading out on the surrounding rocks to avoid incurring the wrath of the winds. Taking the hatchet from his belt, he began cutting these branches, pulling them from the ice and snow to make a pile precisely at the top of the highest peak.

He had to work about two hours and to range for several hundred yards before he assembled a pile of wooden debris about the size of a small automobile. After resting a few minutes he poured all of his gasoline over it. Taking a piece of paper from his wallet, he crumpled it up, lit it and tossed it on the pyre. With a roar the flames shot up a good fifty feet, a fine signal fire for all to see.

Sitting in the orange glow of the fire, he now felt closer to Rosie than he had at any time since her death. For the first time he could tell himself that she might even be proud of the way he'd finally handled himself with Ann. He was also sure that she'd want him to go on, not to be a professional mourner . . . widower. Rosie had never said he was forty-five years old —she'd always used the phrase "only forty-five." He still maybe had something to offer a woman of sensible age, didn't he? Anyone who had lived with Rosie Kelly, never mind how briefly, had to have learned something about hope, and courage, and joy, and especially love.

Staring into the crackling flames, he thought of Rosie as a young girl already with outrageous responsibilities and troubles enough to sink most strong adults, a teenager who dreamt of coming up here with an imaginary lover to build a signal fire on this mountain peak. When he'd asked her what the message of her fire was, she had declined to demean it by spelling it out, had put her fingers over his lips to stop him from asking. Well, now he knew. Now that he needed more than riddles, the simple answer was as clear to him as the dancing flames: even as a lonely young girl Rosie had wanted to signal that hope, and courage, and joy and especially love could blaze up even in the most impossible circumstances— like a fire on ice.

As Ben held his hands out to the flames, he actually felt as though he were absorbing her hope and courage from them, along with the heat that made his wet gloves steam and the orange light that danced on the snow all around him brighter even than the sun. Every year when the first heavy snow fell, he decided, he would return here to light a fire like an enormous candle for Rosie, and to renew himself.

513

Gradually the blaze subsided, leaving a black circle of wet ashes on the mountain peak that Ben covered with snow before making his way to his snowmobile. Going down the steep ravines to the glass forest and the valley below would be more dangerous than coming up. He would be careful. He was sure, after all, that Rosie had intended her legacy as a prescription for life, not death. Who, after all, had loved life with more intensity than Rosie Kelly?